P9-DUX-611

The Company of Animals

Edited and with an Introduction by

Michael J. Rosen

Doubleday

New York   London   Toronto   Sydney   Auckland

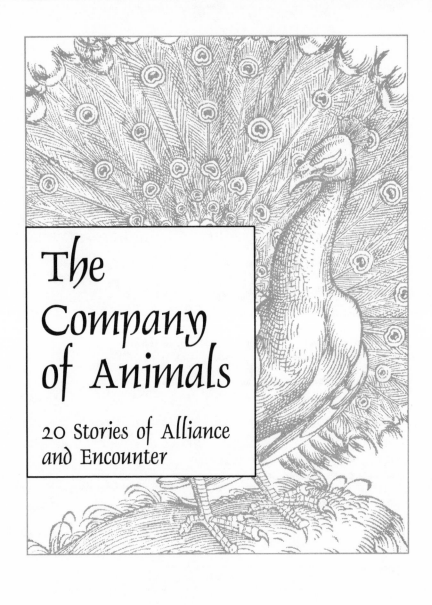

The Company of Animals

20 Stories of Alliance and Encounter

PUBLISHED BY DOUBLEDAY
a division of Bantam Doubleday Dell Publishing Group, Inc.
1540 Broadway, New York, New York 10036

DOUBLEDAY and the portrayal of an anchor
with a dolphin are trademarks of Doubleday,
a division of Bantam Doubleday Dell
Publishing Group, Inc.

Permissions to be found starting on page 277

Book design by Marysarah Quinn

Library of Congress Cataloging-in-Publication Data

The Company of animals : 20 stories of alliance and encounter / edited
    and with an introduction by Michael J. Rosen. — 1st ed.
        p.   cm.
    1. Animals—Fiction.   2. Short stories, American.   I. Rosen,
    Michael J., 1954–
    PS648.A5C65   1993
    808.83′936—dc20   92-43471
                                                       CIP

ISBN 0-385-46817-2

10 9 8 7 6 5 4 3 2 1

First Edition

Profits from this anthology, as with its "companion volumes," will be donated to animal welfare agencies. The efforts of the collective contributors provide emergency and ongoing care for animals throughout the country. Previous grants—geared toward cats and dogs—have included rescue and intervention services, low- and no-cost spaying and neutering projects, adoption and humane education programs, and various forms of assistance to help individuals struggling to keep and care for the companion animals in their lives.

With the publication of this volume, grant giving will be broadened to include grants to agencies that directly affect the health and well-being of animals other than cats and dogs. For more information about The Company of Animals Fund, write to Michael J. Rosen, c/o Doubleday, 1540 Broadway, New York, N.Y. 10036.

It is, therefore, to each contributor, caretaker, and compassionate reader that this collection, too, is dedicated. The editor would like to extend his deepest appreciation to Jacki Spangler, not only for her resourceful and generous commitment to discovering many of these stories, but also for her critical and most compassionate responses that furthered so many of my working ideas of this anthology and its shape.

Contents

CONTENTS

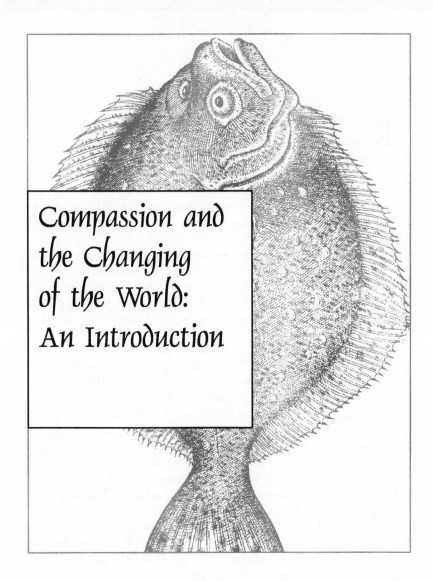

Compassion and the Changing of the World: An Introduction

ANCHOVIES AND THE COURSE OF NATURE

Recently, I visited a major aquarium which housed, among its exhibits and wonders, an enormous wall tank of schooling, hand-sized, silver fish. They glided back and forth in a synchrony that remained inexplicable—and still does, despite the sign's didactic information and the experts' continual hypotheses. Anchovies. If nothing else, this was the first time I had ever seen these fish outside of that square tin with its old-fashioned key.

Fascination genuinely fixed me there as these shimmering shards of mirror wended their collective way behind the window of the great tank. Although I hadn't yet assigned the anchovies the boredom that I was sure to feel were I to continue a vigil beside their repetitive pacing, I had been imagining the vaster ocean in which such compulsion, unrestricted and responsive to the tides, would look more like sense than nonsense, more like necessity than nervousness.

Just then a boy of five or six strolled right to the base of the tank and punched one of two buttons (I hadn't even noticed them) with the palm of his hand. "Watch this!" he implored his lagging teacher and the classmates who now gathered beside me. Instantly, a forceful current charged the tank, whooshing and gurgling, and the school, in one ensemble movement of flaring fins, halted, reversed directions, and headed, face-first, into that current. Each fish matched the water's speed with the propulsion of its fins, maintaining its position: suspended not just in saltwater but in time. Behind the wall, some kind of motor propelled and, perhaps, circulated the current from the left side of the tank to the right side so that the fish could demonstrate, according to a sign I then noticed, *rheotaxis:* a fish's ongoing adjustments that orient the water's flow, and hence oxygen, into its mouth, across the gill's blood vessels, and out its gill covers.

After this brief demonstration, the current subsided and the fish resumed their forward motion as though they'd simply idled, momentarily, en route to a predetermined destination. But, just as all the fish had closed rank and inched ahead, another boy hit the second button which, after a short delay, initiated a flow of current in the opposite, right-to-left direction, causing the anchovies to perform another about-face. And so the school froze again, as if the boy were pressing the pause button on his VCR and this tank were a large screen on which a frame of swimming fish was held fast before our eyes; the translucent fluttering of their fins even resembled the jitteriness of a stilled picture.

Before I could say anything to their teacher (and before I came to regret my misplaced irritation), the students had continued to punch the buttons in as rapid a succession as the display would permit (every two minutes with a few second lull), giving no hint of quitting until everyone in their bickering-for-next-in-line group of eleven had seized a personal opportunity to alter the course of nature, at least in this do-it-yourself, made-for-television, home version of the game.

And so on, I figured, hundreds of times a day, thousands of times a year, the school of anchovies executes its immediate response (hesitation is not only fatal to the fish but altogether ungratifying for the viewer), oblivious to the play-gods of their fickle universe.

While I still would not presume that such habitual performance causes harm to the fish (it clearly doesn't compare to the fate of the anchovies I had eaten before), the persisting thought that I took from this exhibit, however well-intentioned and awe-inspiring the notion of rheotaxis, had something to do with harm. Now, hundreds of visiting children may prove me wrong, but I'd hazard that a great majority are more fascinated by the power buttons than by the pivoting fish. *Watch what this button does!* Were there another visitor, one who could stare down through an overhead skylight into this museum of scrambling human beings, his most notable observations would not be of the modest rheotactic measures of schooling anchovies, but of the schools of children swirling *outside* the tank, impatiently maneuvering themselves toward the source of power.

THE TELEVISION ZOO

Novelist and television critic Michael Arlen recounts a visit to the country home of a friend. A deer—not simply rare for the time of year, but also lame; a specific deer the family had lost track of recently—wandered into the field near their house. When the young son was summoned from watching television to join them at the window, he demurred, saying, "There's sea elephants fighting here," and turned back to the screen.

The obvious irony here is a profound part of our storytelling about animals: the comfortable distance we often require or desire between animals and our tolerance/appreciation of them. Arlen concludes, "Perhaps in response to these age-old and persistent stirrings in his soul, man, who apparently cannot do *without* wild animals and cannot live *with* them, has devised the last animal ghetto: the television zoo."

The stories in *The Company of Animals* may be another kind of ghetto, in that they create environments—safer in some ways, harsher, perhaps, in others—in which we can view these creatures. Moreover, because the authors have provided human characters (endowing them with decidedly nonfictional qualities) we can, from a temporary distance, view our characteristic human attitudes toward those animals as well.

But before considering the fiction specifically, it's worth asking ourselves, how it is, given the progress of ethology, ecology, and all the other sciences, and given the availability or even the onslaught of their findings, how it is we're not better informed and hence more rational and more compassionate regarding animals?

In his book *The Age of Missing Information,* Bill McKibben compares the information gathered from twenty-four hours of television (simultaneously recording every available cable channel, and then systematically viewing these over a period of weeks) with that gleaned from a day of camping in the Adirondack Mountains. Among his conclusions are several regarding nature programming, whose educational value he feels is pathetically overestimated. First: Shows about nature "undercut their message with pictures"; such and such an animal is endangered or nearly extinct, and yet the program offers endless pictures of it. Second: "Something even more insidious happens when you get most of your nature through television . . . the 'real' nature around you, even when it's intact, begins to seem dull." Third: "The nature documentaries are as absurdly action-packed as the soap operas. . . . Trying to understand 'nature' from watching 'Wild Kingdom' is as tough as trying to understand 'life' from watching 'Dynasty.' " And last: Of the "ten million (some say thirty million) species on earth . . . only a few meet the requirements for extensive television coverage—cuteness . . . great amiability or ferocity, accessibility . . . correct size to show up well on camera, and so on. . . ."

McKibben's deductions mirror the basic fabric of the stories collected here and elsewhere, not only in magazines and journals, but in more ephemeral communications such as newspapers and conversations. Animals, he writes, "are not there for you—they are there because the world belongs to them too." And while this is unimpeachably a fact, it's hardly a fact we have learned to live with (or better: live and let live with).

Fiction, I hope this volume argues, is a different way of processing our experiences and even our lack of experiences with animals: a way of learning, a self-education with the hope for a salutary contagion. Perhaps, these stories can move us away from the television (or the glass tank or even the windowpane) and out again into the open.

HUMILITY AND HUMAN TIME ON EARTH

We often define nature by the very terms that estrange us from it: Nature is what we haven't manufactured or mismanaged; what exists outside of houses and cities; places that people neither own nor occupy. This separation is hardly passive. Alternately plundering and worshiping, we wage both sides of the war, hoping to develop nature for human purposes but also to reclaim it from the self-same development. Everywhere the evidence—environmental, economic, and nearly every category of global assessment—suggests that we are incurably ambivalent about most animals, about their place(s) in our society *and* in the unsocialized world, and about our role—caretaker, harvester, warden— as we negotiate (on their behalf as well) our needs with theirs, in abiding their presence, controlling their numbers, appropriating their territories.

The stories we write provide yet another proof of our conflicting feelings, since they are, by their nature, motivated by conflict rather than by peaceable harmony.

Underlying much of this uneasiness about our stewardship is one fundamental question: What do we really know about each animal, since we presume that such knowledge informs, if it can't always answer, any other question, prerogative, or assumption we consider about their lives? Unlike Michael Maslin's beaver, reprinted opposite, we do feel we can arbitrate on behalf of all creation simply because human speech is all we accept in the courtroom. (One notable exception: Criminals have been convicted on the evidence of a tracking dog's scenting ability.) We claim to be judge, jury, each side's attorneys, and all the witnesses in the world's court.

In *Cosmos*, Carl Sagan cites a recently established consequence of our human progress: Aside from the continuing slaughter of whales—a tragedy most of us do understand—here is a subtler and, perhaps, more devastating realization. There were no humans in "99.99 percent of the history of the whales" (That alone should be sufficient to humble any human imagination). Via the deep ocean sound channels, whales were able to "communicate with each other at twenty Hertz essentially anywhere in the world. One might be off the Ross Ice Shelf in Antarctica and communicate with another in the Aleutians." They had, it seems

"I ask that the record show that the witness does not presume to speak for the animal kingdom but is testifying here strictly in his capacity as a beaver."

likely, a "global communications network." Two hundred years ago, for example, two finback whales, separated by 10,000 kilometers, could still communicate. But the noise pollution of steamships, military and commercial vessels, so decreased that distance, that today whales can't hear much beyond a few hundred kilometers. Sagan concludes, "We have cut the whales off from themselves. Creatures that communicated for tens of millions of years have now effectively been silenced."

When I read such a statement, I can't help thinking of myself as responsible in some way; I wish to imagine myself—now enlightened to this plight—among those who could alleviate or abate the situation. And yet here, as in most other situations where human progress has sacrificed the needs (and often the very lives) of other creatures, I confess to having more sympathy than solutions. What kind of response can I offer on my behalf or on behalf of my species to these "silenced" whales? What, even, might I have done at the aquarium in front of the anchovy tank? This stupefying ignorance, with its attendant shame and arrogance, is one source of fiction's endless extrapolations on the inhuman conditions within which we conduct our human lives.

But, for me, this self-implication did become something of an aspiration: It did initiate these anthologies and the granting program funded by their profits. My hope, which I'm honored to say has been shared by so many of my colleagues gathered here, has been to assume some kind of responsibility, if only a personal education in compassion, with the further hope that the concrete action of making these books and stories available might inspire a far-reaching, like-minded response in readers.

Writing in *The Republic of Tea,* a book about the establishing of a new tea company, Mel Ziegler, a self-named "zentrepreneur" speaks of his desire to form a life—and a business—committed to "fundamental change," which he defines as a "society where every individual comes to accept every social problem as a problem of his own making, and sees the wisdom of changing himself (into a happier and compassionate human being) as his way of changing the world."

As I've written in the previous anthologies, my contributors did not claim that animal welfare was their first concern in life; nor were any of them deluded by the idea that ranking either diminishes a problem or prevents someone from making a significant and lasting contribution.

ON THE WITNESS STAND

While I claim that we are plagued and puzzled by questions about our fellow creatures, I believe we are even more disturbed by questions that we must ask, in light of these "Others," about ourselves and our kind. The history of medical science is sufficient to unhinge anyone who might witness (or merely force himself to actually consider) the practices that have roughhewed the shape of knowledge. More than a hundred years ago, Henry J. Bigelow, Professor of Surgery at Harvard University Medical School, wrote, "There will come a time when the world will look back on vivisection, in the name of science, as they do now to burning at the stake in the name of religion."

Desmond Morris suggests that when we scrutinize our own species, the truths we disclose will disrupt the flow of distractions, oversimplifications, and misrepresentations that constitute so much of the self-centered haste we consider our living. In his plea for a worldwide code of ethics for every animal, *The Animal Contract,* he maintains that the "torments suffered in the name of science," "the bloody pleasures of animal fights," and so many other "savageries" humans have inflicted upon animals, constitute "one of the great dilemmas of this topic of man-animal relations: To delve into the subject fully is to encounter aspects of human nature so appalling that anyone wishing to do something about it cannot face the facts, and turns away in disgust. Only a few brave spirits are prepared to grasp the nettle and they are frequently rewarded by being labelled as cranks. In this way the great bulk of the population can keep a discreet distance from the unpalatable and smother their guilt with intense preoccupations elsewhere."

Short stories, once again, may be one way of "facing the facts" and "grasping the nettle," if we allow for my earlier proposal that fiction is the form facts can take when transformed by the accessibility and application of an individual life.

TO EACH HIS OWN TIRE

In another chapter from *Mr. Palomar* (only "The Blackbird's Whistle" is included here), Italo Calvino describes Palomar's observations of a captive albino gorilla. The only thing this animal possesses to occupy his repetitive days is an old tire, to which he clings. "A toy? A fetish? A talisman? Mr. Palomar feels he understands the gorilla perfectly, his need for something to hold tight while everything eludes him, a thing with which to allay the anguish of isolation. . . ." The gorilla preoccupies Palomar, disturbing both his fitful hours and his dreams; Palomar concludes: "Just as the gorilla has his tire, which serves as tangible support for a raving, wordless speech . . . I have this image of a great white ape. We all turn in our hands an old, empty tire through which we try to reach some final meaning, which words cannot achieve."

Consider then, the book you are turning in your hands as a collection of old empty tires, captive gorillas, or pages. Each story is a stand-in for an experience you have not had personally, and yet each offers its occasion for your empathy. The need, as Calvino suggests, is to understand something that words—those struggles for accuracy or metaphor that formulate whatever appreciation we garner from this world—have yet to draft in permanent form. Though I won't propose that any of the stories here are willfully ambiguous, each does possess, like Palomar's haunting image, more than one axiomatic resolution that might banish the unsettling or discrepant emotions it elicits. Indeed, I suspect that these stories have been composed from an individual's sense of ambiguity which, if resolved, might erase the story—or at least the need to retell it—from the waking mind. This insolvable, persistent complexity may motivate all fiction, but I'd suggest that it is all the more urgent when writing about our encounters with animals.

One reason for this urgency, as I've asserted, is that our appreciation of and presumptions about these other creatures are not simply incoherent but truly inchoate. Maurice Maeterlinck speaks of this in his remarkable book *The Life of the Bee*. Almost a century ago, he wrote, "Our intellect is not the proper tribunal before which to summon the bees, and pass their faults in review. Do we not find, among ourselves, that consciousness and intellect long will dwell in the midst of errors and faults without perceiving them, longer still without effecting a remedy? . . . compare the mistakes of the hive with those of our own society." Our own assessments of these other lives are not only inappropriate and often incorrect, but, moreover, they often reveal such faults, misapprehensions, and limitations in human practices. It is in this same volume that he reaches a most sobering conclusion: "There is not yet any truth, but everywhere there are three good probabilities." The introduction of animals challenges our assertion of *human* truth in light of all the other probable truths that animals represent, even if they can't articulate them.

The cultural philosopher William Irwin Thompson reinforces this notion of our insecurity: "After domesticating animals and plants, man went on to domesticate man. It was to be called civilization, but it was also slavery. . . . art became a celebration of power and glory, but since man had only recently emerged from nature's dominance, it was a nervous whistling in the dark; underneath the celebration of glory remained the awareness of death." This tentative dominance is expressed in at least two ways within these stories—in a discomfort with the "privileges" we take by virtue of our piecemeal knowledge of other animals, and also in a deeper uneasiness: Each animal destroys any delusions we try to sustain of our own immortality. (Despite whatever differences we claim, we are identical to animals in death.)

We have, as a culture, frequently used animals to gauge, however inaccurately, some condition that might affect or be inflicted upon a person. Let's simply consider the familiar example of the canaries that miners took into their shafts, whose more sensitive lungs would announce, with the bird's death, the lack of oxygen in the mine and so the need to turn back. An animal in a short story, like those canaries, is often sacrificed—or nearly so—in order to reveal to the humans (characters, author, reader) the intolerable conditions to which we may all, finally, be subjected. This effect is magnified to the degree that we are already used to regarding the short story itself as a kind of canary, offering the example of its characters for the reader's benefit.

Ultimately, the feelings we have for animals are deeply entrenched in religion, unconsciousness, archetype, morality, and memory, and these sustain their power because the animals cannot assuage or un-complicate our emotional reactions with explanations and extenuations. Their speechlessness draws forth our further speech. The true or ob-served occasion that prompted a given story doesn't simply cry out to be recounted, it requires the conventions and conveyances of fiction to recast it—not merely to heighten or mollify the original events, but to seize an opportunity to change the self; it is Carl Jung who reminds us, "The encounter with the creature changes the creator."

PICTURES AT AN EXTINCTION

The photographs of James Balog deal with irreconcilable meanings. Just as the devices of fiction are imposed upon whatever actual en-counters occurred between author and animal, Balog has used the gim-micks and stagings of fashion photography—scrims, photo-white back-drops, strong lighting, and peculiar cropping—to create what he has called "a new vision of endangered wildlife." His new vision clearly reveals that it is not only the animals that have become endangered, but also and more crucially (at least in terms of our chances of preventing further extinctions), our ability to perceive the animals intrinsically—on their own terms, without a human-assigned place, intervention, or function. His work reveals the animal as both a sacred and profaned creature, "capturing" simultaneously its natural beauty and its unnatu-ral displacement, its innate value and its function within a man-made nature. Within an artificial world, each creature is a refugee turned spectacle.

"I have no desire to perpetuate the romantic mirages of traditional wildlife photography," Balog notes in his monograph on these images, *Survivors*. "Instead I have created images of animals in exile from a lost Eden, adrift in the ether of a planet now made alien to them. It is a new kind of landscape, one largely devoid of the old, familiar topography. But it is the place they must now call home."

He has, in many cases, even offered us an animal's responsive gaze, a genuine reciprocation that, as John Berger suggests in "Why Look at Animals," a zoo deprives us from ever experiencing. Zoo animals, he writes, "have been immunised to encounter, because nothing can any more occupy a *central* place in their attention. . . . *You are looking at something that has been rendered absolutely marginal;* and all the concentration you can muster will never be enough to centralise it."

An animal in a story is simultaneously an individual in a specific encounter, and also a representative of the animal kingdom. Likewise, the animal's presence elicits from us more than an individual's response: Just as the animals of the wild live alongside us simply as a collective species, there may be a particular joy or poignancy in sharing their anonymity, humbly conceding that whatever good or even tolerance we offer has been done without the ego's needs for appreciation. When we deal humanely with an animal intruder in our home, when we help some wounded creature, it is not for any gratitude or reciprocation, as in some fable. No, such an act of kindness can be undertaken only as a gesture on behalf of our kind—humankind.

Just as most of nature's individual conflicts occur without our awareness—we simply don't witness most of what befalls the creatures of our backyards and neighborhoods, let alone what occurs counties and continents away—so most of our human doings and undoings do not become the stuff of fiction. But the need for stories often arises at that very moment when we discover or intrude upon some consequence of the struggle for survival and, consequently, struggle ourselves with our interpretations of cruelty, our sense of tragedy and pity, our notions of duty or denial. This is the nervous whistling in the dark to which Thompson alludes.

Consider stories such as Robley Wilson's "Quills," where a man must painfully remove a porcupine's quills from a dog's face; Constance Pierce's "The Red Sea," where a mother discovers her child's first moral defection in the wanton stoning of a small reptile; or Lynne Sharon Schwartz's "What I Did for Love," where a mother tends her daughter's sickly guinea pig in the child's absence: In each case, people are tested by the intrusion of an animal while others watch—others, of course, including us readers.

Every animal—intruder, menace, curiosity, companion—raises the moral stakes in a story, charging the atmosphere in which the rest of the characters conduct their drama. The animal shifts the story into a pastoral realm, a simpler, clearer realm in which moral decisiveness becomes an imperative rather than the option we lazily allow it to be. I mean "pastoral" both in the sense of romantic convention (an isolated place, such as an island or pasture, within which the world's complexities are clarified) and in the sense of a more harmonious nature in which an animal encourages a character's recognition of the self as representative of an allied species within the animal world.

ANIMAL FEELINGS

A writer's struggle with anthropomorphism is central to most of these stories: how to show sympathy and sensitivity for an animal without projecting human feelings, motivations, and desires. But this is a literary fallacy more than a literal one, and an argument—should we assign emotions, sensitivities, and other intangible mental capacities to nonhuman creatures?—that has been renewed throughout our history. The individual qualities of animals were, for centuries, a succinct means by which we metaphorically understood and described ourselves. This goes far beyond "Homeric terms," where people are depicted as possessing one animal's wariness, another's strength, another's self-reliance.

Konrad Lorenz, one of the foremost authorities and founders of modern ethology, addresses this subject head-on in his life-long study of the greylag goose, *Here Am I—Where Are You?:* "If we feel ourselves emotionally affected by the behavior of an animal, it is a clear indication that we have intuitively discovered a similarity between its behavior and human behavior. We should not conceal this in our description." Furthermore, he argues that since we can apply the word "eye" to both a human and to an octopus, and "do not feel that we must always add a qualifier to the effect that the octopus eye is not the same as the vertebrate eye," we should allow ourselves to think of animals as possessing their own versions of our feelings. "Nevertheless, such recognition should not mislead us into thinking that we can fathom or replicate the subjective states of animals. Our feelings are simply an indicator of convergent adaptation."

Until Descartes argued that body and soul were separate entities, claiming that anything like a soul (feelings, intentions, memory) was exclusively human, all creatures were believed to be a part of a single continuum. Our modern-day discomfort with anthropomorphism is simply another means by which we reinforce our self-invented isolation. In fact, the "parallel lives" of animals, as John Berger concludes, "offer man a companionship which is different from any offered by human exchange. Different because it is a companionship offered to the loneliness of man as a species." One challenge, taken up by several writers included here, is to break through this isolation and reintegrate with the larger world that exists beyond the myths of self-importance we sustain.

WITH, WITH QUALIFICATIONS, OR WITHOUT

The animals in the stories I have collected in these three volumes could arguably constitute a current and somewhat complete view of the degree to which our lives are integrated with or detached from our most common fellow inhabitants. The stories and their central animals divide into three sorts, within the guidelines I used for their selection.

I included only fiction, and only short stories, choosing among those I considered the finest examples of the most accomplished and promising authors writing in the last several years. Moreover, each story had to be about people significantly involved with an animal: The story could neither focus entirely on an animal (as in an ethological memoir), nor could it feature animals as merely peripheral to human events (on a par with the incidental staffage of interiors and narratives). Without a doubt, the overwhelming majority of stories fall into this latter category, reflecting the obvious fact that companion animals occupy, even when they don't preoccupy, our imaginations.

I also declined a disproportionate number of stories that, while they met the above qualifications, featured animals gratuitously suffering cruel and cavalier fates. Some of those accounts were certainly powerful and excellent when viewed with an objectivity that, I admit, I had no motive to apply. In none of those stories did I suppose that the author advocated such violences and abuses; nor could I say all the stories vilified the inhumane acts they described. In general, the characters in such fiction confronted or caused haphazard, spiteful, or gratuitous harm to animals in expectation of shocking the reader into participation: Sympathy for the animals was less frequently the idea; more often the reader was supposed to sense the desperate psychological state of a character who would be capable of committing or condoning such heartlessness. Eventually, I came to see this facile turn of events as critically lacking in the broader compassion that would finally convince me of the character's plight; instead, I sympathized with each author, straining for an effect.

Of the stories I have collected, the first group consists of those where humans significantly interact with an animal *we can live with:* a pet, clearly claimed as *family.* These stories are primarily about companion animals and are collected in my two previous anthologies devoted to cats and dogs. The animals are not only incarnations of nature itself, but also family members who have the ability to elucidate a problem or a moral predicament that the benighted characters are otherwise unable to perceive.

While some of the stories collected in this volume—tales of horses, goats, birds, and incidental cats and dogs—make a strong claim to be included in this category, most of the present volume's stories are better suited to these next two categories.

The second lot of stories concerns animals that, make no mistake, *we can't live with.* These are undomesticated creatures of two types: the unapproachable marvel, like a cougar, or the independent menace, like a copperhead. In these stories, suddenly, between their territory and ours, a breach or a blurring occurs: One party wanders into the realm of the other and therein begins the necessary, and often ill-prepared, negotiation: fear, combat, hysteria, curiosity, tolerance. . . .

The two stories set around zoos—those by Haruki Murakami and Graham Swift—hover precisely on this very border, examining the nature of a sustained and artificial separation between ourselves and these other creatures.

Finally, there are stories with animals that cross the boundaries of the first two categories, just as their lives and territories may cross into our own. These are the creatures close enough to our quotidian lives and not so immediately threatening that *we could live with them . . . if only—or as long as . . .* Tameable or abidable under extraordinary circumstances, but otherwise threatening or problematic, here are those creatures that trouble, fascinate, annoy, and worry us in our semipermeable habitations: deer, raccoons, bats, rats, porcupines, bears, lizards. The authors of these fictions create situations where a heightened clarity is required of the human participants. In *The Unbearable Lightness of Being,* novelist Milan Kundera writes, "True human goodness, in all its purity and freedom, can come to the fore only when its recipient has no power. Mankind's true moral test, its fundamental test (which lies deeply buried from view), consists of its attitude toward those who are at its mercy: animals." The short story is often undertaken for the very opportunity to disinter such a buried test and examine its results.

GROWING OLD OURSELVES WITH ANIMALS

In each of these "categories," animals provide—often through the sacrifice of their own lives—a tragic means of understanding our own nature. They afford an access to the forces of grief and rage that are normally subsumed by society's notions of appropriate social behavior and rational conduct. It's as though the "nature" that is an animal flushes out the truer "nature" of human nature—the specific character's nature as well as some characteristic that we readers might recognize as universal.

In her essay, "Growing Old," Doris Grumbach writes of her beloved editor's death from the complications of AIDS. She speaks of the range of emotions she feels—"I rage against my own survival in the darkness of his disappearance, I hate being an age he will never see, I detest his leaving before I can bid him farewell"—emotions as complex as their relationship deserved, and yet her tears do not issue for two weeks. Just before a frost, she transfers her two black goldfish "who live, against all lack of care and expectations, in the small pond in the garden" to a temporary basin. But before she takes them into the house, one fish "commits suicide, leaping out of the basin onto the destructive wooden floor." Grumbach buries the fish in the garden, "placing a cross made of match sticks over his body," and finally manages to cry. "For an hour . . . for the dead, nameless fish, for Lazarus [the just-named, surviving fish] now left alone and lonely, I believe, for my carelessness. . . . I am amazed at my free-flowing tears . . . at the depth of my grief, at my obliviousness to the true cause of my sorrow. Now I know I am crying for my dead friend, not for the newly dead fish alone."

Her essay addresses the very process that defines the art of fiction writing—of locating the means by which to channel tremendous emotion. Yet the undeniable truth is that animals, perhaps by virtue of a commiserative and yet impassive silence, offer us an all-too-limited opening for emotional self-examination and release. And since we are much better at sharing joy than grief, the animals, even when solicited or sustained by love or something even more benign, are often asked to convey our more painful emotions.

THE UNEXPECTED CRUELTY

Among the reviews and letters I received for the first two collections in this series, the subject of cruelty (i.e., "How could you put such a story in a volume that claims to care about animals!"), came up with surprising frequency. That it came up at all surprised me. Cruelty in the treatment of animals is all too common a practice; it's hardly infrequent (though it may be underexposed to the general reader). The fact that our stories record such cruelty, in the context of animal companionships and encounters, seems to be in keeping with fiction's power to help us confront or reconsider such events and their concomitant emotions. Indeed, I could hardly find a story that wasn't a memoir or a nonfiction article about the virtues of particular animals, that didn't allude to such harsh realities as violence, abandonment, or an untimely end. Though it might be needless to reiterate this, all of the stories expressed a distinct compassion, and a sustained affection, even if such joy and devotion had to be compromised.

And yet, many readers were appalled to find evidence of such neglect and hardship in works of fiction—as though stories had to aspire to a more benign world than the one in which we live. I should say that the "cruelty" they most cited in their objections was simply death—and death most often from aging, whether aided or not by a veterinarian. The "literature," however, offered no option: A book about our relationships with animal companions necessitates a range of loving care and neglect, as well as the deaths of these shorter-lived creatures.

I wish I thought ours were a peaceable world that I simply couldn't find aptly recorded in fiction. Had fiction departed from present reality and concocted all the hardships and oppressions these stories recounted? Honestly, I doubt that fiction can rival, either in number or intensity, the inhumanities expressed in the statistics, national averages, and documented cases logged by animal welfare agencies. In every way, the cruelties in the lives of the animals in these collected stories fell far shy of those recorded in this data. Curiously, the humans' plights and travails—their estrangements, injuries, misfortunes, and deaths—did not seem to matter to those responders; only what happened to the animals alarmed them. All that I could conclude is that some of us (perhaps, all of us) are so thoroughly disgusted with people, so inured and accustomed to the repeating tragedies we predictably force upon one another, that only when these same violences or abuses or devastations are visited upon animals—those last innocents, those lone survivors in their particular humanity's lonely protectorate—can they rail with pent-up fury at such injustices. What's more, when these fates occur to an animal, they also violate these individuals' own safety and security, for the animal is the last member and sole representative of an untainted nature.

A FICTIONAL FIELD GUIDE

During college I became an avid, amateur birdwatcher. For all but the winter months, my partner from ornithology lab, Jim Caldwell, and I trooped off at four o'clock every Saturday morning for some prime birding spot where various species migrated or resided: the fish hatcheries near Hebron, the marshes around Lake Erie, the grounds of Greenlawn Cemetery. We carried our new copies of Peterson's guide, hand-me-down binoculars (mine were the ones my parents had used for stadium sports), a backpack of fruit and cheese, and all the nomenclature, song patterns (transcribed from listening-lab tapes), physiognomy, flight theory, and other minutiae we had crammed into our memories from two courses in ornithology.

Our only useful qualification was, no doubt, our eagerness. Every bird was a rare bird by our standards. Our life lists—all the birds seen to this point in our lives—were mainly the backyard visitors of childhood. But we worked well together. In early spring, when there was no obscuring foliage, we could find birds in nearly every direction. And given a large sluggish bird, one tending a nest, or a whole flock, we could usually make a positive identification—or at least narrow it down to a few choices in the field guide. Admittedly, our initial guess was often a common enough bird—if only we were living among the more exotic species in New Mexico or northern Canada rather than in Ohio. Our second guess was often a female or a juvenile of an uncommon species, since we could locate all but, say, the requisite wing bars or the telltale chestnut-colored cheeks. Rarely did a bird hang around for a third guess.

We hiked those sites, no more than a few feet apart, sidling closer whenever one of us sighted something. We had different kinds of binoculars. Jim could see farther than I, but my magnification was greater. Despite our efforts to describe a given bird's location, often only one of us sighted the bird. If Jim spotted a might-be-interesting candidate, he'd direct my gaze to it—first my naked eye and then my fumbled binocs: "See that dead birch? Just left, there's a tulip tree, I think. Where it meets the birch go up about ten feet—there's a warbler, a Cape May, maybe. See it?"

Sometimes I would. Sometimes, after my prolonged efforts, if Jim still had the bird in sight, he'd hold his binocs steady, back up from the eyepiece, and make a ring of his arms so that I could duck under and then slip inside them, assuming his gaze, peering through his sights. Perhaps he had shifted, perhaps his binocs's focus wasn't right for my eyes, perhaps the bird had darted to another branch during that changeover—but often the only bird I'd end up viewing was the color reproduction that Jim would tentatively confirm in the field guide.

The stories in *The Company of Animals* include starlings and Canadian geese, members of the Class Aves, as well as many other vertebrates; still, the creature most conspicuously in sight and in focus is *Homo sapiens*. In scientific study we learn that the observer changes the observed; but fiction takes it a step farther, or closer: Here, the observer becomes the observed. Each author is both our partner in the field, pointing out what we might otherwise miss, and also someone whom, like my birdwatching partner Jim, we can watch making those observations.

I cannot promise that you will see with your own eyes the creation each writer hopes you'll share. Exactly what you or I identify (and whom we identify with) is left to each of us and our own cumulative life lists. Nonetheless, I hope you can think of each story as being held out for you: The author, *deus absconditus,* has moved out of view, and the book you are holding in your hands is a pair of steadied and focused binoculars. Slip inside the embrace each of these twenty fellow observers has made for you, and read on.

Michael J. Rosen

Remote from universal nature, and living by complicated artifice, man in civilization surveys the creature through the glass of his knowledge and sees thereby a feather magnified and the whole image in distortion. We patronize them for their incompleteness, for their tragic fate of having taken form so far below ourselves. And therein we err, and greatly err. For the animals shall not be measured by man. In a world older and more complete than ours they move finished and complete, gifted with extensions of the senses we have lost or never attained, living by voices we shall never hear. They are not brethren, they are not underlings; they are other nations, caught with ourselves in the net of life and time, fellow prisoners of the splendour and travail of the earth.

HENRY BESTON

The Company of Animals

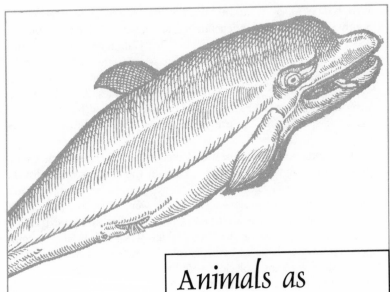

Animals as Brothers and Sisters

BRENDA PETERSON

As a child I played a game with my siblings: *What country are you?*

What body of water? What war? What animal? My sister was Ireland, the South Seas, the War of Independence, and a white stallion. My brother was Timbuktu, the Amazon River, the One Hundred Years' War, and a cobra. I was South America, the Gulf of Mexico, the Civil War, and a dolphin. Sometimes we called upon our animals—my sister galloping away from grown-ups with a powerful snort and a flick of her fine, silver mane; my brother summoning the fierce serpent hiss to ward off his older sisters; and I soaring through sea and air with my tribe of dolphins.

Our parents didn't think it odd then that their children metamorphosed into animals, oceans, or wars right there in the middle of the living room or backyard. My father always planted his family next to a forest, a river, or an ocean—all of which were expansive and natural enough to absorb our wildest play. One of the few times our transformation was curbed was at the dinner table—if, say, my brother as cobra poised above my hand as I cut the cake in exact equal pieces or if my sister was pawing the tablecloth with her pale equine impatience. Then my father, whose own play was raising horses and hunting, might threaten my sister with a tight bit or suggest my brother uncoil himself and cool down until his blood was really reptilian, slow and grounded.

"The cobra can't uncoil until he strikes and eats," my brother would mutter as he sighed and right before us changed back into the youngest child. But his eyes remained hooded.

"The white stallion is never broken," my sister would warn my father, who did raise her with a freer hand as if she were one of his fine, high-strung thoroughbreds.

I was always under water during these discussions, on the green, shady depths of my warm gulf, listening more intently to a language that creaked and chattered like high-speed hinges—dolphin gossip. Or sometimes I just tuned in to their other language: the pictures dolphins send one another in their minds. Because I had to come up for air, and my eyes were as good above water as below, I did keep a lookout on my family's dinner dramas. But if my mother was having one of her bad moods or my father was giving his lectures, back down I'd go to my other family, who welcomed me with wide-open fins. Even without hands, the dolphins embraced me more than most people did. It was body-to-body, full embrace, our eyes unblinking, utterly open as we swam, belly-to-belly, our skin twenty times more sensitive than that of humans.

The play my siblings and I chose as children is mirrored in the way we live as grown-ups. And I suspect it has much to do with our career choices, our relationships, even where we choose to live. My sister finds her South Seas body of water (and reunites with our family's Seminole blood) by living in Florida and marrying into an old Key West family. She is still fighting her War of Independence, a ripsnorting battle, which involves her husband and three daughters as high-spirited playmates. Every so often I see her snort and toss her full mane of hair; and when she really means business, she paws the ground with her delicate, high-heeled hooves. My brother, as a Navy jet navigator, has traveled the world, is caught up in all sorts of military intrigue in far places—enough to last one hundred years easy. His serpentine ways have surrendered more to the feminine aspects of the snake, for at the births of his three daughters, my brother shed his toughened military skin and was reborn. And me, well I now live in a whole city under water: Seattle. And I'm still swimming with dolphins.

This is difficult to do in Puget Sound with its year-round temperature variation from forty-six to forty-eight degrees Fahrenheit. So aside from sighting Dall's Porpoises from shore or ferry, I've had to go to warmer waters to make my psychic life match up with my actual life. How convenient then that my sister's Conch Republic connections carried me to the Florida Keys to find my animal allies.

Actually, it was a kind of coincidence. Five years ago I was sitting in my Seattle study listening to the splatter of rain on my roof, reading a New York *Times* article about a Florida Keys research program that studied human-dolphin interaction with the emphasis on dolphins and their underwater world. As I was reading, my sister

Paula called. Seems she was stranded in a motel along the string of coral keys, en route to a family reunion in Key West. I could just hear her champing at the bit.

"We're stuck here overnight," she snorted. "The girls are bored silly."

"They're not the only ones," I laughed and told her about the research program right there in Key Largo. "It's minutes from your motel," I cajoled her. "Go swim with the dolphins, please . . . do it for me."

"All right, all right," she said. "We'll go play with your imaginary friends."

There was nothing imaginary about them, as my sister who was eight months pregnant with her third daughter, soon discovered. None of Paula's births has ever been easy. But my sister's high spirits make for feisty pregnancies. With her first two children, Lauren and Lindsay, Paula was still wind-surfing into her eighth month.

It was with no fear then, that Paula lowered herself and her swollen belly into the warm tropical depths. Lauren and Lindsay have inherited their mother's thoroughbred staying power. The girls actually dove into the dolphins' lagoon with delighted squeals.

To the four dolphins below it must have seemed that small humans with high-pitched frequencies were crashing down through their watery ceiling. Rather a rude way to come calling, a dolphin might note; and yet the young of all species often enter boisterously. And these children, little mammals who breathe air as dolphins do, who are warm-blooded and may one day nurse their own young—they are mammal kin. Most of all the dolphins welcome children.

The bond was evident as the dolphins played with the girls. My five-year-old niece, Lauren, grabbed hold of a dorsal fin and held on as she was sped around the lagoon at what seemed like the speed of light. She doesn't remember seeing anything but bright bubbles. Careful to keep Lauren's small head above water, her dolphin, who weighed about three hundred pounds and was itself a relative child (only six years old in a lifespan of approximately forty years), carried Lauren as it would a precious baby doll.

Another dolphin swam sister Lindsay, two and a half, round and round until she was dizzy. Then they let her bob about in her life jacket, singing at the top of her lungs. The dolphins showed their approval with some tail slaps, spins, and leaps, always careful about their motors, those great tails. After playing with the children, the dolphins circled my sister, and when their echolocation heard the fetal heartbeat, they got very excited. The high-frequency whines and creaks increased as their sonar sounded my sister's belly, read the fetal blood pressure, and scanned the infant's stomach gases for signs of stress.

"What are they doing?" Paula asked. Her whole body was buzzing.

"Offering to midwife you," the researcher replied. "They seem concerned about the baby. Is . . . is there anything wrong?"

"I don't think so," Paula answered, and for the first time in that lagoon, she felt fear. My sister is a nurse and knows all about ultrasound. But perhaps there was something the dolphins deciphered that our technology didn't.

Then the researcher told my nieces how the dolphins midwife one another, assisting the mother as she swirls and spins in labor by stroking her flanks, and at the moment of birth, when the newborn dolphin eases out of one watery womb into another, the midwives lift the calf with their long, sensitive beaks up to the surface. There the newborn dolphin takes its first breath. "Every breath for the rest of the dolphin's life is taken consciously," the researcher told Paula. "Some scientists think that dolphins exist in an alpha state—like meditation—and since they never really sleep, just switch sides of the brain being used, we wonder what kind of intelligence is this?"

My sister certainly wondered when she gave birth three weeks later to a daughter with a rare blood disease. Had the dolphins diagnosed it? After much trauma and weeks of watching her newborn double as a tiny human pincushion, Paula brought her daughter, Lissy, home from the hospital.

On Lissy's second birthday, in gratitude and out of curiosity, we took her back to meet these dolphin midwives. But the rules had changed: no pregnant women and only children who are excellent swimmers. So little Lissy jumped and leaped on the side of the lagoon, shouting, "I am a dolphin! I am a dolphin!" as her sisters and Paula and I all slipped back into the warm salt water.

This was my first swim with the dolphins at the Dolphins Plus Marine Mammal Research & Education Center in Key Largo. My dolphin companions, Niki, Dreamer, and Sara, were six-year-old females in elective captivity only two years. Exuberant, still quite wild, they are children themselves.

"Remember," our researcher reminded us as we eased into the water, "you'll have to be creative if you want them to play with you—don't just bob about gawking. They've already got enough float toys."

The dolphins here are not rewarded with food for interaction with humans; that is the old model of performance. The real reward for all of us is the play itself.

As I swam, snorkel mask down, arms at my side to signal that I would wait for them to choose to play with me, I heard far below the familiar high-frequency dialogue. It sounded like the high-pitched whine of a jet engine right before takeoff, combined with rapid creaks and bleeps. The sounds encircled my body and then, as the dolphins came closer, there was that astonishing physical sensation of being probed by their sonar. It's as subtle as an X ray, but exhilarating. My whole body tingled, stomach gurgled, head felt pleasurable pricking as if a high-speed ping-pong game played with light was bouncing around my brain. Their sonar's precision made the experience of having my body echo-scrutinized more than simply a physical sensation. I was scanned more profoundly than by anything our medical science has yet invented. But there is another element here, not at all scientific. It is what happens to my heart, not physiologically, but emotionally.

Every time I'm sounded by a cetacean, I feel as if my cells are penetrated, seen, and—what is most remarkable—*accepted*. I've never felt judgment, even if the dolphin chose to bypass me for another playmate. Whether a dolphin spends five or forty-five minutes with a swimmer, everyone will say it was enough, all they needed, as much as they could receive. In fact, every time I've swum with dolphins, my human companions and I have admitted afterward that we each felt like the favorite. Could it be we have something to learn about parenting from dolphins?

As I swam on the surface, peering through my mask into the dense green depth, I wondered what I must look like to a dolphin. Humans are the most ungainly mammals dolphins see in the ocean. We are the only creatures in the sea who splash at both ends of our bodies. Our appendages don't move in sync with the sea as do the long arms of anemones. There is only one dance in the sea, one pulsing movement of all that lives, one law.

The dolphins always come when I'm most distracted, when my mind is not on them at all, but drifting, perhaps dreaming. In my underwater reverie, I was startled by the sensuous skin stroking my legs. I happily recognized the silken, clean, elegant feel of dolphin belly as Dreamer surfaced over me, running her whole body across my back like a bow glides across violin strings. And then she was gone. There were only the sounds fading, then coming closer as suddenly all three young dolphins swam toward me. I still see in my dreams those gray globelike domes with brown, unblinking eyes meeting mine as the dolphins greeted me under water. "Intimate" is the only way I can describe their eye contact. Benevolent, familiar, and again that acceptance. Any fear one feels vanishes once those eyes hold yours.

"Choose one!" the researcher shouted above me. Having been under water so long, I could barely hear his voice. But I remembered his instructions; the dolphins are possessive of their toys and I must bond with only one or else they'll squabble among themselves. So I chose Niki, though Dreamer was my favorite, because if truth be told, Niki made the choice. She slipped her dorsal fin under my arm and raced off with me at such a speed I saw only bubbles and sky. Then she dove with me and we both held our breaths. As we surfaced, I saw in the opposite lagoon two dolphins leaping with my nieces like calves in tow. No time to see anything else—I inhaled and dove down again.

Thrilling, this underwater ballet, as I twirled with my dolphin, my hands along her flanks. Fluid, this liquid life below where all is weightless and waves of warmth enfolded my body as I breathed air in this watery element. And I was not alone. Everywhere was sound—my nieces singing, and the dolphins' dialogue. My mind suddenly filled with pictures. Then I realized that every time I imagined my dolphin doing something, a split second later she did it. It was not a performance at my request; it was an answer to my wondering. Call and response. It was also an anticipation of my delight, a *willingness* that is the purest form of play.

I pictured myself spinning round, one hand on Niki's heart—it happened. I saw both my arms outstretched, a dolphin's dorsal offered each hand—and suddenly I was flying between Niki and Dreamer. It was impossible to tell who was sending whom these pictures. But they all happened. It was like instant replay of everything imagined. And now I understood why the child in me chose dolphins. What more perfect playmates?

Ahead in the water swam my sister. Paula was galloping with her dolphin; and my niece Lauren had a dolphin gently resting its long beak on her legs like a paddle to push her through the water. Distracted, I broke one of the basic rules: I got too close to a dolphin and her favorite toy (Paula). Suddenly a wallop to my shoulder. My world turned upside down and though I was face-up in the air, I breathed water. Sputtering, I broke another rule: my body tilted vertically, a sign to the dolphins of distress. Another whack of a pectoral in the lower back, then a beak thrust under my bottom to raise me above the water.

"Horizontal!" the researchers yelled. "They think you're drowning."

I would rather play with a dolphin than be rescued by one. Blowholes fiercely expelled their air everywhere around me. Surrounded by all three dolphins, I started to cry. I failed, I felt. I was a fool. And for the first time ever, I was afraid of them.

It was hard not to cower there in the water with them. All the pictures flooding my mind overwhelmed me and I couldn't figure anything out. Except I remembered to float, though my body was rigid and what I would most have liked to do was curl up into a fetal ball and be safe on shore the way long ago I'd surface from my own darker daydreams to find myself at the comfortingly ordinary dinner table I first sought to escape. But this was real; I couldn't imagine my way out of it. Or could I?

Again and again one picture floated in my mind. It was I, still shaken, but surrendering to all three dolphins at once. I breathed raggedly, the snorkel like an intruding fist into my mouth. But after closing my eyes, I allowed it. Yes, they could come back and find me again where I floated in fear. At first Niki and Sara were tentative, their beaks very gently stroking my legs. Now that I wasn't going to drown, would I play with them again?

I am small, I thought, and hoped they could hear. *I am just a human being—afraid and fragile in your element. Be careful with me?*

And they were. Together the three of them floated me so slowly my body barely rippled water. Then began the deepest healing. Dreamer gently eased me away from the others with a nudge of her dorsal fin. Her eyes steadily held mine as she swam gracefully in wide arcs of figure eights around the lagoon. In and out through warm water. My body surrendered to the massage, not of hands, but of water and sound. I thought of the others who come here who are not as healthy as I—the autistic and Down's syndrome children, the handicapped, the terminally ill, all of them nursed by these dolphins who embraced me. Deeper than the play, more moving than the sense of another mind in these waters, is the simple kindness of the creatures. I do not understand it. I want to.

As Dreamer circled with me, I was so relaxed I barely recognized the voices far above in the high, harsher air. "Come back," the researcher called. "It's time . . . but the dolphins are having so much fun with you, they're not going to let you get out easily."

There was a firmness to our researcher's voice, like a parent calling children in from play. We'd been swimming with the dolphins three times longer than the allotted half hour and I suddenly realized I was utterly exhausted. I felt like I'd been moving heavy furniture for days. My snorkel mask fogged and the balmy wind felt abrupt. I remembered gravity and how it works against me.

"You'll all have to link arms to signal the dolphins that you're serious about getting out. They'll respect your tribe. But they'll protest!"

As my sister and my nieces and I moved toward the dock, the dolphins leapt over our heads, chided us for spoiling their sport, and swam figure eights between our legs. Even as we hoisted ourselves up onto the platform, Niki cajoled my niece by opening her long beak and running it up and down Lauren's small leg.

"She's tasting you," the researcher told Lauren and laughed. "They only do that when they *really* like you."

"It's a compliment," Lauren confirmed in her most matter-of-fact voice. "She likes me best."

Of course we all secretly felt that way. I still feel that way, after 5 years of swimming with the same dolphins. In my Seattle study I sit surrounded by my photos—Dreamer's eyes still hold mine as she glides by in a shining green background; Niki exuberantly leaps above the surface; Sara offers her abiding companionship. My niece Lauren sends me drawings of dolphins and whales; her sister Lindsay has decided to speak nothing but dolphin dialect when I call long-distance. We cluck and click and make sounds deep in our throats like a Geiger counter. Anyone crossing wires on our conversations might think there was electronic equipment trouble on the line.

This summer I took my eight-year-old nephew Timothy to swim with the dolphins whom my nieces now call "our other relatives." A sturdy swimmer, Timothy was stunned when Samantha offered him her dorsal fin the instant he eased off the dock into that warm lagoon. She

swept Timothy away so swiftly that I rarely saw him again except underwater when boy and dolphin glided past me like one sleek body, a
ballet half-dolphin, half-human. I felt like a slow, gangly jellyfish afloat
in their fast wake.

Later on the dock the dolphins jumped over Timothy's dangling
legs, chattering to him. My nephew didn't want to leave them.

"It's the most fun I've had in *all* my eight years," he said solemnly
and tried his manly best to hold back tears at leavetaking. "I wish I
could be a dolphin," he sighed.

"Maybe you can," I laughed. "Maybe you already are. After all, they
welcomed you with open dorsals."

"Maybe they recognized me," he suggested and when I didn't dispute him, he added with quiet authority, "It's like thinking you were all
alone and then finding your long-lost brother."

"Or sister," I said and held him close.

Look How
the Fish Live

J. F. POWERS

It had been a wonderful year in the yard, which was four city lots and full of trees, a small forest and game preserve in the old part of town. Until that day, there hadn't been a single casualty, none at least that he knew about, which was the same thing and sufficient where there was so much life coming and going: squirrels, both red and grey, robins, flickers, mourning doves, chipmunks, rabbits. These creatures, and more, lived in the yard, and most of these he'd worried about in the past. Some, of course, he'd been too late for, and perhaps that was best, being able to bury what would have been his responsibility.

Obviously the children had been doing all they could for some time, for when he happened on the scene the little bird was ensconced in grass twisted into a nesting ring, soggy bread and fresh water had been set before it—the water in a tiny pie tin right under its bill—and a birdhouse was only inches away, awaiting occupancy. Bird, food and drink, and house were all in a plastic dishpan.

"Dove, isn't it?" said his wife, who had hoped to keep him off such a case, he knew, and now was easing him into it.

"I don't know," he said, afraid that he did. It was a big little bird, several shades of grey, quills plainly visible because the feathers were only beginning. Its bill was black and seemed too long for it. "A flicker maybe," he said, but he didn't think so. No, it was a dove, because where were the bird's parents? Any bird but the dove would try to do something. Somewhere in the neighborhood this baby dove's mother was posing on a branch like peace itself, with no thought of anything in her head.

"God," he groaned.

"Where *are* the worms?" said his wife.

"We can't find any," said the oldest child.

"Here," he said, taking the shovel from her. He went and dug near some shrubbery with the shovel, which was probably meant for sand and gravel. With this shovel he had buried many little things in the past. The worms were deeper than he could go with such a shovel, or they were just nowhere. He pried up two flagstones. Only ants and one many-legged worm that he didn't care to touch.

He had found no worms, and when he came back to the bird, when he saw it, he was conscious of returning empty-handed. His wife was going into the house.

"That bird can't get into that house," he said. "It's for wrens."

"We know it," said the oldest child.

He realized then that he had pointed up an obvious difficulty that the two girls had decently refrained from mentioning in front of the bird and the two younger children, the boys. But he hadn't wanted them to *squeeze* the dove into the wrenhouse. "Well, you might as well leave it where it is. Keep the bird in the shade."

"That's what we're doing."

"We put him in the dishpan so we could move him around in the shade."

"Good. Does it eat or drink anything?"

"Of course."

He didn't like the sound of that. "Did you *see* it eat or drink anything?"

"No, she did."

"You saw it eat or drink?" he said to the younger girl.

"Drink."

"It didn't eat?"

"I didn't see him eat. He maybe did when we weren't watching."

"Did it drink like this?" He sipped the air and threw back his head, swallowing.

"More like this." The child threw back her head only about half as far as he had.

"Are you sure?"

"Of course."

He walked out into the yard to get away from them. He didn't know whether the bird had taken any water. All he knew was that one of the children had imitated a bird drinking—rather, had imitated him imitating a chicken. He didn't even know whether birds threw back their heads in drinking. Was the dove a bird that had to have its mother feed it? Probably so. And so probably, as he'd thought when he first saw the bird, there was no use. He was back again.

"How does it seem? Any different?"

"How do you mean?"

"Has it changed any since you found it?"

The little girls looked at each other. Then the younger one spoke: "He's not so afraid."

He was touched by this, in spite of himself. Now that they'd found the bird, she was saying, it would be all right. Was ever a bird in worse shape? With food it couldn't eat, water it probably hadn't drunk and wouldn't, and with a house it couldn't get into—and *them!* Now they punished him with their faith in themselves and the universe, and later, when these had failed and the bird began to sink, they would punish him some more, with their faith in him. He knew what was the best thing for the bird. When the children took their naps, then maybe he could do the job. He was not soft. He had flooded gophers out of their labyrinthine ways and beheaded them with the shovel; he had purged a generation of red squirrels from the walls and attic of the old house when he moved in, knowing it was them or him. But why did animals and birds do this to him? Why did children?

"Why'd you pick this bird up? Why didn't you leave it where it was? The mother might've found it then."

"She couldn't lift him, could she?"

"Of course not."

"Well, he can't fly."

"No, but if you'd left it where it fell, the mother might see it. The mother bird has to feed a baby like this." Why couldn't she lift it? Why couldn't the two parents get together and just put it back in the nest? Why, down through the ages, hadn't birds worked out something for such an emergency? As he understood it, they were descended from reptiles and had learned how to grow feathers and fly. The whale had gone to sea. But he didn't know whether he believed any of this. Here was a case that showed how incompetent nature really was. He was tired of such cases, of nature passing the buck to him. He hated to see spring and summer come to the yard, in a way. They meant death and mosquitoes to him.

It had been the worst year for mosquitoes that anyone could remember, and in Minnesota that was saying a lot. He had bought a spraying outfit, and DDT at $2.50 a quart, which, when you considered that there was no tax on it, made you think. A quart made two gallons, but he was surprised how quickly it went. The words on the bottle "Who enjoys your yard—you or the mosquitoes?" had stayed with him, however. He had engaged professionals, with a big machine mounted on a truck, to blow a gale of poison through the yard. (In other years, seeing such an operation in other yards, he had worried about the bees.) The squirrels and rabbits in residence had evacuated the trees and lily beds while he stood by, hoping that they and the birds understood it was an emergency measure. He believed, however, that the birds received too much credit for eating annoying insects. Wasps, he knew, consumed great numbers of mosquitoes—but what about *them?* The mosquito hawk, a large, harmless insect, was a great killer of mosquitoes, but was itself killed by birds—by martins. That was the balance of nature for you. Balance for whom? You had to take steps yourself—drastic steps. Too drastic?

"Now I want you to show me exactly where you found this bird."

The little girls looked at each other.

"Don't say anything. Just take me to the exact spot."

They walked across the yard as if they really knew where they were going, and he and the little boys followed. The girls appeared to agree on the spot, but he supposed the one was under the influence of the other. The older one put out a foot and said, "Here."

He hadn't realized they were being that exact. It was surprising how right they were. Fifty or sixty feet overhead, in a fork of a big white oak, he saw a nest, definitely a dove's nest, a jerry-built job if he ever saw one, the sky visible between the sticks, and something hanging down. He moved away and gazed up again. It was only a large dead leaf, not what he'd feared, not a baby bird hanging by its foot. He felt better about having had the yard sprayed. The machine on the truck was very powerful, powerful enough to bend back the bushes and small trees, but he doubted that it had blown the baby dove out of the nest. This was just an unusually bad nest and the bird had fallen out. Nature had simply failed again.

"The nest! I see it! See?"

"Yes." He walked away from them, toward the garage. He hadn't called the nest to their attention because restoring the bird was out of the question for him—it was a job for the fire department or for God, whose eye is on the sparrow—but that didn't mean that the children might not expect him to do it.

"Just keep the bird in the shade," he called from the garage. He drove down to the office, which he hadn't planned to visit that day, and spent a few hours of peace there.

And came home to another calamity. In the kitchen, the little girls were waiting for him. Something, they said, had jumped out of the lilies and pushed one of the young bunnies that hadn't been doing anything, just eating grass near the playhouse. A weasel, they thought. Their mother hadn't seen it happen, had only heard the bunny crying, and had gone up to bed. There was no use going to her. They were in possession of what information there was. He should ask them.

"Don't go out there!"

"Why not?"

"Mama says if the bunny has the rabies it might bite."

He stood still in thought. Most of his life had been spent in a more settled part of the country. There was a great deal he didn't know about wildlife, even about the red squirrel and the yellow-jacket wasp, with which he had dealt firsthand, and he knew it. He could be wrong. But there was something ridiculous about what they were suggesting. "Did you see whatever it was that pushed the rabbit?"

"Of course!" said the older girl. It was this that distinguished her from all others in the house.

"What did it look like?"

"It went so fast."

This was ground they'd covered before, but he persevered, hoping to flush the fact that would explain everything. "What color was it?"

"Kind of—like the rabbit. But it went so fast."

This, too, was as before. "Maybe it was the mama rabbit," he said, adding something new. The more he thought about it, the more he liked it. "Maybe she didn't want the young one to come out in the open —in the daytime, I mean. Maybe she was just teaching it a lesson." He didn't know whether rabbits did that, but he did know that this particular mother was intelligent. He had first noticed her young ones, just babies then, in a shallow hole alongside a tiny evergreen that he had put a wire fence around, and that he'd draped with Shoo—rope soaked with creosote, advertised as very effective against dogs, rabbits, and rodents of all kinds. And as for the punishment the young rabbit had taken from whatever it was, he had once seen a mother squirrel get tough with a little one that had strayed from the family tree.

"Would she hurt the young rabbit?" said the younger girl.

"She might. A little."

"This one was hurt a lot," said the eyewitness. She spoke with authority.

"Maybe it was a cat," he said, rallying. "You say it was about the same size."

The children didn't reply. It seemed to him that they did not trust him. His mama-rabbit theory was too good to be true. They believed in the weasel.

"A weasel would've killed it," he said.

"But if he saw *me?*"

"*Did* he see you?"

"Of course."

"Did you see *him?*"

"Of course!" cried the child, impatient with the question. She didn't appear to realize that she was cornered, that having seen the attacker she should be able to describe it. But she was under no obligation to be logical. He decided to wait a few years.

Out in the yard he scrutinized the ground around the playhouse for blood and fur, and saw none. He stepped to the edge of the lilies. Each year the lilies were thicker and less fruitful of flowers, and a gardener would have thinned them out. A gardener, though, would have spoiled this yard—for the fairies who, the children told him, played there. He didn't enter the lilies because he didn't want to encounter what he might.

Passing through the kitchen, he noticed that the children were cutting up a catalogue, both pasting. Apparently the older one could no longer get the younger one to do all the scissor work. "How's the bird?"

"We don't know."

He stopped and got them in focus. "Why don't you know?"

"We haven't looked at it."

"Haven't looked at it! Why haven't you?"

"We've been doing this."

"This is why."

It was a mystery to him how, after crooning over the helpless creature, after entangling him in its fate, they could be this way. This was not the first time, either. "Well, get out there and look at it!"

On the way out to look at it himself, he met them coming back. "He's all right," the older one said grumpily.

"Looks the same, huh?" He didn't catch what they said in reply, which wasn't much anyway. He found the bird where he'd last seen it, beside the back porch. He had expected it to be dying by now. Its ribs showed clearly when it breathed, which was alarming, but he remembered that this had worried him when he first saw the bird. It did seem to be about the same.

He passed through the kitchen and, seeing the children all settled down again, he said, "Find a better place for it. It'll soon be in the sun."

A few moments later, he was intervening. They had the whole yard and yet they were arguing over two patches of shade, neither of which would be good for more than a few minutes. He carried the dishpan out into the yard, and was annoyed that they weren't following him, for he wanted them to see what he was doing and why. He put the dishpan down where the sun wouldn't appear again until morning. He picked it up again. He carried it across the yard to the foot of the white oak. On the ground, directly below the nest, there was and would be sun until evening, but near the trunk there would be shade until morning.

The bird was breathing heavily, as before, but it was in no distress —unless this was distress. He thought not. If the bird had a full coat of feathers, its breathing wouldn't be so noticeable.

He was pleasantly surprised to see a mature dove high above him. The dove wasn't near the nest, wasn't watching him—was just looking unconcerned in another part of the tree—but it was in the right tree. He tried to attract its attention, making what he considered a gentle bird noise. It flew away, greatly disappointing him.

He knelt and lifted the tin of water to the bird's mouth. This he did with no expectation that it would drink, but it did, it definitely did. The bird kept its bill in the water, waggling it once or twice, spilling some, and raised its head slightly—not as a chicken would. He tried a little bread, unsuccessfully. He tried the water again, and again the bird drank. The bread was refused again and also the water when it was offered the third time. This confirmed him in his belief that the bird had been drinking before. This also proved that the bird was able to make decisions. After two drinks, the bird had said, in effect, no more. It hadn't eaten for some time, but it was evidently still sound in mind and body. It might need only a mother's care to live.

. . .

He went into the house. In the next two hours, he came to the window frequently. For a while he tried to believe that there might be maternal action at the foot of the oak while he wasn't watching. He knew better, though. All he could believe was that the mother might be staying away because she regarded the dishpan as a trap—assuming, of course, that she had spotted the baby, and assuming also that she gave a damn, which he doubted.

Before dinner he went out and removed the birdhouse and then the bird from the dishpan, gently tipping it into the grass, not touching it. The nest the children had twined together slid with it, but the bird ended up more off than on the nest. There was plenty of good, growing grass under the dove, however. If, as the children claimed, the bird could move a little and if the mother did locate it, perhaps between them—he credited the baby with some intelligence—they might have enough sense to hide out in the lilies of the valley only a few feet away. There would be days ahead of feeding and growth before the little bird could fly, probably too many days to pass on the ground in the open. Once the mother assumed her responsibility, however, everything would become easier—that is, possible. *He* might even build a nest nearby. (One year there had been a dove's nest in a chokecherry tree, only ten feet off the ground.) Within a few yards of the oak there were aged lilac bushes, almost trees, which would be suitable for a nest. At present, though, with the mother delinquent, the situation was impossible.

He looked up into the trees for her, in vain, and then down at the orphan. It had moved. It had taken up its former position precisely in the center of the little raft of grass the children had made for it, and this was painful to see, this little display of order in a thing so small, so dumb, so sure.

It would not drink. He set the water closer, and the bread, just in case, and carried away the dishpan and the birdhouse. He saw the bowel movement in the bottom of the dishpan as a good omen, but was puzzled by the presence of a tiny dead bug of the beetle family. It could mean that the mother had been in attendance, or it could mean that the bug had simply dropped dead from the spraying, a late casualty.

After dinner, standing on the back porch, he heard a disturbance far out in the yard. Blue jays, and up to no good, he thought, and walked toward the noise. When he reached the farthest corner of the yard, the noise ceased, and began again. He looked into the trees across the alley. Then he saw two catbirds in the honeysuckle bushes only six feet away and realized that he had mistaken their rusty cries for those of blue jays at some distance. The catbirds hopped, scolding, from branch to branch. They moved to the next bush, but not because of him, he thought. It was then that he saw the cat in the lilies. He stamped his foot. The cat, a black-and-white one marked like a Holstein cow, plowed through the lilies and out into the alley where the going was good, and was gone. The catbirds followed, flying low, belling the cat with their cries. In the distance he heard blue jays, themselves marauders, join in, doing their bit to make the cat's position known. High overhead he saw two dopey doves doing absolutely nothing about the cat, heard their little dithering noise, and was disgusted with them. It's a wonder you're not extinct, he thought, gazing up at them. They chose that moment to show him the secret of their success.

He walked the far boundaries of the yard, stopping to gaze back at the old frame house, which was best seen at a distance. He had many pictures of it in his mind, for it changed with the seasons, gradually, and all during the day. The old house always looked good to him: in spring when the locust, plum, lilacs, honeysuckle, caragana, and mock orange bloomed around it; in summer, as it was now, almost buried in green; in autumn when the yard was rolling with nuts, crashing with leaves, and the mountain-ash berries turned red; and in winter when, under snow and icicles, with its tall mullioned windows sparkling, it reminded him of an old-fashioned Christmas card. For a hundred years it had been painted barn or Venetian red, with forest-green trim. In winter there were times when the old house, because of the light, seemed to be bleeding; the red then was profound and alive. Perhaps it knew something, after all, he thought. In January the yellow bulldozers would come for it and the trees. One of the old oaks, one that had appeared to be in excellent health, had recently thrown down half of itself in the night. "Herbal suicide," his wife had said.

Reaching the other far corner of the yard, he stood considering the thick black-walnut tree, which he had once, at about this time of year, thought of girdling with a tin shield to keep off the squirrels. But this would have taken a lot of tin, and equipment he didn't own to trim a neighboring maple and possibly an elm, and so he had decided to share the nuts with the squirrels. This year they could have them all. Few of the birds would be there when it happened, but the squirrels—there were at least a dozen in residence—were in for a terrible shock.

He moved toward the house, on the street side of the yard, on the lookout for beer cans and bottles that the college students from their parked cars tossed into the bushes. He knew, from several years of picking up after them, their favorite brand.

He came within twenty yards of the white oak, and stopped. He didn't want to venture too near in case the mother was engaged in feeding the baby, or was just about to make up her mind to do so. In order to see, however, he would have to be a little closer. He moved toward the white oak in an indirect line, and stopped again. The nest was empty. His first thought was that the bird, sensing the approach of darkness, had wisely retreated into the shelter of the lilies of the valley nearby, and then he remembered the recent disturbance on the other side of the yard. The cat had last been seen at what had appeared a safe distance then. He was looking now for feathers, blood, bones. But he saw no such signs of the bird. Again he considered the possibility that it was hiding in the lilies of the valley. When he recalled the bird sitting in the very center of the nest, it did not seem likely that it would leave, ever—unless persuaded by the mother to do so. But he had no faith in the mother, and instead of searching the lilies, he stood where he was and studied the ground around him in a widening circle. The cat could've carried it off, of course, or—again—the bird could be safe among the lilies.

He hurried to the fallen oak. Seeing the little bird at such a distance from the nest, and not seeing it as he'd expected he would, but entire, he had been deceived. The bird was not moving. It was on its back, not mangled but dead. He noted the slate-black feet. Its head was to one side on the grass. The one eye he could see was closed, and the blood all around it, enamel-bright, gave the impression, surprising to him, that it had poured out like paint. He wouldn't have thought such a little thing would even have blood.

He went for the shovel with which he'd turned up no worms for the bird earlier that day. He came back to the bird by a different route, having passed on the other side of a big tree, and saw the little ring of grass that had been the bird's nest. It now looked like a wreath to him.

He dug a grave within a few feet of the bird. The ground was mossy there. He simply lifted up a piece of it, tucked in the bird, and dropped the sod down like a cover. He pounded it once with the back side of the shovel, thinking the bird would rest easier there than in most ground.

When he looked up from his work, he saw that he had company: Mr. and Mrs. Hahn, neighbors. He told them what had happened, and could see that Mr. Hahn considered him soft. He remembered that Mr. Hahn, who had an interest such as newspapers seemed to think everybody ought to have in atomic explosions, didn't care to discuss the fallout.

The Hahns walked with him through the yard. They had heard there were no mosquitoes there now.

"Apparently it works," he said.

"The city should spray," said Mrs. Hahn.

"At least the swamps," said Mr. Hahn, who was more conservative.

He said nothing. They were perfectly familiar with his theory: that it was wet enough in the lily beds, in the weeds along the river, for mosquitoes to breed. When he argued that there just weren't enough swamps to breed that many mosquitoes, people smiled, and tried to refute his theory—confirmed it—by talking about how little water it took, a birdbath, a tin can somewhere. "In my opinion, they breed right here, in this yard and yours."

"Anyway, they're not here now," said Mrs. Hahn.

He received this not as a compliment but as a polite denial of his theory. They were passing under the mulberry tree. In the bloody atmosphere prevailing in his mind that evening, he naturally thought of the purple grackle that had hung itself from a high branch with a string in the previous summer. "I'm sick of it all."

"Sick of *what?*" said Mrs. Hahn.

The Hahns regarded him as a head case, he knew, and probably wouldn't be surprised if he said that he was sick of them. He had stopped trying to adjust his few convictions and prejudices to company. He just let them fly. Life was too short. "Insects, birds, and animals of all kinds," he said. "Nature."

Mr. Hahn smiled. "There'd be too many of those doves if things like that didn't happen."

"I suppose."

Mr. Hahn said: "Look how the fish live."

He looked at the man with interest. This was the most remarkable thing Mr. Hahn had ever said in his presence. But, of course, Mr. Hahn didn't appreciate the implications. Mr. Hahn didn't see himself in the picture at all.

"That includes children," he said, pursuing his original line. It was the children who were responsible for bringing the failures of nature to his attention.

Mrs. Hahn, who seemed to feel she was on familiar ground, gaily laughed. "Everybody who has them complains about them."

"And women," he added. He had almost left women out, and they belonged in. They were responsible for the children and the success of *Queen for a Day.*

"And men," he added when he caught Mr. Hahn smiling at the mention of women. Men were at the bottom of it all.

"That doesn't leave much, does it?" said Mr. Hahn.

"No." Who *was* left? God. It wasn't surprising, for all problems were at bottom theological. He'd like to put a few questions to God. God, though, knowing his thoughts, knew his questions, and the world was already in possession of all the answers that would be forthcoming from God. Compassion for the Holy Family fleeing from Herod was laudable and meritorious, but it was wasted on soulless rabbits fleeing from soulless weasels. Nevertheless it was there just the same, or something very like it. As he'd said in the beginning, he was sick of it all.

"There he is now!" cried Mrs. Hahn.

He saw the black-and-white cat pause under the fallen oak.

"Should I get my gun?" said Mr. Hahn.

"No. It's his nature." He stamped his foot and hissed. The cat ran out of the yard. Where were the birds? They could be keeping an eye on the cat. Somewhere along the line they must have said the hell with it. He supposed there was a lesson in that for him. A man couldn't commiserate with life to the full extent of his instincts and opportunities. A man had to accept his God-given limitations.

He accompanied the Hahns around to the front of the house, and there they met a middle-aged woman coming up the walk. He didn't know her, but the Hahns did, and introduced her. Mrs. Snyder.

"It's about civil defense," she said. Every occupant of every house was soon to be registered for the purposes of identification in case of an emergency. Each block would have its warden, and Mrs. Snyder thought that he, since he lived on this property, which took up so much of the block . . .

"No."

"No?"

"No." He couldn't think of a job for which he was less suited, in view of his general outlook. He wouldn't be here anyway. Nor would this house, these trees.

While Mr. and Mrs. Hahn explained to Mrs. Snyder that the place was to become a parking lot for the college, he stood by in silence. He had never heard it explained so well. His friends had been shocked at the idea of doing away with the old house and trees—and for a parking lot!—and although he appreciated their concern, there was nothing to be done, and after a time he was unable to sympathize with them. This they didn't readily understand. It was as if some venerable figure in the community, only known to them but near and dear to him, had been murdered, and he failed to show proper sorrow and anger. The Hahns, however, were explaining how it was, turning this way and that, pointing to this building and that, to sites already taken, to those to be taken soon or in time. For them the words "the state" and "expansion" seemed sufficient. And the Hahns weren't employed by the college and they weren't old grads. It was impossible to account in such an easy way for their enthusiasm. They were scheduled for eviction themselves, they said, in a few years.

When they were all through explaining, it must have been annoying to them to hear Mrs. Snyder's comment. "Too bad," she said. She glanced up at the old red house and then across the street at the new dormitory going up. There had been a parking lot there for a few years, but before that another big old house and trees. The new dormitory, apricot bricks and aluminum windows, was in the same style as the new library, a style known to him and his wife as Blank. "Too bad," Mrs. Snyder said again, with an uneasy look across the street, and then at him.

"There's no defense against that *either,*" he said, and if Mrs. Snyder understood what he meant, she didn't show it.

"Well," she said to Mr. Hahn, "how about you?"

. . .

They left him then. He put the shovel away, and walked the boundaries of the yard for the last time that day, pausing twice to consider the house in the light of the moment. When he came to the grave, he stopped and looked around for a large stone. He took one from the mound where the hydrant was, the only place where the wild ginger grew, and set it on the grave, not as a marker but as an obstacle to the cat if it returned, as he imagined it would. It was getting dark in the yard, the night coming sooner there because of the great trees. Now the bats and owls would get to work, he thought, and went into the doomed house.

A Folio
of Photographs

JAMES BALOG

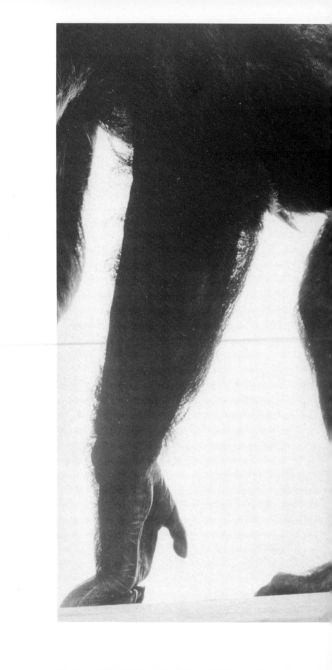

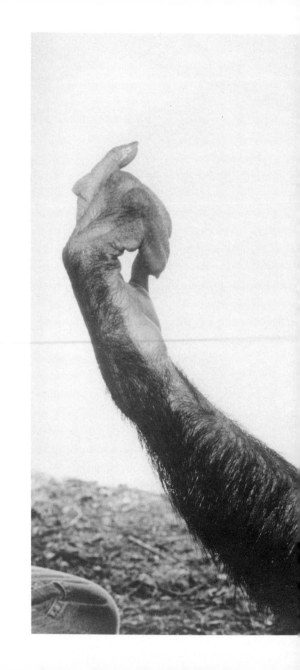

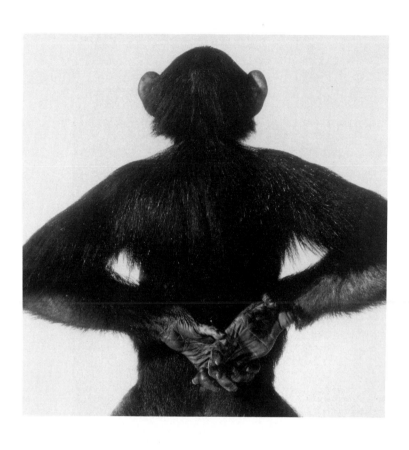

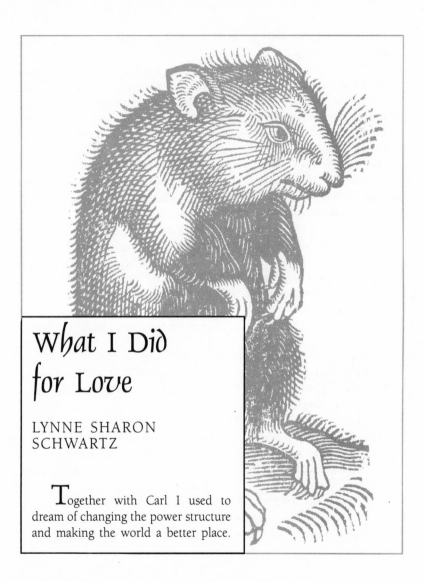

What I Did for Love

LYNNE SHARON SCHWARTZ

Together with Carl I used to dream of changing the power structure and making the world a better place.

Never that I could end up watching the ten o'clock news with a small rodent on my lap.

He was the fourth. Percy, the first, was a bullet-shaped dark brown guinea pig, short-haired as distinct from the long-haired kind, and from the moment he arrived he tried to hide, making tunnels out of the newspapers in his cage until Martine, who was just eight then, cut the narrow ends off a shoebox and made him a real tunnel, where he stayed except when food appeared. I guess she would have preferred a more sociable pet, but Carl and I couldn't walk a dog four times a day, and the cat we tried chewed at the plants and watched us in bed, which made us self-conscious, and finally got locked in the refrigerator as the magnetic door was closing, so after we found it chilled and traumatized we gave it to a friend who appreciated cats.

Percy had been living his hermit life for about a year when Martine noticed he was hardly eating and being unusually quiet, no rustling of paper in the tunnel. I made an appointment with a vet someone recommended. On the morning of the appointment, after I got Martine on the school bus, I saw Percy lying very still outside the tunnel. I called the vet before I left for work to say I thought his patient might be dead.

"Might be?"

"Well . . . how can I tell for sure?"

He clears his throat and with this patronizing air doctors have, even vets, says, "Why not go and flick your finger near the animal's neck and see if he responds?"

Since I work for a doctor I'm not intimidated by this attitude, it just rolls off me. "Okay, hold on a minute. . . ." I went and flicked. "He doesn't seem to respond, but still . . . I just don't feel sure."

"Raise one of his legs," he says slowly, as if he's talking to a severely retarded person, "wiggle it around and see if it feels stiff." He never heard of denial, this guy. What am I going to tell Martine?

"Hang on. . . ." I wiggled the leg. "It feels stiff," I had to admit.

"I think it's safe to assume," he says, "that the animal is dead."

"I guess we won't be keeping the appointment, then?" I'm not re-tarded. I said it on purpose, to kind of rile him and see what he'd say.

"That will hardly be necessary."

To get ready for the burial, I put Percy in a shoebox (a new one, not the tunnel one), wrapped the tissue paper from the shoes around him, and added some flowers I bought on the way home from work, then sealed it up with masking tape. Carl and I kept the coffin in our room that night so Martine wouldn't have to be alone in the dark with it. She didn't cry much, at least in front of us. She keeps her feelings to herself, more like me in that way than Carl. But I knew she was very attached to Percy, hermit that he was. The next morning, a Saturday, the three of us set out carrying the box and a spade and shovel we borrowed from the super of the building. Carl's plan was to bury him in the park, but it was the dead of winter, February, and the ground was so frozen the spade could barely break it.

"This isn't going to work," he said.

Martine looked tragic. She's always been a very beautiful child, with a creamy-skinned face and an expression of serene tragic beauty that, depending on the situation, can make you want to laugh or cry. At that moment I could have done either. We were huddled together, our eyes and noses running from the cold, Martine clutching the shoebox in her blue down mittens.

"I know what," Carl said. "We'll bury him at sea."

Martine's face got even more tragic, and I gave him a funny look too. What sea? It was more than an hour's drive to Coney Island and I had a million things to do that day.

"The river. It's a very old and dignified tradition," he told her. "For people who die on ships, when it would take too long to reach land. In a way it's nicer than an earth burial—in the course of time Percy's body will drift to the depths and mingle with coral and anemone instead of being confined in—"

"Okay," she said.

So we walked up to the 125th Street pier on the Hudson River. This is a desolate place just off an exit of the West Side Highway, where the only buildings are meat-processing plants and where in the daytime a few lone people come to wash their cars, hauling water up in buckets, and even to fish, believe it or not, and at night people come to buy and sell drugs. I looked at Martine. She handed me the box like she couldn't bear to do it herself, so I knelt down and placed it in the river as gently as I could. I was hoping it would float for a while, at least till we could get her away, but my romantic Carl was saying something poetic and sentimental about death and it began to sink, about four feet from where we stood. It was headed south, though, towards the Statue of Liberty and the open sea, I pointed out to her. Free at last.

We got her another guinea pig, a chubby buff-colored one who did not hide and was intelligent and interested in its surroundings, as much as a guinea pig can be. We must have had it—Mooney, it was called—for around a year and a half when Carl began talking about changing his life, finding a new direction. He was one of those people—we both were—who had dropped out of school because it seemed there was so much we should be doing in the world. I was afraid he would be drafted, and we had long searching talks, the way you do when you're twenty, about whether he should be a conscientious objector, but at the last minute the army didn't want him because he had flat feet and was partially deaf in one ear. Those same flat feet led all those marches and demonstrations. Anyhow, he never managed to drop back in later on when things changed. Not that there was any less to do, but somehow no way of doing it anymore and hardly anyone left to do it with, not to mention money. You have to take care of your own life, we discovered. And if you have a kid . . . You find yourself doing things you never planned on.

He started driving a cab when Martine was born and had been ever since. It's exhausting, driving a cab. He spent less and less time organizing demonstrations and drawing maps of the locations of nuclear stock-piles. Now he spent his spare time playing ball with the guys he used to go to meetings with, or reading, or puttering with his plants, which after me, he used to say, were his great passion. It was not a terrible life, he was not harming anyone, and as I often told him, driving a cab where you come in contact with people who are going places was more varied than what I do all day as an X-ray technician, which you could hardly call upbeat. Most of the time, you find the patients either have cancer or not, and while you naturally hope for the best each time, you can't help getting to feel less and less, because a certain percentage are always doomed regardless of your feelings. Well, Carl was not satisfied, he was bored, so I said, "Okay, what would you do if you had a totally free choice?"

"I would like to practice the art of topiary."

"What's that?"

"Topiary is the shaping of shrubberies and trees into certain forms. You know, when you drive past rich towns in Westchester, you some-times see bushes on the lawns trimmed to spell a word or the initials of a corporation? You can make all sorts of shapes—animals, statues. Have you ever seen it?"

"Yes." I was a little surprised by this. You think you know all about a person and then, topiary. "Well, maybe there's someplace you can learn. Take a course in, what is it, landscape gardening?"

"It's not very practical. You said totally free choice. I don't think that there could be much of a demand for it in Manhattan."

"We could move."

"Where, Chris?" He smiled, sad and sweet and sexy. That was his kind of appeal. "Beverly Hills?"

"Well, maybe there's something related that you can do. You know those men who drive around in green trucks and get hoisted into the trees in little metal seats? I think they trim branches off the ones with Dutch elm disease. Or a tree surgeon?"

This didn't grab him. We talked about plants and trees, and ambition, and doing something you cared about that also provided a living. Finally he said it was a little embarrassing, but what he really might like, in practical terms, was to have a plant store, a big one, like the ones he browsed in down in the twenties.

"Why should that be embarrassing?"

"When you first met me I was going to alter the power structure of society and now I'm telling you I want to have a plant store. Are you laughing at me, Chris? Tell the truth."

"I haven't heard you say anything laughable yet. I didn't really expect you to change the world, Carl."

"No?"

"I mean, I believed you meant it, and I believed in you, but that's not why I married you." Lord no. I married him for his touch, it struck me, and the sound of his voice, and a thousand other of those things I thought I couldn't exist without. It also struck me that I had never truly expected to change the power structure but that I had liked hanging out with people who thought they could. It was, I would have to say, inspiring.

"Do you think I'm having a mid-life crisis?"

"No. You're only thirty-three. I think you want to change jobs."

So we decided he should try it. He could start by getting a job in a plant store to learn about it, and drive the cab at night. That way we could save some money for a small store to begin with. He would have less time with me and Martine, but it would be worth it in the long run. Except he didn't do it right away. He liked to sit on things for a while, like a hen.

That summer we scraped together the money to send Martine to a camp run by some people we used to hang out with in the old days, and since it was a camp with animals, sort of a farm camp, she took Mooney along. Her third night away she called collect from Vermont and said she had something very sad to tell us. From her tragic voice for an instant I thought they might have discovered she had a terminal disease like leukemia, and how could they be so stupid as to tell her—they were progressive types, maybe they thought it was therapeutic to confront your own mortality—but the news was that Mooney was dead. Someone had left the door of the guinea pigs' cage open the night before and he got out and was discovered in the morning in a nearby field, most likely mauled by a larger animal. I sounded relieved and not tragic enough, but fortunately Carl had the right tone throughout. At the age of eleven she understood a little about the brutalities of nature and the survival of the fittest and so on, but it was still hard for her to accept.

Martine is a peacefully inclined, intuitive type. She would have felt at home in our day, when peace and love were respectable attitudes. We named her after Martin Luther King, which nowadays seems a far-out thing to have done. Not that my estimation of him has changed or that I don't like the name, only it isn't the sort of thing people do anymore. Just as, once we stayed up nights thinking of how to transform the world and now I'm glad I have a job, no matter how boring, and can send her to camp for a few weeks.

Anyway, the people running the camp being the way they were, they immediately bought her a new guinea pig. Aside from her tragedy she had a terrific time, and she came home with a female pig named Elf, who strangely enough looked exactly like Mooney, in fact if I hadn't known Mooney was dead I would have taken Elf for Mooney. I remember remarking to Carl that if things were reversed, if Mooney had been left at home with us and died and we had managed to find an identical bullet-shaped replacement, I might have tried to pass it off as Mooney, in the way mothers instinctively try to protect their children from the harsher facts of life. But Carl said he wouldn't have, he would have told her the truth, not to make her confront harsh reality but because Martine would be able to tell the difference, as mothers can with twins, and he wouldn't want her catching him in a lie. "You know she has such high standards," he said.

In the dead of winter, even colder than in Percy's era, Martine told us Elf wasn't eating. Oh no, I thought. *Déjà vu.* The stillness, then the stiffness, wrapping it in the shoebox, burial at sea . . . Nevertheless, what can you do, so I made an appointment with the vet, the same old arrogant vet—I didn't have the energy to look for a new one. I was feeling sick when the day arrived, so Carl took off from work and went with Martine and Elf.

"There's good news and bad news," he said when they got home. "The good news is that she doesn't have a dread disease. What's wrong with her is her teeth."

I was lying in bed, trying to sleep. "Her teeth?"

"You've got it. Her top and bottom teeth are growing together so she can't eat. She can't separate them to chew." He gave me a demonstration of Elf's problem, stretching his lips and straining his molars.

"Please, this is no time to make me laugh. My stomach is killing me."

"What is it? Your period?"

"No. I don't know what."

"Well, listen—the bad news is that she needs surgery. Oral surgery. It's a hundred twenty-five including the anesthetic."

"This is not the least bit funny. What are we going to do?" Martine was putting Elf back in her cage, otherwise we would have discussed this with more sensitivity.

"Is there a choice? You know how Martine feels—Albert Schweitzer Junior. I made an appointment for tomorrow. She'll have to stay overnight."

"I presume you mean Elf, not Martine."

"Of course I mean Elf. Maybe I should call a doctor for you too."

"No, I'll be okay. What's a stomach ache compared to oral surgery?"

"I don't want you getting all worked up over this, Chris." He joined me on the bed and started fooling around. "Thousands of people each year have successful oral surgery. It's nothing to be alarmed about."

"I'll try to deal with it. Ow, you're leaning right where it hurts." Martine came into the room and Carl sat up quickly.

"She's looking very wan," she said.

"Two days from now she'll be a new person," Carl said.

"She's never been a person before. How could she be one in two days?"

"Medical science is amazing."

"I have no luck with guinea pigs." She plopped into a chair, stretched out her legs, and sat gazing at her sneakers. I noticed how tall she was growing. She was nearly twelve and beginning to get breasts. But she wasn't awkward like most girls at that stage; she was stunning, willowy and auburn-haired, with green eyes. There was sometimes a faint emerald light in the whites of her eyes that would take me by surprise, and I would stare and think, What a lucky accident.

"Maybe none of them live long," I said. "I doubt if yours are being singled out."

"They have a four-to-six-year life span. I looked it up in the encyclopedia. But in four years I've gone through almost three."

That night I had such terrible pains in my stomach that Carl took me to the emergency room, where after a lot of fussing around—they tried to send me home, they tried to get me to sleep—they found it was my appendix and it had to come out right away. It was quite a few days before I felt like anything resembling normal, and I forgot completely about Elf's oral surgery.

"Chris, before we go inside, I'd better tell you something." Carl switched off the engine and reached into the back seat for my overnight bag. He was avoiding my eyes.

"What happened? I spoke to her on the phone just last night!" I was about to leap out of the car, but he grabbed my arm.

"Hold it a minute, will you? You're supposed to take it easy."

"Well what's wrong, for Chrissake?"

He looked at me. "Not Martine. Jesus! Elf."

"Elf." I thought I would pass out. I was still pretty drugged.

"She got through the surgery all right. We brought her home the next day. But . . . I don't know whether she was too weak from not eating or what, but she never started eating again. And so . . ."

"I never liked that doctor. How did Martine take it this time?"

"Sad but philosophical. I think she's used to it by now. Besides, she was more concerned about you."

"I'm glad to hear that. So where is the corpse? At sea again?"

"Well, no, actually. That's why I wanted to tell you before you went in the apartment. The temperature has been near zero. The river is frozen."

"Just give it to me straight, Carl."

"She's wrapped in some plastic bags on the bathroom windowsill. Outside. The iron grating is holding her in place. I was going to put her in the freezer with the meat, but I thought you might not care for that."

"Couldn't you find a shoebox?"

"No. I guess nobody's gotten new shoes lately."

"And how long is she going to stay there?"

"They're predicting a thaw. It's supposed to get warm, unseasonably warm, so in a few days we'll take her out to the park. Anyway, welcome home. Oh, there's another thing."

"I hope this is good."

It was. He had found a job working in the greenhouse at the Botanical Garden.

Since Martine never brought the subject up again after the thaw and the park burial, I assumed the guinea pig phase of her life was over. Two weeks after she returned from camp that summer, the super who had loaned us the spade and shovel for Percy came up to say there was a family in the next building with a new guinea pig, but their baby was allergic to it and couldn't stop sneezing. Maybe we wanted to do them a favor and take it off their hands?

Martine and I turned to each other. "What do you think?" I said.

"I'm not sure. They're a lot of expense, aren't they?"

"Not so bad. I mean, what's a little lettuce, carrots . . ."

"The medical expenses. And you don't like them too much, do you, Mom?"

I tried to shrug it off with a blank smile. I looked at Mr. Coates—what I expected I'll never know, since he stood there as if he had seen and heard everything in his lifetime and was content to wait for this discussion to be over. I wondered how much of a tip he would get for the deal. Nothing from us, I vowed.

"I've noticed," Martine said. "You don't like to handle them. You don't like small rodents."

"Not a whole lot, frankly." They looked to me like rats, fat tailless rats. For Martine's sake I had wished them good health and long life, but I tried not to get too close. When she was out with her friends and I had to feed them, I used to toss the lettuce in and step back as they lunged for it. I didn't like the eager squeaks they let out when they smelled the food coming, or the crunching sounds they made eating it. And when I held them—at the beginning, when she would offer them to me to stroke, before she noticed how I felt about small rodents—I didn't like the nervous fluttery softness of them, their darting squirmy little movements, the sniffing and nipping and the beat of the fragile heart so close to the surface I could feel it in my palms. "But they don't bother me so long as they're in the cage in your room." Which was true.

"You could go over and take a look," said Mr. Coates finally. "I'll take you over there if you want."

"Maybe I'll do that, Mom. Do you want to come too?"

"No. I know what guinea pigs look like by now."

"What color is it?" Martine was asking him on the way out.

"I don't know the color. I ain't seen it myself yet."

I didn't pay any more attention to Rusty, named for his color, than I had to the others. I made sure to be in another room while Martine and Carl cut his nails, one holding him down, the other clipping—they took turns. Martine started junior high and got even more beautiful, breasts, hips, the works, with a kind of slow way of turning her head and moving her eyes. She also started expressing intelligent opinions on every subject in the news, test tube babies, airplane hijackings, chemicals in packaged foods, while Carl and I listened and marveled, with this peculiar guilty relief that she was turning out so well—I guess because we were not living out our former ideals, not changing the world or on the other hand being particularly upwardly mobile either. Carl was happier working in the greenhouse, but we still hadn't managed to save enough to rent a store or qualify for a bank loan.

At Martine's thirteenth birthday party in May, we got to talking in the kitchen with one of the mothers who came to pick up her kid. I liked her. She was about our age, small and blonde, and she had dropped out of school too but had gone back to finish and was even doing graduate work.

"What field?" I asked. I was scraping pizza crusts into the garbage while Carl washed out soda cans—he was very big on recycling. In the living room the kids were dancing to a reggae song called "Free Nelson Mandela," and the three of us had been remarking, first of all, that Nelson Mandela had been in prison since we were about their age and in the meantime we had grown up and were raising children and feeling vaguely disappointed with ourselves, and secondly, that dancing to a record like that wouldn't have been our style even if there had been one back then, which was unlikely. Singing was more our style. And the fact that teen-agers today were dancing to this "Free Nelson Mandela" record at parties made their generation seem less serious, yet at this point who were we to judge styles of being serious? The man was still in prison, after all.

"Romance languages," she said. She was playing with the plastic magnetic letters on the refrigerator. They had been there since Martine was two. Sometimes we would use them to write things like Merry Xmas or, as tonight, Happy Birthday, and sometimes to leave real messages, like Skating Back at 7 M. The messages would stay up for the longest time, eroding little by little because we knocked the letters off accidentally and stuck them back any old place, or because we needed a letter for a new message, so that Happy Birthday could come to read Hapy Birda, and at some point they would lose their meaning altogether, like Hay irda, which amused Martine no end. This woman wrote, *"Nel mezzo del cammin di nostra vita."*

"What does that mean?" Carl asked her.

" 'In the middle of the journey of our life.' It's the opening of *The Divine Comedy*. What it means is, here I am thirty-five years old and I'm a graduate student."

"There's nothing wrong with that," said Carl. "I admire your determination. I'm driving a cab, but one day before I die I'm going to learn to do topiary, for the simple reason that I want to."

She said what I knew she would. "What's topiary?"

He stopped rinsing cans to tell her.

I never read *The Divine Comedy*, but I do know Dante goes through Hell and Purgatory and eventually gets to Paradise. All the parts you ever hear about, though, seem to take place in Hell, and so a small shiver ran up my spine, seeing that message on the refrigerator above Happy Birthday. Then I forgot about it.

In bed that night I asked Carl if he was serious about learning topiary. He said he had been thinking it over again. Since he had gotten a raise at the greenhouse, maybe he might give up the cab altogether, he was so sick of it, and use the money we'd saved for the store to study landscape gardening.

"Well, okay. That sounds good. I can work a half day Saturdays, maybe."

"No, I don't want you to lose the little free time you have. We'll manage. Maybe there's something you want to go back and study too."

"I'm not ambitious. Why, would I be more attractive, like, if I went to graduate school?"

"Ha! Did I hear you right?" He let out a comic whoop. "I don't even remember her name, Chris. Listen, you want me to prove my love?"

That was the last time. The next day he came down with the flu, then Martine and I got it, and just when we were beginning to come back to life he had a heart attack driving the cab. He might have made it, the doctor said, except he was alone and lost control of the wheel. They told me more details about it, just like a news report, more than I could bear to listen to, in fact. I tried to forget the words the minute I heard them, but no amount of trying could make me stop seeing the scene in my mind. They offered me pills, all through those next insane days, but I wasn't interested in feeling better. Anyhow, what kind of goddamn pill could cure this? I asked them. I also kept seeing in my mind a scene on the Long Island Expressway when Martine was a baby and we were going to Jones Beach. About three cars ahead of us over in the right lane, a car started to veer, and as we got closer we could see the driver slumping down in his seat. Before we could even think what to do, a state trooper appeared out of nowhere and jumped in on the driver's side to grab the wheel. Sirens started up, I guess they took him to the hospital, and a huge pile-up was averted. Watching it, I felt bad about how we used to call cops pigs. That sounds a little simple-minded, I know, but so was calling them pigs. And now I wondered how come a miracle in the form of a cop happened for that person and not for Carl, which is a question a retarded person might ask—I mean, an out-of-the-way street in Queens at eleven at night . . . It happened the way it happened, that's all. A loss to all those who might have enjoyed his topiary. I do think he would have done it in his own good time. If only we had had a little more time, I could have taken care of him. I wouldn't have been a miracle, but I would have done a good job. The way he vanished, though, I couldn't do a thing, not even say goodbye or hold his hand in the hospital or whatever it is old couples do—maybe the wife whispers that she'll be joining him soon, but I have no illusions that I'll ever be joining him, soon or late. I just got a lot less of him than I expected. Another thing is that the last time we made love

I was slightly distracted because of the graduate student he admired for her determination, not that anything transpired between them except some ordinary conversation, but it started me wondering in general. Stupid, because I know very well how he felt, he told me every night. Those words I don't forget. I let them put me to sleep. I lie there remembering how it felt with his arms and legs flung over me and can't believe I'm expected to get through decades without ever feeling that again.

So I did end up working half days on Saturdays. In July Martine was supposed to go back to the camp run by the progressives and pacifists, where she had always had such a great time except for her tragedy with Mooney, and I didn't want to begin my life alone by asking for help.

"I don't have to go," she said, "If we don't have the money it's all right. I don't think I even feel like going anymore." My beautiful child with the tragic face. Now she had something worthy of that face.

"You should go, however you feel. When you get there you'll be glad."

"Except there's a slight problem," she said.

"What's that?"

"Rusty. I'm not taking him. Not after what happened to Mooney."

"No," I agreed.

"Which means . . ."

"Oh God! All right, I can do it. How bad can it be? A little lettuce, cabbage, right? A few handfuls of pellets . . ."

"There's the cage to clean too."

"The cage. Okay."

It was hard, her going off on the bus, with the typical scene of cheery mothers and fathers crowding around waving brown lunch bags, but I forced myself through it and so did she. I would force myself through the rest of my life if I had to.

First thing every morning and before I went to bed I put a handful of pellets in Rusty's bowl and fresh water in his bottle, and when I left for work and came home I dropped a few leaves of something green into the cage. Since I never really looked at him I was shocked, the fourth night after Martine left, when Mr. Coates, who had come up to fix the window lock in her room, said in his usual unexcited way, "Your pig's eye's popping out."

The right eye was protruding half an inch out of the socket and the cylindrical part behind it was yellow with gummy pus, a disgusting sight. "Jesus F. Christ," I said.

"He won't be no help to you. You need a vet."

The thought of going back to that arrogant vet who I always suspected had screwed up with Elf was more than I could take, so I searched the yellow pages till I found a woman vet in the neighborhood. When I walked in the next day carrying Rusty in a carton, I knew I had lucked out. She had curly hair like a mop, she wore jeans and a white sweatshirt, and she seemed young, maybe twenty-nine or thirty. Her name was Doctor Dunn. Very good, Doctor Dunn, so there won't be all that other shit to cope with.

To get him on the examining table I had to lift him up by his middle and feel all the squirminess and the beat of the scared delicate heart between my palms.

"It looks like either a growth of some kind pushing it forward, or maybe an abscess. But in either case I'm afraid the eye will have to go. It's badly infected and unless it's removed it'll dry up and the infection will spread and . . . uh . . ."

"He'll die?"

"Right."

Seventy-five dollars, she said, including his overnight stay, plus twenty-five for the biopsy. Terrific, I thought, just what I need. It was lower than the other vet's rates, though.

"I want to explain something about the surgery. He's a very small animal, two pounds or so, and any prolonged anesthesia is going to be risky. What this means is, I can't make any guarantees. I'd say his chances are . . . seventy-thirty, depending on his general condition. Of course, we'll do everything we can. . . ."

"And if I don't do it he'll die anyhow?"

"Right."

Squirming there on the table was this orange rat whose fate I was deciding. I felt very out of sync with reality, as if I was in a science fiction movie and how did I ever arrive at this place. "Okay. I guess we'd better do it."

The receptionist I left him with told me to call around four the next day to see how he came through the surgery. *If* was what she meant. That evening out of habit I almost went in to toss him some celery, then I remembered the cage was empty. There was no reason to go into Martine's room. But I decided to take the opportunity to clean the cage and the room both. I had found that the more I moved around the more numb I felt, which was what I wanted.

On the dot of four, I called from work. Doctor Dunn answered herself.

"He's fine! What a trouper, that Rusty! We had him hooked up to the EKG the whole time and monitored him, and he was terrific. I'm really pleased."

"Thank you," I managed to say. "Thank you very much." In one day she had established a closer relationship with him than I had in a year. That was an interesting thought. I mean, it didn't make me feel emotionally inadequate; I simply realized that's why she went through years of veterinary school, because she really cared, the way Carl could have about topiary, I guess.

"Can you come in and pick him up before seven? Then I can tell you about the post-op care."

Post-op care? I had never thought of that. I had never even thought of how the eye would look. Would it be a hole, or just a blank patch of fur? Would there be a bandage on it, or maybe she could fix him up with a special little eye patch?

I found Rusty in his carton on the front desk, with the receptionist petting him and calling him a good boy. "We're all crazy about him," she said. "He's quite a fella, aren't you, Rusty-baby?"

Where his right eye used to be, there was a row of five black stitches, and the area around it was shaved. Below the bottom stitch, a plastic tube the diameter of a straw and about an inch long stuck out. That was a drain for the wound, Doctor Dunn explained. He had a black plastic collar around his neck that looked like a ruff, the kind you see in old portraits of royalty. To keep him from poking himself, she said.

"Was he in good condition otherwise?" I thought I should sound concerned, in this world of animal-lovers.

"Oh, fine. Now . . . The post-operative care is a little complicated, so I wrote it down." She handed me a list of instructions:

1. Cold compresses tonight, 5–10 minutes.
2. Oral antibiotics, 3× a day for at least 7 days.
3. Keep collar on at all times.
4. Feed as usual.
5. Call if any excessive redness, swelling, or discharge develops.
6. Come in 3–4 days from now to have drain pulled.
7. Call early next week for biopsy results.
8. Make appointment for suture removal, 10–14 days.
9. Starting tomorrow, apply warm compresses 5–10 minutes, 2× a day for 10 days.

"Here's a sample bottle of antibiotics. Maybe I'd better do the first dose to show you how." She held him to her chest with one hand, while with the other she nudged his mouth open using the medicine dropper and squeezed the drops in, murmuring, "Come on now, that's a good boy, there you go." As she wiped the drips off his face and her sweatshirt with a tissue, I thought, Never. This is not happening to me. But I knew it was, and that I would have to go through with it.

When I went to get some ice water for the cold compress that night, I saw the message the graduate student mother had left on the refrigerator near Happy Birthday, which was now Happ Brhday. *"Ne mezz I camn di nstr vita,"* it read. I knew some letters were missing though not which ones, and those that were left were crooked, but I remembered well enough what it meant. I sat down to watch the ten o'clock news with Rusty on my lap and put the compress on his eye, or the place where his eye used to be, but he squirmed around wildly, clawing at my pants. Ice water oozed onto my legs. I told him to cut it out, he had no choice. Finally I tried patting him and talking to him like a baby, to quiet him. Don't worry, kiddo, you're going to be all right—stuff like that, the way Carl would have done without feeling idiotic. It worked. Only hearing those words loosened me a little out of my numbness and I had this terrible sensation of walking a tightrope in pitch darkness, though in fact I was whispering sweet nothings to a guinea pig. I even thought of telling him what I'd been through with my appendix, a fellow sufferer, and God knows what next, but I controlled myself. If I freaked out, who would take care of Martine?

I figured seven and a half minutes for the compress was fair enough —Doctor Dunn had written down 5–10. Then I changed my mind and held it there for another minute so if anything happened I would have a clear conscience when I told Martine. I held him to my chest with a towel over my shirt, feeling the heart pulsing against me, and squirted in the antibiotic. I lost a good bit, but I'd have plenty of chances to improve.

In the morning I found the collar lying in the mess of shit and cedar chips in his cage. I washed it and tried to get it back on him, but he fought back with his whole body—each time I fitted it around his neck he managed to squirm and jerk his way out, till beyond being repelled I was practically weeping with frustration. Two people could have done it easily. Carl, I thought, if ever I needed you . . . Finally after a great struggle I got it fastened in back with masking tape so he wouldn't undo it. But when I came home from work it was off again and we wrestled again. The next morning I rebelled. The drops, the compresses, okay, but there was no way I was going to literally collar a rodent morning and night for ten days. There are limits to everything, especially on a tightrope in the dark. I called Doctor Dunn from work.

"Is he poking himself around the eye?" she asked. "Any bleeding or discharge? Good. Then forget it. You can throw the collar away."

I was so relieved.

"How is he otherwise? Is he eating?"

"Yes. He seems okay. Except he's shedding." I told her how when I lifted him up, orange hair fluttered down into his cage like leaves from a tree. When leaves fell off Carl's plants, which I was also trying to keep alive though that project wasn't as dramatic, it usually meant they were on their way out. I had already lost three—I didn't have his green thumb. It seemed my life had become one huge effort to keep things alive, with death hot on my trail. I even had nightmares about what could be happening to Martine at camp. When I wrote to her, though, I tried to sound casual, as if I was fine, and I wrote that Rusty was fine too. Maybe Carl would have given her all the gory details, but I didn't mind lying. He was going to be fine. I was determined that pig would live even if it was over my dead body. Luckily I wasn't so far gone as to say all this to Doctor Dunn. "Is that a bad sign?"

"Shedding doesn't mean anything," she said. "He doesn't feel well, so he's not grooming himself as usual. It'll stop as he gets better."

I also noticed, those first few days, he would do this weird dance when I put the food in his cage. It dawned on me that he could smell it but not see it. While he scurried around in circles, I kept trying to shove it towards his good side—kind of a Bugs Bunny routine. Then after a while he developed a funny motion, turning his head to spot it, and soon he was finding it pretty well with his one eye. I told Doctor Dunn when I brought him in to have the drain removed. She said yes, they adapt quickly. They compensate. She talked about evolution and why eyes were located where they were. Predators, she said, have close-set eyes in the front of their heads to see the prey, and the prey have eyes at the sides, to watch out for the predators. How clever, I thought, the way nature matched up the teams. You couldn't change your destiny, but you had certain traits that kept the game going and gave you the illusion of having a fighting chance. We talked about it for a good while. She was interesting, that Doctor Dunn.

A few days later she plucked out the stitches with tweezers while I held him down.

"I have to tell you," she said, "not many people would take such pains with a guinea pig. Some people don't even bother with dogs and cats, you'd be amazed. They'd rather have them put away. You did a terrific job. You must really love animals."

I didn't have the heart to tell her that although it didn't turn my stomach anymore to hold him on my lap and stroke him for the compresses, he was still just a fat rat as far as I was concerned, but a fat rat which fate had arranged I had to keep alive. So I did.

"Well, you could say I did it for love."

She laughed. "Keep applying the warm compresses for another day or two, to be on the safe side. Then that's it. Case closed."

"What about the biopsy?"

"Oh yes, the lab report. It's not in yet, but I have a feeling it wasn't malignant. He doesn't look sick to me. Call me on it next week."

In eleven days Martine will be back. Beautiful Martine, with her suntan making her almost the color of Rusty. I'll warn her about the eye before she sees him. It doesn't look too gruesome now, with the stitches out and the hair growing back—soon it'll be smooth blank space. In fact, if not for the missing eye she would never have to know what he went through. The house will feel strange to her all over again without Carl, because whenever you're away for a while you expect to come home to some pure and perfect condition. She'll be daydreaming on the bus that maybe it was all a nightmare and the both of us are here waiting for her. But it'll be an altogether different life, and the worst thing is—knowing us, sensible, adaptable types—that one remote day we'll wake up and it'll seem normal this way, and in years to come Carl will turn into the man I had in my youth instead of what he is now, my life. I even envy her—he'll always be her one father.

So I'm applying the warm compresses for the last time, sitting here with a one-eyed guinea pig who is going to live out his four-to-six year life span no matter what it takes, in the middle of the journey of my life, stroking him as if I really loved animals.

Uncle Tony's Goat

LESLIE MARMON SILKO

We had a hard time finding the right kind of string to use. We knew we needed gut to string our bows the way the men did, but we were little kids and we didn't know how to get any. So Kenny went to his house and brought back a ball of white cotton string that his mother used to string red chili with. It was thick and soft and it didn't make very good bowstring. As soon as we got the bows made we sat down again on the sand bank above the stream and started skinning willow twigs for arrows. It was past noon, and the tall willows behind us made cool shade. There were lots of little minnows that day, flashing in the shallow water, swimming back and forth wildly like they weren't sure if they really wanted to go up or down the stream; it was a day for minnows that we were always hoping for—we could have filled our rusty coffee cans and old pickle jars full. But this was the first time for making bows and arrows, and the minnows weren't much different from the sand or the rocks now. The secret is the arrows. The ones we made were crooked, and when we shot them they didn't go straight—they flew around in arcs and curves; so we crawled through the leaves and branches, deep into the willow groves, looking for the best, the straightest willow branches. But even after we skinned the sticky wet bark from them and whittled the knobs off, they still weren't straight. Finally we went ahead and made notches at the end of each arrow to hook in the bowstring, and we started practicing, thinking maybe we could learn to shoot the crooked arrows straight.

We left the river each of us with a handful of damp, yellow arrows and our fresh-skinned willow bows. We walked slowly and shot arrows at bushes, big rocks, and the juniper tree that grows by Pino's sheep pen. They were working better just like we had figured; they still didn't fly straight, but now we could compensate for that by the way we aimed them. We were going up to the church to shoot at the cats old Sister Julian kept outside the cloister. We didn't want to hurt anything, just to have new kinds of things to shoot at.

But before we got to the church we went past the grassy hill where my uncle Tony's goats were grazing. A few of them were lying down chewing their cud peacefully, and they didn't seem to notice us. The billy goat was lying down, but he was watching us closely like he already knew about little kids. His yellow goat eyes didn't blink, and he stared with a wide, hostile look. The grazing goats made good deer for our bows. We shot all our arrows at the nanny goats and their kids; they skipped away from the careening arrows and never lost the rhythm of their greedy chewing as they continued to nibble the weeds and grass on the hillside. The billy goat was lying there watching us and taking us into his memory. As we ran down the road toward the church and Sister Julian's cats, I looked back, and my uncle Tony's billy goat was still watching me.

My uncle and my father were sitting on the bench outside the house when we walked by. It was September now, and the farming was almost over, except for bringing home the melons and a few pumpkins. They were mending ropes and bridles and feeling the afternoon sun. We held our bows and arrows out in front of us so they could see them. My father smiled and kept braiding the strips of leather in his hand, but my uncle Tony put down the bridle and pieces of scrap leather he was working on and looked at each of us kids slowly. He was old, getting some white hair—he was my mother's oldest brother, the one that scolded us when we told lies or broke things.

"You'd better not be shooting at things," he said, "only at rocks or trees. Something will get hurt. Maybe even one of you."

We all nodded in agreement and tried to hold the bows and arrows less conspicuously down at our sides; when he turned back to his work we hurried away before he took the bows away from us like he did the time we made the slingshot. He caught us shooting rocks at an old wrecked car; its windows were all busted out anyway, but he took the slingshot away. I always wondered what he did with it and with the knives we made ourselves out of tin cans. When I was much older I asked my mother, "What did he ever do with those knives and slingshots he took away from us?" She was kneading bread on the kitchen table at the time and was probably busy thinking about the fire in the oven outside. "I don't know," she said; "you ought to ask him yourself." But I never did. I thought about it lots of times, but I never did. It would have been like getting caught all over again.

The goats were valuable. We got milk and meat from them. My uncle was careful to see that all the goats were treated properly; the worst scolding my older sister ever got was when my mother caught her and some of her friends chasing the newborn kids. My mother kept saying over and over again, "It's a good thing I saw you; what if your uncle had seen you?" and even though we kids were very young then, we understood very well what she meant.

The billy goat never forgot the bows and arrows, even after the bows had cracked and split and the crooked, whittled arrows were all lost. This goat was big and black and important to my uncle Tony because he'd paid a lot to get him and because he wasn't an ordinary goat. Uncle Tony had bought him from a white man, and then he'd hauled him in the back of the pickup all the way from Quemado. And my uncle was the only person who could touch this goat. If a stranger or one of us kids got too near him, the mane on the billy goat's neck would stand on end and the goat would rear up on his hind legs and dance forward trying to reach the person with his long, spiral horns. This billy goat smelled bad, and none of us cared if we couldn't pet him. But my uncle took good care of this goat. The goat would let Uncle Tony brush him with the horse brush and scratch him around the base of his horns. Uncle Tony talked to the billy goat—in the morning when he unpenned the goats and in the evening when he gave them their hay and closed the gate for the night. I never paid too much attention to what he said to the billy goat; usually it was something like "Get up, big goat! You've slept long enough," or "Move over, big goat, and let the others have something to eat." And I think Uncle Tony was proud of the way the billy goat mounted the nannies, powerful and erect with the great black testicles swinging in rhythm between his hind legs.

We all had chores to do around home. My sister helped out around the house mostly, and I was supposed to carry water from the hydrant and bring in kindling. I helped my father look after the horses and pigs, and Uncle Tony milked the goats and fed them. One morning near the end of September I was out feeding the pigs their table scraps and pig mash; I'd given the pigs their food, and I was watching them squeal and snap at each other as they crowded into the feed trough. Behind me I could hear the milk squirting into the eight-pound lard pail that Uncle Tony used for milking.

When he finished milking he noticed me standing there; he motioned toward the goats still inside the pen. "Run the rest of them out," he said as he untied the two milk goats and carried the milk to the house.

I was seven years old, and I understood that everyone, including my uncle, expected me to handle more chores; so I hurried over to the goat pen and swung the tall wire gate open. The does and kids came prancing out. They trotted daintily past the pigpen and scattered out, intent on finding leaves and grass to eat. It wasn't until then I noticed that the billy goat hadn't come out of the little wooden shed inside the goat pen. I stood outside the pen and tried to look inside the wooden shelter, but it was still early and the morning sun left the inside of the shelter in deep shadow. I stood there for a while, hoping that he would come out by himself, but I realized that he'd recognized me and that he wouldn't come out. I understood right away what was happening and my fear of him was in my bowels and down my neck; I was shaking.

Finally my uncle came out of the house; it was time for breakfast. "What's wrong?" he called out from the door.

"The billy goat won't come out," I yelled back, hoping he would look disgusted and come do it himself.

"Get in there and get him out," he said as he went back into the house.

I looked around quickly for a stick or broom handle, or even a big rock, but I couldn't find anything. I walked into the pen slowly, concentrating on the darkness beyond the shed door; I circled to the back of the shed and kicked at the boards, hoping to make the billy goat run out. I put my eye up to a crack between the boards, and I could see he was standing up now and that his yellow eyes were on mine.

My mother was yelling at me to hurry up, and Uncle Tony was watching. I stepped around into the low doorway, and the goat charged toward me, feet first. I had dirt in my mouth and up my nose and there was blood running past my eye; my head ached. Uncle Tony carried me to the house; his face was stiff with anger, and I remembered what he'd always told us about animals; they won't bother you unless you bother them first. I didn't start to cry until my mother hugged me close and wiped my face with a damp wash rag. It was only a little cut above my eyebrow, and she sent me to school anyway with a Band-Aid on my forehead.

Uncle Tony locked the billy goat in the pen. He didn't say what he was going to do with the goat, but when he left with my father to haul firewood, he made sure the gate to the pen was wired tightly shut. He looked at the goat quietly and with sadness; he said something to the goat, but the yellow eyes stared past him.

"What's he going to do with the goat?" I asked my mother before I went to catch the school bus.

"He ought to get rid of it," she said. "We can't have that goat knocking people down for no good reason."

I didn't feel good at school. The teacher sent me to the nurse's office and the nurse made me lie down. Whenever I closed my eyes I could see the goat and my uncle, and I felt a stiffness in my throat and chest. I got off the school bus slowly, so the other kids would go ahead without me. I walked slowly and wished I could be away from home for a while. I could go over to Grandma's house, but she would ask me if my mother knew where I was and I would have to say no, and she would make me go home first to ask. So I walked very slowly, because I didn't want to see the black goat's hide hanging over the corral fence.

When I got to the house I didn't see a goat hide or the goat, but Uncle Tony was on his horse and my mother was standing beside the horse holding a canteen and a flour sack bundle tied with brown string. I was frightened at what this meant. My uncle looked down at me from the saddle.

"The goat ran away," he said. "Jumped out of the pen somehow. I saw him just as he went over the hill beyond the river. He stopped at the top of the hill and he looked back this way."

Uncle Tony nodded at my mother and me and then he left; we watched his old roan gelding splash across the stream and labor up the steep path beyond the river. Then they were over the top of the hill and gone.

Uncle Tony was gone for three days. He came home early on the morning of the fourth day, before we had eaten breakfast or fed the animals. He was glad to be home, he said, because he was getting too old for such long rides. He called me over and looked closely at the cut above my eye. It had scabbed over good, and I wasn't wearing a Band-Aid any more; he examined it very carefully before he let me go. He stirred some sugar into his coffee.

"That goddamn goat," he said. "I followed him for three days. He was headed south, going straight to Quemado. I never could catch up to him." My uncle shook his head. "The first time I saw him he was already in the piñon forest, halfway into the mountains already. I could see him most of the time, off in the distance a mile or two. He would stop sometimes and look back." Uncle Tony paused and drank some more coffee. "I stopped at night. I had to. He stopped too, and in the morning we would start out again. The trail just gets higher and steeper. Yesterday morning there was frost on top of the blanket when I woke up and we were in the big pines and red oak leaves. I couldn't see him any more because the forest is too thick. So I turned around." Tony finished the cup of coffee. "He's probably in Quemado by now."

I looked at him again, standing there by the door, ready to go milk the nanny goats.

"There wasn't ever a goat like that one," he said, "but if that's the way he's going to act, O.K. then. That damn goat got pissed off too easy anyway."

He smiled at me and his voice was strong and happy when he said this.

The Red Sea

CONSTANCE PIERCE

Brenda was standing at the window, spying on her two daughters, who were supposed to be raking leaves in the yard between the house and barn. They were blond and slender, nearly the same size. One was twelve, the other thirteen. They were moving z-shaped, jabbing one rigid hand forward, the other behind, and making languid snake-like motions with their heads to the music from an enormous radio blaring from the grass. The radio had been the self-selected birthday present of the oldest girl. It was the size of Brenda's microwave, bigger than the computer she used to keep the farm's accounts. It had an alien look, like something from another planet.

Her daughters' plaid flannel shirts were swaying above their jeans and Pumas. Suddenly, the girls froze to a hesitation in the music, and Brenda saw them, not as her daughters, but as stylized Egyptians in a frieze: Painted on the red barn arching behind them.

She shifted to clear her eyes of this odd vision. Out in the field beyond the yard, the bay gelding Jim had bought the girls was nosing its way across the bright green grass, its tail swatting at something. It was an in-between season, with things still alive that ought to be dead or hibernating. She wished it would get cold, just to get things settled. Maybe the leaves would blow off somewhere, and at least Jim could put the horse in the barn and she wouldn't be reminded every day that the girls never rode it.

I thought young girls were supposed to love horses, she thought. All her girls cared about was junior-high social life, music, expensive play shoes. She'd wanted them to be responsible farm kids, smelling like horse-sweat and hay, with hayseed in their hair. She had thought they would be in 4-H, that they would husband animals and win prizes at the State Fair. She'd imagined them streaking across the field, doubled up on the horse, their hair bright and flying. They were wearing simple plaid shirts and jeans in her daydreams, but in life she was lucky if they'd even dress like that to rake the leaves.

The song finished and the girls fell on the ground, red-faced and laughing. Every few seconds one of them would sing out "Eei-oh!" in imitation of the women on the record, the Bangles. Brenda watched Millie, the youngest, unbutton her shirt and fan it against her bare chest.

"Stop that!" Sadie yelled. Millie hesitated, and then she rebuttoned her shirt, not looking at Sadie. "You're too much," Sadie said with disgust.

Then there was another song on the radio and they were both on their feet again, pawing at the grass with their soft shoes and swinging their arms from the elbows, busily snapping their fingers.

Brenda watched them a little longer. Am I going to be able to take this? she wondered.

Sadie had been wearing a bra for less than a week, and not quite needing it, and already she was making Millie self-conscious. Twice Brenda had come upon Sadie scrutinizing the figures on the tape measure wrapped very loosely around her chest, maybe even around a couple of fingers too, the contents of the sewing box strewn on the carpet in the spare room. How much progress could women have made?

Brenda turned away from her daughters. Through another window she could see their old orange cat, Chloe, ambling across another square of lawn, heading for the barn. A snatch of lyric, odd as her daughters frozen on the barn, ran through her head: Joe MacDonald had a farm.

She watched Chloe stop, as if blasted by the heat from the girls' music. The cat put her ears back. If she were human, she'd be frowning, Brenda thought, frowning herself. Country Joe and the Fish? She hadn't thought about them since the days when she used to go to rock concerts, decked out in an Indian headband and bellbottom jeans with a peace sign sewn on the tailpocket, her other pockets stuffed with sunflower seeds. Life. Now she had a flagpole in a bed of peonies on the front lawn and flew the flag on Flag Day and the Fourth of July, like folk art.

The cat gave the girls one last indignant look and changed her course, her white-socked feet breaking into a run for several yards.

"I'm going," Brenda called to Jim, who was watching the Bengals and the Colts fight it out on the TV, in between feeding the cattle and feeding the cattle. He was trying to get them ready to sell. When he didn't answer, she stepped into the living room and saw him sleeping on the sofa, sitting up. And this was a game he'd been waiting for all week.

She tiptoed over and turned up the sound. He was exhausted, she knew, but he'd feel worse if he missed this game, and the last thing he'd want was for her to catch him sleeping in the afternoon. She wished he'd give himself a break. If she had known how hard life was going to be, on all of them, and if she hadn't loved Jim, she'd have married somebody in another line of work, or just kept on living in town and teaching school.

"Don't let them cut it too short," he mumbled suddenly, his eyes still closed. It gave her a start, like he'd heard her thoughts.

"I thought you were sacked out," she said, digging into her purse for the keys. "You could give somebody a heart attack like that."

"I'd like to give you a heart attack, Baby," Jim said, opening his eyes and flirting with her.

"Well, it wouldn't take much these days. I'm too old for this."

"Too old for what," Jim said, turning back to the game, where the Bengals were slaughtering the Colts. Brenda watched the Bengals' bright tiger-striped helmets against the turf.

"Breasts," she said.

Jim gave her a puzzled look.

"Loud music, expensive fads, dates." She found her keys and strung her purse back on her shoulder. "Cranky moods. Sulking."

"You need some interests," Jim said.

"Yes," Brenda said. "Maybe I'll start riding Tony-the-Pony. They're never going to ride him." She paused. "I thought they'd ride him," she said, looking back to the TV set where her husband had fixed his eyes again. "I thought they'd wear their jeans and Dingos and ride across the hayfield like little Calamity Janes." She could feel herself near tears.

"You ought to figure out what's bothering you," Jim said, sitting forward a little to follow a play.

"Mummy!" Sadie's scream brought Jim to his feet. Brenda turned as her daughter burst into the room, her face glowing.

"There's a big lizard out there," Sadie said, excitedly. "Millie raked it up with the leaves."

Jim sat back down.

"Well, are you scared or hot-to-trot?" Brenda asked, giving her daughter a look. "I can't tell with you anymore. Where's Millie?"

"That child," Sadie said, suddenly calming down, sounding about thirty years old. "She's hiding in the barn."

"From a lizard?" Brenda said.

"Well, it might be a snake," Sadie said indifferently. "It's out in the yard crawling around. Are you going to shoot it?" she asked her father, in the new world-weary voice she used these days.

"If it's a snake, I guess a hoe'll take care of it," Jim said, looking longingly at the football players rolling around in living color.

"I'll do it," said Brenda, her heart beating faster.

Jim looked at her.

"Really. I've killed a snake before," she lied. "Get me the hoe, Sadie."

"Don't cut it too short," Jim said, looking back at the TV.

Brenda was confused. "The snake?" she asked.

"Your hair."

"Lisa cuts it however she wants to," Brenda said irritably. "I don't seem to have much influence with her. Or anybody else."

Outside, holding the hoe like a club out in front of her, both her daughters on her heels (Millie snuffling, Sadie walking in a contemptuous silence that could be felt), Brenda approached the area where the animal had last been seen.

"You let it get away," Sadie said, as they stood on the empty lawn, looking around. "Daddy should've come."

"I see it!" Millie yelled, shrinking back toward the barn.

"Where?" Brenda asked. Then she saw it. "Oh," she said.

"Kill it," Sadie said.

Brenda lowered her hoe. A snake-like lizard, a skink, was lying still in the grass about ten feet away. Brenda moved closer. It had about six inches of head and torso and six inches of tail. It had frozen in all of the commotion, its body stiff and raised slightly off the ground on impossibly tiny legs; but its eyes seemed to move a little, as if it were trying to assess the danger it was in without calling extra attention to itself. At its throat, a half-transparent ruff expanded in creamcolored poufs and then collapsed, a motion so regular and precise that Brenda stood transfixed for a moment, watching the wrinkled skin bloom in slow motion, the dull color of collapse swelling again and again to a taut luminescence, like a little dawn.

Is this the snake in my garden? she wondered. A small wary snake, poised to run?

"You girls are something," she said, finally. "That's just a skink."

"Well, kill it," Sadie said. "It almost bit Millie."

Already Sadie was drifting off in her head. Brenda saw her eyes disengage, watched her dig into the pocket of her jeans and bring out a barrette and begin to rearrange her hair.

"Can we have pizza for supper?" she asked Brenda.

"No. Bad for your skin and hair," Brenda said. "You're going to go bald if you don't stop pulling your hair up like that. It makes your skin look pulled back." Sadie was fashioning a wild new-style ponytail, pulled to the side. Brenda could see gold stars that looked like the ones she used to put besides the names of her best students on a bulletin-board chart, studding her daughter's earlobes, one of the several holes there dangling a golden half-moon. The stars and moon together looked like the logo of Proctor and Gamble, who bought all Jim's cows that got struck by lightning or just died, and made them into soap and shampoo. The logo was also an old symbol for Satan, some fundamentalists said. They'd had P & G on the run, and Brenda thought she had read that the logo had been changed, but she couldn't be sure.

"Those animals are good for my garden," Brenda said, turning to squint at the skink, then urging it toward the bushes with her hoe. It moved several feet and stopped, its eyes frozen now, too, within their small pouches of wrinkles; even the miraculous throat seemed still. "Just leave it alone," she said to the girls, turning and heading for the barn to put away the hoe. "What kind of farm kids are you anyway?"

"No kind," Sadie said, glumly. Brenda stopped and looked back. Sadie picked up a small rock and tossed it near the skink. Millie was looking at the skink and then at her mother, then at the skink again.

Brenda resumed walking. She could hear Sadie's rocks landing in the grass with soft thuds, like a sluggish heartbeat. "Leave it alone," she said, not looking back. She felt Millie's clammy hand catch up to hers and tug on it a little before it settled in. Then they walked together to the barn, palm to damp palm.

Chloe was sitting, sphinx-like, on the walk when Brenda got home. "You old cat," Brenda said, affectionately, pausing to scratch the cat's head. She was going to miss Chloe, just as she missed her litter-mate, Cleo, who had died last year. Cleo had died out in the barn and had frozen up and thawed out half the spring, Jim said, before Brenda found her when she went out for her gardening tools. Cleo had been dismantling in bits out there, and Jim hadn't said a word. "Why didn't you take her out and throw her in the field," Brenda had asked, wiping away tears of fury at her husband. She'd had Chloe and Cleo as long as she'd had Sadie and Millie. She'd found Cleo only half-frozen at noon on the prettiest day of the year, a day when she'd been so happy, her pockets stuffed with seed packets, everything sunny and warm, bright blue sky, high clouds—and she'd ended up digging a grave, making a little casket for Cleo out of the straw she'd planned to put between her vegetable rows to keep down the weeds.

"I didn't have time to do it whenever I thought about it," Jim had said, shrugging. "Then when I had time, I never thought about it."

"Good old cat," Brenda said again, rising up. Chloe had a sagging belly with two lines of sagging tits, a broken fang, and a cloudy spot on her eye, two permanent bare spots on the back of her neck where the neighbors' male cats had left their vampire's mark for years. Chloe had a scar on her nose from fighting one of them when he'd come back to kill her male kittens, a losing battle. They always came back and killed the kittens. Did Chloe remember any of that now, the murky sea of kinship? Or had all the old battles, the many lost and the several won, receded into a haze deeper than memory? The stuff of life, gone, and yet you'd never know it, the cat seemed so content. It was like getting a little sun was enough now, that and staying out of the way of the girls, who never knew where anything was except themselves.

Brenda lingered, touching her haircut. She wondered if there would be a time when everyone she knew now would be lost to her, when they would be only thin surfaces of themselves in their relations with her, like most of her own old selves. Sometimes it seemed like you survived life because nothing much accumulated.

She looked out across her yard, feeling the soft fur of Chloe against her leg, aware of the winding-down clock inside the cat, contradicted by the wound-up motor purring. The yard was a sea of red leaves now, and beyond, the field was circled with red trees, burning as if in their finest hour. Tony-the-Pony broke into a little trot at the field's edge, then settled down quickly and began to graze again. Probably the last of the bees or a fly on its last wing, Brenda thought, breathing in the queer mixed season, shaking her hair out, which was not too short, she had reassured herself all the way home in the rearview mirror. She'd been pleased with how she'd handled Lisa at the beauty shop. It had seemed a small engineering of Fate, which she imagined as a vast ectoplasm, scrunching invisibly on the horizons of her life. How could you do much, when everybody else was going through stages? When love fell on you like a disease, leading you into a life you weren't trained for.

When business, and trends, and adolescence, and death disrupted households all over the world, and your muscles and bones began to separate within you, nothing you could do about it.

Was all this what was bothering her? She didn't think that was all of it. She couldn't seem to get at all of it.

"Oh," Sadie said, stumbling out of the door, onto Brenda and Chloe before she slowed down. "Sorry." She looked at Brenda a moment. "Your hair looks nice, Mummy."

"Thanks," Brenda said, smiling at her daughter, who had exchanged her raking clothes for a soft pink sweatshirt, against which her little breasts, absurdly high on her chest, pushed like two crabapples. "I told Lisa to pay attention to me for once. It seemed to work. Where's your Dad?"

"Feeding the cows," Sadie said. "Where else?"

"Don't be smart *every* chance you get," Brenda warned, already weary of Sadie's pouty, whiny voice, which she knew she'd be listening to for the next four or five years, until the girls came back into the human world. "Where's Millie?"

"Who cares?" Sadie said. "I wish I could get a new haircut."

"Why don't you?" Brenda said lightly, feeling a sudden release of her daughter's weight, which she'd been carrying around inside her head for months, she realized, as if her brain were a womb and Sadie was back in it. "Why don't you do whatever you want to do to your hair? Wear anything you want, eat junk? Rake the leaves or don't rake them. Kill skinks." Brenda felt her face loosening in the loss of tension. She didn't have to struggle with these kids every step of the way, over every little thing.

"I did kill the skink," Sadie pouted.

Brenda felt a shock. Chloe's fur, still against her leg, gave her a creepy feeling. "What do you mean?"

"I didn't exactly mean to," Sadie said. "But I hit it with a rock and stunned it a little, and I just couldn't quit."

"You stoned it to death?" Brenda said, looking at her daughter in horror of all she was that her mother didn't know about. The cat got up and walked to the edge of the walk, swishing her tail.

"Well, so what?" Sadie said, pushing past her mother. "It was just an old snake with legs. It almost bit Millie anyway."

"I think that's the worst thing you've ever done in your life," Brenda said, and meant it. "Where is Millie anyway? Did she help you?" Brenda almost reeled with the possibility that both of her daughters were propelled, inside, by something darker than what was inside herself, or in Jim, who never hurt anything uselessly, even if he did forget about things that weren't business sometimes.

Sadie scoffed. "Millie cried about it. She's about five years old, if you ask me. It was her that almost got bit."

"And you're about a hundred," Brenda said, relieved that Millie, at least, hadn't crossed beyond the pale. "I want those leaves raked before dark or you can just forget about a haircut or junk-food, or radio music or skink-hunting or anything you like to do."

"I plan to rake the leaves," Sadie said, indignant. "Why do you think I came out here?"

"Yes, in your spiffy clothes. What did you do with the skink? Hi, honey," she said as Millie came out of the house, still wearing her raking clothes, her face drawn into a knot. Brenda held out her arm and let Millie walk into its circle, as if under a wing.

"Sadie killed the skink," Millie said.

"I know," Brenda said. "Just try to forget it."

"That's what *I'm* going to do," Sadie said, walking toward the rakes still lying on the lawn, making Chloe jump out of her way and disappear into the safety of the shrubs along the house.

"No, you're not," Brenda said, gathering steam against the facts: that her daughters scared her, that the next four or five years would decide, one way or the other, how and how much they would stay in her life, for the rest of her life. And how and how much she would want to stay in theirs, she asserted now, knowing it was a lie. She would want to stay in theirs, whatever happened. "You're going to go over there and pick up that animal and carry it out in the field and cover it up with something," Brenda said. "I'm not going to have it rotting out here on the lawn."

Sadie and Millie both gave her a horrified look.

"Did you think I was going to do it?" Brenda said. "Or your Daddy? Those days are over. Come on. We'll all go."

"Oh, Mummy, no," Millie pleaded. "Then I won't be able to forget it."

"Well, maybe I was wrong to say you should forget," Brenda said. "On second thought, I think it's something you both need to see, close-up: an act and its consequences. Which will give you some idea of what really growing up is all about."

"I wish you wouldn't preach all the time," Sadie said over her shoulder, already fuming toward the dead skink like a steam engine, kicking up a spray of red leaves.

Is that true? Brenda wondered, as she and Millie followed. She thought about it for a moment. Maybe I do preach. Maybe I'm just pretending this is something they have to see, to make an impression on them, any way I still can.

At the edge of the yard, the skink lay in a thin wave, as if it had just stopped and would be scooting off again any moment. Brenda could see the small white line of its underbelly. Its undersized legs curled against its body like tiny question marks.

"Maybe he isn't dead," Millie said, letting go of Brenda's hand and moving closer to the skink.

"Well, he is," Sadie said. "Look at his head."

Brenda saw its head for the first time, a little mound of disconnected tissue, mashed up like berries or fruit. "You beat his head in," Millie said, reproaching her sister.

Sadie picked up a thin forking limb nearby and poked at the skink, flipping it over and then back on its stomach. Brenda could see now the small tears in its body where her daughter's rocks had found their mark. The ruff at its throat was limp now and the throat itself slack and dun-colored.

Millie, wide-eyed and fearless with sympathy, was crouching down by the skink. Amazed, Brenda watched her put a finger on its back. She felt a deep chill, in spite of knowing what it said about Millie. She felt like she was finding an orphan-child in the bulrushes—one much more noble than herself.

"I thought it would feel slimy," Millie said, her voice miserable. "It feels like my felt board."

"You make me sick," Sadie said. "Get up so I can do what she wants me to do."

"What's going on out here," Jim said, coming up on them.

"We're having a sermonette," Brenda said, struggling for the banter he expected. "We're learning about Paradise Lost, and growing up. Life. And Death."

"Well, you sure let him have it with that hoe," Jim said. "It's nothing but a skink, though."

"I didn't kill it," Brenda exclaimed. "Your daughter Sadie stoned it to death in a fit. She sounded possessed. She said she couldn't help herself."

Jim looked at Sadie.

"I just want to forget the whole thing," Sadie said, her mouth a pout the color of her pink sweatshirt.

"Mummy says we shouldn't forget it, Daddy," Millie said. "I'll never forget it. Its skin felt like felt."

"Well, you'd better do something with it, Sadie," Jim said. "They say that a dead reptile's mate will come and wrap around it and stay there. You don't want two dead lizards on your conscience."

"She hasn't got a conscience," Millie said solemnly.

Sadie began to lift the skink onto her tree-limb. Brenda turned away, pulling Millie with her. She felt like somebody had died. She wished Jim would notice how well Millie was behaving, though.

"I don't want to walk back through those leaves," Millie said.

"Why not?" Brenda said.

"Because the skink's mate might be there."

"I thought you'd made your peace with the skink," Brenda said, disappointed. This would be the story of the rest of her life, this constant shifting around, always having to put a new face on things.

"Daddy?" Millie said.

Jim bent down and swung her up on his shoulders. "You're getting your last piggyback," he said. "You're too big."

The three of them headed back. "You should have raked the leaves," Brenda said to Millie. "Then you wouldn't have to worry about hiding places for skinks. Is that true?" she asked Jim. "About the skink's mate?" The idea moved her.

"I've always heard it," Jim said. "About snakes, anyway. But I've never seen it. I heard a skink will brood its eggs just like a chicken— that's rare for a lizard. I've heard a scared lizard would drop its tail, too, and that it would grow another one in its place."

"Really?" Millie said.

"It's called regeneration," Jim said. "I read about it in *The Progressive Farmer.*"

"Will the tail grow another body?" Millie said.

"I don't think so," Jim said. "But you never know. They're always shedding whole suits of skin and growing new ones, snakes anyway."

"I think that's creepy," Millie said.

"I guess so," Jim said. "Dead things ought to stay dead. It's natural."

Brenda looked at her husband and Millie. Their heads were close together, Millie's arms around Jim's neck. Millie still looked a little scared, and Jim looked a little tired, but otherwise they looked normal as apple pie.

"Regeneration is natural too," Brenda said, to nobody. It was. A natural miracle, for a few chosen creatures of the earth. The rest just had to reproduce, something different from themselves.

Sometimes *very* different. She looked back at Sadie, out in the field, scraping doggedly at the ground with a stick. She wondered if Sadie would hold in her mind the day when something ugly had welled up inside her and taken over. Brenda hoped her daughter would remember the smell of the earth, getting ready to die for a while itself as she dug into it, the moment when she committed the skink back to earth, the private funeral. She hoped that it all wouldn't be sloughed off, or lost, like Chloe's forgotten babies.

But maybe she'd even forget it herself, until it surfaced after thirty years, like that blast-from-the-past this afternoon, Country Joe and The Fish. Recalling a few minutes out of all the minutes of life. Where were all the others?

"I like your hair," Jim said.

"Good," Brenda said. "Who won the game?"

"The Bengals," Jim said.

"Watch out, Daddy," Millie warned as they headed into the leaves, Brenda slightly ahead, her hair stirring in the breeze.

Brenda walked slowly, sneaking looks back toward the field, where Tony-the-Pony was a grazing shadow behind his shadowy fence—content or lonely and tormented by flies, who could know? She couldn't think about him now. He was a backdrop for Sadie now, a lesser mystery. Brenda was looking for something in the posture or gestures of her prodigal daughter to reassure her. She could see Sadie lifting the skink up on her tree-branch out on the deserted field. She seemed rigid, stoical, like a prophet of old.

Brenda stopped looking back. Walking through the leaves, she suddenly felt scared too. You never knew what lay ahead of you. It would be nice if you could know, unless you couldn't do anything to change your course. When she was young, she'd imagined that all the time: How awful it would be to live your life over and know everything you knew now and not be able to warn anybody or change the course of things. She had concluded that that was God's Fate, and she had thought, Poor God, unable to warn his creatures, and had even prayed for him.

She felt a gust of wind whip by them. A moment later it attacked the leaves, blowing them out of her path, a brief happy accident. Chloe seized her chance and darted by, then disappeared into the shadows. The bright green grass seemed to stretch out like a narrow carpet for about a dozen feet as the red leaves rolled back before piling up again. Neither Millie nor Jim had noticed. For a moment Brenda felt herself suspended—how to use it: a lesson for Millie or a joke to lighten her husband's load?

She decided not to mention it. "Come on, Sadie," she called over her shoulder, but looking straight ahead. "Just cover it enough to keep the cat from digging it up." Let bygones be bygones, for now. She was lost in a desert herself. She would take the parted leaves as a small, good sign, like Chloe had. Wily old cat. Wily, and doomed anyway.

"Let's go make a pizza," she said. "It's getting cold out here." She sped up, determining to lead her people, if just for this evening, out of something too big for every living thing.

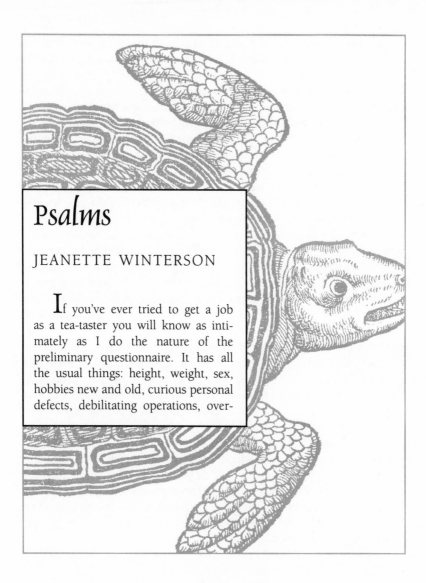

Psalms

JEANETTE WINTERSON

If you've ever tried to get a job as a tea-taster you will know as intimately as I do the nature of the preliminary questionnaire. It has all the usual things: height, weight, sex, hobbies new and old, curious personal defects, debilitating operations, over-long periods spent in the wrong countries. Fluency, currency, contacts, school tie. Fill them in, don't blob the ink and, if in doubt, be imaginative.

Then, on the last page, before you sign your name in a hand that is firm enough to show spirit, but not enough to show waywardness, there is a large empty space and a brief but meaningful demand.

You are to write about the experience you consider to have been the most significant in the formation of your character. (You may interpret 'character' as 'philosophy' if such is your inclination.) This is very shocking, because what we really want to talk about is that time we saw our older sister compromised behind the tool shed, or the time we very deliberately spat in the communion wine.

When I was small, I had a tortoise called Psalms. It was bought for me and named for me by my mother in an effort to remind me continually to praise the Lord. My mother had a horror of graven images, including crucifixes, but she felt there could be no harm in a tortoise. It moved slowly, so I could fully contemplate the wonders of creation in a way that would have been impossible with a ferret. It wasn't cuddly, so that I wouldn't be distracted as I might with a dog, and it had very little visible personality, so there was no possibility of us forming an intimate relationship as I might with a parrot. All in all, it seemed to her to be a satisfactory pet. I had been agitating for a pet for some time. In my head I had a white rabbit called Ezra that bit people who ignored me. Ezra's pelt was as white as the soul in heaven but his heart was black . . .

My mother drew me a picture of a tortoise so that I would not be too disappointed or too ecstatic. She hated emotion. I hoped that they came in different colours, which was not unreasonable since most animals do, and, when they were all clearly brown, I felt cheated.

"You can paint their shells," comforted the man in the shop. "Some people paint scenes on them. One chap I know has 26 and if you line 'em end to end in the right order you got the Flying Scotsman pulling into Edinburgh station."

I asked my mother if I could have another twelve so that I could do a tableau of the Last Supper, but she said it was too expensive and might be a sin against the Holy Ghost.

"Why?" I demanded as the man left us arguing in front of the gerbils. "God made the Holy Ghost, and he made these tortoises, they must know about each other."

"I don't want the Lord and his disciples running round the garden on the backs of your tortoises. It's not respectful."

"Yes, but when sinners come into the garden they'll be taken aback. They'll think it's the Lord sending them a vision." (I imagined the heathen being confronted by more and more tortoises; they weren't to know I had thirteen, they'd think it was a special God-sent tortoise that could multiply itself.)

"No," said my mother firmly. "It's Graven Images, that's what. If the Lord wanted to appear on the backs of tortoises he'd have done it already."

"Well can I just have two more then? I could do The Three Musketeers."

"Heathen child," my mother slapped me round the ears. "This pet is to help you think about our Saviour. How can you do that if you've got The Three Musketeers staring up at you?"

The man looked sympathetic, but he didn't want to get involved so we packed up the one tortoise in a box with holes and went to catch the bus home. I was excited. Adam had named the animals, now I could name mine. "How about The Man in the Iron Mask?" I suggested to my mother who was sitting in front of me reading her *Band of Hope Review*. She turned round sharply and gave a little screech.

"I've cricked my neck, what did you say?"

I said it again. "We could call it Mim for short, but it looks like it's a prisoner doesn't it?"

"You are not calling that animal The Man in the Iron Mask, or anything for short, you can call it Psalms."

"Why don't I call it Ebenezer?" (I was thinking that would match Ezra.)

"We're calling it Psalms because I want you to praise the Lord."

"I can praise the Lord if it's called Ebenezer."

"But you won't, will you? You'll say you forgot. What about the time I bought you that 3-D postcard of the garden of Gethsemane? You said that would help you think about the Lord and I caught you singing 'On Ilkley Moor Baht 'at.' "

"Alright then," I sulked. "We'll call it Psalms."

So we did, and Psalms lived very quietly in a hutch at the bottom of the garden and every day I went and sat next to him and read him one of his namesakes out of the Bible. He was an attentive pet, never tried to run away or dig anything up; my mother spoke of his steadfastness with tears in her eyes. She felt convinced that Psalms was having a good effect on me. She enjoyed seeing us together. I never told her about Ezra the demon bunny, about his ears that filtered the sun on a warm day through a lattice of blood vessels reminiscent of orchids. Ezra the avenger didn't like Psalms and sometimes stole his lettuce.

When my mother decided it was time for us to go on holiday to Llandudno she was determined to take Psalms with us.

"I don't want you being distracted by Pleasure," she explained. "Not now that you're doing so well."

I was doing well; I knew huge chunks of the Bible by heart and won all the competitions in Sunday School. Most importantly, for an evangelical, I was singing more, which you do, inevitably, when you're learning Psalms. On the train my mother supplied me with pen and paper and told me to make as many separate words as I could out of Jerusalem. My father was dispatched for coffee and she read out loud interesting snippets from her new paperback, *Portents of the Second Coming.*

I wasn't listening; practice enabled me to pour out the variations on Jerusalem without even thinking. Words slot into each other easily enough once sense ceases to be primary. Words become patterns and shapes. Tennyson, drunk on filthy sherry one evening, said he knew the value of every word in the language, except possibly "scissors." By value he meant resonance and fluidity, not sense. So while my mother warned me of the forthcoming apocalypse I stared out of the window and imagined that I was old enough to buy my own Rail Rover ticket and go off round the world with only a knapsack and a penknife and a white rabbit. A white rabbit? I jumped a little at this intrusion into my daydream. Ezra's pink eyes were gleaming down at me from the frayed luggage rack. Ezra wasn't invited on this trip; I had been determined to control him and make him stay behind. In the box next to me I felt Psalms fidgeting. My mother was oblivious.

"Just think," she said enthusiastically. "When the Lord comes back the lion will lie down with the lamb."

But will the rabbit come to terms with the tortoise?

Like Psalms, I was feeling nervous, as one would when one's fantasy life gets out of control. Ezra's eyes bored into my soul and my own black heart. I felt transparent, the way I do now when I meet a radical feminist who can always tell that I shave my armpits and have a penchant for silk stockings.

"I'm trying to be good," I hissed. "Go away."

"Yes," continued my mother, all unknowing. "We'll live naturally when the Lord comes back, there'll be no chemicals or aerosol deodorants. No fornicating or electric guitars." She looked up sharply at my father. "Did you put saccharine in this coffee? You know I can't drink it without." My father smiled sheepishly and tried to placate her with a packet of Bourbons, which was a mistake because she hated anything that sounded foreign. I remembered how it had been when my auntie had come back from Italy and insisted on having us round for pasta. My mother was suspicious and kept turning it over with her fork and saying how much she liked hot pot and carrots. She didn't mind natives so much or people who lived in the jungle and other hot places because she felt they couldn't help it. Europe, though, was close enough to Britain to behave properly and, in not behaving properly, was clearly perverse and due to be rolled up when the Lord came back. (In the Eternal City there will be no pasta.)

I tried to distract myself from her gathering storm by concentrating on the notices in our carriage. I took in the exhortation to leave the train clean and tidy and felt suitably awed by the dire warnings against frivolously pulling the communication cord. Ezra began to chew it. Tired and emotional, though fondly imagining we shared a common ground other than the one we were standing on, we reached our boarding house at nightfall and spent the holiday in various ways. One morning my mother suggested we take Psalms with us to the beach.

"He'll enjoy a change of air."

I hadn't seen Ezra for a couple of days otherwise I might have been more alive to the possibilities of catastrophe. We set off, found a patch that wasn't too windy, said a prayer and my father fell asleep. Psalms seemed comforted by the sand beneath his feet and very slowly dug a very small hole.

"Why don't you take him to that rock in the breakers?" My mother pointed. "He won't have seen the sea before." I nodded, and picked him up pretending I was Long John Silver making off with booty. As we sat on the rock sunning ourselves a group of boys came splashing through the waves, one of them holding a bow and arrow. Before my eyes he strung the bow and fired at Psalms. It was a direct hit in the centre of the shell. This was of no matter in itself because the arrow was rubber-tipped and made no impression on the shell. It did make an impression on Psalms, though, who became hysterical and standing on his back legs toppled over into the sea. I lunged down to pick him out but I couldn't distinguish between tortoise and rocks. If only my mother had let me make him into one of The Three Musketeers I could have saved him from a watery grave. He was lost. Dead. Drowned. I thought of Shelley.

"Psalms has been killed," I told my mother flatly.

We spent all afternoon with a shrimping net trying to find his corpse, but we couldn't and at six o'clock my mother said she had to have some fish and chips. It was a gloomy funeral supper and all I could see was Ezra the demon bunny hopping up and down on the prom. If it had not been for my father's devotion and perseverance in whistling tunes from the war in a loud and lively manner we might never have recovered our spirits. As it was, my mother suddenly joined in with the words, patted me on the head and said it must have been the Lord's will. Psalms's time was up, which was surely a sign that I should move onto another book of the Bible.

"We could go straight onto Proverbs," she said. "What kind of pet would be proverbial?"

"What about a snake?"

"No," she refused, shaking her head. "Snakes are wily, not wise."

"What about an owl?"

"I don't want an owl in my room. Owls are very demanding and besides when your Uncle Bert parachuted into the canal by mistake, it was an owl I saw just before I got the telegram."

Death by water seemed to be a feature of our family, so why not have something that was perpetually drowned? "Let's get some fish, they're proverbial, and they'll be quiet like Psalms was, and they'll remind us of the Flood and our own mortality." My mother was very taken with this, especially since she had just eaten a fine piece of cod. She liked it when she could experience the Bible in different ways.

As for me, I was confronted with my own black heart. You can bury what you like but, if it's still alive when you bury it, don't look for a quiet life. Is this what the tea board wants to know about? Is it hoping to read of tortoises called Psalms?

I don't believe it. They must have an identikit picture of what constitutes a suitable forming experience, like playing quarterback in the school team and beating Wales, or saving a rare colony of worker bees from extinction.

My mother bought some brown ink in Llandudno and sketched

Psalms on a few square inches of stiff card. She caught his expression very well, though I still feel the burden of being the only person who has ever seen what emotion a tortoise can express when about to drown. Such things are sobering and stretch down the years. I could have saved him, but I felt he limited my life. Sometimes I take out the sketch and stare at his mournful face. He was always mournful, though I think that was a characteristic of the breed because I have never met a jubilant tortoise. On the other hand, perhaps I never made him happy. Perhaps we were at emotional odds like Scarlett O'Hara and Rhett Butler. Perhaps a briny end was better than a gradual neglect. I ponder these things in my heart. My mother, always philosophical in her own way, enjoyed a steady stream of biblical pets: the Proverbial fish, Ecclesiast the hen who never laid an egg where we could find it, Solomon the Scotch terrier and, finally, Isaiah and Jeremiah, a pair of goats who lived to a great age and died peacefully in their pen.

"You can always depend on the prophets," declared my mother whenever anyone marvelled at the longevity of her goats. The world was a looking glass for the Lord—she saw him in everything. Though I do warn her, from time to time, never to judge a bunny by its pelt . . .

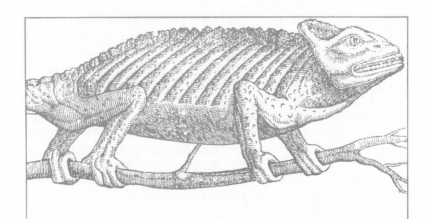

The Bath

YŪKO TSUSHIMA

TRANSLATED BY J. MARTIN
HOLMAN

It had been a long time since I
had seen the shadow of a gecko, but
now one was clinging to the outside of

the frosted glass window of the bath. Its image was like a small, care-fully wrought design of cut paper. It was quite showy. A moment after I noticed it, I called to my six-year-old son.

My mother had continued to live alone in this old house. I went to visit her every week or two, since we lived in the same part of the city. With nothing in particular to do, I would just lounge about, watching my two children as they played around the house, so I rarely had occasion to look in on the bath. After finishing supper with my mother and children one Sunday toward summer, the temperature was rather high. I couldn't stand the sweaty feeling of my own body, so I told the children, who were eager to start setting off the fireworks we had brought, to wait until they had refreshed themselves in a hot bath. I turned on the light in the bath at the end of the hall and lit the heater. It was only then that I noticed the shadow of the gecko.

My son has always been fond of reptiles and amphibians, and he never fails to bring along a net and an insect cage whenever we come here. Frogs, lizards, snails and such are constantly appearing and disap-pearing here around this old house, but he seems incapable of catching anything but the snails. "This time I'm gonna do it," he always says, eagerly prowling around outside until dark.

"What about snakes?" he once asked.

"I've never seen a snake," his grandmother replied.

I was raised in this house and I've never seen one either.

"Now geckos, there *are* geckos," his grandmother continued. "But not as many as there used to be. This was long ago, but when I was asleep at night, occasionally I'd think something had run across my face. And when I felt for it with my hand, I'd realize it had been a gecko."

My son was filled with awe as he stared at his grandmother. This was the grandmother who had even found a long-tailed lizard and caught it for him. Ever since he'd heard that story, a gecko was one of the animals that my son wanted to add to his collection, which already included creatures he had gotten at a festival—newts and big tadpoles with legs growing. He had received a toad in trade from a friend in the neighborhood. Sometimes other kinds of lizards would dart in front of him, as if to tease him, but as yet he had never seen even a trace of a gecko.

As soon as my son caught sight of the gecko on the window of the bath, he flew out the back door with his insect net in hand. I stayed in the bath. I was hardly wide-eyed with wonder about what would happen. Still, I kept my eye on the gecko, as if it were my duty to watch. Before I knew it, my daughter and mother were standing behind me.

Just as I saw the shadow of my son's net flail about, the gecko twisted around and fell to the grass below the window, as if it had lost its balance. Much too late, the insect net struck the window glass two or three times in vain. We in the bathroom sighed. "Give it up. It's dark. And the gecko is in the grass now. You'll never find it," we called to my son through the glass. He answered in an angry voice, but I could not understand him. My daughter and mother went back to the parlor, but I continued to speak to my son from within the bathroom: "Hurry back in. It's hopeless now. There'll be a bigger one next time."

I didn't think to go outside to be with him. Even at noon, the weed-tangled yard outside the bathroom would have seemed too much for me. My son would have to scream before I'd get near that tall grass, submerged as it was in darkness.

About 30 minutes later my son finally came back inside. He was angry and full of remorse for having lost his prey. His eyes were red and his face was smudged with tears.

My daughter and her grandmother had already started setting off the fireworks when I stepped out to the veranda almost carrying my son under my arm. His emotions were still inflamed. As I gazed at the fireworks, I remembered when I was a child and my mother had picked up a gecko that she had found hibernating between the pieces of firewood she was breaking up. I told my son about it. "That's it. You should look for one in the winter. If you search under old boards and rocks, you're sure to find a gecko or some other kind of lizard. It would be sleeping so you could catch it with no trouble at all."

My mother's old house is in a residential area wedged between tall buildings in the heart of the city. She lives alone, so she can hardly take care of everything around the house. Ants come and go as they please from the cracks in the walls. In the summer weeds grow in wild profusion, and all kinds of creatures sleep securely there, confident that there are few human beings around.

My children and I live about a ten-minute walk away in a sixth-floor apartment on a six-lane street. To my children, who were raised in this apartment, geckos, other lizards, and even snails, are legendary creatures, like their own father, who also never makes an appearance. My children love to go to their grandmother's house, but not to see her face. They go to see the faces of the tiny creatures. There, my children taste the excitement of peering into a world they do not know.

But the creatures have not multiplied simply because my mother has grown old and lives alone. The last time I saw a gecko from the bath of my mother's house was probably when I was twenty years old. My mother and I had lived alone since I entered high school. My father died when I was a child, and my older brother died when I was in middle school. Then my older sister moved out. When I was twenty-three, I left home to chase after a young man—not the one who became the father of my children. It wasn't that I was all that much in love with him; it was just that the thought of living enveloped in my mother's solitude, as if in a dark cloud, was frightening. Rather than feel sympathy for my mother's loneliness, I found myself stifled by it. No matter how I loved her, I could not bring myself to obtain my security cradled in my mother's arms.

At the time, I had been startled, "Oh, a gecko!" So I must not have seen them very often, even then. Or perhaps I had merely avoided noticing them. I was in the bath, so of course I was naked. When I saw the shadow of the gecko on the translucent glass, I stood up. There was a second gecko on the glass—and others, too. Amazed at how many there were, I counted them. There were eight geckos clinging to the six-foot-wide lattice window. They looked rather repulsive. Preoccupied with thoughts of my own life at the time, I felt a sense of irritation at the number of geckos on the glass. So angry that I was about to cry, I scooped up some bath water and threw it against the window. I hated this frosted glass that mysteriously blurred the darkness outside. Only the place where the water had struck transmitted the darkness honestly as the color black. Several geckos fled, but one or two obstinately remained. They did not even move when I finally knocked on the glass to scare them.

Speaking of which, some time before I saw the eight geckos, I had begun to dream that my dead brother was standing outside the bath window trying to communicate with me. Surprisingly enough, it was the geckos that reminded me of this dream. The window of the bath is different from the others in a house: We usually see it only at night. Naked, I stared at that night window. There is no other window before which a person becomes so defenseless. It would have been impossible for my dead brother to avoid this window; at night when the light went on in the bath, he would approach, drawn by memories, and press his face to the glass. I had that dream again and again. In the bath, I held my breath, and with my whole body I sensed my brother's presence outside. How long did he plan to keep coming here like this, even though he could no longer enter the house? I wanted to let him in, but I realized that it would be impossible for a living person to do so. I thought of my brother's despair outside the window, and I was afraid. I was overwhelmed with grief, as if my body would melt. If only I could let him know that death meant he would never be able to pass through that window no matter how long he clung there. Although he was sixteen when he died, my brother had still not been able to count past ten or to express his pain in appropriate words. Perhaps I feared that he could not completely become one of the dead, because, even after he had died, he still did not know the meaning of death. Until then, as his sister, I had always taken the responsibility of explaining new things to him if he was going to try them. Alone now, he could not have understood what had happened. As he drew near the window, he would cry out, "Why can't I come in? This is weird. What did I do wrong?" He would remain there for years, decades, not knowing what to do.

I sometimes wondered if I could put the meaning of death into words my brother could understand—just a few words that I could call out to him through the window.

But there was no way for me to find these words. My father had died before I could understand such things, so to me his death meant merely his absence. Though I had shed tears when my dog died, the dog was a creature that lived outside the house. With my brother's death, I finally began vaguely to grasp the meaning of a death that occurs in a place where people actually live—but not enough to explain it to other people, much less to someone like my brother who did not understand reason. Now, though more than twenty years have passed, the meaning of death is still obscure.

In early spring the cat we had kept in our sixth-floor apartment suddenly quit eating and became lethargic. It was a male, one-and-a-half years old. My daughter had picked him up from the park when he was still a kitten with his eyes closed. After he joined our household, my children and I felt as though our family had grown by one. Until then, there had always seemed to be something missing when we did things with just the three of us. That gap was filled by the cat. My daughter, the older of my children, felt a particularly deep satisfaction. Unlike her brother, she could probably still recall what it was like when her father lived with us, as though the memory were a faint, indistinct odor. My daughter would not let the cat take one step outside. Most days I was at work and my son was at the day-care center through the afternoon, so the cat was always left alone until my daughter came home from school about three o'clock. When he heard the sound of the door being unlocked, the cat would come flying to the entryway. Since my daughter usually came straight home, she was the one who best knew the joy of being greeted by the cat, as he sat primly, meowing sweetly when she opened the heavy steel door.

The cat came to be the center of her life. When she woke up in the morning, the first thing she did was to hug the cat. Before she went to school—the cat. When she got home—the cat. Before she went to bed —the cat. When she wrote a composition or drew a picture at school— the cat. I would have thought it ridiculous to spend money on a cat we had picked up, but swayed by my daughter's passion, I took him for shots and examinations, knowing it would be rather expensive.

I thought the cat had probably lost his vigor because of a cold, but to make sure, the next morning I asked my daughter to take the cat to the animal hospital. That day I wasn't able to get all my work done, so I called my daughter at home and asked her to pick up her brother at the day-care center because I would be home late. Then I remembered. "How is the cat?" I asked.

"I took him to the hospital," she answered. "They told me he has a lump on his stomach or something. Anyway, the veterinarian said for you to be sure to call him. He said he would probably know by evening what sort of disease it is."

I called the animal hospital right away, but I was annoyed at all this trouble.

"Thank you for calling," the young veterinarian said in a gracious tone. "Actually, I didn't know if this was something I could tell your daughter, considering her age."

I felt uneasy and my pulse quickened.

"The results of the blood test aren't back yet, so I can't say this for sure," the veterinarian began to explain. "All I can say is that some big lymphatic tumors seem to have formed on the stomach and heart, and . . ."

"In other words, it's cancer," I rushed him.

"Yes. I think you'll have to consider it cancer of the blood," the veterinarian said. "I hope my diagnosis is mistaken, but if it's not, I'm very sorry."

"So he will die, won't he?" I asked. "Will he die tonight? Or in two or three days?"

"No, I don't think it will be anything like that," the veterinarian reassured me.

"Then he will be all right—for tonight?"

"Yes, and even if it really is a lymphatic tumor, with drugs the cat could live six months, or maybe as long as a year."

"I see."

I felt deflated. I made an appointment to go to the clinic the next day to learn the results of the test. Then I hung up the phone. My legs trembled. I doubted whether the cat would really be all right tonight. I was frightened. It was repulsive to think that the flow of the day's events might end in the death of the cat. I would rather go to sleep tonight and leave the whole matter to be settled tomorrow. I was afraid. I wanted this one day to end without incident, and I breathed a sigh of relief now that it seemed that it would. But the cat would eventually die. I could not imagine what that would mean for my children and me. I was afraid.

"The cat will live at least another ten years and by then I'll be twenty years old." As she held the cat, my daughter had calculated their ages. The cat would die. And wouldn't a valuable part of my child also crumble? Her grief, her terror, her despair—I was afraid of all of them. How I had always wanted to let her stay as she was! Why had this cat that she brought home come down with this strange disease? As I returned from work, I began to feel an unreasonable bitterness. My daughter was a child who was terrified by the sight of her own parents glaring at one another, forgetting about their own children. Although I was her mother, she already knew that I would forget about her and think only about myself when I was driven into a corner.

When I got home, however, far from being on the verge of death, the cat was eating well again. When I asked my daughter what had happened, she said the doctor had given the cat a shot to restore his appetite. "Really—is there such a drug? Anyway, we can't help him if he doesn't eat."

For the time being I felt relieved. I nodded. I could not tell her what the veterinarian had told me. Even after I found out the next day that it was a lymphatic tumor, even after the cat continued to live with the medicine we gave it, even after I began secretly to think of putting the cat to sleep because the veterinarian's fees worried me, I still could not tell my daughter what sort of disease it was. I just nodded vaguely when she said that the cat would be better in a little while.

The medicine worked and the cat's condition seemed to improve. He had been reduced to skin and bones, but now he began to gain weight. The veterinarian looked pleased when he announced the drug didn't work on all cats. "You know, the lump has grown smaller, so he might live a long time like this." I wasn't able to muster the courage to tell him to stop treatment if there was no hope of saving the cat. I continued to pay for the drug.

About three weeks later I noticed a new lump on the cat's throat. Although I realized that the disease had progressed, I didn't tell my daughter or the veterinarian. In two or three days my daughter noticed it too, but not knowing what it was, she didn't rush to tell the veterinarian. Then the cat's appetite disappeared. Two days after he quit eating, the cat became unsteady on his feet. And suddenly he became incontinent. At close inspection, I noticed that the hair around his genitals had started falling out. Being away all day, we were unable to check on the cat, but that evening I had to tell my daughter to be sure to take the cat to the animal hospital right after school the next day. "But if he's going to die anyway . . . ," I thought to myself. Still, now that death seemed imminent, I felt hesitant.

The next day that cat was taken to the animal hospital. He came back having been given all kinds of injections. His appetite was a little better, but by evening, though he would open his mouth to cry, the cat could no longer make a sound.

Late at night, I awoke to a sound like that of a person snoring. I wondered if it was one of my children, but it wasn't. I was facing the cat as he lay sprawled beside me. He stared at me, his transparent green eyes wide open in the dark. My eyes were looking into his, so the cat opened his mouth a bit. A sound like a snore came out. Two or three times the cat opened his mouth, releasing this sound into the stillness of the deep night. I finally realized that the cat could no longer cry. Unable to sleep, I continued to stare at the cat's face, while the cat stared fixedly back at me. His large eyes were transparent, unclouded, and didn't try to ask anything. Sentimentality could not even prompt me to stroke his diseased body.

The cat died the next day. When I came home from work, my daughter met me at the sliding partition. "Mother, he died" was all she said. She clung to the pillar and broke into tears.

My older brother's death had been quite sudden to me. He had been in bed sick, and one day when I came home from school he was gone. He had been admitted to the hospital. I had mistakenly thought he had a cold, but my sister told me it had been diagnosed as pneumonia. She said that it had weakened him, but there was nothing to worry about. Even when I saw what my mother looked like when she came back to get my brother's things, there seemed to be no cause for concern about his condition. "It was a mistake to think it was just a cold, wasn't it?" I asked my mother.

"I don't know how long he'll be in the hospital, but I think it would be good for you to stop by on the way home from school to visit him. He'd enjoy that."

When my mother said this, I imagined the visit would be a pleasant experience. I recalled that when you went to see someone in the hospital there were always delicious treats that visitors had brought, things you seldom ate at home.

The next day I was excited as I went to the hospital, which was near spirits of babies and animals always go to heaven and, though we can't see them, they can see us clearly from the other side.

I looked up at the ginkgo tree where my daughter was pointing. It must have been twenty feet tall. The branches of unfolding new leaves were brilliant, bathed in unobstructed light from the sky.

When we arrived at the animal hospital, the veterinarian took the cat out of something like a refrigerator. It was lying in a small cage, its four legs stretched out to the side, its eyes closed. Because of the fur covering its body, the changes brought on by death were less noticeable than they would be in a human.

"Let me hold him," my daughter said as she patted the cat's body with her fingers through the bars of the cage.

"Don't try to pick it up. If you move the body, all the dirty stuff left inside will come out." The veterinarian opened the lid of the cage to make it easier for my daughter to touch the cat. My daughter nodded and began to stroke the cat's body. It seemed she could not help but stroke the cat all the way down to the tip of its tail. Silent, her head cast down, my daughter continued simply to move her hand.

The veterinarian and I went to the next room to settle the bill. I also paid the fee for the pet cemetery.

"I'm exhausted by this, too. She's sharp, that girl. I thought I'd have to watch what I said since she's just a child. She's loved that cat for a long time, hasn't she? My inept consolation just wouldn't work. But I explained what kind of disease it was and she understood."

I was thankful for the veterinarian's consideration. As I bowed my head, I felt as though I were about to sob.

Five minutes later we returned to my daughter's side. "That's enough, isn't it?" The veterinarian urged her to close the top of the cage. My daughter nodded silently.

After my daughter washed and sterilized her hands, we went outside. Refreshed, she lifted her face toward the brilliant sky and inhaled deeply. Then smiling slightly, she looked at me. No part of her had been crushed by the cat's death. She looked at me with lively eyes.

my home. I peeped into the second-floor room that my mother had given me directions to. But no one was there, only a metal bed with the sheets made up neatly. Instantly I sensed in the depths of my heart what had become of my brother; nevertheless, I promptly decided that I must have mistaken the room number. How strange. I leaned my head to one side and looked at the number again. Then I glanced up and down the hall. Which room might it have been? I wondered if my brother had been released from the hospital since there had been nothing to worry about. Absent-mindedly, I stood in the hallway. I could neither bring myself to ask at the reception desk nor could I go straight home. I didn't know what I should do.

A middle-aged woman, perhaps a nurse's aide, was climbing the stairs to the second floor. I didn't think she would know about other patients so I decided to call to her. I expected her to answer that she didn't know anything.

"The fifteen- or sixteen-year-old boy who was here, did he get moved to . . ."

Before I had finished speaking, the woman opened her mouth. Her eyes filled with sympathy. She stared at me, a girl dressed in a middle-school uniform and carrying a school bag. "Oh, that boy. It's such a shame. I suppose the woman was his mother—she cried so."

"What do you mean 'such a shame'?" I asked, still pretending not to understand.

"He's gone. . . . And he was so young, too. Cerebral palsy, wasn't it? Are you a relative? Didn't you know anything about it before you came?"

I don't remember precisely what words followed. The woman repeated her question, but, realizing that she was bracing herself to try to comfort me, I lowered my head and fled. When I looked back from the top of the stairs, she was still standing there, gazing at me with deep emotion, and it made me shudder.

The weather was beautiful that day. At a normal pace it was less than a ten-minute walk from the hospital to my home, but that day it took half an hour. As I plodded, I continued foolishly to cock my head to one side and wonder where my brother had gone. I was offended. You could never trust what some senseless woman like that would say. Her words were off. She must have meant he had gone *somewhere*. And my brother certainly did not have cerebral palsy. He was just mentally retarded, so she must not have been talking about my brother. I thought there must have been some other boy with cerebral palsy there, too, and surely he was the one who had died. I was sorry I hadn't looked into some of the other rooms. My legs became so heavy they would only move a little at a time, but eventually I made my way home. I tried to open the wooden gate as forcefully as I always did. Then I went inside.

The dog, chained to its doghouse, looked at me and jumped up, putting its front paws on me. I stared at the dog, unable to turn my head toward the glass of the back door. Although fear had changed my color, I continued to think how disgusting it was that I had gone to so much trouble to see my brother in the hospital and hadn't even known which room he was in. I was playing with the dog, pretending to relieve my boredom, when my aunt rushed out of the house and found me. Had she not called to me, I wonder how long I would have had to keep up my pretense of playing with the dog.

"Oh, hello," I responded casually to my aunt. Surprisingly, my theatrics went over well. When I started to go inside, my aunt said, "Don't you know yet? You . . . well, your brother . . . he died." She covered her face and burst out crying. Even at this, I maintained a blank look. I stood on the porch. Finally, with my aunt holding onto my shoulders, I was able to go into the house.

Even when I was shown my brother's face and saw my mother crying, even after I passed the night at the wake without changing from my school uniform, even when my brother's altar was built and his classmates and teachers came, and even when I went to the crematorium, I never abandoned the pose I had unwittingly struck at the hospital room when I had pretended not to realize what had happened.

I stubbornly continued to flee from knowing the me death.

More than two years after my brother died, I started h dream about the bath.

The cat also died at a hospital. The veterinarian asked i pick up the body. If not, I could have it sent directly to a pet I told my daughter what he said. "That's all right. Let's not pi my daughter replied. She had already been to the animal h herself to confirm the cat's death.

That night, after I went to bed, I knew it was impossible, how I kept hearing the cat's voice. Once I decided that I hearing it, the sound truly seemed to echo. I got up and around the room, but there was no cat.

"Why don't you cry?" my son asked quietly. His sister w but he was able to avoid it.

"Because I've heard your sister crying," I said.

"I'll cry." He pretended to wail.

Indeed, I never shed a single tear for the cat.

The next day I came home early. I waited for my daugh home so we could go to the animal hospital to view the cat f time and pay the bills that had accumulated. It was a warm The sky was high and beautifully clear.

"I cried all I need to yesterday, so I won't cry anymore," ter said.

"Yes, you did cry all day yesterday."

"No, yesterday when I got the phone call and went to t hospital, the veterinarian was still working on the cat, but I ready dead. Still, I thought it was strange that I should be s was after I saw your face that I started crying. . . . I wor already gone as high as that tree?"

"What?"

"His spirit going to heaven." She laughed, embarrassed. The night before, I had blurted out to my sobbing daught

About a month later, a friend of hers gave her two kittens that, come to think of it, were born about the same time the other cat died. One was for her and one was for her brother.

Cat-centered life began again. The two kittens were raised within the confines of our sixth-floor apartment. Growing up in this apartment, the kittens determined that this was the only world they would live in. We had forced this life upon them, but, in contrast, my children and I were not living in just any old place; we had settled in this apartment to make this special place our home.

Here, we were able to go home assured, to sleep at night assured, and face the morning assured. We were out all day long, but the cats stayed in the apartment. They were so curious about the newts and frogs my son kept that they never tired of watching them. Thanks to these cats that played constantly with the curtains and the children's pencils and their underwear, our home never lost its warmth.

Whenever we were in the bath, our old cat had been so concerned about what we were doing in there that he could hardly stand it. Although he hated getting wet, he would plant himself at the door of the bath and meow in a strange voice, as if to ask if someone wouldn't open the door for him. We were all accustomed to the image of this black cat on the other side of the glass, but after he became ill he no longer came as far as the bath. Finally, we even forgot about this old habit of his.

Late one night, about two months after we were given the kittens, I was taking a bath after the children had settled down to sleep. When I looked at the glass door, I couldn't believe my eyes. There was an image of a cat, not a bit different from the one I had been used to seeing, except that the color was brown. I knew immediately that it was one of the kittens, but sitting properly with its paws together and its chest out, facing me, motionless, it looked just like our old cat. The kitten had grown and had finally extended its sphere of curiosity as far as the bath.

Naked, I was unable to take my eyes off the cat's image. I wondered if we were going to become accustomed to the shadow of this brown cat in the glass door of the bath.

From within the bath, I entrusted all my memories to the image transmitted by the frosted glass.

My own mother, on the other hand, saw not a cat, but the image of geckos through her bath window. I don't know what kind of memories she drew to herself as she looked at these shadows, but she continued to wash herself beside the window to which the geckos clung.

A Suite
of Cartoons

MICHAEL MASLIN

"When I say 'jump,' I expect everybody to jump."

"I'm a people person—Roger's a sandpiper person."

"I thought you should hear this from me before you heard it from anyone else, Irene. I'm an arboreal tropical American edentate of the family Bradypodidae. In other words, a two-toed sloth."

"Shall we?"

"Stay."

"Mitchell—herd of four."

"Ladies and gentlemen, the chicken and, in a related development, the egg."

"You're a great actor, Mortey—an artist, but never ever forget
that you're also a gorilla."

"Have you met our feathered friends?"

"Just between the two of us, there are three of us."

"Surprise!"

Wild Goose Chase

DAVID WAGONER

The fields of corn stubble in the flat river valley had been half flooded by a week of storms, and though it wasn't actually raining at the moment, it was going to. He could taste it, smell it, and feel it coming, even inside the car as they drove slowly along the zigzagging humpbacked macadam road between barbed-wire fences, past groves of black cottonwood and red alder, then into the stubble fields again.

Suddenly he slowed, stopped half on the weedy shoulder, ran his window down, and focused his field glasses. He said, "Four shovelers, two cinnamon teals, and a lesser scaup."

Leaning nearly into the driver's seat with him, she used her own less heavy glasses while he pressed backward to make room. "*Five* shovelers," she said. "Three females. And a bufflehead."

He looked again at the shallow fifty-foot-long temporary pond in the middle of the field, knowing she would be right.

She said, "Aren't they beautiful."

He nodded, agreeing genuinely, but her voice had in it the soft edges of reverence she kept strictly for the animal kingdom, and an old uneasiness stirred in him. He'd never heard her speak that feelingly and benevolently about any human being, including him. He hoped it would be a healing day for a change. She almost always felt better after looking at anything wild, preferably not through cage bars, and even though this was duck season and her main enemies in life—killers of animals—were out in red-faced force all over the state, there had been enough No Hunting and No Trespassing signs for the past mile to make her feel reassured. They hadn't heard a shotgun go off for half an hour.

The open window had chilled the car in a hurry, and with her unspoken agreement he rolled it up and began driving again, going slow, letting his eyes flick from the leafless wild rosebushes to the tops of split-cedar fenceposts to the silhouettes of tree branches against the gray sky and back down to the pools in the next field, the restless scanning of a bird watcher.

He saw it first—the Canada goose standing by itself in the two-inch stubble, not dabbling in the nearby pond, but rigid, oddly alert, more like a decoy than a real goose. At first, he didn't put into words what seemed wrong about it, just knew it, and he found himself wishing she wouldn't see it at all.

"Canada goose," she said, the way some women mentioned the names of famous dress designers or prize dahlias. But she turned uneasy almost as quickly as he had. "It's wounded."

He didn't contradict her right away. While she rolled her window down to use her glasses better, he stopped the car half on the road, idling, and began hoping no damage would be noticeable, no blood, no disarranged feathers, no wing-crooking. He let her do the inspecting.

"I can't see anything," she said. "Let me use yours."

He unlooped his stronger glasses and handed them over. "It's probably all right," he said without enough conviction in his voice. The trouble was the bird shouldn't have been alone: it was very ungooselike behavior. He waited.

"I still can't see anything. Turn off the engine."

He switched off the ignition to reduce the slight jiggling the motor always gave to a magnified image.

After staring for a few more seconds, she said, "What's it doing alone?"

He let out the breath he'd been holding. "Maybe it's waiting for a friend."

"They mate for life like eagles. Where's the mate?"

"Maybe it's immature." But even with the naked eye he could see the plumage was fully developed, the neck, head, and bill as black as they would ever be, the breast fully rounded, so he wasn't surprised when she didn't bother to answer.

"We've got to go see," she said.

He didn't bother to ask why. It wasn't necessary to hear, again, about his moral responsibility in matters like this. Their house through the fifteen years of their marriage had been a combination zoo, pet store, veterinary clinic, and pet cemetery, and he personally had undertaken the private burial services of water turtles and land tortoises, four kinds of lizards, a woodpecker, a rabbit, three tropical songbirds, a raccoon, a weasel, a mountain beaver, and other creatures which he had momentarily and mercifully forgotten, some of which they'd found injured, some acquired sick from careless shops or grateful owners, all given a clean, warm place to die.

So he opened the driver's door without protesting and slid out, clicking it shut, snapping his parka against the cold breeze. "He's watching. One false move, and he'll be heading back to Canada."

"Prove it," she said through her open window. "Make a false move."

All his moves felt false: the tug at his Irish tweed hat, the stomping to make sure his feet hadn't gone to sleep in his rubber hikers, the sidling away from the car so the goose could get the full benefit of his manshape. He tried to *will* the goose to fly, but it stayed put, staring, fifty yards away beyond the wire fence. He shouted, "Hey!" at the gruffest, most intimidating pitch of his voice.

"Don't scare it!" she said.

"I thought that was the idea." But the goose hadn't budged. Moving along the fence for a slightly closer look, he wondered whether it might not be a newfangled plastic decoy after all.

The car door opened and closed quietly behind him, and he turned to see her unfolding their old red-plaid car blanket, giving it a tentative shake.

Trying to forestall what she obviously had in mind, he said, "Take a better look at it. It's holding both wings in tight. Not a hitch. It's standing on both feet, and it's alert."

"We can take it to the Wild Bird Clinic."

"Now let's just back up a minute," he said. "Do you have any idea how strong a wild goose is?"

"A wounded goose isn't as strong."

He turned his back to the breeze, hunching his shoulders. "A wounded wild goose is even more irrational close to human beings than an unwounded wild goose. We'd do it more damage than it's already had. *If* it's wounded."

"It's wounded. I can tell."

"How?"

Immediately he wished he hadn't asked, and instead of replying to her silence with *It takes one to know one* or some other hazardous, flip remark, he turned to the barbed wire, set one boot hard against the lowest strand, grabbed the second wire between barbs, pulling it taut as a bowstring, and managed to duck through without damaging himself or losing his hat or even looking particularly awkward—more from luck than experience. Turning, he held out his hands for the blanket. "Let me do it," he said. "If it can be done. You've got good slacks on."

But she held on to the moth-eaten red wool, clutching it close as if for comfort. "No, I'm coming too."

"Take a look at that mud."

"I know what mud looks like, and I know what a healthy Canada goose looks like. Hold the wires for me."

He spread the gap again, helping unsnag the blanket when it caught briefly, and watched her skim through with the dancer's agility she'd never lost, in spite of the year-old operation in which she'd lost so much else.

"Thank you very much, sir."

Instead of reacting to her mock formality, he looked toward the goose, hoping all this bustle and activity had sent it into its short takeoff scamper, but it had only waddled a few yards and was keeping its right eye on them in full profile. The ground between the long rows of stubble was mucky, even here in a relatively well-drained area, and he glanced ahead to the swampier patches with depressed resignation. "Somebody's going to get hurt trying this," he said.

"Something's already hurt." She began a slow stalk of the goose, exaggerated by the need to pick her boots all the way out of the upper layer of mud before she could put them down again.

"Have you ever caught anything in a blanket?" he said. "Besides me and your feet?"

"Don't talk."

The bird, leaner-necked and more agile-looking than a domestic goose, was watching them intently—a little insanely, he thought, and certainly with no hint of welcome. "It doesn't like the look of us, and I don't blame it."

She made clucking noises he'd heard farm women use when scattering scratch, but the goose gave no sign of interest in becoming domesticated. With its long neck up straight, it began a steady waddle at an oblique angle away from them. She stopped, he stopped, and after a few more waddles the goose stopped, still watchful. "If it could fly, it would've flown by now, so it *is* wounded," she whispered.

"All right, suppose it is. This is posted land. It's safe. They spend most of their time on the ground anyway. They don't want to be flying all that goosefat around twenty-four hours a day. Let it make a living around here. On foot."

"It's *not* safe. There are dogs and foxes and farmers."

"There's probably a farmer right now aiming a .30-30 at us from his hayloft. We're in his posted cornfield, stalking a game bird. We've got a shorter life expectancy than the goose."

"You're just quibbling because you want to get out of it."

The goose was standing equidistant between them and a stand of brush-filled alders, and beyond that—if he had his local geography straight—was the swollen river, only a few feet below flood stage. It seemed unlikely the goose would want to enter the brush, that being poor flying territory for anything larger than a wren or a warbler, and so it was just possible they might be able to corner it long enough to use the blanket. If it was crippled.

Even so, he tried again. "Couldn't we just drive back to a feed store and get a sack of hen scratch for it? Let it build up its strength? Lots of them winter around here. They don't *all* have to go to California." He could see her face souring on the idea, rejecting it, so he let it turn foolish. "Then in the spring when the flocks start coming over again, it can come out of hiding and honk for a mate."

"That's really likely, isn't it," she said. "If you're so scared, go on back to the car and be a coward. Nobody's asking you to stay."

"I'm not a coward." He examined her blue lips as if identifying fieldmarks on a subspecies that could easily be mistaken for a common variety. "Why don't you at least wear that blanket till we catch up with the damn thing, which we won't."

"I'm not cold, and I don't want to spook it by flapping a blanket around."

He wanted to tell her he was being prudent and judicious, as thoughtful of her and the goose as of himself, but it didn't seem worth the effort.

When she started her muddy, clodhoppery walk again, he followed, and the goose headed for the alder thicket, picking up speed when she did, its black legs beginning to scuttle. It unfolded its wings halfway, and for the first time they could see the gap in the scapulars on the left side and the dark wound there, probably a wing shot. The right wing flapped momentarily, but the left stayed half folded while the goose stretched its neck forward and did its best to run.

And its best was as good as theirs across the slippery, puddle-filled furrows.

"Stop it!" she said, either to him or the goose or both.

As he lumbered past her, managing not to fall down, he grabbed at the blanket, ready to take over leadership of the Cause with the enthusiasm of a convert, but she kept hold of one end of it, hauling him back off balance, and by the time they'd recovered, arms out like people crossing ice and the blanket between them like an improvised sail, the goose had gone scooting into the brush, head down and forward, as neatly as a pheasant taking cover.

"Where in the hell did it learn how to do that?" he said, skidding to a halt just shy of the sagging rail fence between them and the alder grove. He expected her to stop too and talk it over with him, to consider the chase ended and to go back, honor intact, both having tried their damnedest to do some good.

Instead, she yanked his end of the blanket away from him, bundled it quickly, and clambered over the fence, knocking the rotten top rail loose, and blundered straight into the thicket, not taking her eyes away from the direction the goose had been headed.

"Wait a minute," he said. "You'll get scratched up." The ground cover among the forty-foot, gray-and-white-splotched alders was a mixture of salmonberry and trailing blackberry, and though it could have been denser, it looked like uncomfortable going. But she wasn't hesitating except when the tough vines and withes caught at her slacks or jacket or the blanket, or when they half tripped her.

Worried about her doggedness and the trouble it might make for her (and therefore him), he scissored his legs over the fence and kept on her trail. Whether it was also the trail of the goose was problematical: He had no idea whether it also had a pheasant's gift for lying doggo or veering unexpectedly.

Raising his voice, he said, "The river's just ahead. For godsake, be careful." Already he could hear its full, steady rush, and even though nearly all the banks in this district were low and she wasn't in much danger of falling in where she couldn't scramble out, the high water was full of snags and other debris, and the currents were more complicated than usual.

Suddenly she stopped cold ten feet ahead of him, frozen like a bird dog pointing. But when he caught up with her, he saw that her eyes—those gun-metal blue eyes that had used to soften whenever they looked into his—were darting from all the way left to all the way right, saw she was listening hard, and he'd already held still before she hushed him.

They stood together in the middle of the thicket, trying to hear through the increased noise level of the river. She stood slightly bent, as if ready to spring, and he leaned sideways against one of the alders, remembering other times he'd admired the mottled bark up close, the pale-green lichen clinging to it in patches. Even without sunlight, the tall, slim, closely palisaded tree trunks cast an uncanny light. It would have been a wonderful place to sit and think and watch and learn, but at the moment there seemed to be nothing to think about, only something clumsy and dangerous to do, and he felt lost beside her, displaced. A man with an impossible assignment. He thought of kissing her to make up for the sense of estrangement, but her usually soft, sensual mouth was as thin-lipped as one of the lizards she'd tried to keep, whose mucous membranes didn't compromise with the tough exterior by allowing anything as vulnerable as lips.

They heard it at the same time—a brushy scuffling that had nothing to do with the sound of the river—and at first he thought a dog or a raccoon had caught it and they'd all wind up in a catch-as-catch-can free-for-all, everyone a loser. But then he saw the goose struggling to wedge itself through the last patches of salmonberry, catching its half-crooked wings sometimes but churning away with its flat black webfeet.

She ran toward it, her shoulders glancing off tree trunks, stumbled, and fell short, only cushioning herself partly with the blanket, and he saw her face collide with an alder.

He caught up while she was still thrashing to get to her knees, and he tried to touch her scraped cheek and the puffed split lower lip.

Shaking his hands away, she scrambled forward, sometimes on her knees, sometimes on her feet, and he followed her into a shallow grassy clearing at the river's abrupt edge. The goose stood on the two-foot cutbank above the heavily silted, roiling current full of small branches and all the clutter from flooded tributaries, not so much poised there as beside itself. It wasn't used to being chased on the ground, especially not through bushes, and it looked ready to get back to its own kind of territory.

They were only ten feet away, and she said, "Don't let it fall in! It might drown."

"Geese don't drown." He was short of breath and worried about her lip.

"Be quiet!" she said, then took a moment to spit blood.

The goose was still hesitating, and never having been this close to one before, he stared at its wild black eye and the white face-patch, feeling like apologizing for all this harassment. The hunter who'd shot it was probably half shot himself by now in a tavern somewhere, enjoying the exchange of lies with other shotgunners, and he wished the man a bad night and a bad day and weeks more of the same.

When the goose saw the blanket come up in her hands and she made a short rush at it mostly on her knees, it squatted to slide down the bank. Even with her clumsiness, she nearly caught it: One edge of the blanket momentarily covered it halfway, but the goose slid from underneath and went into the water with only a small splash and began paddling downstream.

He saved her from going in too by hanging on to her snagged jacket, then eased her back to a sitting position while they both watched the goose heading out of sight beyond a low-hanging willow branch, not battling the current but using it with an easy skill.

She started weeping silently. "It's hurt."

"It doesn't swim with its wings," he said. "And it's doing what it *wants* to do."

"Except flying." She glared at him. "Right now it doesn't know what's good for it."

He let that pass and offered her his fairly clean handkerchief, but she shoved it aside, spitting more blood. He tried to think of something, anything, to distract or comfort her. "Don't worry. It'll swim ashore at a safe place."

"There aren't any safe places," she said with a contemptuous superiority, like a disciplinarian whose star student was failing in an exam.

And he felt, with a weird certainty, that she would have preferred going down the river, even under it, with the goose instead of staying where she was. Trying to regain some kind of advantage, he said, "I mean, that goose is a survivor. It knows exactly what to do, day or night, one wing or two, on the ground, in the air, on water. It would probably even know what to do in a cage."

"That's not true." She was probing the inside of her mouth with her tongue and spitting more blood, and again she refused the handkerchief as if refusing a blindfold. She said, "I broke a tooth."

He could tell from her look she was turning away from not trusting him and the rest of the world, at least for the time being, and was beginning to concentrate on not trusting her body, the still beautiful body she now considered ugly. He saw on her face a kind of bitter pleasure, and he blinked and half turned from it, wishing he hadn't noticed. She let him help her to her feet, and could see she was going to need stitches in her lip. He felt panicky, inadequate, responsible, compassionate, tired, and raggedly geared up, a bad combination of emotions for the ambulance driver he was going to have to be in a few minutes.

And he knew he would come out of this fiasco looking bad. He'd done something wrong, maybe everything. Or maybe just *felt* the wrong way. She would know what he'd done wrong and would tell him sooner or later and probably over and over. She began to groan rhythmically, and he walked with her through the tangled thicket and helped her climb over the fence. It was drizzling and turning darker as he half guided and half followed her across the empty stubble field.

Hands

GREGORY BLAKE SMITH

Here in New England we sit in chairs.

It's from my porch rocker that I watch the raccoon. He usually comes at dusk, that time of day half dog and half wolf, when the downturned leaves seem to glow with the sunset and the

upturned ones glimmer with moonlight. I watch him pad through autumn weeds while the sweat of my chairmaking dries on my skin. He lingers in the shadows, still woodside, the sun falling further with each moment, and then waddles onto my lawn. He looks like a house cat, once the woods are behind him. He tosses a wary look at me and then slowly disappears behind the chair shop. After another minute I hear the enormous crash of my garbage can lid falling on the stones. He doesn't even bother to run off as he used to, dawdling at the wood's edge until it's safe to come back. He seems to know I won't leave my chair.

"A twenty-two," my neighbor Moose says while I pare stretchers. "A twenty-two and then we won't blow the b'Jesus out of the pelt."

I take a few more cuts with my gouge and then ask him how he thinks the raccoon has missed his trap line all this time. He peers at me with that cold menace of old age. He has a white beard that rims his chin like frost.

"It probably don't run my way," he says. "But if you want it trapped I can trap it. It's just a pissload easier to shoot it if it's coming every night like you're ringing the dinner bell. Right here," he says and he goes over to the window just above my workbench and taps at a pane. His fingers are scarred with patches of old frostbite. "We'll take this here pane out. I can rest the barrel on the mullion. If it's close enough I'll get it clean through the head and I'll be richer one pelt and you'll be poorer one dinner guest."

I tell him I'm not sure I want to kill him.

"*Him?*" he says. "How d'you know it's a *him?*" And he spits on my woodstove so the cast iron sizzles and steams.

Outside, my moaning tree sends up a regular howl.

"*Please* cut that tree down, Smitty," my sister Jaxxlyn says every weekend when she comes up from New York. "It's driving me positively psychotic."

I tell her it's a poplar. I can't cut it down. I don't use poplar in my chairs.

"But you heat with wood," she says. "Don't you? Don't you heat with wood?"

Not poplar wood I don't, I say. Too soft.

"It's driving me positively psychotic, Smitty."

I say what about New York. What about the car horns and the sirens. She says they don't have trees that moan in New York, Smitty.

Smitty, she says.

My name is Smith. I'm a chairmaker with a tree that's grown itself tight around a telephone pole and a raccoon that's taken a fancy to my garbage. I've never minded the name Smith. I like the ancestral whiff of fashioning and forging in its single syllable. And I don't mind the moaning tree and its outrage over the telephone poles that have been stabbed into the landscape like stilettos, rubbing its insulted bark in the slightest breeze and howling when the wind blows in earnest. But the raccoon has unsettled me and I don't know why. My sister—who hates her last name and is being driven psychotic by my moaning tree—is not bothered by the raccoon.

"I think he's *cute*," she says, sitting on my porch with me as the fat creature moves from shadow into moonlight and back into shadow. "My friend Flora in the west seventies has a skunk for a pet. You should see him, Smitty! His little claws go clack-clack-clack on the linoleum, you know? Of course he's been desmelled or whatever they do to them. Oh, Smitty!" she says as the garbage can lid crashes on the stony ground. "Isn't that the cutest thing? How does he do it? Just *how* does he do it? Do you leave the lid on loose for him? Is that how he does it?"

Hands, I tell her, and I feel a faint panic at the word. They've got hands. And I hold my own hands up in the gloom, the backs reddish with dusk, the palms silver with moonlight.

When Monday comes I try tying the lid shut with mason's twine. That night there is no aluminum crash and I think: so much for hands, so much for raccoons, so much for half dog and half wolf! The next day I start in on a set of eight Queen Anne chairs, carefully designing the S-shaped legs to Hogarth's line of beauty. But that evening the raccoon comes trotting along the forest floor, hiking up onto my lawn behind the shop. It takes him a few minutes longer, but eventually the harsh, bright crash shatters the dusk. I sit in a stupor. In ten minutes he emerges from behind the shop trundling happily along. He pauses partway to the wood's edge and tosses me a scornful look over his shoulder and then vanishes into the now-dark bushes.

"You might open up a motel," Moose suggests, "seeing as what you already got yourself a rest'rant."

My cabriole legs aren't right. I can't strike the balance between knee and foot. It's never happened like this before. I get out Hogarth's *Analysis of Beauty* and look his S's over, and I print S S S S S on my graph paper, write my own name: Smith, Smith, Smith, Smith, but when I go to draft my Queen Anne leg I can't balance the knee to the foot, the foot to the knee, the S's top orb to its bottom. I spend a whole day at my drafting table, trying, and end up tossing a sheaf of rejected legs into the stove. That night the raccoon dines on pumpkin and old cantaloupe.

I get my bucksaw and my knapsack and my spool of pink ribbon. If I can't work I'll hunt wood, do the felling now and wait until the first decent snow to find the marker ribbons and sledge the logs out with Moose's snowmobile. I plan on a two-day roam, bringing my sleeping bag and some food. At the sight of my bucksaw, my moaning tree groans.

I'm going to forget about raccoons.

I poach my lumber, and maybe that's why I have a feeling of trespassing when I go into the woods, of being where I only half belong. There are stone walls everywhere, built in earlier centuries and now running mute and indecipherable through the forest. Walking, I try to picture perfect S's in the air, but the stone walls distract me. They are like hieroglyphs on the land. From time to time I come across an old foundation, a sprinkle of broken glass in the weeds and a small graveyard a ways off. I find a bottle or two, an old auger, but they look as alien there as I do. Farther on, the stone walls are so tumble-down they have ceased to look like walls. There is a feeling of low menace all around.

I mark my wood as I go, but on this trip I keep my eyes open for hollowed trees, for trees with holes, a cicatrix, disease. I climb up several and look inside, peer up the trunk of one, but there's no sign of habitation. That night, lying on dark pine needles, I have a recurring picture of the raccoon back at my house, sitting at the kitchen table in one of my chairs, with knife and fork in hand—perhaps a napkin—eating.

By noontime on the second day I've swung around to where I know there's a stand of tiger maple near a marshy pond two miles from the house. I spend the afternoon carefully harvesting the rare, figured wood, dragging the delimbed trunks down to the pondside and sticker-ing them off the ground so they won't rot. The work puts the raccoon out of my mind. I feel healthy, feel the steel teeth of my bucksaw sharp and vengeful, the rasp of the sawn wood like the sound of defeat. But after the last haul, just as I sit content and forgetful on a stump, I catch sight of a tiny footprint in the soft silt that rings the water. Farther on, there's another one.

There's a hush over the pond. The marsh reeds stand like pickets along the shore. Across the way the shadows between the junipers and low laurels seem to breathe in and out. I have a feeling of having been tricked, of having been watched all along. On the water the whirligigs hover like spies. A scarlet leaf flutters through the blue air and lands a foot or so from the raccoon's footprint, then cartwheels slyly until it covers the print. But it's too late. In the west, where my house is, the sun is kindling nests of reddish fire in the blue tops of the spruces.

You've got yourself a comfy den, I'm saying half an hour later after I've found the raccoon's beech tree. I've brought a crotched branch from the pondside for a leg up, and I'm peering into a yawning hole maybe ten feet off the ground. I say it out loud. I do. I say: leaves and dried reeds, decaying wood for heat, some duck down. You've done all right. Yes, you have. You've done all right.

The trees seem to stir at the sound of my voice. I pull my head out and listen. They sound baffled, outraged. I want to say to them: "Do you think so? Do you think so? So *I'm* the intruder? Do you think so?" But I don't. I just look at the hasty illogic of the shadows. Trees don't come on all fours and pry your garbage can lid off, I say. Even Darwin can't see to that, I say, and I go back to looking inside the raccoon's den.

I'm not afraid he's in there somewhere. I *know* what time of day it is. I *know* where he is. But off to the side, in a decaying burl, something has caught my eye, something shiny and unnatural. I look closer and realize he's got himself a cache of junk, bottle caps and aluminum can rings. Then in the next instant I recognize a piece of old coffee cup I'd broken in the summer, and then, too, a router bit I'd chipped and thrown out, then an old ballpoint, a spoon, screws.

Are you a user of spoons, too, raccoon? I finally say out loud. And screws? And pens? Are you a writer of sonnets? I say.

But even as I talk I hear footsteps behind me on the leaves. I pull my head out and look around, but there's nothing moving, just the vagrant leaves falling. I listen again, hear them coming closer. Is it the raccoon returning? I hang fire a moment and then start hurriedly down the trunk. But before I do I reach in and steal back my old ballpoint. I hide the crotched limb in some bushes nearby.

For the next few days I wonder just how much the raccoon knows. There's no new contempt evident in his regard as he bellies up out of the woods onto my lawn—but he may be a master of his emotions. Jaxxlyn has put a bowl of water out for him. She says she's going to move it nearer to the house each day until the raccoon gets used to being with us. She wants me to do the moving on the weekdays.

My West Hartford client calls and asks how her Queen Anne chairs are coming. I start to tell her about the raccoon. I start to tell her about William Hogarth and beauty and order, about how a man can't work when a raccoon's eating his garbage, about how I've allowed eagle's claws for chair feet in the past, lion's paws too. But this raccoon is asking too much, I tell her. There's a silence on the line when I stop— and then she asks again how her chairs are coming.

"Six inches each day," Jaxx tells me as she gets into her car. "Six inches, Smitty."

Monday I can't work. Tuesday I can't either. Tuesday evening I wander off into the woods again, walk the two miles to the raccoon's tree. Somewhere on the way I know we cross paths. I get the crotched limb out of its hiding place and steal back a screw.

The next morning I get the mating S's of the cabriole legs down perfectly in ten minutes, and by sundown I have all sixteen legs squared up and cut. That night I take the router bit back.

Thursday it's another screw. Friday a piece of china. I'm going great guns on my chairs.

Jaxxlyn doesn't understand why the raccoon won't drink her water. She asks if I've moved it each day. Then she talks to the raccoon from the porch, talks to him so he pauses in his jaunty walk and looks our way. She alternates from a low, cooing voice to a high, baby voice. The raccoon and I exchange looks. He knows, I think to myself. He knows. He can hardly cart things off as fast as I can steal them back. He knows.

For the next week I am a maker of chairs in the daytime and a sitter of chairs at night. I'm a happy man. Only during the in-between hours do I venture through the woods to the raccoon's house and then venture back in the near-dark. I've taken to putting my booty back in the trash can.

My West Hartford lady drives cross-state to see how her chairs are coming along. I let her run her wealthy fingers across the soft wood, up and down the smooth legs. She shivers and says it feels alive still. "Doesn't it feel alive still?" she says.

Back in the woods I take a different route to the raccoon's tree. I figure I might catch him out this time, but it turns out we've merely switched paths, and he's trying to catch me out. I round the pond quickly, the last fall leaves floating like toy boats on the water, and hurry to the bushes where the crotched branch is hidden. The trees are quiet. I throw the crotch up against the tree-trunk, climb quickly up, and in the half-light see that the raccoon has taken the ballpoint pen back.

Still writing sonnets, raccoon? I say and I reach in and take the pen back. But just as I do the den bursts into a flurry of fur and claws and teeth. I hear a hiss, a growling sibilance, and just before I fall see two leathery hands gripped around my wrist and a furry mouth set to bite. An instant later I am lying scratched and hurt in the laurel below. Above me the raccoon peers fiercely down at me from his hole. His eyes are black and fanatical, and he seems to say: "All right? All right? Understand? All right?"

Violence! I spit through my teeth, stumbling back through the woods. I don't even try to staunch the blood coming from the punctures on my wrist. *Violence! Violence!*

Moose laughs. He laughs and asks how much the first of my rabies series costs. I'm sitting in his living room feeding bark into his stove. I don't answer him at first. I'm sick and I ache from the shot. Finally I tell him twenty dollars.

"Well, let's see," he says and he sights down the barrel of his twenty-two. "A raccoon pelt brings thirty dollar nowadays. You already used up twenty of them dollars on that shot. But I figure my half is still fifteen. So I figure you owe me five dollar."

I muster enough character to tell him he's getting a little ahead of himself, he's getting a little eager.

"No eagerer than that raccoon's getting," he says. The frostbite on his face crumples with his laugh, as if the skin there were half alive. I sit sullen and witless. I feel wasted. I don't know what to do. The raccoon comes and ravages my garbage.

I lie in bed for two days. When I'm up again I ask Moose for one of his box traps. I tell him I don't want to shoot the raccoon, I want to trap him. And once I've trapped him I want to let him go. He looks at me like this is confirmation of some suspicion he's had about me all along, never mind raccoons, some suspicion he'd had since he met me and my chairs.

"I ain't altogether sure a raccoon will trap so near a house," he says. "Raccoons ain't dumb."

This one will, I say. He's a modern raccoon.

But that night, sitting in my warm chair shop on a half-finished Queen Anne chair, I watch the raccoon stop and inspect the trap, puff at the acorn squash inside and then waddle over to the garbage can. He knocks the lid off with a professional air, but before he crouches into the garbage, he tosses a disdainful look through the windowpane at me and my chair. Behind him the trap sits in a state of frozen violence.

Beauty is the visible fitness of a thing to its use, I say to the raccoon in my dreams. Order, in other words. In a Yale-ish voice he answers back: "Not entirely different from that beauty which there is in fitting a mortise to its tenon."

I wake in a sweat. My wound itches under its bandage.

On the second night, kneeling on the wooden floor in my shop, the chairs empty behind me, I watch the raccoon sniff a moment longer at the squash but again pass it up. This time it's contempt in his face when he catches sight of me through the windowpane. That night the air turns cold.

What do you want? I whisper to the raccoon in my sleep. *What do you want?*

"*What do you want?*" the raccoon whispers back. "*What do you want?*"

On the third night I forsake the chair shop for the junipers, hiding myself long before dusk in the green shrubbery that skirts the forest's edge. It's snowing. The flurries make an icy whisper in the trees overhead. I watch the sun fall through autumn avatars and set in blue winter. The snowflakes land on my eyelashes and melt New England into an antique drizzle. I blink my eyes to clear them and wait with my joints stiffening, my toes disappearing.

By the time the raccoon comes I am iced over, a snowy stump among the evergreens. He pads silently through the snow, leaving tiny handprints behind him on the slushy ground. He doesn't see me. I watch him with frost inside me, my breathing halted, my hands clubbed. He looks for me on the porch, in my rocker, then tries to spy me through my shop window. For an instant he seems stunned by my absence, by the change in things. He turns and peers straight across at where I sit in the frozen junipers. I am certain he sees me, even nod my head at him. For a moment we are poised, balanced, the one against the other. He blinks, acknowledging my presence in the snow, and then with an air of genteel reciprocation, turns and walks straight into the trap.

When I reach him he has his paws up on the trap's sides, the fingers outstretched on the fencing. He peers up at me as if to see if I'll take his hands as evidence after all. There are snowflakes on his eyelashes. When I bend over him our breaths mingle in the cold gray New England air.

Antlers

RICK BASS

The woods can be a bit strange.
It takes a long time to feel you belong
there and then you never again
really belong in town.
—*Jim Harrison*

Halloween brings us all closer,
in the valley. The Halloween party at

the saloon is when we all, for the first time since last winter, realize why we are all up here—all three dozen of us—living in this cold, blue valley. Sometimes there are a few tourists through the valley in the high green grasses of summer, and the valley is opened up a little; people slip in and out of it; it's almost a regular place. But in October the snows come, and it closes down. It becomes our valley again, and the tourists and less hardy-of-heart people leave.

Everyone who's up here is here because of the silence. It is eternity up here. Some are on the run, and others are looking for something; some are incapable of living in a city, among people, while others simply love the wildness of new untouched country. But our lives are all close enough, our feelings, that when winter comes in October there's a feeling like a sigh, a sigh after the great full meal of summer, and at the Halloween party everyone shows up, and we don't bother with costumes because we all know one another so well, if not through direct contact then through word of mouth—what Dick said Becky said about Don, and so forth—knowing more in this manner, sometimes. And instead of costumes, all we do is strap horns on our heads—moose antlers, or deer antlers, or even the high throwback of elk antlers—and we have a big potluck supper and get drunk as hell, even those of us who do not drink, that one night a year, and we dance all night long, putting nickels in the jukebox (Elvis, the Doors, Marty Robbins) and clomping around in the bar as if it were a dance floor, tables and stools set outside in the falling snow to make room, and the men and women bang their antlers against each other in mock battle. Then around two or three in the morning we all drive home, or ski home, or snowshoe home, or ride back on horses—however we got to the party is how we'll return.

It usually snows big on Halloween—a foot, a foot and a half. Sometimes whoever drove down to the saloon will give the skiers a ride home by fastening a long rope to the back bumper, and we skiers will hold on to that rope, still wearing our antlers, too drunk or tired to take them off, and we'll ride home that way, being pulled up the hill by the truck, gliding silently over the road's hard ice across the new snow, our heads tucked against the wind, against the falling snow. . . .

Like children being let off at a bus stop, we'll let go of the rope when the truck passes our dark cabins. It would be nice to leave a lantern burning in the window, for coming home, but you don't ever go to sleep or leave with a lantern lit like that—it can burn your cabin down in the night and leave you in the middle of winter with nothing. We come home to dark houses, all of us. The antlers feel natural after having been up there for so long. Sometimes we bump them against the door going in and knock them off. We wear them only once a year: only once a year do we become the hunted.

We believe in this small place, this valley. Many of us have come here from other places and have been running all our lives from other things, and I think that everyone who is up here has decided not to run anymore.

There is a woman up here, Suzie, who has moved through the valley with a regularity, a rhythm, that is all her own and has nothing to do with our—the men's—pleadings or desires. Over the years, Suzie has been with all the men in this valley. All, that is, except for Randy. She won't have anything to do with Randy. He still wishes very much for his chance, but because he is a bowhunter—he uses a strong compound bow and wicked, heart-gleaming aluminum arrows with a whole spindle of razor blades at one end for the killing point—she will have nothing to do with him.

Sometimes I wanted to defend Randy, even though I strongly disagreed with bowhunting. Bowhunting, it seemed to me, was wrong—but Randy was just Randy, no better or worse than any of the rest of us who had dated Suzie. Bowhunting was just something he did, something he couldn't help; I didn't see why she had to take it so personally.

Wolves eviscerate their prey; it's a hard life. Dead's dead, isn't it? And isn't pain the same everywhere?

I would say that Suzie's boyfriends lasted, on the average, three months. Nobody ever left her. Even the most sworn bachelors among us enjoyed her company—she worked at the bar every evening—and it was always Suzie who left the men, who left us, though I thought it was odd and wonderful that she never left the valley.

Suzie has sandy-red hair, high cold cheeks, and fury-blue eyes; she is short, no taller than anyone's shoulders. But because most of us had known her for so long—and this is what the other men had told me after she'd left them—it was fun, and even stirring, but it wasn't really that *great*. There wasn't a lot of heat in it for most of them—not the dizzying, lost feeling kind you get sometimes when you meet someone for the first time, or even glimpse them in passing, never to meet. . . . That kind of heat was missing, said most of the men, and it was just comfortable, they said—*comfortable*.

When it was my turn to date Suzie, I'm proud to say that we stayed together for five months—longer than she's ever stayed with anyone— long enough for people to talk, and to kid her about it.

Our dates were simple enough; we'd go for long drives to the tops of snowy mountains and watch the valley. We'd drive into town, too, seventy miles away down a one-lane, rutted, cliff-hanging road, just for dinner and a movie. I could see how there was not heat and wild romance in it for some of the other men, but for me it was warm, and *right,* while it lasted.

When she left, I did not think I would ever eat again, drink again. It felt like my heart had been torn from my chest, like my lungs were on fire; every breath burned. I couldn't understand why she had to leave; I didn't know why she had to do that to me. I'd known it was coming, someday, but still it hurt. But I got over it; I lived. She's lovely. She's a nice girl. For a long time, I wished she would date Randy.

Besides being a bowhunter, Randy was a carpenter. He did odd jobs for people in the valley, usually fixing up old cabins rather than ever building any new ones. He kept his own schedule, and stopped working entirely in the fall so that he could hunt to his heart's content. He would roam the valley for days, exploring all of the wildest places, going all over the valley. He had hunted everywhere, had seen everything in the valley. We all hunted in the fall—grouse, deer, elk, though we left the moose and bear alone because they were rarer and we liked seeing them—but none of us were clever or stealthy enough to bowhunt. You had to get so close to the animal, with a bow.

Suzie didn't like any form of hunting. "That's what cattle are for," she'd say. "Cattle are like city people. Cattle expect, even deserve, what they've got coming. But wild animals are different. Wild animals enjoy life. They live in the woods on purpose. It's cruel to go in after them and kill them. It's cruel."

We'd all hoo-rah her and order more beers, and she wouldn't get angry, then—she'd understand that it was just what everyone did up here, the men and the women alike, that we loved the animals, loved seeing them, but that for one or two months out of the year we loved to hunt them. She couldn't understand it, but she knew that was how it was.

Randy was so good at what he did that we were jealous, and we admired him for it, tipped our hats to his talent. He could crawl right up to within thirty yards of wild animals when they were feeding, or he could sit so still that they would walk right past him. And he was good with his bow—he was deadly. The animal he shot would run a short way with the arrow stuck through it. An arrow wouldn't kill the way a bullet did, and the animal always ran at least a little way before dying— bleeding to death, or dying from trauma—and no one liked for that to happen, but the blood trail was easy to follow, especially in the snow. There was nothing that could be done about it; that was just the way bowhunting was. The men looked at it as being much fairer than hunting with a rifle, because you had to get so close to the animal to get a good shot—thirty-five, forty yards was the farthest away you could be —but Suzie didn't see it that way.

She would serve Randy his drinks and would chat with him, would be polite, but her face was a mask, her smiles were stiff.

What Randy did to try to gain Suzie's favor was to build her things. Davey, the bartender—the man she was dating that summer—didn't really mind. It wasn't as if there were any threat of Randy stealing her away, and besides, he liked the objects Randy built her; and, too, I think it might have seemed to add just the smallest bit of that white heat to Davey and Suzie's relationship—though I can't say that for sure.

Randy built her a porch swing out of bright larch wood and stained it with tung oil. It was as pretty as a new truck; he brought it up to her at the bar one night, having spent a week sanding it and getting it just right. We all gathered around, admiring it, running our hands over its smoothness. Suzie smiled a little—a polite smile, which was, in a way, worse than if she had looked angry—and said nothing, not even "thank you," and she and Davey took it home in the back of Davey's truck. This was in June.

Randy built her other things, too—small things, things she could fit on her dresser: a little mahogany box for her earrings, of which she had several pairs, and a walking stick with a deer's antler for the grip. She said she did not want the walking stick, but would take the earring box.

Some nights I would lie awake in my cabin and think about how Suzie was with Davey, and then I would feel sorry for Davey, because she would be leaving him eventually. I'd lie there on my side and look out my bedroom window at the northern lights flashing above the snowy mountains, and their strange light would be reflected on the river that ran past my cabin, so that the light seemed to be coming from beneath the water as well. On nights like those I'd feel like my heart was never going to heal—in fact, I was certain that it never would. I didn't love Suzie anymore—didn't think I did, anyway—but I wanted to love someone, and to be loved. Life, on those nights, seemed shorter than anything in the world, and so important, so precious, that it terrified me.

Perhaps Suzie was right about the bowhunting, and about all hunters.

In the evenings, back when we'd been together, Suzie and I would sit out on the back porch after she got in from work—still plenty of daylight left, the sun not setting until very late—and we'd watch large herds of deer, their antlers covered with summer velvet, wade out into the cool shadows of the river to bathe, like ladies. The sun would finally set, and those deer's bodies would take on the dark shapes of the shadows, still out in the shallows of the rapids, splashing and bathing. Later, well into the night, Suzie and I would sit in the same chair, wrapped up in a single blanket, and nap. Shooting stars would shriek and howl over the mountains as if taunting us.

This past July, Randy, who lives along a field up on the side of the mountains at the north end of the valley up against the brief foothills, began practicing: standing out in the field at various marked distances —ten, twenty, thirty, forty yards—and shooting arrow after arrow into the bull's-eye target that was stapled to bales of hay. It was unusual to drive past in July and not see him out there in the field, practicing— even in the middle of the day, shirtless, perspiring, his cheeks flushed. He lived by himself, and there was probably nothing else to do. The bowhunting season began in late August, months before the regular gun season.

Too many people up here, I think, just get comfortable and lazy and lose their real passions—for whatever it is they used to get excited about. I've been up here only a few years, so maybe I have no right to say that, but it's what I feel.

It made Suzie furious to see Randy out practicing like that. She circulated a petition in the valley, requesting that bowhunting be banned.

But we—the other men, the other hunters—would have been doing the same thing, hunting the giant elk with bows for the thrill of it, luring them in with calls and rattles, right in to us, hidden in the bushes, the bulls wanting to fight, squealing madly and rushing in, tearing at trees and brush with their great dark antlers. If we could have gotten them in that close before killing them, we would have, and it would be a thing we would remember longer than any other thing. . . .

We just weren't good enough. We couldn't sign Suzie's petition. Not even Davey could sign it.

"It's wrong," she'd say.

"It's personal choice," Davey would say. "If you use the meat, and apologize to the spirit right before you do it and right after—if you give thanks—it's okay. It's a man's choice, honey," he'd say—and if there was one thing Suzie hated, it was that man-woman stuff.

"He's trying to prove something," she said.

"He's just doing something he cares about, dear," Davey said.

"He's trying to prove his manhood—to me, to all of us," she said. "He's dangerous."

"No," said Davey, "that's not it. He likes it and hates it both. It fascinates him is all."

"It's sick," Suzie said. "He's dangerous."

I could see that Suzie would not be with Davey much longer. She moved from man to man almost with the seasons. There was a wildness, a flightiness, about her—some sort of combination of strength and terror—that made her desirable. To me, anyway, though I can only guess for the others.

I'd been out bowhunting with Randy once to see how it was done. I saw him shoot an elk, a huge bull, and I saw the arrow go in behind the bull's shoulder where the heart and lungs were hidden— and I saw, too, the way the bull looked around in wild-eyed surprise, and then went galloping off through the timber, seemingly uninjured, running hard. For a long time Randy and I sat there, listening to the clack-clack of the aluminum arrow banging against trees as the elk ran away with it.

"We sit and wait," Randy said. "We just wait." He was confident and did not seem at all shaky, though I was. It was a record bull, a beautiful bull. We sat there and waited. I did not believe we would ever see that bull again. I studied Randy's cool face, tiger-striped and frightening with the camouflage painted on it, and he seemed so cold, so icy.

After a couple of hours we got up and began to follow the blood trail. There wasn't much of it at all, at first—just a drop or two, drops in the dry leaves, already turning brown and cracking, drops that I would never have seen—but after about a quarter of a mile, farther down the hill, we began to see more of it, until it looked as if entire buckets of blood had been lost. We found two places where the bull had lain down beneath a tree to die, but had then gotten up and moved on again. We found him by the creek, a half-mile away, down in the shadows, but with his huge antlers rising into a patch of sun and gleaming. He looked like a monster from another world; even after his death, he looked noble. The creek made a beautiful trickling sound. It was very quiet. But as we got closer, as large as he was, the bull looked like someone's pet. He looked friendly. The green-and-black arrow sticking out of him looked as if it had hurt his feelings more than anything; it did not look as if such a small arrow could kill such a large and strong animal.

We sat down beside the elk and admired him, studied him. Randy, who because of the scent did not smoke during the hunting season— not until he had his elk—pulled out a pack of cigarettes, shook one out, and lit it.

"I'm not sure why I do it," he admitted, reading my mind. "I feel kind of bad about it each time I see one like this, but I keep doing it." He shrugged. I listened to the sound of the creek. "I know it's cruel, but I can't help it. I have to do it," he said.

• • •

"What do you think it must feel like?" Suzie had asked me at the bar. "What do you think it must feel like to run around with an arrow in your heart, knowing you're going to die for it?" She was furious and righteous, red-faced, and I told her I didn't know. I paid for my drink and left, confused because she was right. The animal had to be feeling pain—serious, continuous pain. It was just the way it was.

In July, Suzie left Davey, as I'd predicted. It was gentle and kind—amicable—and we all had a party down at the saloon to celebrate. We roasted a whole deer that Holger Jennings had hit with his truck the night before while coming back from town with supplies, and we stayed out in front of the saloon and ate steaming fresh meat on paper plates with barbecue sauce and crisp apples from Idaho, and watched the lazy little river that followed the road that ran through town. We didn't dance or play loud music or anything—it was too mellow. There were children and dogs. This was back when Don Terlinde was still alive, and he played his accordion: a sad, sweet sound. We drank beer and told stories.

All this time, I'd been uncertain about whether it was right or wrong to hunt if you used the meat and said those prayers. And I'm still not entirely convinced, one way or the other. But I do have a better picture of what it's like now to be the elk or deer. And I understand Suzie a little better, too: I no longer think of her as cruel for hurting Randy's proud heart, for singling out, among all the other men in the valley, only Randy to shun, to avoid.

She wasn't cruel. She was just frightened. Fright—sometimes plain fright, even more than terror—is every bit as bad as pain, and maybe worse.

What I am getting at is that Suzie went home with me that night after the party; she had made her rounds through the men of the valley, had sampled them all (except for Randy and a few of the more ancient ones), and now she was choosing to come back to me.

"I've got to go somewhere," she said. "I hate being alone. I can't stand to be alone." She slipped her hand in mine as we were walking home. Randy was still sitting on the picnic table with Davey when we left, eating slices of venison. The sun still hadn't quite set. Ducks flew down the river.

"I guess that's as close to 'I love you' as I'll get," I said.

"I'm serious," she said, twisting my hand. "You don't understand. It's *horrible*. I can't *stand* it. It's not like other people's loneliness. It's worse."

"Why?" I asked.

"No reason," Suzie said. "I'm just scared, is all. Jumpy. Spooky. Some people are that way. I can't help it."

"It's okay," I said.

We walked down the road like that, holding hands, walking slowly in the dusk. It was about three miles down the gravel road to my cabin. Suzie knew the way. We heard owls as we walked along the river and saw lots of deer. Once, for no reason, I turned and looked back, but I saw nothing, saw no one.

If Randy can have such white-hot passion for a thing—bowhunting— he can, I understand full well, have just as much heat in his hate. It spooks me the way he doesn't bring Suzie presents anymore in the old, hopeful way. The flat looks he gives me could mean anything: they rattle me.

It's like I can't *see* him.

Sometimes I'm afraid to go into the woods.

But I do anyway. I go hunting in the fall and cut wood in the fall and winter, fish in the spring, and go for walks in the summer, walks and drives up to the tops of the high snowy mountains—and there are times when I feel someone or something is just behind me, following at a distance, and I'll turn around, frightened and angry both, and I won't see anything, but still, later on into the walk, I'll feel it again.

But I feel other things, too: I feel my happiness with Suzie. I feel the sun on my face and on my shoulders. I like the way we sit on the porch again, the way we used to, with drinks in hand, and watch the end of day, watch the deer come slipping down into the river.

I'm frightened, but it feels delicious.

This year at the Halloween party, it dumped on us; it began snowing the day before and continued on through the night and all through Halloween day and then Halloween night, snowing harder than ever. The roof over the saloon groaned that night under the load of new snow, but we had the party anyway and kept dancing, all of us leaping around and waltzing, drinking, proposing toasts, and arm-wrestling, then leaping up again and dancing some more, with all the antlers from all the animals in the valley strapped to our heads—everyone. It looked pagan. We all whooped and danced. Davey and Suzie danced in each other's arms, swirled and pirouetted; she was so light and so free, and I watched them and grinned. Randy sat on the porch and drank beers and watched, too, and smiled. It was a polite smile.

All of the rest of us drank and stomped around. We shook our heads at each other and pretended we were deer, pretended we were elk.

We ran out of beer around three in the morning, and we all started gathering up our skis, rounding up rides, people with trucks who could take us home. The rumble of trucks being warmed up began, and the beams of headlights crisscrossed the road in all directions, showing us just how hard it really was snowing. The flakes were as large as the biggest goose feathers. Because Randy and I lived up the same road, Davey drove us home, and Suzie took hold of the tow rope and skied with us.

Davey drove slowly because it was hard to see the road in such a storm.

Suzie had had a lot to drink—we all had—and she held on to the rope with both hands, her deer antlers slightly askew, and she began to ask Randy some questions about his hunting—not razzing him, as I thought she would, but simply questioning him—things she'd been wondering for a long time, I supposed, but had been too angry to ask. We watched the brake lights in front of us, watched the snow spiraling into our faces and concentrated on holding on to the rope. As usual, we all seemed to have forgotten the antlers that were on our heads.

"What's it like?" Suzie kept wanting to know. "I mean, what's it *really* like?"

We were sliding through the night, holding on to the rope, being pulled through the night. The snow was striking our faces, caking our eyebrows, and it was so cold that it was hard to speak.

"You're a real asshole, you know?" Suzie said, when Randy wouldn't answer. "You're too cold-blooded for me," she said. "You scare me, mister."

Randy just stared straight ahead, his face hard and flat and blank, and he held on to the rope.

I'd had way too much to drink. We all had. We slid over some rough spots in the road.

"Suzie, honey," I started to say—I have no idea what I was going to say after that—something to defend Randy, I think—but then I stopped, because Randy turned and looked at me, for just a second, with fury, terrible fury, which I could *feel* as well as see, even in my drunkenness. But then the mask, the polite mask, came back down over him, and we continued down the road in silence, the antlers on our heads bobbing and weaving, a fine target for anyone who might not have understood that we weren't wild animals.

Bears

SARA BURNABY

There's something about bears. Like love. Every time I see one it grips my heart like a fist, and I whisper. Songs. Incantations. The power of a bear is in its paw.

It woke me without a sound at dawn. Just there, outside my window, testing the thin ice bridge over the stream, I watched it lap at wellings along the melting edges. A bear with cubs and a den nearby. Our paths first crossed last summer, which was more startling to me than the bear. Contrary to popular myth, bears see just fine. But they don't let on to it. When you come up on one, it will avert its gaze ignoring you and so, on a windless evening with dust muffling sound, you're the only one who's surprised. Suddenly. Shadows go solid. Also a bear has no collarbone and if it is facing you, you can see an arc of light between the front legs. Just below the neck where they join in the shape of a Gothic arch. It is bad to look a bear in the eye. Look, but look away, and make noise and move slowly so it can figure out exactly what you intend. When it is gone, but still in sight—there is a moment when that happens, when the mind won't let go of form and goes on filling in the edges—the whispering begins. You'll hear just afterwards, but not as you say it. Songs, chants: Amen. I believe.

The bears came down the mountain early last year in the drought. August came and went without berries and the streams dried up. It was so dry. The joke in town was that we were serving *truites au bleu* up here. That's how bad it was: the water so low and warm it poached the fish. So the bear is double hungry this spring, and it's too soon for her to forage far from her young. You can tell by the way she stands: undecided beneath an outsize winter coat, still groggy, sniffing the air for green, hungry for sap. Now she is clawing the roots of an aspen. She pulls a willow branch through her teeth.

"Stay," I whisper. "Eat."

But there is nothing to feed on and she turns away. Goes slab-sided and swaying back in under the night shadow of the mountain. "One more week," I tell her, seeing the den, the cubs clamoring to their feet, whimpering, the great head blocking the light. A growl warns them out from under her paws. That's how it is: the bear settles softly, her cubs suckling, kneading her with their claws. And in the dim quiet of half-sleep I wonder if bears are born tame or if people are born wild and the rest is training. If the outcome just depends on who you belong to. I could go wild very calmly, learn to dare black ice, swallow wind, endure hunger, and denned, blink slowly awake, licking last year's salt from musky fur: a bear in the heavy quiet of its single mind.

The vision lulls me. At midmorning, I dress slowly, afraid of losing it, and trying not to be because then it will happen. You can't propitiate a bear in this day and age. There are no bear gods to grant your prayers and, anyway, we've lost the art for that sort of thing. Nor are we wise enough or savage. For that you need a single mind and you'd have to get it right the first time. No middle way and no going back. No wondering if this was it, your right mind. You'd just have to trust what was taking you over, like a bear. A single mind is not something to experiment with. That's why I whisper. Even now, the sense of it is fading fast. I take the dog out. There is pink ice where crystals cut the bear's tongue. That's all there is, a little blood and the track, almost human, always ghostly. Round and round the house.

In the afternoon, in the cafe where I go for coffee and the paper, no one notices that I am late. Beth and Julie are in back talking to "the girls." Every one who works for them becomes a sort of daughter to be mothered, worried over. Right now it is Mirta and since it's the lull time before closing and Mirta doesn't speak any English, the three of them are practicing whatever it is they don't speak. Everyone in back, prepping for tomorrow. That leaves Jennifer to run the counter. But she's there too. All of them, crossing to and fro, chopping, rolling out, frying, stacking the cold room. No one is in charge and everything is getting done. I like it like this, coming in late, with no one up front and the sun coming full on the windows and the voices and the radio and the fan at a million decibels. I take a roll and pour my coffee, listening to Jennifer. Right now she is the only one making sense. She doesn't even try to speak "Spanglish," as we call it. She is announcing to all of them that she is pregnant.

"Oh, Jen!" cries Beth and hugs her. Julie tries to explain in English to Mirta that Jennifer has tried to have a baby for two years, then Beth takes over and I am called in. Pretty soon we are all crowded together poking out our stomachs, grinning, arms extended miming gargantuan pregnancies. A man looks in the window. We quit, feeling dumb. Mirta hides her face in her hands. Beth reaches for the CLOSED sign.

"Too late," says Julie. "He's coming in."

On the glass two greasy prints make it true.

"He's the one," says Beth, "who shot the bear. But we have to be nice."

"If you want him to build flower boxes," warns Julie.

They introduce me to the building janitor. His skin looks sticky; his no-color clothes match his face. Lewis is his no-color name, and we hate him in unison, all chirpy like schoolgirls. Being nice. When he is gone, I ask if the flower boxes are worth it.

"Well, they're something," says Julie.

"Hate is useless," says Beth.

"I saw a bear, today," I tell them. "At dawn, outside my window."

"He was . . . ," Mirta mimes eating, but her eyes are looking for a better word than "hunger."

"It was just hungry," Beth answers. Bears don't scare her, but she doesn't love them either. To Beth, they're more of a nuisance. Once at the old mine where she used to live, she tug-of-warred a bear for a cold box full of food. She'd left it open on the porch, barely turned her back and the bear was into it. "It was the lettuce," she said. "I wasn't going to ski all the way down for more. And the bear knew it. He saw how mad I was and let go."

I walk home thinking that hunger to the well-fed is only discomfort. To the underfed it is the first hold of death. In the bear's track around my house was the slow, dull panic of a creature looking at its end. "A week or two," I whisper and wonder if being nice to hateful people is very useful—outside the personal, I mean—if it really keeps peace in the world. Punishment has to do some good, except that no one wants the job of punisher. If justice came from God's hand like in the Old

Testament, or even like His mercy in the New, the way He uses it in endless supply—the sense that payback is coming and nobody knows for sure what it will be—that would be perfect prevention: fear and uncertainty for all. It's the unknown that keeps us in line. For good or bad, and somehow, lately, things seem out of balance.

As I think about it, laws seem too predictable for the taking of life—any life—and every time I go to the cafe from spring through summer, I think of the shot bear and unseen punishment. Maybe that's what it is to really wish a person to hell. It comes over me like a power. From outside. If I see Lewis I think of the bear and I can watch that man from behind the window as if I were invisible. Studying the way he is bundled up in his cold stickiness, even at the height of day. Faceless. He's just a hat and an oily pair of old gloves, jerking along like something you'd drag for a cat, and it puts me up on edge. Every time. Makes me sit up straighter to see what he's doing. Today he's out there by the dumpster, on his hands and knees, back and forth, like a wind-up thing. The snow has melted on the farthest peaks; only the gnarled trees on the wind-scarred crests attest to winter's force and the bear has been dead long since. It is August and heat is baking grease into the pavement, but I can't let up.

"What's he doing?" I ask Julie.

"You don't want to know," she says.

Beth pours me more coffee. "Scrubbing the pavement," she says.

"Oh," I say and know enough to wait.

"Blood," she says. "They moved the dumpster this morning. It was awful. A big dried pool right underneath."

Behind the newspaper, I am filled with weeping.

"I feel so terrible," Julie says, counting the register. "We told him not to sit in here at night."

"He really did that?" I ask. "Came in here, and waited for the bear?"

She rolls her eyes up in her head. "Definitely," she says. "I could tell from his smell. It lingered like metal. Oil. Something."

"Not food," I say to show I understand.

· · ·

From the cafe I take the long way home, cutting through the forest and down to the creek. Not really watching it, just following the sound of water still high for late summer. It was a decent winter, this last, and with the drought over, I don't expect to see the bears. Their tracks this spring told me all I wanted to know. That they'd made it from last year to this. They're probably way in the back country by now, and in their absence, I've taken to reading about them: bears lie down in November, but they don't always sleep all winter. They come and go. This month, August, they are gorging on berries: it's the sugar that fattens them for winter. Sometimes the black bear, that lives here on the east side of the Sierra, is brown, deep cinnamon. A bear is wild, intelligent. It can learn with two rewards. It is curious, most always hungry, a scavenger, which brings it in contact with people. The stories abound. So the sow and her cubs survive to give me a memory. And a worry. For the first time in our county this year, they're going to let hunters take bears. For a week.

Ahead, the tin roofs of the Forest Service cabins vein through the trees like a mother lode. That's what got this side of the mountains started with people: silver, not gold. And there are mules at the pack station across the way. They move in the brush against the late sun, as quiet and sudden as stick figures, watching me cross through the few old cabins that the Forest Service rents. The oldest were torn down, one dating as far back as the mine, which makes me sad. Still, there's something original about this place: the tall grass, the aspens and alder. And the creek. There's an open space along a pebbly riffle where they say the bear fell and died. I heard Julie tell someone just after, that it cried like a human as it fled. It was 5 a.m. and she was coming in to bake when Lewis fired. She called Fish and Game as soon as they opened, but it was too late to shorten the bear's misery. I stare back toward the town, picking out the tiny cafe parking lot, trying to esti- mate the miles the wounded creature ran in panicked, agonized circles.

You cannot kill a bear with a single shot. It takes two: one to shatter the shoulder's bony plate, the second to pierce the heart. I go over and peer into the riffling water, thinking how deceptive it is. Horrible things happening in peaceful places. Inside, my own voice cries out, stripped, primal. If I were a child right now, I'd be running from here. Instead, I turn. And look straight at one of the cabins. Its roof sags inward. There are gaps in the shingles that make you wonder who'd ever live in such a freezing place. Someone does. There's an old bedspread nailed over the window, the screen is torn and hanging. Nearer, I can smell spilt grease and fuel oil coming out of the ground. Above, two old trees rub together with a sound like crows, but the rhythm is wrong for calling. The place is a mess and the wind warning me to go home. But I stay, puzzling something out.

Standing in front of the sorry cabin and hearing the creek, I think that what runs in our family is a love for animals, wild or tame. For instance, my mother's fish. The Great Trout. Mother fell in love with that fish two years before she took it. Used to go visit his hole and speak to him, like a Siren, until the day he gave up, charmed onto her hook. And she played him on its barbless curve down the river, and fell and kept him, holding her arm up until the water gave her back her feet. Afterwards, I suspect she talked to her fish in the freezer. I remember her hand on him, stroking, soothing, pulling little bits of paper off. She kept him there for years and even after his color faded into dull silver the color of ice, she'd bring him out for us to admire, and tell the story, which was the entire point of asking. To see her eyes burning over the freezer light. I suspect there's something wild in my mother that got passed on to me.

"Leave the bears alone, Helen," she said. "They know you are thinking about them."

She's right, but I can't help it. I go on finding things out.

Within a week of visiting her, I found Herb Severns dragging a trap to the back of some condos, trying to catch a garbage bear. "The sows teach the cubs," he said. "Then there's a generation of bears that can't hunt. They don't know how."

"What do you do?" I asked, eyes on his badge. Department of Fish and Game has a rule: three tags and the bear gets shot.

"I don't tag 'em the first time."

"It's awful," I said.

Herb tapped the cage. It is a length of culvert pipe barred at both ends. "Had one in here, once. Kept her up nights, beating on this thing, lights, the works."

He noticed me wince and got indignant.

"You ever try to get enough rodents for a bear, or berries? Lug enough water? Christ."

He saw that I was catching on. Rewards for a bear to learn, punishment to unlearn. "Bear retraining," I offered.

"Look," he pointed inside the cage, mollified. "Bacon rind. Bears love smoked stuff, or cat food. And sugar. I saw one, once, lick jelly from the back of his paw. Like this." He lowered his head, raised his hand, deftly. Put out his tongue like a kid.

"And afterwards," I asked, "when they're caught?"

"That's the good part," he said. "I give 'em a lift home. About a hundred and fifty miles from here."

"And they stay?" I asked.

"Most do. I've never seen the bear I kept, again."

"But you . . ." I wanted reassurance. Proof. Certainty.

"Do you know what it would take to teach them all?" he demanded. I didn't mention my bears. The point, after all, is to keep people and bears apart. Herb risks his life for it.

"The worst," he said, "is turning your back, lifting this thing." He hefted the tongue of the cage to the truck hitch.

"Make it longer," I suggested.

"Cage swings too much," he said.

It's embarrassing to advise someone whose job is putting his life on the line. What more can he do? I tried to make it up to Herb, telling him about seeing a sow sitting up, braced against a rock, to nurse her cub . . . not here . . . a long time ago . . . through field glasses.

"You saw that!" He straightened up with wonder, not disbelief. And regret. Just a little, that it wasn't him, and smiled it away, saying, "It's funny how people like bears for the ways they seem human: stand on their back legs, wave their paws for food. They never think a bear weighs four hundred pounds. Cute, they say. Christ, it can climb a tree as fast as you can run. Tell them that," he said, getting into the truck. "There's forty pounds alone, in a bear's paw!"

I wanted to protest that bears were the only thing on my mind. Not people. Bears are not like us, no matter how it appears on the surface. They are not afraid of existence. Things are clear to them; in the wild it takes no time to die and there is no other way. While we, fearing the end, slide into our own disorder. Go right to the bottom of it. But I let Herb go, certain his disgust was my own. Surely anyone who had looked at his own death would agree that hunting was a secondhand way to examine it. A wrongheaded way of getting some animal courage. Herb would never put a wild life in the sights of a gun, a creature unafraid, its gaze still and alert. But you can't discuss things like that with someone whose job is keeping wild things and people separate. Sometimes, I think, you are just given things to know whole and forever, and when they stop, they stay yours. That's how it is with me and bears. Time is something we have to walk through.

That is what I am thinking as I watch sunset's red thorny light crown the manzanita around the cabin. Even so, it doesn't hide the patches of brown. The month of berries is ending. Already, the days have shifted to earth's great downward pitch. In the dusk I turn home and stumble over a paper wrapping, startle at the weight inside it. Catch my breath against the sweet, deep stench of rotting meat. Kicking the wrapping free of my shoe I end up hopping to keep clear of the bear track, perfectly pressed in soft oily earth. Broad, five-toed, left rear foot, heel like a moccasin print. "An average bear weighs four hundred pounds: its paw, forty pounds." I already know that. But just to get a better idea, I take off my shoe and sock, ease my foot into the dank print, leaving an outline inside it, tender and inefficient. A foot needing to be shod. A domestic foot that will never carry me to the heart of wilderness.

"Get out!" His yell shoots through me. The cafe janitor is half out the door of the ruined cabin, reaching back for something.

In shock, no particular name comes to mind. It just slips my guard: "Bear killer!" I yell. It's out, green hate snaking between us. He raises the gun. I grab up the meat in its greasy wrapper. Shake out dense rancid chunks. Yell: "I know what you're doing!"

He comes toward me. Walking and mumbling. Holding the gun like a stick. Once, as a kid, I yelled at a tramp. At the train track where I was forbidden to go and he came at me like this: threw a vanilla bottle. I heard it shatter. I grab my shoe and run.

All evening my pulse pounds in my head. Herb's phone just rings. The sound of it comes back at me out of the empty house. I want to tell him about the track and the meat in the paper. Ask him to come and save the bear. Come out and take it right now, right out from under Lewis's nose. He'll know what's going on because last year two Indian women at the pack station did the same thing. Baited a bear and when they thought no one was around . . . bam. The janitor is doing exactly what it looks like he's doing. Getting ready for bear season.

And earlier, this spring? I shut my eyes against what is certain to be true—Lewis after hours at the cafe—and only see it better. The janitor taking food to the dumpster, laying the top open as far as it will go. Lounging in the dark booths, waiting, leaving his smell. Bringing the bear in for two nights, four. Who knows, and afterward telling the judge that it was a garbage bear . . . that it had "menaced" him. That he had only shot the thing and run, because he couldn't fly! The news reporter liked that. He wrote about Lewis several times and people took to saying whenever they could that they had seen a bear and run because they couldn't fly. But the town council still voted against installing bear-proof dumpsters. Too expensive, they said, which had put even more scared people in Lewis's camp. And now, by hunting season, the janitor meant to bring a bear to his cabin and, at least to all appearances, to have the law on his side as well.

Through the night I go over and over it, making sure. At daybreak give the light time to spread out. To touch the peaks, which makes far crags and cliffs appear closer, leaves the meadow below a dim unknown. Dawn reverses distance, bringing me closer to the bears. Up on the heights they are already taking up the day's layout of planes and angles.

At the cafe, I call Herb again. Don't care if I wake him. Stand smelling bread, looking at the dumpster, listening to his phone shrill through the empty house. Lewis pulls up in his truck. On time. I go invisible in my own breath, slide into a booth.

"Looks like you worked all night," says Julie.

What interests me about Julie is that she thinks living alone and writing stories which are unpublished is harder than what anyone else is doing. "I chose it," I say. "It's what I know how to do."

"Still . . ." she says.

That's the argument. She thinks I'm some kind of martyr. Beth comes out now, with a book by a woman who won the Nobel Peace Prize, hugging it like the prize itself, certain she has found an answer for us all: "It is not worthy," she reads, "of human beings to give up hope."

"Hope lulls you," I say. "It excuses you from doing anything." I could hope that the bear survived and went home, but it would not be enough. Would never end there in spite of the release I might feel at first. "Hope," I exclaim, "can keep you from acting and all the while life is running out!"

"But that's the point," Beth beams. "Human beings have the gift of eternity . . . and endless hope. You can't give that up!"

"I'd settle for right now!" I grumble, and take a big breath, letting up on Beth. You can't spoil an idea for her. She is indestructible, a Catholic, and even if you proved that hope was gone, bam, splattered all over the universe, she would still pray that there was some, so I don't say what the janitor is doing.

Outside, the aspens have begun taking up the shades of fall. I want the summer back and dawn's washy impermanence. Want to feel my feet caught up in the sway of valley and steep like last week when I didn't know what I do now. But the trail is sharp with shadows, the lakeshore dented with prints, animals coming lower as the heights grow cold even as sun takes away the chill. Beside the water, I choose a warm sandy spot, lie back, feel little breezes twist my hair in dried grass, and sleep and dream of rings licked from my fingers, the turquoise, the jade, the ruby and gold. And am not afraid. Let love tongue the bonds over my knuckles one by one. Triumphant and certain, licking them away into the water's lapping, leaving white bands where my rings have been all summer, my insect-bitten hands healed and smoothed beneath my head. The last shadings of sleep dissolve in the lake's cold mirror. There, under day's broadest light, is the bear. Lowering and raising its head amid bushes stripped of berries. I raise up on my elbow. It swings toward me massive and peering, a face as undefended as the sightless faces of the blind. Lowering, casting for my scent along the ground. Mosquitos swarming over its back, humming in fall's last heat. I freeze, trying not to alter the solitude. Moments pass. The mosquitos insist. The bear cleaves the mirror, with a stroke liquifies everything that was. All that is left is the faint fishy smell of lake sand at noon and long stalks of fallen mullein, not frost killed. Not yet. But flattened between two logs. I kneel beside the wide indentation of the bear's bed, lay my hand on broken stalks. Sun warmth and animal presence intersect. Close my fingers, walk me home.

In the shower, I look down on my frame, still fairly smooth and tan, but stiff and tired, and think how a bear swims. In a straight line not to be deflected. Picture it denned, heavy and soft in the arms of winter. Imagine it asleep under half a ton. "They lie down in November." That's what Herb said, not as a fact—we both know that—but as a prayer. It occurs to me that I am praying now. For an instant. Not with my whole mind. Half. The other half aware of age. The signs come over you in notches. You learn what to look for in others: the unruly gray hair, dates forgotten, lines under hard light, the mention of prayer. But here in the shower-steamed mirror I am looking at myself. There's no use calling Herb again. I've left a message on the machine. He'll be home in a few days with coffee-bean eyes, small and bright as a bear's, puffed from campfire smoke and watching into the dark. His work is in the field. He doesn't know yet, the field is here.

I sleep through the afternoon and wake at twilight with salt sticking my hand to my cheek. Once, my mother told me, when she was little, she slept through dinner and in the morning insisted on meat for breakfast. That's how I get up, wanting what's not being served. And feel a shift in the planking from my room to the porch. Find it with both feet. Step quickly to the switch. Watch the porch light eclipsed by hugeness. An outline of fur over muscle and spine, at its edges, silver: rain just turning to snow. The bear with espresso eyes and two and a half million years of evolution, staring back over its shoulder. And me with such lightness. I could go now. It would be just the two of us, survivors of the last ice age. I, the one who can count but not enough to follow. In me the ages do not add up. I am the curiosity, the anomaly: the one who thinks she'll live forever. That's the trap; you have to see it yourself or not at all. And if there is wildness in getting older, it is the joy of being able to go further than you think toward what you are. There's a roundness in it, too. It is what the young and the old have in common. Maybe even animals and people. Maybe that's what binds us.

The bear has gone its way. Outside my window is the meadow; above it, the shades of peaks; at the sides, the shadows of leaves. This is what I have. This night, and silence, my interrogator and the questions asked so often that I begin to disbelieve the answers. I lie back down on the bed on my heart side. Listen to its thump reverberate over the springs. Things repeated from the inside. Me, singly, in the bear's mind. The idea plays in waves along the solid edges that the mind fills in. Tunes my ears to something softly steering me through the night, padding over the room, edging between me and daybreak. Dry snuffing, stiff pelt against the wall bring me to my feet. I follow its brushing through the dim room, keep to the wall, slide between tables, chairs. Outside, the bear is always in motion. Sound or silence, I match its pace. Clothes clinging with the chill of fever. The wall, nothing between us. The dark, too close.

"Get out!" I shout. "Get out of my ears!"

And dress. And follow.

Outside the house nothing stirs. The last hours of night smell of frost-killed meadow. I do not need the bear in sight. We both know where we are going. Along the creek to the Forest Service pasture which held cattle a week ago, sleek and drowsing in dusty grass. Now, its loading pens are still with the stench of fear and urine. There are no lights at this hour in the cabin tract, no sheen of tin roofs. Haze sits over Lewis's place. From the oil stove. His truck is hunched like a ghost, gathered up at the cab and beside it I am invisible, crouched, spreading my arms into the flat shadows, my hands on the wrapper. Its corners poke like white flowers through the wet snow. Slowly, the roots of frost let go. Beneath is the meat where it fell. And I know what I am going to do. I'm going to give Lewis to the bear. The chunks, out for two days, are gummy and cold against my chest, but I keep one hand free for the logs that go up like stairs at the cabin's corner. Softly, set my feet in the crossings where the walls meet. Three steps to the roof eaves. Five to the pitch above. The porch rattles with melting. Hush is mine. I ease the meat onto the tar paper, careful of my weight against the sway-backed roof. Like an old horse, it can't carry much more.

The bent center beam tremors with the nerve of vengeance, its impulses traveling down the rafters beneath my glove. I sense the brief stir inside. A breath, a shiver—a reflex. And stay still as the death I intend for Lewis, one hand curved, hanging on. With the other lay the meat up, as far as it will go. And back down, going wide where shadows meld with the trees. Sensing the bear nearby. Somewhere. Both of us trying to unlock the dark with a combination long forgotten. It is in my whispering: Come on. Amen. I believe. And is there at the edge of the trees, listening to the silent cabin. The bear approaches, lifts its slow dark length toward the roof, balances softly against the eaves. Casts for the scent above and climbs, ears, snout, head, shoulders, emerging under thin blue light. The decrepit roof sways. Walls shift. The center beam yaws; nails tear. A corner of the cabin collapses. Somewhere glass pops, rattling to the ground, and the bear slips. Leaps from its place on the sky. Old wood splinters. Logs override. Jam. Release and roll as roof and walls drop into the dark. On the path home, I look back once, at blue dust swirling up over the moon's arc.

The newspaper photo of the ruined cabin is different from what I saw in that backward glance. Under floodlights the clearing has an inner dark and an outer dark. Like a whirlpool. There are no shadows on the bright snow. It is blotched instead, by paths of mud. Newly trodden, too wide. Dried iris and dandelion spike up into the sickly bubble of electric glare sheeting the wreckage. The sheriff has Lewis by the elbow, guiding him over the ground. Lewis is shouting into the camera, his teeth bright with menace, eyes flat against the light and I know now, why they never let you see the executioner. Lewis is going to stick in my mind. Maybe forever. Blot out everything else, if the bear gets shot. It never occurred to me that I was proving Lewis's point and right now it's taking all I have to keep on coming back to this clearing, watching for the bear. Still trying to save it.

Everyday, the wind giggles in the trees, stirs the coyotes to the taste of winter. Together, we wait on the numb time when the blood is dull, and it is slow to come. The deer have passed through. Bear season ends today, and the grease will never come out of my parka. I can't even smell it anymore. There's just a dark stain across my heart with a zipper going through. A line where Lewis and I are crossing over. Changing places. Waiting for the bear. Each of us for a different reason though more and more, it seems, we resemble each other. But I don't know what else to do. Bears lie down in November. It chants my mind, keeps me going.

At the cafe they are talking about what happened. "Lewis almost killed. By a bear."

"Maybe," says a doubter.

"Roof didn't cave in by itself."

"Maybe he went up there . . . and fell through."

"He's too scared to go out at night. There's bait all over the place."

The spooky justice of it. That's what puts people in awe, but if Lewis were to walk in right now I wouldn't jump. Because he's already here. On everyone's mind.

"Killer Bear," they say over and over. And with the season ended, I feel Lewis pushing everyone with his intent. Pretty soon someone is going to kill the bear for him just like he wants. And out of the same misbegotten sense of preservation. Bland faced, without concern for repercussion or the jubilation of the hunt. Saying it's the sensible thing to do. As I said, it's pure Lewis, hell-bent on enjoying the fruits of his horrible labors. And there is no going back from it. Nor am I invisible anymore. Beth and Julie and Jennifer and Mirta want me to show them where the cabin was because I said I'd seen the wreckage, and they told Herb, who wants to know what I know.

Across the table from me, he is measuring to see if it is good or bad. Not suspicious, but wary. It's the way he lets the yolk out of his egg. Slowly, considering, someone who keeps God in reserve.

This morning I took the bird feeder down from its place in the window because it catches my eye from the side and I startle easily enough as it is. Also, there's a new story about the Killer Bear—how it followed Lewis at night through the trees to his cabin. He's been cornering people in the post office, saying Fish and Game won't get rid of it. All they care about is keeping bears out of dumpsters. That's what Lewis claims: Fish and Game is soft on bears. So the heat's on Herb.

"Did Lewis really come to you?" I ask.

"I get a lot of calls," he replies. "When I'm in the field." He won't look at me. Just waits. Fussing with that egg.

Desperate, afraid Herb will give in to the pressure, I say: "Lewis made a lot of trouble, taking matters into his own hands."

But Herb just listens to the talk around us.

"Bear has to be shot."

"Maybe, already is."

"Can't anyone prove it?"

"Proof," a big guy chuckles, "when it claws off your roof and eats your wife and kids!"

You, I rage silently, will be home with them, but my mind is less with logic than Herb's stillness. It gathers on his right side, and he's eating left-handed like me, only clumsier, jammed up against the window. Someone too big for corners.

"It's a sow bear." Herb pushes his plate aside, angry, not hungry. He doesn't like me watching him, either. "She's bred by now." And leaning forward into my thoughts, he says, "That's three dead bears, Helen. That's what they're asking for."

"Which bear?" I insist. "How can anyone tell?"

Around us the talk hushes, everyone straining to hear. Trying to chew quietly, foreheads shiny with listening, backs stiff with it. From the corner of my eye I catch sight of the trailer hitched to Lewis's ghostly pickup.

Without warning, Herb raises his eyes, fixing me. "I called you."

"When?"

"The night I got back." His tone makes everything glow as if it had been freshly painted, because there's only one night to be talking about and inside me more of the myth explodes. I want to yell out that you can be motivated by a passion for life so great it makes you deadly. Follow it, barely sensing what is happening. Feel only love burning out the edges of fear. That's how it was out there. Right and unbridled and humbled in my darkness with the bear. Instead, I whisper. Words. A plea, "What to do?"

Grimacing, Herb pushes himself up from the seat one-handed. At the cash register lays out his check for Julie. Hauls out his wallet, shoves it between puffed knuckles. With his good hand, pulls out the bills and snaps it shut with his thumb.

Outside, I calm down enough to ask how he got hurt.

"Bear graze." He says it flat, jerking his head toward faces knotted together in the cafe window, opens the pickup door.

Breath pours out of me and I don't care if it is the entire store of prayers allotted me in this life. "She's safe?"

"Yes." Herb admits it slowly, almost tenderly. Pulls the battered green truck onto the road, watching in the rearview mirror. I can tell by the angle of his head. And between us a presence settles into place at last. Subtle and low in its disturbance of the air. Miles too far for hearing, seeing, or smelling.

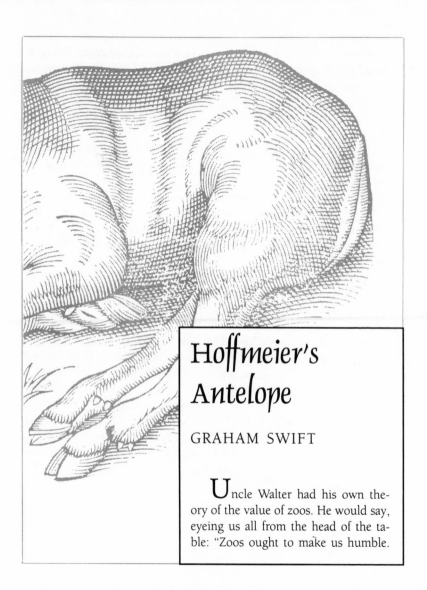

Hoffmeier's Antelope

GRAHAM SWIFT

Uncle Walter had his own theory of the value of zoos. He would say, eyeing us all from the head of the table: "Zoos ought to make us humble.

When we visit them we ought to reflect—mere humans, mere evolutionary upstarts that we are—that we shall never have the speed of the cheetah, the strength of the bear, the grace of the gazelle, the agility of the gibbon. Zoos curb our pride; they show us our inadequacies. . . ."

Having launched on this favourite theme, he would proceed inexorably to elaborate it, cataloguing joyously the virtues of animal after animal, so that I (a precocious boy, doing "A" levels), for whom zoos were, in one sense, places of rank vulgarity—tormenting elephants with ice-cream wrappers, grinning at monkeys copulating—could not resist punctuating his raptures with the one word: "Cages."

Uncle Walter would not be daunted. He would continue his speech, come to rest again on the refrain, "Show us our inadequacies," and, leaving us free once more to gobble his wife's rock cakes and lemon-meringue pie, lean back in his chair as if his case were beyond dispute.

My uncle was not, so far as I knew, a religious man; but sometimes, after declaiming in this almost scriptural fashion, his face would take on the serene, linear looks of a Byzantine saint. It made one forget for a moment the real uncle: pop-eyed, pale skinned, with stains of tobacco, like the ink smudges of schoolboys, on his fingers and teeth, a mouth apt to twitch and to generate more spittle than it was capable of holding —and a less defined, overall awkwardness, as if the mould of his own features somehow constricted him. Every time we visited him for Sunday tea—in that cramped front room laden with books, photos, certificates and the odd stuffed insectivore, like a Victorian parlour in which "enthusiasts" would regularly meet—he would not fail to instill in us the moral advantages of zoos. When he came at last to a halt and began to light his pipe, his wife (my Aunt Mary), a small, mousy, but not unattractive woman, would get up embarrassedly and start to remove plates.

He lived in Finchley and was deputy keeper at one of the mammal houses at the Zoo. Martyr to his work, he would leave his home at all hours for a quite different world. After twenty-five years of marriage, he treated his wife like something he was still not quite certain how to handle.

We lived in the country not far from Norwich. It was perhaps because I regarded myself as closer to nature than Uncle Walter that I felt obliged to sneer at the artifice of zoos. Near our house were some woods, vestiges of a former royal hunting forest, in which you could sometimes glimpse wild fallow deer. One year, when I was still a boy, the deer vanished. About every six weeks we used to travel down to London to see my grandparents who lived in Highgate. And the weekend would always be rounded off by a visit to my uncle, who would meet us, usually, at the Zoo, then take us home to tea.

I scorned London, for the same reason that I despised zoos and remained loyal to my rural heritage. In fact I liked animals—and couldn't deny my uncle's knowledge of them. At the same time I developed interests which were hardly likely to keep me in the countryside. I took a degree in mathematics.

It was on one of those Sundays as guests of Uncle Walter that we were first introduced to the Hoffmeier's Antelopes. There were a pair of these rare and delicate animals at the Zoo, which, just then, to the great joy of the staff (my uncle in particular) had produced a solitary issue—a female. Neither adults nor young were as yet on view to the general public but we were ushered in on a special permit.

Rufous-brown, twig-legged, no more than eighteen inches off the ground when mature, these tender creatures looked up at us with dark, melting eyes and twitching flanks as Uncle Walter enjoined us not to come too near and to make only the gentlest movements. The newborn female, trembling by its mother, was no bigger and more fragile than a puppy. They were, so Uncle Walter told us, one of a variety of kinds of tiny antelope native to the dense forests of west and central Africa. The particular species before us had been discovered and recorded as a distinct strain only in the late forties. Twenty years later a survey had declared it extinct in the wild.

We looked at these plaintive, captive survivors and were suitably moved.

"Oh, *aren't* they *sweet!*" said my mother, with a lack, perhaps, of true decorum.

"Er, notice," said Uncle Walter, crouching inside the pen, "the minute horns, the large eyes—nocturnal animals of course—the legs, no thicker, beneath the joint, than my finger, but capable of leaps of up to ten feet."

He wiped the spit from the corner of his mouth, and looked, challengingly, at me.

The reason for my uncle's attachment to these animals lay not just in their extreme rarity but in his having known personally their discoverer and namesake—Hoffmeier himself.

This German-born zoologist had worked and studied at Frankfurt until forced to leave his country for London during the nineteen-thirties. The war years had suspended an intended programme of expeditions to the Congo and the Cameroons, but in 1948 Hoffmeier had gone to Africa and come back with the remarkable news of a hitherto unidentified species of pygmy antelope. In the interval he had made his permanent home in London and had become friends with my uncle, who started at the Zoo more or less at the time of Hoffmeier's arrival in England. It was by no means a common thing, then, for a serious and gifted zoologist to befriend a zealous but unscholarly animal keeper.

Hoffmeier made three more trips in the next ten years to Africa and carried out intensive studies of the "Hoffmeier" and other species of forest antelope. Then in 1960, fearing that the already scant Hoffmeier's Antelope, prized for its meat and pelt by local hunters, would be no more within a few years, he had brought back three pairs for captivity in Europe.

This was the period in which blacks and Europeans killed each other mercilessly in the Congo. Hoffmeier's efforts to save not only his own skin but those of his six precious charges were a zoological feat with few parallels. Two of the pairs went to London, one to Frankfurt, Hoffmeier's old zoo before the rise of the Nazis. The animals proved extremely delicate in captivity, but a second, though, alas, smaller generation was successfully bred. The story of this achievement (in which my uncle played his part), of how a constant and anxious communication was kept up between the mammal departments at Frankfurt and London, was no less remarkable than that of Hoffmeier's original exploits in the Congo.

But the antelopes stood little real chance of survival. Four years after Uncle Walter showed us his little trio there remained, out of a captive population that had once numbered ten, only three—the female we had seen as a scarcely credible baby, and a pair in Frankfurt. Then, one winter, the Frankfurt female died; and its male companion, not a strong animal itself, which had never known the dark jungle of its parents, was rushed, in hermetic conditions, accompanied by veterinary experts, by jet to London.

So Uncle Walter became the guardian of the last known pair of Hoffmeier's Antelopes, and therefore, despite his lowly status, a figure of some importance and the true heir, in the personal if not the academic sense, of Hoffmeier.

"Hoffmeier," my uncle would say at those Sunday afternoon teas, "Hoffmeier . . . my friend Hoffmeier . . ." His wife would raise her eyes and attempt hastily to change the subject. And I would seem to see the chink in his none too well fitting armour.

I was to live with him for some four months (it would be more accurate perhaps to say, "those last four months") when I first came to London after taking my degree. This was only a short while after my Aunt

Mary's death following a sudden illness. I had got a job at the North London Polytechnic, and while I found my feet and looked for a flat it was agreed between Uncle Walter and my family that his home in Finchley, now half empty, should also be my own.

I accepted this kindness with misgivings. Uncle Walter welcomed me with morose hospitality. The house, with its little traces of femininity amongst the books and pipe-stands, was imbued with the sense of a presence which could not be replaced. We never spoke about my aunt. I missed her rock cakes and lemon-meringue. My uncle, whose only culinary knowledge had been acquired in preparing the diet of hoofed animals, ate large quantities of raw and semi-cooked vegetables. At night, across the passage-way that separated our rooms, I would hear him belch and snore vibrantly in the large double bed he had once shared, and, waking myself later in the night, would listen to him mutter solemnly in his sleep—or perhaps not in his sleep, for he wore now the shrouded look of a man wrapped in constant internal dialogue with himself.

Once, finding the bathroom light on at three in the morning, I heard him weeping inside.

Uncle Walter left before I woke to start his day at the Zoo; alternatively he worked late shifts in the evening—so that days passed in which we scarcely met. When we did he would speak coldly and shortly as if attempting to disguise that he had been surprised in some guilty undertaking. But there were times when we coincided more happily; when he would fill his pipe and, forgetting to light it, talk in that pedantic, pontifical, always "dedicated" way, glad to have me to debate with. And there were times when I was glad—since Uncle Walter had procured for me a free pass to the Zoo—to slip from the traffic, the blurred faces of a city still strange to me, into the stranger still, but more comfortingly strange community by the banks of the Regent's Canal. He would meet me in his keeper's overalls, and I would be led, a privileged visitor, required to wear special rubber boots, into the breeding units closed to the public, to be shown—snuffling disconsolately at their concrete pen—the pair of frail, timid, wan-faced Hoffmeier's Antelopes.

"But what does it mean," I once said to Uncle Walter, "to say that a species exists which no one has ever observed?" We were talking in his front room about the possibility of undiscovered species (as the Hoffmeier's Antelope had once been) and, conversely, of near-extinct species and the merits of conservation. "If a species exists, yet is unknown—isn't that the same as if it did not exist?"

He looked at me warily, a little obtusely. In his heart, I knew, there lurked the slender hope that somewhere in the African forest there lived still a Hoffmeier's Antelope.

"And therefore," I continued, "if a thing which was known to exist ceases to exist, then doesn't it occupy the same status as something which exists but is not known to exist?"

My uncle furrowed his pasty brows and pushed forward his lower lip. Two nights a week, to make a little extra money, I was taking an evening class in philosophy (for which I had no formal qualification) at an adult institute, and I enjoyed this teasing with realities. I would have led my uncle to a position where one might still assume the existence of an undiscoverable Dodo.

"Facts," he replied, knocking his pipe, "scientific data—sound investigatory work—like Hoffmeier's for example"—in a jerky shorthand which betrayed unease. I knew he was not a scientist at heart. Well read enough, privately, to pass for a professional zoologist, he would never have done so, for he liked, as he put it, to work "with" not "on" animals. But science, nonetheless, was the power he called, reluctantly, guiltily, to his aid whenever his ground was threatened.

"Science—only concerned with the known," he flung out with a pinched, self-constraining look; though a glint deep in his eye told me that he had already fully pursued and weighed my arguments, was open, despite himself, to their seduction.

"Whatever is found to exist or ceases to exist," I went on, "nothing is altered, since the sum of what exists is always the sum of what exists."

"Quite!" said my uncle as if this were a refutation. He settled back in his chair and raised to his lips the glass of frothy stout that stood on the arm-rest (Guinness was my uncle's one indulgence).

I wished to manoeuvre him towards the vexed question of why it was that—if we were prepared to admit the possibility of species that might never be discovered, that might live, die and vanish altogether, unrecorded, in remote forests and tundra—we should yet feel the obligation to preserve from oblivion, merely because they were known, creatures whose survival was threatened—to the extent, even, of removing them from their natural habitat, transporting them in planes, enclosing them, like the Hoffmeier's Antelopes, in antiseptic pens.

But I stalled at this. It seemed too sharp an assault upon a tender spot. Besides, I really felt the opposite of my own question. The notion that creatures of which we had no knowledge might inhabit the world was thrilling to me, not meaningless, like the existence, in math, of "imaginary" numbers. Uncle Walter eyed me, moving his pipe from side to side between his teeth. I thought of the word "ruminant" which in zoology means "cud-chewer." I said, instead of what I had intended: "The point is not what exists or doesn't, but that, even given the variety of known species, we like to dream up others. Think of the animals in myth—griffins, dragons, unicorns. . . ."

"Ha!" said my uncle, with a sudden piercing of my inmost thoughts which jolted me, "You are jealous of my antelope."

But I answered, with a perception which equally surprised me: "And you are jealous of Hoffmeier."

.   .   .

The plight of the two antelopes at this time was giving cause for anxiety. The pair had not mated when first brought together, and now, in a second breeding season, showed little further sign of doing so. Since the male was a comparatively weak specimen there was fear that the last chances of saving the animal from extinction, at least for another generation, were empty ones. Uncle Walter's role during this period, like that of other zoo officials, was to coax the two animals into union. I wondered how this was contrived. The antelopes when I saw them looked like two lonely, companionless souls, impossibly lost to each other even though they shared a species in common.

Yet my uncle was clearly wrapped in the task of producing an offspring from the creatures. Throughout those weeks after my aunt's death his face wore a fixed, haunted, vigilant look, and it would have been hard to say whether this was grief for his wife or concern for his issueless antelopes. It struck me for the first time—this was something I had never really considered, despite all those Sunday teas as a boy— that he and my aunt were childless. The thought of my uncle—lanky and slobbery, fingers and teeth stained indelibly amber, exhaling fumes of stout and raw onion—as a begetter of progeny was not an easy one. And yet this man, who could reel off for you, if you asked, the names of every known species of *Cervinae*, of *Hippotraginae*, teemed, in another sense, with life. When he returned home late on those March evenings, a dejected expression on his face, and I would ask him, with scarcely a trace, now, of sarcasm in my voice, "No?" and he would reply, removing his wet coat, shaking his bowed head, "No," I began to suspect—I do not know why—that he had really loved my aunt. Though he hardly knew how to show affection, though he had forsaken her, like a husband who goes fishing at weekends, for his animals, yet there was somewhere, unknown to me, in that house in Finchley a whole world of posthumous love for his wife.

My own love-life, in any case, occupied me enough at this time. Alone in an unfamiliar city, I acquired one or two short-lived and desultory girlfriends whom I sometimes took back to Uncle Walter's.

Not knowing what his reaction might be, fearing that some spirit of scholarly celibacy lurked in the zoological tomes and in the collection of taxidermies, I took care to ensure these visits took place while he was out, and to remove all traces, from my front bedroom, of what they entailed. But he knew, I soon sensed, what I was up to. Perhaps he could sniff such things out, like the animals he tended. And my exploits prompted him, moreover, to a rare and candid admission. For one night, after several bottles of stout, my uncle—who would not have flinched from examining closely the sexual parts of a gnu or okapi—confessed with quivering lips that in thirty years of marriage he could never approach "without qualms" what he called his wife's "secret regions."

But this was later, after things had worsened.

"Jealous of Hoffmeier?" said my uncle. "Why should I be jealous of Hoffmeier?" His lips twitched. Behind his head was an anti-macassar, with crochet borders, made by my aunt.

"Because he discovered a new species."

Even as I spoke I considered that the discovery might be only half the enviable factor. Hoffmeier had also won for himself a kind of immortality. The man might perish, but—so long at least as a certain animal survived—his name would, truly, live.

"But—Hoffmeier—zoologist. Me? Just a dung-scraper." Uncle Walter reverted to his self-effacing staccato.

"Tell me about Hoffmeier."

Hoffmeier's name, Hoffmeier's deeds sounded endlessly on my uncle's lip, but of the man himself one scarcely knew anything.

"Hoffmeier? Oh, expert in his field. Undisputed . . ."

"No—what was he like?" (I said "was" though I had no certain knowledge that Hoffmeier was dead.)

"Like—?" My uncle, who was preparing himself, pipe raised to stress the items, for the catalogue of Hoffmeier's credentials, looked up, his wet lips momentarily open. Then, clamping the pipe abruptly between his teeth and clutching the bowl with his hand, he stiffened into almost a parody of "the comrade recalled."

"The man you mean? Splendid fellow. Boundless energy, tremendous dedication. Couldn't have met a kinder . . . Great friend to me . . ."

I began to doubt the reality of Hoffmeier. His actual life seemed as tenuous and elusive as that of the antelope he had rescued from anonymity. I could not picture this stalwart scientist. He had the name of a Jewish impresario. I imagined my uncle going to him and being offered the antelope like some unique form of variety act.

I asked myself: Did Hoffmeier exist?

My uncle, poking his head forward oddly, in one of those gestures which made me think he could see my thoughts, said: "Why, he used to come here, stay here. Many a time. Sat in that armchair you're sitting in now, ate at that table, slept—"

But then he broke off suddenly and began to suck hard at his pipe.

I was having no luck in my attempts to find a suitable flat. London grew more faceless, more implacable, the more I grew accustomed to it. It did not seem a place in which to be a teacher of math. My philosophy lectures became more esoteric. I gave a particularly successful class on Pythagoras, who, besides being a mathematician, believed one should abstain from meat and that human souls entered the bodies of animals.

Four weeks after my talk with Uncle Walter about Hoffmeier, things took a sudden bad turn. The male antelope developed a sort of pneumonia and the fate of the pair and—so far as we may know—of a whole species, seemed sealed. My uncle came in late from the Zoo, face drawn, silent. Within a fortnight the sick animal had died. The remaining female, which I saw on perhaps three subsequent occasions, looked up, sheepishly, apprehensively, from its solitary pen as if it knew it was now unique.

Uncle Walter turned his devotion to the remaining antelope with all the fervour of a widowed mother transferring her love to an only child. His eyes now had a lonely, stigmatized look. Once, on one of my Sunday visits to the Zoo (for these were often the only occasions on which I could be sure of seeing him), the senior keeper in his section, a burly, amiable man called Henshaw, drew me to one side and suggested that I persuade Uncle Walter to take a holiday. It appeared that my uncle had requested that a bed be made up for him in the antelope's pen, so that he need not leave it. A bundle of hay or straw would do, he had said.

Henshaw looked worried. I said I would see what I could do. But, for all that I saw of my uncle, I scarcely had an opportunity to act on my promise. He came home after midnight, leaving a reek of stout in the hall, and sneaked straight upstairs. I felt he was avoiding me. Even on his off-duty days he would keep to his room. Sometimes I heard him muttering and moving within; otherwise an imprisoned silence reigned, so that I wondered should I, for his own sake, peer through the keyhole or leave behind the door a tray of his favourite fibrous food. But there were times when we met, as though by accident, in the kitchen, amongst his books in the front room. I said to him (for I thought only an aggressive humour might puncture his introspection) didn't he think his affair with the female antelope was going too far? He turned on me the most wounded and mortified look, his mouth twisting and salivating; then he said in a persecuted, embattled tone: "You been speaking to Henshaw?"

He seemed conspired against from all sides. One of the things that distressed him at this time was a proposal by the Council to build a new inner link road which, though it would not touch his own house, would cleave a path through much of the adjacent area. Uncle Walter had received circulars about this and subscribed to a local action group. He called the council planners "arse-holes." This surprised me. I always imagined him as living in some remote, antiquated world in which the Zoological Society, august, venerable, was the only arbiter and shrine.

So long as he could travel to the warm scent of fur and dung, it did not seem to me that he noticed the traffic thundering on the North Circular, the jets whining into Heathrow, the high-rises and flyovers—or that he cared particularly where he lived. But one Saturday morning when, by rare chance, we shared breakfast and when the noise of mechanical diggers could be heard through the kitchen window, this was disproved.

My uncle looked up from his bowl of porridge and bran and studied me shrewdly. "Don't like it here, do you? Want to go back to Norfolk?" he said. His eyes were keen. Perhaps my disillusion with London—or maybe the strain of sharing a house with him—showed in my face. I murmured non-committally. Outside some heavy piece of machinery had started up so that the cups on the table visibly shook. My uncle turned to the window. "Bastards!" he said, then turned back. He ate with his sleeves rolled up, and his bare forearms, heavily veined and covered with gingery hairs, actually looked strong, capable. "Bastards," he said. "Know how long I've lived here? Forty years. Grew up here. Your Aunt and I—. Now they want to. . . ."

His voice swelled, grew lyrical, defiant. And I saw in this man whom I had begun to regard as half insane, a grotesque victim of his own eccentricities, a glimpse of the real life, irretrievably lost, as if the door to a cell had momentarily opened.

I began to wonder who my true uncle was. A creature who was not my uncle inhabited the house. When not at the Zoo he retired ever more secretively to his room. He had begun to remove to his bedroom from his "library" in the corner of the front room certain of his zoological volumes. He also took, from on top of the bookcase, the framed photographs of his wife. At three, at four in the morning, I would hear him reading aloud, as if from the Psalms or the works of Milton, passages from Lane's *Rare Species,* Ericdorf's *The African Ungulates* and from the work which I had already come to regard as Uncle Walter's Bible, Ernst Hoffmeier's *The Dwarf and Forest Antelopes.* In between these readings there were sporadic tirades against certain absent opponents, who included the borough planning committee and "that shit-can" Henshaw.

The fact was that he had developed a paranoiac complex that the world was maliciously bent on destroying the Hoffmeier's Antelope. He was under the illusion—so I learnt later from Henshaw—that, like children who believe that mere "loving" brings babies into the world, he could, solely by the intense affection he bore the female antelope, ensure the continuation of its kind. He began to shun me as if I too were a member of the universal conspiracy. We would pass on the stairs like strangers. Perhaps I should have acted to banish this mania, but something told me that far from being his enemy I was his last true guardian. I remembered his words: "The speed of the cheetah, the strength of the bear . . ." Henshaw phoned to suggest discreetly that my uncle needed treatment. I asked Henshaw whether he really liked animals.

One night I dreamt about Hoffmeier. He had a cigar, a bow tie and a pair of opera glasses and was marching through a jungle, lush and fantastic, like the jungles in pictures by Douanier Rousseau. In a cage carried behind him by two bearers was the pathetic figure of my uncle. Watching furtively from the undergrowth was a four-legged creature with the face of my aunt.

The attendances at my philosophy classes fell off. I devoted two lessons to Montaigne's "Apology of Raymond Sebond." Students complained I was leading them along eccentric and subversive paths. I did not mind. I had already decided to quit London in the summer.

My uncle suddenly became communicable again. I heard him singing one morning in the kitchen. A thin, reedy, but strangely youthful tenor was crooning "Our Love is Here to Stay." He had changed to the afternoon shift of duty and was preparing himself an early lunch before heading for the Zoo. There was a smell of frying onions. When I entered he greeted me in the way he used to when I was a Sunday guest, just grown into long trousers. "Ah Derek! Derek, me lad—have a Guinness," he said, as though there were something to celebrate. He offered me a bottle and the opener. There were already four empties on the draining board. I wondered whether this was a miraculous recovery or the sort of final spree people are apt to throw before flinging themselves off balconies. "Uncle?" I said. But his sticky lips had parted in an inscrutable grin; his face was contained and distinct as if it might disappear; his eyes were luminous, as though, should I have looked close, I might have seen in them the reflections of scenes, vistas known only to him.

I had with me a file of students' work in preparation for my afternoon's math classes. He looked scoffingly at it. "All this—" he said. "You ought to have been a zoo-keeper."

He wiped his mouth. His long sallow face was creased. I realized that nowhere could there be anyone like my uncle. I smiled at him.

That night I had a telephone call from Henshaw. It must have been about one in the morning. In a panic-stricken voice he asked me if I had seen Uncle Walter. I said no; I had been teaching at the adult institute, finished the evening at a pub and come home to bed. My uncle was probably already in bed when I came in. Henshaw explained that a security officer at the Zoo had found various doors to the special care unit unlocked; that on further investigation he had discovered the pen of the Hoffmeier's Antelope empty. An immediate search of the Zoo precincts had begun but no trace was to be found of the missing animal.

"Get your uncle!" screamed Henshaw maniacally. "Find him!"

I told him to hang on. I stood in the hallway in bare feet and pajamas. For one moment the urgency of the occasion was lost in the vision I had of the tiny creature, crossing the Prince Albert Road, trotting up the Finchley Road, its cloven feet on the paving stones, its soft eyes under the street-lamps, casting on North London a forlorn glimmer of its forest ancestry. Without its peer in the world.

I went up to Uncle Walter's room. I knocked on his door (which he would often keep locked), then opened it. There were the books scattered on the floor, the fetid remnants of raw vegetables, the shredded photos of his wife. . . . But Uncle Walter—I had known this already —was gone.

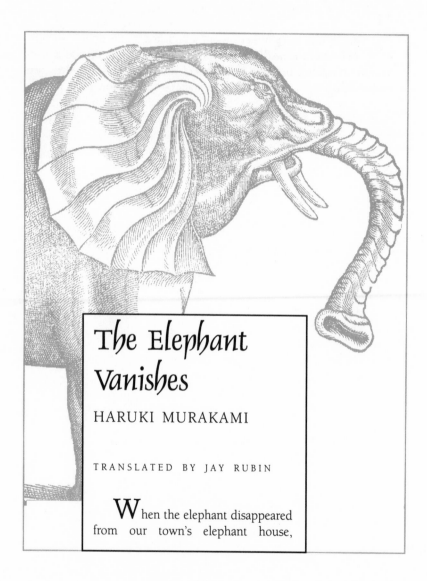

The Elephant Vanishes

HARUKI MURAKAMI

TRANSLATED BY JAY RUBIN

When the elephant disappeared
from our town's elephant house,

I read about it in the newspaper. My alarm clock woke me that day, as always, at six-thirteen. I went to the kitchen, made coffee and toast, turned on the radio, spread the paper out on the kitchen table, and proceeded to munch and read. I'm one of those people who read the paper from beginning to end, in order, so it took me a while to get to the article about the vanishing elephant. The front page was filled with stories on S.D.I. and the trade friction with America, after which I plowed through the national news, international politics, economics, letters to the editor, book reviews, real-estate ads, sports reports, and finally the regional news.

The elephant article was the lead story in the regional section. The unusually large headline caught my eye: "ELEPHANT MISSING IN TO-KYO SUBURB," and, beneath that, in type one size smaller, "CITIZENS' FEARS MOUNT. SOME CALL FOR PROBE." There was a photo of policemen inspecting the empty elephant house. Without the elephant, something about the place seemed wrong. It looked bigger than it needed to be, blank and empty like some huge, dehydrated beast from which the innards had been plucked.

Brushing away my toast crumbs, I studied every line of the article. The elephant's absence had first been noticed at two o'clock on the afternoon of May 18th—the day before when men from the school-lunch company delivered their usual truckload of food (the elephant mostly ate leftovers from the lunches of children in the local elementary school). On the ground, still locked, lay the steel shackle that had been fastened to the elephant's hind leg, as though the elephant had slipped out of it. Nor was the elephant the only one missing. Also gone was its keeper, the man who had been in charge of the elephant's care and feeding from the start.

According to the article, the elephant and keeper had last been seen sometime after five o'clock the previous day (May 17th) by a few pupils from the elementary school, who were visiting the elephant house, making crayon sketches. These pupils must have been the last to see the elephant, said the paper, since the keeper always closed the gate to the elephant enclosure when the six-o'clock siren blew.

There had been nothing unusual about either the elephant or its keeper at the time, according to the unanimous testimony of the pupils. The elephant had been standing where it always stood, in the middle of the enclosure, occasionally wagging its trunk from side to side or squinting its wrinkly eyes. It was such an awfully old elephant that its every move seemed a tremendous effort—so much so that people seeing it for the first time feared it might collapse at any moment and draw its final breath.

The elephant's age had led to its adoption by our town a year earlier. When financial problems caused the little private zoo on the edge of town to close its doors, a wildlife dealer found places for the other animals in zoos throughout the country. But all the zoos had plenty of elephants, apparently, and not one of them was willing to take in a feeble old thing that looked as if it might die of a heart attack at any moment. And so, after its companions were gone, the elephant stayed alone in the decaying zoo for nearly four months with nothing to do— not that it had had anything to do before.

This caused a lot of difficulty, both for the zoo and for the town. The zoo had sold its land to a developer, who was planning to put up a high-rise condo building, and the town had already issued him a permit. The longer the elephant problem remained unresolved, the more interest the developer had to pay for nothing. Still, simply killing the thing would have been out of the question. If it had been a spider monkey or a bat, they might have been able to get away with it, but the killing of an elephant would have been too hard to cover up, and if it ever came out afterward the repercussions would have been tremendous. And so the various parties had met to deliberate on the matter, and they formulated an agreement on the disposition of the old elephant:

(1) The town would take ownership of the elephant at no cost.

(2) The developer would, without compensation, provide land for housing the elephant.

(3) The zoo's former owners would be responsible for paying the keeper's wages.

I had had my own private interest in the elephant problem from the very outset, and I kept a scrapbook with every clipping I could find on it. I had even gone to hear the town council's debates on the matter, which is why I am able to give such a full and accurate account of the course of events. And while my account may prove somewhat lengthy, I have chosen to set it down here in case the handling of the elephant problem should bear directly upon the elephant's disappearance.

When the mayor finished negotiating the agreement—with its provision that the town would take charge of the elephant—a movement opposing the measure boiled up from within the ranks of the opposition party (whose very existence I had never imagined until then). "Why must the town take ownership of the elephant?" they demanded of the mayor, and they raised the following points (sorry for all these lists, but I use them to make things easier to understand):

(1) The elephant problem was a question for private enterprise—the zoo and the developer; there was no reason for the town to become involved.

(2) Care and feeding costs would be too high.

(3) What did the mayor intend to do about the security problem?

(4) What merit would there be in the town's having its own elephant?

"The town has any number of responsibilities it should be taking care of before it gets into the business of keeping an elephant—sewer repair, the purchase of a new fire engine, etc.," the opposition group declared, and while they did not say it in so many words, they hinted at the possibility of some secret deal between the mayor and the developer.

In response, the mayor had this to say:

(1) If the town permitted the construction of high-rise condos, its tax revenues would increase so dramatically that the cost of keeping an elephant would be insignificant by comparison; thus it made sense for the town to take on the care of this elephant.

(2) The elephant was so old that it neither ate very much nor was likely to pose a danger to anyone.

(3) When the elephant died, the town would take full possession of the land donated by the developer.

(4) The elephant could become the town's symbol.

The long debate reached the conclusion that the town would take charge of the elephant after all. As an old, well-established residential suburb, the town boasted a relatively affluent citizenry, and its financial footing was sound. The adoption of a homeless elephant was a move that people could look upon favorably. People like old elephants better than sewers and fire engines.

I myself was all in favor of having the town care for the elephant. True, I was getting sick of high-rise condos, but I liked the idea of my town's owning an elephant.

A wooded area was cleared, and the elementary school's aging gym was moved there as an elephant house. The man who had served as the elephant's keeper for many years would come to live in the house with the elephant. The children's lunch scraps would serve as the elephant's feed. Finally, the elephant itself was carted in a trailer to its new home, there to live out its remaining years.

I joined the crowd at the elephant-house dedication ceremonies. Standing before the elephant, the mayor delivered a speech (on the town's development and the enrichment of its cultural facilities); one elementary-school pupil, representing the student body, stood up to read a composition ("Please live a long and healthy life, Mr. Elephant"); there was a sketch contest (sketching the elephant thereafter became an integral component of the pupils' artistic education); and each of two young women in swaying dresses (neither of whom was especially good-looking) fed the elephant a bunch of bananas. The elephant endured these virtually meaningless (for the elephant, entirely meaning-less) formalities with hardly a twitch, and it chomped on the bananas with a vacant stare. When it finished eating the bananas, everyone applauded.

On its right rear leg, the elephant wore a solid, heavy-looking steel cuff from which there stretched a thick chain perhaps thirty feet long, and this in turn was securely fastened to a concrete slab. Anyone could see what a sturdy anchor held the beast in place: the elephant could have struggled with all its might for a hundred years and never broken the thing.

I couldn't tell if the elephant was bothered by its shackle. On the surface, at least, it seemed all but unconscious of the enormous chunk of metal wrapped around its leg. It kept its blank gaze fixed on some indeterminate point in space, its ears and the few white hairs on its body waving gently in the breeze.

The elephant's keeper was a small, bony old man. It was hard to guess his age; he could have been in his early sixties or late seventies. He was one of those people whose appearance is no longer influenced by their age after they pass a certain point in life. His skin had the same darkly ruddy, sunburned look both summer and winter, his hair was stiff and short, his eyes were small. His face had no distinguishing characteristics, but his almost perfectly circular ears stuck out on either side with disturbing prominence.

He was not an unfriendly man. If someone spoke to him he would reply, and he expressed himself clearly. If he wanted to he could be almost charming—though you always knew he was somewhat ill at ease. Generally, he remained a reticent, lonely-looking old man. He seemed to like the children who visited the elephant house, and he worked at being nice to them, but the children never really warmed to him.

The only one who did that was the elephant. The keeper lived in a small prefab room attached to the elephant house, and all day long he stayed with the elephant, attending to its needs. They had been together for more than ten years, and you could sense their closeness in every gesture and look. Whenever the elephant was standing there blankly and the keeper wanted it to move, all he had to do was stand next to the elephant, tap it on a front leg, and whisper something in its ear. Then, swaying its huge bulk, the elephant would go exactly where the keeper had indicated, take up its new position, and continue staring at a point in space.

On weekends, I would drop by the elephant house and study these operations, but I could never figure out the principle on which the keeper-elephant communication was based. Maybe the elephant understood a few simple words (it had certainly been living long enough), or perhaps it received its information through variations in the taps on its leg. Or possibly it had some special power resembling mental telepathy and could read the keeper's mind. I once asked the keeper how he gave his orders to the elephant, but the old man just smiled and said, "We've been together a long time."

And so a year went by. Then, without warning, the elephant vanished. One day it was there, and the next it had ceased to be.

I poured myself a second cup of coffee and read the story again from beginning to end. Actually, it was a pretty strange article—the kind that might excite Sherlock Holmes. "Look at this, Watson," he'd say, tapping his pipe. "A very interesting article. Very interesting indeed."

What gave the article its air of strangeness was the obvious confusion and bewilderment of the reporter. And this confusion and bewilderment clearly came from the absurdity of the situation itself. You could see how the reporter had struggled to find clever ways around the absurdity in order to write a "normal" article. But the struggle had only driven his confusion and bewilderment to a hopeless extreme.

For example, the article used such expressions as "the elephant escaped," but if you looked at the entire piece it became obvious that the elephant had in no way "escaped." It had vanished into thin air. The reporter revealed his own conflicted state of mind by saying that a few "details" remained "unclear," but this was not a phenomenon that could be disposed of by using such ordinary terminology as "details" or "unclear," I felt.

First, there was the problem of the steel cuff that had been fastened to the elephant's leg. This had been found *still locked.* The most reasonable explanation for this would be that the keeper had unlocked the ring, removed it from the elephant's leg, *locked the ring again,* and run off with the elephant—a hypothesis to which the paper clung with desperate tenacity despite the fact that the keeper had no key! Only two keys existed, and they, for security's sake, were kept in locked safes, one in police headquarters and the other in the firehouse, both beyond the reach of the keeper—or of anyone else who might attempt to steal them. And even if someone had succeeded in stealing a key, there was no need whatever for that person to make a point of returning the key after using it. Yet the following morning both keys were found in their respective safes at the police and fire stations. Which brings us to the conclusion that the elephant pulled its leg out of that solid steel ring without the aid of a key—an absolute impossibility unless someone had sawed the foot off.

The second problem was the route of escape. The elephant house and grounds were surrounded by a massive fence nearly ten feet high. The question of security had been hotly debated in the town council, and the town had settled upon a system that might be considered somewhat excessive for keeping one old elephant. Heavy iron bars had been anchored in a thick concrete foundation (the cost of the fence was borne by the real-estate company), and there was only a single entrance, which was found locked from the inside. There was no way the elephant could have escaped from this fortresslike enclosure.

The third problem was elephant tracks. Directly behind the elephant enclosure was a steep hill, which the animal could not possibly have climbed, so even if we suppose that the elephant somehow managed to pull its leg out of the steel ring and leap over the ten-foot-high fence, it would still have had to escape down the path to the front of the enclosure, and there was not a single mark anywhere in the soft earth of that path that could be seen as an elephant's footprint.

Riddled as it was with such perplexities and labored circumlocutions, the newspaper article as a whole left but one possible conclusion: the elephant had not escaped. It had vanished.

Needless to say, however, neither the newspaper nor the police nor the mayor was willing to admit—openly, at least—that the elephant had vanished. The police were continuing to investigate, their spokesman saying only that the elephant either "was taken or was allowed to escape in a clever, deliberately calculated move. Because of the difficulty involved in hiding an elephant, it is only a matter of time till we solve the case." To this optimistic assessment he added that they were planning to search the woods in the area with the aid of local hunters' clubs and sharpshooters from the national Self-Defense Force.

The mayor had held a news conference, in which he apologized for the inadequacy of the town's police resources. At the same time, he declared, "Our elephant-security system is in no way inferior to similar facilities in any zoo in the country. Indeed, it is far stronger and far more fail-safe than the standard cage." He also observed, "This is a dangerous and senseless anti-social act of the most malicious kind, and we cannot allow it to go unpunished."

As they had the year before, the opposition-party members of the town council made accusations. "We intend to look into the political responsibility of the mayor; he has colluded with private enterprise in order to sell the townspeople a bill of goods on the solution of the elephant problem."

One "worried-looking" mother, thirty-seven, was interviewed by the paper. "Now I'm afraid to let my children out to play," she said.

The coverage included a detailed summary of the steps leading to the town's decision to adopt the elephant, an aerial sketch of the elephant house and grounds, and brief histories of both the elephant and the keeper who had vanished with it. The man, Noboru Watanabe, sixty-three, was from Tateyama, in Chiba Prefecture. He had worked for many years as a keeper in the mammalian section of the zoo, and "had the complete trust of the zoo authorities, both for his abundant knowledge of these animals and for his warm, sincere personality." The elephant had been sent from East Africa twenty-two years earlier, but little was known about its exact age or its "personality." The report concluded with a request from the police for citizens of the town to come forward with any information they might have regarding the elephant.

I thought about this request for a while as I drank my second cup of coffee, but I decided not to call the police—both because I preferred not to come into contact with them if I could help it and because I felt the police would not believe what I had to tell them. What good would it do to talk to people like that, who would not even consider the possibility that the elephant had simply vanished?

I took my scrapbook down from the shelf, cut out the elephant article, and pasted it in. Then I washed the dishes and left for the office.

I watched the search on the seven-o'clock news. There were hunters carrying large-bore rifles loaded with tranquillizer darts, Self-Defense Force troops, policemen, and firemen combing every square inch of the woods and hills in the immediate area as helicopters hovered overhead. Of course, we're talking about the kind of "woods" and "hills" you find in the suburbs outside Tokyo, so they didn't have an enormous area to cover. With that many people involved, a day should have been more than enough to do the job. And they weren't searching for some tiny homicidal maniac: they were after a huge African elephant. There was a limit to the number of places a thing like that could hide. But still they had not managed to find it. The chief of police appeared on the screen, saying, "We intend to continue the search." And the anchorman concluded the report, "Who released the elephant, and how? Where have they hidden it? What was their motive? Everything remains shrouded in mystery."

The search went on for several days, but the authorities were unable to discover a single clue to the elephant's whereabouts. I studied the newspaper reports, clipped them all, and pasted them in my scrapbook —including editorial cartoons on the subject. The album filled up quickly, and I had to buy another. Despite their enormous volume, the clippings contained not one fact of the kind that I was looking for. The reports were either pointless or off the mark: "ELEPHANT STILL MISS-ING," "GLOOM THICK IN SEARCH HQ," "MOB BEHIND DISAP-PEARANCE?" And even articles like this became noticeably scarcer after a week had gone by, until there was virtually nothing. A few of the weekly magazines carried sensational stories—one even hired a psychic —but they had nothing to substantiate their wild headlines. It seemed that people were beginning to shove the elephant case into the large category of "unsolvable mysteries." The disappearance of one old ele-phant and one old elephant keeper would have no impact on the course of society. The earth would continue its monotonous rotations, politi-cians would continue issuing unreliable proclamations, people would continue yawning on their way to the office, children would continue studying for their college-entrance exams. Amid the endless surge and ebb of everyday life, interest in a missing elephant could not last for-ever. And so a number of unremarkable months went by, like a tired army marching past a window.

Whenever I had a spare moment, I would visit the house where the elephant no longer lived. A thick chain had been wrapped round and round the bars of the yard's iron gate, to keep people out. Peering inside, I could see that the elephant-house door had also been chained and locked, as though the police were trying to make up for having failed to find the elephant by multiplying the layers of security on the now empty elephant house. The area was deserted, the previous crowds having been replaced by a flock of pigeons resting on the roof. No one took care of the grounds any longer, and thick, green summer grass had sprung up there as if it had been waiting for this opportunity. The chain coiled around the door of the elephant house reminded me of a huge snake set to guard a ruined palace in a thick forest. A few short months without its elephant had given the place an air of doom and desolation that hung there like a huge, oppressive rain cloud.

I met her near the end of September. It had been raining that day from morning to night—the kind of soft, monotonous, misty rain that often falls at that time of year, washing away bit by bit the memories of summer burned into the earth. Coursing down the gutters, all those memories flowed into the sewers and rivers, to be carried to the deep, dark ocean.

We noticed each other at the party my company threw to launch its new advertising campaign. I work for the P.R. section of a major manufacturer of electrical appliances, and at the time I was in charge of publicity for a coördinated line of kitchen equipment, which was scheduled to go on the market in time for the autumn-wedding and winter-bonus seasons. My job was to negotiate with several women's magazines for tie-in articles—not the kind of work that takes a great deal of intelligence, but I had to see to it that the articles they wrote didn't smack of advertising. When magazines gave us publicity, we rewarded them by placing ads in their pages. They scratched our backs, we scratched theirs.

As an editor of a magazine for young housewives, she had come to the party for material for one of these "articles." I happened to be in charge of showing her around, pointing out the features of the colorful refrigerators and coffeemakers and microwave ovens and juicers that a famous Italian designer had done for us.

"The most important point is unity," I explained. "Even the most beautifully designed item dies if it is out of balance with its surroundings. Unity of design, unity of color, unity of function: this is what today's *kit-chin* needs above all else. Research tells us that a housewife spends the largest part of her day in the *kit-chin*. The *kit-chin* is her workplace, her study, her living room. Which is why she does all she can to make the *kit-chin* a pleasant place to be. It has nothing to do with size. Whether it's large or small, one fundamental principle governs every successful *kit-chin,* and that principle is unity. This is the concept underlying the design of our new series. Look at this cooktop, for example. . . ."

She nodded and scribbled things in a small notebook, but it was obvious that she had little interest in the material, nor did I have any personal stake in our new cooktop. Both of us were doing our jobs.

"You know a lot about kitchens," she said when I was finished. She used the Japanese word, without picking up on *"kit-chin."*

"That's what I do for a living," I answered with a professional smile. "Aside from that, though, I do like to cook. Nothing fancy, but I cook for myself every day."

"Still, I wonder if unity is all that necessary for a kitchen."

"We say *'kit-chin,'* " I advised her. "No big deal, but the company wants us to use the English."

"Oh. Sorry. But still, I wonder. Is unity so important for a *kit-chin?* What do *you* think?"

"My personal opinion? That doesn't come out until I take my necktie off," I said with a grin. "But today I'll make an exception. A kitchen probably *does* need a few things more than it needs unity. But those other elements are things you can't sell. And in this pragmatic world of ours, things you can't sell don't count for much."

"Is the world such a pragmatic place?"

I took out a cigarette and lit it with my lighter.

"I don't know—the word just popped out," I said. "But it explains a lot. It makes work easier, too. You can play games with it, make up neat expressions: 'essentially pragmatic,' or 'pragmatic in essence.' If you look at things that way, you avoid all kinds of complicated problems."

"What an interesting view!"

"Not really. It's what everybody thinks. Oh, by the way, we've got some pretty good champagne. Care to have some?"

"Thanks. I'd love to."

As we chatted over champagne, we realized we had several mutual acquaintances. Since our part of the business world was not a very big pond, if you tossed in a few pebbles one or two were bound to hit a mutual acquaintance. In addition, she and my kid sister happened to have graduated from the same university. With markers like this to follow, our conversation went along smoothly.

She was unmarried, and so was I. She was twenty-six, and I was thirty-one. She wore contact lenses, and I wore glasses. She praised my necktie, and I praised her jacket. We compared rents and complained about our jobs and salaries. In other words, we were beginning to like each other. She was an attractive woman, and not at all pushy. I stood there talking with her for a full twenty minutes, unable to discover a single reason not to think well of her.

As the party was breaking up, I invited her to join me in the hotel's cocktail lounge, where we settled in to continue our conversation. A soundless rain went on falling outside the lounge's panoramic window, the lights of the city sending blurry messages through the mist. A damp hush held sway over the nearly empty cocktail lounge. She ordered a frozen Daiquiri and I had a Scotch-on-the-rocks.

Sipping our drinks, we carried on the kind of conversation that a man and woman have in a bar when they have just met and are beginning to like each other. We talked about our college days, our tastes in music, sports, our daily routines.

Then I told her about the elephant. Exactly how this happened, I can't recall. Maybe we were talking about something having to do with animals, and that was the connection. Or maybe, unconsciously, I had been looking for someone—a good listener—to whom I could present my own, unique view on the elephant's disappearance. Or, then again, it might have been the liquor that got me talking.

In any case, the second the words left my mouth, I knew that I had brought up one of the least suitable topics I could have found for this occasion. No, I should never have mentioned the elephant. The topic was—what?—too complete, too closed.

I tried to hurry on to something else, but, as luck would have it, she was more interested than most in the case of the vanishing elephant, and once I admitted that I had seen the elephant many times she showered me with questions—what kind of elephant was it, how did I think it had escaped, what did it eat, wasn't it a danger to the community, and so forth.

I told her nothing more than what everybody knew from the news, but she seemed to sense constraint in my tone of voice. I had never been good at telling lies.

As if she had not noticed anything strange about my behavior, she sipped her second Daiquiri and asked, "Weren't you shocked when the elephant disappeared? It's not the kind of thing that somebody could have predicted."

"No, probably not," I said. I took a pretzel from the mound in the glass dish on our table, snapped it in two, and ate half. The waiter replaced our ashtray with an empty one.

She looked at me expectantly. I took out another cigarette and lit it. I had quit smoking three years earlier but had begun again when the elephant disappeared.

"Why 'probably not'? You mean you could have predicted it?"

"No, of course I couldn't have predicted it," I said with a smile. "For an elephant to disappear all of a sudden one day—there's no precedent, no need, for such a thing to happen. It doesn't make any logical sense."

"But still, your answer was very strange. When I said, 'It's not the kind of thing that somebody could have predicted,' you said, 'No, probably not.' Most people would have said, 'You're right,' or 'Yeah, it's weird,' or something. See what I mean?"

I sent a vague nod in her direction and raised my hand to call the waiter. A kind of tentative silence took hold as I waited for him to bring me my next Scotch.

"I'm finding this a little hard to grasp," she said softly. "You were carrying on a perfectly normal conversation with me until a couple of minutes ago—at least until the subject of the elephant came up. Then something funny happened. I can't understand you anymore. Something's wrong. Is it the elephant? Or are my ears playing tricks on me?"

"There's nothing wrong with your ears," I said.

"So then it's you. The problem's with you."

I stuck my finger in my glass and stirred the ice. I like the sound of ice in a whiskey glass.

"I wouldn't call it a 'problem,' exactly. It's not that big a deal. I'm not hiding anything. I'm just not sure I can talk about it very well, so I'm trying not to say anything at all. But you're right—it's very strange."

"What do you mean?"

It was no use: I'd have to tell her the story. I took one gulp of whiskey and started.

"The thing is, I was probably the last one to see the elephant before it disappeared. I saw it after seven o'clock on the evening of May 17th, and they noticed it was gone on the afternoon of the eighteenth. Nobody saw it in between, because they lock the elephant house at six."

"I don't get it. If they closed the house at six, how did you see it after seven?"

"There's a kind of cliff behind the elephant house. A steep hill on private property, with no real roads. There's one spot, on the back of the hill, where you can see into the elephant house. I'm probably the only one who knows about it."

I had found the spot purely by chance. Strolling through the area one Sunday afternoon, I had lost my way and come out at the top of the cliff. I found a little flat open patch, just big enough for a person to stretch out in, and when I looked down through the bushes there was the elephant-house roof. Below the edge of the roof was a fairly large vent opening, and through it I had a clear view of the inside of the elephant house.

I made it a habit after that to visit the place every now and then to look at the elephant when it was inside the house. If anyone had asked me why I bothered doing such a thing I wouldn't have had a decent answer. I simply enjoyed watching the elephant during its private time. There was nothing more to it than that. I couldn't see the elephant when the house was dark inside, of course, but in the early hours of the evening the keeper would have the lights on the whole time he was taking care of the elephant, which enabled me to study the scene in detail.

What struck me immediately when I saw the elephant and keeper alone together was the obvious liking they had for each other—something they never displayed when they were out before the public. Their affection was evident in every gesture. It almost seemed as if they stored away their emotions during the day, taking care not to let anyone notice them, and took them out at night when they could be alone. Which is not to say that they did anything different when they were by themselves inside. The elephant just stood there, as blank as ever, and the keeper would perform those tasks one would normally expect him to do as a keeper: scrubbing down the elephant with a deck broom, picking up the elephant's enormous droppings, cleaning up after the elephant ate. But there was no way to mistake the special warmth, the sense of trust between them. While the keeper swept the floor, the elephant would wave its trunk and pat the keeper's back. I liked to watch the elephant doing that.

"Have you always been fond of elephants?" she asked. "I mean, not just that particular elephant?"

"Hmm . . . come to think of it, I do like elephants," I said. "There's something about them that excites me. I guess I've always liked them. I wonder why."

"And that day, too, after the sun went down, I suppose you were up on the hill by yourself, looking at the elephant. May—what day was it?"

"The seventeenth. May 17th at 7 P.M. The days were already very long by then, and the sky had a reddish glow, but the lights were on in the elephant house."

"And was there anything unusual about the elephant or the keeper?"

"Well, there was and there wasn't. I can't say exactly. It's not as if they were standing right in front of me. I'm probably not the most reliable witness."

"What did happen, exactly?"

I took a swallow of my now somewhat watery Scotch. The rain outside the windows was still coming down, no stronger or weaker than before, a static element in a landscape that would never change.

"Nothing happened, really. The elephant and the keeper were doing what they always did—cleaning, eating, playing around with each other in that friendly way of theirs. It wasn't what they *did* that was different. It's the way they looked. Something about the balance between them."

"The balance?"

"In size. Of their bodies. The elephant's and the keeper's. The balance seemed to have changed somewhat. I had the feeling that to some extent the difference between them had shrunk."

She kept her gaze fixed on her Daiquiri glass for a time. I could see that the ice had melted and the water was working its way through the cocktail like a tiny ocean current.

"Meaning that the elephant had gotten smaller?"

"Or the keeper had gotten bigger. Or both simultaneously."

"And you didn't tell this to the police?"

"No, of course not," I said. "I'm sure they wouldn't have believed me. And if I had told them I was watching the elephant from the cliff at a time like that I'd have ended up as their Number One suspect."

"Still, are you *certain* that the balance between them had changed?"

"Probably. I can only say 'probably.' I don't have any proof, and, as I keep saying, I was looking at them through the air vent. But I had looked at them like that I don't know how many times before, so it's hard for me to believe that I could make a mistake about something as basic as the relation of their sizes."

In fact, I had wondered at the time whether my eyes were playing tricks on me. I had tried closing and opening them and shaking my head, but the elephant's size remained the same. It definitely looked as if it had shrunk—so much so that at first I thought the town might have got hold of a new, smaller elephant. But I hadn't heard anything to that effect, and I would never have missed any news reports about elephants. If this was not a new elephant, the only possible conclusion was that the old elephant had, for one reason or another, shrunk. As I watched, it became obvious to me that this smaller elephant had all the same gestures as the old one. It would stamp happily on the ground with its right foot while it was being washed, and with its now somewhat narrower trunk it would pat the keeper on the back.

It was a mysterious sight. Looking through the vent, I had the feeling that a different, chilling kind of time was flowing through the elephant house—but nowhere else. And it seemed to me, too, that the elephant and the keeper were gladly giving themselves over to this new order that was trying to envelop them—or that had already partially succeeded in enveloping them.

Altogether, I was probably watching the scene in the elephant house for less than half an hour. The lights went out at seven-thirty—much earlier than usual—and, from that point on, everything was wrapped in darkness. I waited in my spot, hoping that the lights would go on again, but they never did. That was the last I saw of the elephant.

"So, then, you believe that the elephant kept shrinking until it was small enough to escape through the bars, or else that it simply dissolved into nothingness. Is that it?"

"I don't know," I said. "All I'm trying to do is recall what I saw with my own eyes, as accurately as possible. I'm hardly thinking about what happened after that. The visual image I have is so strong that, to be honest, it's practically impossible for me to go beyond it."

That was all I could say about the elephant's disappearance. And, just as I had feared, the story of the elephant was too particular, too complete in itself to work as a topic of conversation between a young man and woman who had just met. A silence descended upon us after I had finished my tale. What subject could either of us bring up after a story about an elephant that had vanished—a story that offered virtually no openings for further discussion? She ran her finger around the edge of her cocktail glass, and I sat there reading and rereading the words stamped on my coaster. I never should have told her about the elephant. It was not the kind of story you could tell freely to anyone.

"When I was a little girl, our cat disappeared," she offered after a long silence. "But still, for a cat to disappear and for an elephant to disappear—those are two different stories."

"Yeah, really. There's no comparison. Think of the size difference."

Thirty minutes later, we were saying goodbye outside the hotel. She suddenly remembered that she had left her umbrella in the cocktail lounge, so I went up in the elevator and brought it down to her. It was a brick-red umbrella with a large handle.

"Thanks," she said.

"Good night," I said.

That was the last time I saw her. We talked once on the phone after that, about some details in her tie-in article. While we spoke, I thought seriously about inviting her out for dinner, but I ended up not doing it. It just didn't seem to matter one way or the other.

I felt like this a lot after my experience with the vanishing elephant. I would begin to think I wanted to do something, but then I would become incapable of distinguishing between the probable results of doing it and of not doing it. I often get the feeling that things around me have lost their proper balance, though it could be that my perceptions are playing tricks on me. Some kind of balance inside me has broken down since the elephant affair, and maybe that causes external phenomena to strike my eye in a strange way. It's probably something in me.

The papers print almost nothing about the elephant anymore. People seem to have forgotten that their town once owned an elephant. The grass that took over the elephant enclosure has withered now, and the area has the feel of winter.

Quills

ROBLEY WILSON, JR.

Tor, the big Airedale, has been up all night, barking. He barks not only at the moon, but at the wind, at the passage of wild animals in the Ontario darkness, at the lights that burn inside and outside the farmhouse where Alan Asher and Kathleen Clarke live in edgy sin. Tor loves to bark; it is his talent, his calling, the thing he does best. When Alan stops at the bedroom window on his way from the bathroom he sees Tor prancing at the base of the yardlight, and if he puts his fingers against the windowpane he imagines he can feel the glass shiver with the force of every bark.

Finn, the Irish wolfhound, is a different story. Kathleen calls him "the lummox," which Alan in his own mind has amended to "lovable lummox." No matter what he may think of dogs—and Alan does not care for them—it is impossible not to like Finn, an enormous beast who on his hind legs stands taller than Alan, and down on all fours is able to rest his chin on the windowsills of Alan's vintage Mercedes. Finn's weight is an obstacle to both Alan and Kathleen whenever they try to cross the farmyard, and his slobber is a perpetual threat; the dog shoulders them off balance and drools on their clothes. Kathleen strikes out at him with her fists. "Christ," she shouts, "can't you back off from me, you lummox!" It is as if she feels Finn has singled her out for persecution, but sympathetic Alan understands it is only Finn's way—he can see in the dog's luminous sad eyes and in the bedraggled gray fur of his muzzle a craving for affection that is of human proportions. "He means well," Alan always tells Kathleen. All day, Finn sleeps between the pickup truck and the shed, his sad face turned toward the house; almost any time Alan looks out a window, one or two of the several barn cats are curled for warmth on Finn's snarled, broad back.

Kathleen is up early this morning. She has let into the kitchen one of the cats—the young black one, named Vincent Black Shadow after a motorcycle on display at the Royal Ontario Museum—and rolls a stunted red crayon for it to chase over the linoleum. A fire is crackling in the woodstove; the doughy perfume of biscuits fills the house.

"Smells wonderful," Alan says. He pours himself coffee from the Melitta flask, and peers into a cupboard for the sugar bowl. "But I thought the rule was no animals in the house."

Kathleen rolls the crayon toward the cellar door. "I thought we didn't have rules," she says.

"The agreement," Alan amends. "I thought we had an agreement."

Kathleen shrugs. A few days ago she marked her twenty-sixth birthday, and now that she is half as old as Alan she is peevish about aging. And about the money she brought to Canada with her, which Alan has already managed to spend on oil for the furnace, and gas for his car, and an overdue bill for electricity from the Hydro. It isn't as if the money has been squandered, but Kathleen had anticipated spending it in Toronto; she reads the ads in the *Star* and wants to buy clothes at Eaton's, shoes at Roots. Alan feels that they have to pool their funds and be practical—that first they have to survive until he finishes writing the novel that he hopes will lift them both to a higher standard of living.

"Poor little Vinnie isn't worth an argument," Kathleen says. "That's what I think."

Upstairs in the study, Alan stands at the window and looks down on the farmyard. The snow that fell two weeks ago has vanished, and everything below him is brown and dry and hard: the earth, the remains of the garden, the fields between this rented farm and the Hardin place. The sky is iron-gray, ominous, laden with the threat of fresh snow. The outside Celsius thermometer registers five-below—somewhere in the middle twenties, Fahrenheit.

Tor is prancing about the yard, throwing and chasing after some large brown object Alan finally recognizes as a woodchuck. The woodchuck population of this part of Ontario is considerable; Peter Hardin claims to go out of his way to run them over when he drives to and from the town. "You see them on the shoulders, eh?" he says. "They sit up on their fat brown bums and watch you steer at them, and it doesn't enter their furry little heads until it's too late that you're going to decorate their carcasses with the lovely tread design of your Goodyears." Tor tosses the dead chuck into the air, then pounces on it where it falls, grabbing it in his jaws and shaking it before he hurls it away again. Ordinarily Finn would be nearby, watching, during such performances. Finn never participates—this is Tor's game; it fits Tor's character—and today Finn isn't even in view.

Alan turns away from the window. He ought to sit down at the typewriter, review yesterday's work, move on from there into the deeper reaches of the book. What impedes him this dreary morning is Kathleen's testiness. She despises Canada, misses the States, and her temper gets worse and worse as the winter comes on. She cooks but does not enjoy it. She sleeps with Alan but perhaps does not love him. What they do to each other in bed is habit, motions remembered from the days when the wiles they practiced to steal time together added a fevered excitement to their adultery. Now they are like a husband and wife blaming each other for everything.

By ten o'clock the snow has begun, dry flakes that eddy across the farmyard like sheets of salt and begin to collect in the corners of the study windowpanes. The wind has whipped up; it whistles under the shingles. Alan is distracted from his work, goes to look outside for the hundredth time this morning. He wonders what the actual arrival of winter will do to Kathleen's state of mind. Perhaps the two of them can bring the cross-country skis up from the cellar, sit in the kitchen waxing them, walk out tomorrow into a clean new world that will invigorate their lives. The snow is piling up in the lee of the shed; the windshield of the truck is already blank with whiteness.

Finn appears. Like the ghost of a dog—a gray shade within the falling snow—he trots toward the house. As he comes closer, nearly under the study window now, Alan sees that the dog's snout is ice-covered, and when Finn reaches the back door he raises one front paw to scratch at his muzzle. Then he sits and waits.

Alan goes to the head of the stairs, almost colliding with Kathleen, who is just coming out of the bedroom. She is wearing her baby blue jogging clothes, her running shoes, has put her hair up under a white sweatband.

"What?" she says.

"Finn's at the back door," he says.

"And?"

"On your way out, could you let him in?"

"I can't believe this," Kathleen says. "What happened to 'No animals in the house'?"

He shrugs. "Exception that proves the rule," he says. "Weather emergency."

"You do it," she says. "I have to take the biscuits out to cool. And *you* clean up the mud afterward."

"You're going to run in this snow?"

"Before it gets worse," she says. "While I still can."

But it is not ice he has seen covering Finn's muzzle; it is porcupine quills—a lot of them. When he follows Kathleen to the back door, to let the dog inside, Alan sees the array of quills like a mustache, and when he kneels in the vestibule to look closely, he sees that they are in the poor dog's nose, jaws, the roof of its mouth. He cannot imagine the level at which dogs feel pain, but surely Finn feels pain.

"No," he says grimly, "not inside the house."

He holds the dog out of the living room and closes the door behind him so the two of them, man and dog, are enclosed in the five-foot square of the vestibule with its collection of overshoes and boots, its tool boxes and snow shovels and garden rakes, its leftover summer squash that Alan and Kathleen despair of ever being able to use before rot begins. The dog whines, tail wagging, haunches shaking, feet prancing in the confined space of the vestibule.

"It's all right," Alan says. But it is not all right, and he isn't sure what he will do. Certainly the quills have to come out. He has read, somewhere, in a book taken down from an upstairs bookshelf or recollected from summer-camp reading when he was a boy, that if the quills are not extracted, they work their way deeper into the roof of the mouth until they penetrate the brain, turn from painful to lethal. "All right, boy," he says. "We'll fix you up."

He rummages in the red toolbox, clattering through hammers and screwdrivers and box wrenches until he finds a pair of pliers—the obvious instrument for dealing with porcupine quills. He lifts out the pliers, lets the box lid drop shut.

"Lie down, Finn," he says. The dog remains standing, whimpering, looking up at him with its tail thumping against the gum-rubber rain-coats hung along one wall. Alan takes hold of the dog's leather collar and gives it a hard twist. "Down, boy," he says. He grits his teeth and forces the dog down by twisting its head and pushing. "Down, Finn; down, boy."

The dog goes down at its front legs. The haunches follow—slowly, and then all at once, as in a gymnastic exercise. Now Finn is on his side, filling more than half the vestibule's floor space. Alan kneels over him, his right knee pinning the dog's chest, left knee holding the forelegs to the floor. "Don't bite me, God damn it," he says. "I'm trying to help."

He holds one hand hard against Finn's neck; he has the unhappy feeling that if the head moves, he will all at once find his hand clamped in the dog's jaws. The prospect frightens him. If Finn bites him. If the porcupine was rabid—as some wild animals are. If, if, if. He positions his left hand to hold Finn's muzzle, and gets a purchase with the pliers on the protruding end of a quill in the dog's black upper lip. He pulls. The dog yelps softly and flinches, but does not try to escape, does not try to bite. *There's one,* Alan thinks.

He holds the quill for a moment. Studying it, holding it up to the light that comes into the vestibule from the two small panes of glass in the outer door, he sees that it is about an inch long, black at the tip, gray along the shaft, white where it attached itself to its natural owner. He sets it carefully aside, and goes after the next one.

. . .

Finn is a model of patience and decorum. Sometimes he yelps and struggles under the pressures of Alan's knees and elbows and palms, but mostly he is silent. Finn is like a human in a doctor's office, Alan thinks; you may not like the doctor, may even resent him, but you say to yourself that the doctor knows best and it is useless to argue with him. You resign yourself. You learn fatalism, even if you have not studied it.

So it is with Finn. Quill after quill comes out, gripped in the plier jaws, and Finn endures everything. The quills drawn out of the nose, the lips, the gums—even the roof of the mouth, where there are three extraordinarily long quills that Alan can get at only by forcing Finn's jaws apart with his free elbow. "Good dog," he keeps repeating. Little pin-pricks of blood appear in the wake of the quills. "What a good, stupid dog you are." Trying to swallow a porcupine! "In fact, you are the dumbest goddamned mutt I ever met." But he speaks softly, gently, patiently.

Finally he has them all. He counts them as he goes: three, nine, seventeen, thirty-two—that's the final count. Thirty-two quills, some of them broken off at the base, most of them whole; the shortest perhaps a half inch, the longest nearly two inches. He gathers them all together and displays them on the open palm of his left hand.

"Look at this, Finn," Alan says. He holds the quills under the dog's muzzle; Finn struggles to his feet and butts against the man. Alan stands; the dog tries to jump to lick his face. Gratitude. Dumb gratitude.

"All right, Finn. All right, boy. Out you go." He opens the door to the outside world and Finn bounds away. The air is full of swirls of windblown snow. Through the snowflakes, Alan sees Kathleen jogging up the driveway toward him, one hand lifted to shield her eyes so she can see where she's going. Finn is all over her in a moment, boisterous and mindlessly joyful.

"Lummox!" Kathleen shrieks, almost bowled over by the bounding wolfhound. "Crazy fucking lummox!"

In the warmth and calm of the kitchen she sips the coffee Alan has poured her and nibbles at a fresh biscuit. She pulls off the damp sweatband while she studies the tidy pile of porcupine quills.

"Look at them," she says. "Aren't they marvelous?" She holds one of them—one of the longest—up to the diminished daylight from the yard and squints at it. "They have little barbs at the tip. They look like miniature arrows."

"I'd never seen anything like them."

"And these were all stuck in Finn? Was he trying to swallow the porcupine whole?"

"Something like that," Alan says.

"Because they can't be thrown, you know. They just let go more easily when the porcupine is threatened." She looks at him over the top of the coffee mug. "Girl Scouts," she says. "Wildlife Merit Badge."

"I believe it."

"And Finn let you pull out how many?"

"I counted thirty-two."

"That's amazing. That he'd let you, and not go for you."

"Trust," Alan says. "I inspire it."

She raises her hand, motions him toward her. He comes, and she touches her hand to his face and kisses him. "I'm impressed," she says.

"You're always impressed when I do anything for myself."

She drops her hand. "Not called for," she says.

And it's true that he needn't have baited her, for the fact is that he is feeling somewhat smug about his success with the quills. He doesn't even like dogs, he reminds himself, but he figured out what to do, and he did it without being squeamish, and Finn adores him for it.

"Sorry," he says.

"I knew we had porcupines in the neighborhood," Kathleen says.

"Remember that night we drove home from watching television with Graham and Brenda? The eyes at the top of the driveway? That was porcupine; their eyes shine red instead of the usual yellow." She stops, fingers the quills in front of her. "Like mean little needles," she says.

"I should send some of these to my kids," Alan says. "They've never seen porcupine quills."

"That's nice," Kathleen says. "That's a thoughtful thing to do."

The snow persists. By the second morning the snow is a foot deep in sheltered areas and one drift is high enough to have swept over the hood of the truck. Only a patch of yard near the back door is blown clear, and that is where the food for the dogs and cats is put down.

"We'll have to call Peter to plow us out," Kathleen says at lunch. "Otherwise we'll be stuck with no food in the house."

Peter Hardin owns a snowthrower that attaches to his Massey-Ferguson tractor, and Alan has a standing agreement with him about keeping the driveway open. Peter is an affable, earthy man who tends to speak without thinking, and the two households have become friendly only because it is from the Hardins that Alan and Kathleen also buy their milk—trudging to the Hardin milk house once a week to fill a pitcher from the stainless steel tank, stopping off in the Hardin kitchen to socialize. Graham and Brenda Palgrave, the only other near neighbors, live in a brick house beyond the Hardins.

"I'll give him a call," Alan says.

By the time Peter arrives, late in the afternoon, both the snow and the wind have tapered off. In less than an hour the driveway is open and enough of the farmyard is cleared for the truck to be usable, and for Alan to make a path to the shed for stovewood.

Kathleen is standing at the kitchen window when the sound of the tractor ceases.

"He's coming in," she says. "I hope you've got a beer for him."

"He'd rather have whiskey," Alan says. He hears the back door creak open, hears Peter stamping the snow off his boots. Then comes a knock on the inside door, and Peter is inside the house before Alan can respond to the knocking.

"There you are," Peter says, "free to come and go, eh?" He pulls off his work gloves and tucks them in a jacket pocket. When he sees Kathleen in the kitchen behind Alan he takes off his cap.

"Come get warm," Kathleen says. "Can we offer you a beer?"

"I think we've got a little bourbon left," Alan says.

"Ah," Peter says. "A bit of bourbon might not go badly." He sits at the kitchen table and hangs his cap on one knee. "A lovely clean snowfall," he says. "The first of many."

Alan finds ice and pours a modest amount of whiskey for Peter and himself; when he gestures toward Kathleen with the bottle, she shakes her head.

"Is it going to be a hard winter?" she says.

Peter grins and takes a sip of whiskey. "Was there ever a soft Canadian winter? I don't recall one." He reaches into his glass and slides the ice cubes out, then leans to drop them into Alan's drink. "Dilution," Peter says. He winks at Kathleen. "My dear mother always taught me neatness counts."

"Well," Alan says, "we had an adventure here this morning. Finn tried to eat a porcupine." He points to the quills on the table, conscious of how proud he is of his accomplishment. "I pulled out thirty-two quills."

Peter picks up a couple of the quills and holds them toward the light. "Finn is not celebrated for his brainpower," he says. "These are wicked weapons. How did you get them out?"

"Pliers. I just got the dog immobilized and yanked them out one at a time."

Peter nodded. "Painful," he says. "You're lucky you weren't bitten."

"Finn was very patient."

"Because you see—" Peter leans forward and extends one of the quills, "—you see here, these little devils are hollow. What the porcupine does when he's threatened, you see, is fill each quill with a puff of air, and the pressure of the air pushes out these tiny raggedy barbs at the tip, so when the quills go in, the barbs keep them in, and the enemy gets no respite."

"Clever," Alan says. He glances at Kathleen, who is taking in Peter's lecture with one slightly raised eyebrow.

"So you see," Peter says, "if you'd taken a scissors, and just snipped off the shaft of the quill, you'd have released the air and let the barbs retract. Then you'd have pulled it out painlessly, slick as a whistle." He leans back and tosses down the whiskey. "I'm obliged for the refreshment," he says. He stands and puts on his cap, digs into his pocket for the gloves.

"Say hello to Peggy for us," Kathleen says.

"I will. You two come over soon."

Pausing for a moment in the vestibule, Peter shakes Alan's hand before he puts on his gloves. "That's a lovely young lady you've got there," he says. "Very nice, very quiet. You should try not to lose such a prize, eh?"

"I'm doing my best," Alan says.

That night, the supper dishes done and put away, a couple of hours given over to marking up the latest book pages, Alan is in bed with the pillows propped against the headboard. He is thinking about the porcupine and its weaponry, about Finn's patience and pain, about his own ignorance. Kathleen is sitting cross-legged on the bed, trimming her nails. Outside in the dark, Tor is pursuing his noisy calling.

"I didn't know that, about the porcupine quills," Alan says.

"Neither did I."

"All that air pressure stuff, and releasing the barbs by cutting the quill first." He presses his head back against the pillows, sighs and looks at the ceiling. "God," he says, "I can just *feel* those barbs ripping Finn's mouth when I pulled them out. Poor dumb animal, suffering because of an ignorant human."

"I'm not so sure Peter knows what he's talking about; that air business." She leans to put the scissors on the windowsill, then slides under the covers beside Alan. "It isn't logical," she says.

"Made sense to me," he says.

"No, but think about it. Yes, the quills are hollow, but they're also open at the end. If the barbs are going to retract, they'll retract anyway, whether you cut the shaft or not. I think the barbs open when the quill starts to slip out the way it came in. I don't think air has a damned thing to do with it."

"Still," Peter says. "To think I *might* have caused Finn a lot of unnecessary pain—"

Kathleen sits up and kneels on the bed, facing him. She kisses him on the mouth, softly but firmly, her hands on his shoulders. Then she puts one hand against his jaw and obliges him to look at her.

"Listen," she says. "You didn't hurt Finn any more than you absolutely had to, and Peter Hardin is just full of himself and his stupid folk wisdom. Please ignore him. Please stop feeling guilty over nothing. You're a very gentle man, a very kind man; you'd never inflict pain if you could possibly avoid it."

Alan reaches for her and hugs her against him, her hair soft on his face, her breath warm against his cheek. He feels her letting go of her reticence, of herself, permitting him to bear her full weight for the first time in weeks. He holds her and turns her so she is lying on her back, half beside him, half under him. He nuzzles her, kisses her.

"Thank you," he says.

She gives him a small, tired smile. "God, Alan," she says softly, "it's going to be such an awful winter. It's good to know that you have feelings."

He raises one eyebrow. Kathleen covers her eyes with the back of her wrist. "Damn it, you know what I mean," she says.

Otter

JILL PEACOCK

Light in Frank's garage isn't for much, one orange bulb rigged to the automatic garage opener on the ceiling, and light in Frank's car isn't for much, the little overhead light has been broken over a year, all he's got is the speedometer glow coming from the dash. So when Frank gets his old body settled into the driver's seat of his long blue car, he can only guess that the shadows in the passenger seat are those of an otter, and he lets the guess stand until he gets the car pulled out onto the street where the afternoon autumn sun is shining sidelong into the day.

First, Frank presses the button that lowers the garage door. Then, he looks to his right and sees that his guess is correct: whiskers, little brown eyes, stubby ears, light-brown fur, a tail. Frank reminds himself to participate with what he perceives, and he puts the car into drive and travels down Oleander Street to the right of the line, keeping his eyes on the road. The otter smells of mud and musk.

Woilo, where Frank lives, is a decent-sized farming town at the faint corner of a desert with only one skinny river, the Makella, running through town when she gets the spring spirit. People in Woilo, as much as Frank's heard or read in the Woilo *Californian,* aren't paid visits by otters. Normally, the cutoff for animal kingdom visits is a small weasel, usually a skunk. Never in Frank's eighty-one years has he asked for any such visit.

Frank notices he is speeding by fifteen miles an hour. He reminds himself to participate with the laws of the town, and he slows and continues down the road at an average speed.

What he did ask for was a little help on this meeting with Olivia in the afternoon, Cottonwood Coffee Shop, tomorrow. When he telephoned her a few days ago, he was holding tight onto an old prescription of heart pills to get through the short conversation. His voice was shaky when he asked her to meet him, and then she'd hesitated before she said, "Okay." Other than that call, Frank has not once spoken to Olivia in a one-on-one conversation in twenty-five years, just a hello from across the self-serve banquet table at some of their grandchildren's weddings, or a nod from behind a car window every great once in a while when they arrive at an intersection at the same moment. At the intersections when he sees her, she is always so small down in her driver's seat, and Frank would like to know why she's got her big white steering wheel angled to hide her face. What is she thinking about behind that wheel, driving all over town? Is she sad? Is he bent looking? Does he look a wreck?

Frank takes a right onto Chester Avenue. The otter sighs, in a small whistling twitter. Frank isn't going to glance over. All is clear to him now: The breath of the cosmos has ushered this otter into his car to remind him, as he goes into this meeting he's arranged for tomorrow, that he looks a wreck.

In his mind's eye, Frank sees himself: thin white hair, white mustache, nine real teeth and the rest false, an ample stomach, wrinkled olive skin, and up and down on his arms, his legs, his face, his whole body, the liver spots in different sizes and shapes, purple-brown spots all helter-skelter like they'd been put on by one of those alcoholic modern artists. Frank breathes in as deeply as he can, which is not so deeply.

Approaching the Chester-Truxton intersection, Frank slows and sees that Olivia is not in any of the cars also approaching. He stops behind a dented yellow compact under a red light. Also at the intersection are an extra-long Cadillac, a maroon compact and a tractor. If, Frank asks himself in the gathering of idling motors, the otter is here to put him in mind of his looking terrible, then is the animal also here to put him in mind of the subject of death?

The otter has been poking in the fold of the car seat where the back and seat cushions meet and has pulled out an ancient, broken cigarette and an empty package of medicated gum. Now she pulls out two dimes and a paper clip. She keeps poking.

Frank surveys the faces at the intersection, a face watching the light, a face putting on lipstick, a face watching the light. Obviously, the fact that these people's bodies are falling apart has slipped these people's minds. And the death issue isn't anywhere near their thoughts, let alone searching through the solemn debris in their car seat.

Busy all of his life with his dairy business, Frank has a feeling for where these people are. These people are tortured by whom to hire as a new route manager for the milk and cottage cheese deliveries, they are tormented why every little gesture at an improvement for the plant results in run-ins with the town planners, they are angry at the Guernseys who won't produce down here like they do up in Oregon. These people are devising something charming to say to the new dark-skinned beauty handling the Tulare accounts. These people smoke. The light changes and Frank moves through the intersection while the otter keeps digging.

"There isn't any death!" Frank says suddenly in a voice that comes out closer to a yell than not. The otter makes a small high-pitched sound and retreats to her corner. "I mean there's death, sure there is, I know dead people who've proved it! But there's the way you participate! You can practice it, lying on your grave. You participate, don't you?"

The otter holds very still. She does not blink. Driving down block after block, Frank waits until he feels, in the corner of his eye, he has seen her blink. Frank takes a half-breath as deeply as he can. He pulls into the parking lot of the Cottonwood Coffee Shop.

"I'm here," he says in a voice as steady as he can locate, "to feel the place out for tomorrow. I was thinking of going in and sitting at a booth to get to know the waitress. Then I can also talk to the waitress tomorrow. Olivia and I never had much of a rapport. No rapport was our central problem."

The otter blinks again. Does she already know all of this?

Frank looks in his rearview mirror. A nun and two priests walk by toward the coffee shop.

Participating, as far as Frank is concerned, is talking to whomever is in your passenger seat despite your puzzlement about what she's doing there in the first place. Participating is a theme that he has been trying to incorporate into his life since he's retired. He doesn't want to use his brain on anything too hard; he did that for forty-five years. All he wants to do is participate. All he wants to do is watch and say some things and take naps.

"If people don't care for the way I've retired," he says out loud, starts up his car and then hesitates. He does not know what he was going to say next, so he simply participates with where the phrase seems to be headed, "then they don't."

An example of someone who has not taken to the way Frank has retired is his second wife of fifteen years. Last week when he telephoned her and was in the middle of relating a story, telling her, "I was sitting out back last night and I got to thinking . . . ," she interrupted him.

"Yahoo," she said. "You got to thinking. Now that's an occasion."

She lives in Florida.

Frank pulls out of the parking lot.

After dinner, Frank puts on his pajamas and watches his cop show. The cop is very talented. He solves everything lickety-split, and, Frank supposes, during commercials he has only to comb his thick head of hair. Before the show ends, Frank switches it off. He finds a yellowed, never-used accounting book, and he writes down in it: "practicing lying on my gravesite," and, "crying into the pillow, muffled."

Then he leans out from the sliding glass door into his backyard to see whether the otter ate the breaded filet of sole TV dinner he set outside along with a large bowl of water though he doesn't know if otters get thirsty. Food in the sectioned plate is untouched. The otter is making a pile of dirt in the grass. Frank walks out and sits on one of the outdoor chairs, resting his accounting book on his lap.

"I'm not saying I should have divorced Olivia," he says. "I didn't know up or down when I left her. I had a business. I'd started to run around with some gal. But now when I drive out to the cemetery and lie down on my gravesite for twelve minutes every Tuesday and Thursday morning, I hear her crying. I've bought one of those watches with the timer-beeper, and I set it for twelve minutes and lie down, but after a while I hear her crying into her pillow, muffled, like she did when we were divorcing. I was always standing outside our bedroom door because it was locked."

The otter finishes with that pile and moves farther back in the yard. As far as Frank can see into the shadows, she's making another pile.

Frank raises his voice, "I'm going to get there and I'm going to find out we don't have any rapport." Frank hesitates. After the divorce, she never once dated. Eventually, everyone said she'd got herself busy with the grandchildren. Frank hesitates awhile longer, then he says, "What kind of a steering wheel is that one for her to have?"

Frank stands up and walks inside, closing the door after him. A few minutes later, he comes outside, picks up the tray and brings it inside. He eats the breaded sole himself. Afterward he wishes he hadn't. He wishes, instead, that he'd gone ahead and felt whatever it was that he was feeling.

Under his cover, Frank arranges himself and sets his watch alarm for the morning. He is attached to his watch. The timer-beeper never fails to go off, and he's missed hearing it only once, not in his bedroom, but one morning on his gravesite when he fell asleep and didn't wake up until thirty-seven minutes later when the caretaker was getting close with a lawn mower going. He had fallen asleep with Olivia crying in his inner ear, their bedroom door was locked, and he'd awakened to the loud broken rumbling of the mower.

Frank closes his eyes, but he doesn't feel tired. The night passes and through the most part he is arranging himself in different ways with the blankets and pillow and not sleeping. Somewhere in the middle of the night, he gets up and goes into the living room and finds the accounting book. He writes in it, then looks out through the sliding glass windows for the otter. When his eyes become somewhat adjusted to the shadows, he locates her by the garden hose, flipping herself over. In the next moment she is still and in the next, she stands on her head.

Watching her, Frank's own head begins to throb. He goes back to bed.

The following day, Frank arrives at the coffee shop in his good pants and white shirt, only a few minutes late. The otter is in the passenger seat. She was nowhere to be found all morning, but when Frank got in the car to go, he saw her in the shadows on the passenger seat. Now, pulled into their space in the parking lot, the otter is looking toward the entrance to the coffee shop, and Frank expects that she wants to go inside. He picks up his accounting book and reads his notes:

"She always liked your island-water blue eyes."

And, "The only mirrors in the place will be tilted for the pies."

Frank gets out of his car and locks his door, then he walks around and opens the passenger door. The otter bounds down on the asphalt, and he shuts and locks the passenger door. He walks, and down by his shins, she waddles, as they both move toward the coffee shop entrance. Are people seeing all of this? Frank asks himself. If they are, he reminds himself, they are. They did not own and operate a business for forty-five years, that's simple. He yanks open the glass door to the coffee shop and the otter precedes him.

Inside are the sounds of voices going up and down, of a telephone ringing, of piles of silverware clattering. Frank spots Olivia nearby at a booth next to a window. Her hair is light brown from the beauty parlor, and she wears delicate gold jewelry and a tulip-print dress. As usual, she does not appear to be two years older than he is.

When he arrives at her booth, Frank looks down at her and says, "Hello, 'Livia."

"Hello," she says, looking at him quickly.

He sits down in the booth. "How is your health?"

"Fine."

He nods. "You look like a poem."

"Well," she says, embarrassed.

Frank stops. Isn't she going to comment? What did she come for? Frank reminds himself to participate. He is quiet. He listens to hear her breathe in and wonders if she can fill every last one of her lung sacs. He gets himself to rest his hands on either side of him.

In the far corner of the shop where no customers have seated themselves and there seems to be no customer traffic, Frank can see the otter has found a place to sit, around the bend of the counter, under some hanging plants. He looks down at one of his wrinkled hands for a moment.

" 'Livia!" Frank bursts. "You think about death and the theme of participation in any way? What did you marry me for? Why did you put up with me running around? Why am I responsible for the sounds that go with eternity? For all time, 'Livia! We're going to be dead!"

Olivia looks away. Finally, she puts her hands in her lap, and looks back toward him. She starts angrily, "I didn't say . . ." and she stops.

Frank feels his face crowd with emotion. He is angry and dizzy. He should have written down things to tell to her. She didn't date even once after the divorce. She didn't participate with one telephone call from one man. What does she expect from him?

"Coffee or decaf?" asks the waitress, standing next to their booth, a hectic globe of red hair on her head. She pours into their cups, has an exchange with both of them, then she leaves the booth and returns with two slices of pie à la mode. She moves away.

Olivia picks up her fork, but she doesn't do much with it. She puts it down, letting it make a noise. Frank tries to sip his coffee, but now he's starting to hear something in his ear. It seems to start out like the muffled crying and then it turns into a low, fuzzy sound. He doesn't look at Olivia, and he won't look to the far corner of the shop. Finally, he clears his throat and gets himself to pick up his fork. Then, he's putting it down.

Leaning toward him as if she's going to say something long and, possibly, angry, Olivia looks hard at him. Frank leans slightly toward her. Her face changes, and she leans back. More time passes during which Olivia looks out the window and fingers her coffee cup. Frank waits as long as he can.

Shakily, he speaks, "I'm not saying that I don't look a wreck."

Olivia squints at him. Then she looks at a point out the window over his shoulder. When she speaks, her voice has some anger in it, some melancholy, and it comes from a place far off.

"Door wasn't locked," she says. "It was summertime, so the bedroom door would get swollen, so it'd be stuck. It was just a little sticking in it, just stuck."

Frank swallows. He leans toward Olivia. Then he leans back. Is she just on the other side of the door? What does he do? He tries to breathe deeply, but he can't breathe deeply. If he shoved open the door, all those years would pour out.

Again, he tries to breathe deeply. He's feeling more dizzy than ever and the fuzzy sound is turning into a buzz. Into the far corner of the coffee shop he looks and finds that the otter, for the first time, is looking directly at him. Frank vaguely senses that maybe he hasn't found the subject that the otter came to put him in mind of.

Frank looks into Olivia's eyes. Steadily, she looks back for a moment. Then, she picks up her purse and puts it in her lap.

"I thought I had a whole list what I'd say, but now I don't. I guess there's just that summer door." She waits a moment and when she speaks again, her voice has almost faded away, "I guess I'm going now."

She looks to her purse and then she's picking it up and getting herself out of the booth. Frank stands up as she stands, and he wants them to talk some more, but the expression on her face says that she wants to go. Past the booth, the counter, the cash register and out the door, she walks.

Frank sits back down and sits still for a long while as the sound in his ear lessens. Eventually, he finds himself taking a sip of his lukewarm coffee.

Not until he stands up does he notice the commotion in the far corner of the restaurant. He walks over and finds that someone has got the otter into a booth where two kids are petting her, adults are crowding around to look, a busboy shines a flashlight into her eyes, and a voice calls out that it's going to call the health department for a second time, what's taking so long? Frank can see that the otter is looking tired and possibly sickly. The more he looks at her, the more he recognizes that she probably didn't come to put him in mind of a certain subject, the more she looks like an animal who, simply, wants to live.

He watches her for a while longer and then he steps through the crowd, leans over the kids and lifts her up. He holds her in his arms and carries her out of the shop, past the counter and booths and register. With his hands full, he reaches the glass door and waits. From the parking lot, a young couple is approaching, and when they arrive at the door, they hold it open as Frank and the otter pass through. Across the parking lot, Frank walks to his car, sets the otter on the warm hood, unlocks the door and places her on the passenger seat. He shuts the door. He gets into the driver's seat and takes the car out of the lot and moves along Chester, and then onto the highway. She is lying down with her eyes shut.

After a while, Frank is driving up along the cliffs of the winding road that follows the Makella River up the steep Makella Canyon. This far up, past where the Makella is dammed, it rampages through the narrow canyon, steep and wild. He drives farther and farther. Finally, he pulls into a shoulder of the road and stops. He looks over at the otter whose eyes are open now but whose breathing is labored.

When he shoves open the car door, he pushes on it so hard it cracks at the hinges. The car is filled with the sound of the roaring river. He stands at the top of a rocky, skinny-treed slope. From the bottom of the slope comes the tossing and roaring of the Makella, and more and more as he stands over it, the roar fills up his ears.

Frank takes the otter out of the passenger seat, and very slowly, watching every step, he carries her down the slope. When he arrives at the shore of the river, he follows alongside it until he finds a pool he can wade into. In shoes, socks, pants, he steps into the cold river and sets the otter into the water. She goes under, turns over, pokes her head up downstream, then ducks under and swims away.

Down on the river, the roar is deafening. Frank slowly walks out of the water and pulls off his shoes, socks, long pants and underwear. He sets the timer-beeper on his watch for twelve minutes. He wades back into the river, holding onto a large rock set halfway out in the pool where the cold water rises to his waist. His white shirttails float on either side of him, and he has to hold onto the rock to keep his balance in such a way that he can't see the time on his wrist. In the cold water, he waits and looks around him and feels how the water and the air feel.

After a while, he recognizes that he doesn't want to be swimming downriver with the otter, and he doesn't want to get out of the river just yet either. He recognizes that he feels all right, and it doesn't frighten him that when the timer-beeper goes off, he won't hear it for the roar.

Jack:
A Memoir

MAXINE KUMIN

Full moon in February casts extraordinary shadows on snow. Tree trunks and branches, fence posts and rails, all are doubled by moonlight so palely white that the illusion is of a landscape under water. At 4 a.m. Helen comes awake, pricked out of sleep by some sense of things askew. The house feels colder than warranted; prudence dictates that she go downstairs and check the woodstoves.

Russell, who tended the stoves so professionally, sizing up the stack of split logs and choosing two that nestled inside for a perfect fit, died early last winter. She got through the rest of that season the hard way— day by day and nights of bitter tears. This year, things are going a bit easier. She no longer obsessionally thinks of mingling her ashes with his, for instance. She is resigned, a little better than resigned, to going on without him.

They always both said they wanted their ashes to sweeten the farthest field, and he got his wish. Helen isn't sure their two grown sons will be faithful to hers; they may have something else in mind. A religious service with flowers. That prospect horrifies her.

Once up, she glances by habit out the bedroom window at the paddock. There he is, a gaunt ghost horse, an Ichabod Crane-carrier of a horse, hanging his head over the top rail of the gate, facing downhill as if awaiting the Messiah. She is not at all surprised to see him. There was no latch Jack could not unseat with hours of patient effort. She and Russ used to joke about teaching Jack to untie their shoelaces; it would save all that bending down.

Jack's presence echoes something she was working on in the dream that jolted her awake. Something Russell was doing, freshly glimpsed as in real life, a secret event tearing past her as elusive as a coyote she caught sight of out of the corner of her eye. She feels she is living a double life, going on with the one they shared the long slow years of his cured cancer and then his new cancer and its remission, and the final recurrence. Days, she tends the farm, reduced now to three broodmares and a crop of youngsters. Nights, she rejoins Russ in a shadowy space full of bizarre events. There are ocean liners and snowmobiles in it. Planes take off for wild destinations. The grown sons frequently appear as children again, and horses long gone reappear as weanlings. Rampant and unpredictable as they are, Helen welcomes these dreams. But what was the one now eluding her?

Jack stands motionless in the spectral light. The temperature hovers near zero, but he appears oblivious to it, breathing out little frost-puffs that hang in the air like nimbuses by his shaggy, oversize head. As Helen watches, prickly with cold and premonition, he turns toward the house and lifts his gaze to the blind windows as if he could feel her line of sight interlock with his. After a long moment of attention, he turns back to continue his downhill vigil.

They are on the verge of a true exchange, that haunted moment when their eyes meet. She watches for a long time as he stands guard at the gate facing the serpentine road that winds down to the valley. Perhaps he is there not to stare down, but to invite up, or in. Perhaps something is about to be born.

When she dreams Russ back (it happens less frequently now), she feels pregnant with his presence. The first time, he sat bolt upright in his coffin (there hadn't been a coffin, his remains were cremated) and said, "Boo! I was only fooling!" Later, he called her on the phone but was cagey as to his whereabouts. Even inside the dream she knew she couldn't return the call. Lately, he came and went like the coyote's handsome brush, barely but thrillingly experienced. She hated waking up, knowing he had been there but unable to remember the context.

How she and Russ felt about Jack says something about how they felt about each other. They were bonded—that's a word animal people use, Helen says to herself, to express the rapport they've developed with their dogs or cats or horses. You don't go around loosely saying you love your horse. It's okay to love your dog and it's almost okay with cats, but horses are too big, too dangerous, you might say too sexual.

She and Russ belonged to a generation that didn't verbalize affection in public. They used to say they were dinosaurs, so long married as to be an embarrassment to their kids, whose playmates all had multi-parents, stepfathers, half brothers, four sets of grandparents. So they put a lot of tenderness into the barnyard, side by side wheeling sawdust or shavings, lifting hay bales. Like old Calvinists who saw salvation through grace and grace through hard work, she and Russ anointed themselves daily hauling water, mucking stalls, paring hoof abscesses till they bled, poulticing sore ligaments and keeping up a soothing banter with their herd of home-raised standardbreds.

Helen and Russ met half a century ago, give or take a couple of years, in Providence, Rhode Island, when her Wellesley College swim team lost the last meet of the season to Pembroke. Russell, who had hitchhiked down from Boston, hopped on their bus for a free ride back. Although he was still in uniform, the war was over and the Army was about to muster him out.

In the Oxford Grille in Cambridge the next night, over his beer and her beer which she did not drink but ceded to him, Helen found out Russell had majored in chemistry at Cornell; was shy a couple of credits of an advanced degree; loved motorcycles and horses about equally.

Back then he had been pursuing a diver on the team named Pat Thornbury, but his feeling was not reciprocated. In fact, when Pat saw him on the bus that day she turned to the other squad members and made a little moue of deprecation for the benefit of the girls. They called themselves girls; it had not yet occurred to them to do otherwise. Favoring Veronica Lake hairdos angled over one eye, they were gorgeous well-fed girls in sloppy joe sweaters that hung low and loose over their plaid skirts, the hems of which brushed their thick white ankle socks.

Helen was a freestyle swimmer, best at long distances. The 400-meter was her event. She swam for Wellesley because it was free, required no outlay for equipment, and balanced her fierce dedication to the classics, which she was later destined to teach to a broad mix of indifferent and enthusiastic high school students. Her passion for horses, developed in early childhood, had to wait almost two decades for gratification.

Russ's passion for her—it took her a long time to forgive him for choosing her as second-best—was not immediately evident. It bloomed sturdily, though, like an antique rose. By Christmas they were engaged and the following June they married, which was the way, Helen reflected, their entire generation had responded. If you survived the war, you were programmed to sign the contract and procreate.

Their first child was born ten months later, the second, eighteen months after that. Because the babies came so close together and because Helen and Russ prided themselves on being in the avant-garde of child-rearing, parenting for them was a fifty-fifty affair. Helen now thinks it prepared them for these last twenty years of heavy horsekeeping. She wonders if they were slightly worse than average parents. Awfully absorbed in each other, it is possible that they stinted the little boys (whom she loves and resents in their adult phase, in about equal measure).

Russ had a good job as a research chemist with a large pharmaceutical house, but it didn't last, nor did the next one. By then, Helen had found a terrific situation teaching Latin part-time in a private girls' school. It wasn't that Russ ever exactly lost a job; it was more that the job lost him, lost his attention, his respect, his desire. He moonlighted on the side in a variety of small businesses, but nothing quite scratched the itch to be free.

They bought an old farm in western Massachusetts on their eighteenth anniversary. Old farms could still be had back then for the back taxes and a little something to sweeten the deal. Helen moved out there for the summer with Nick and Donnie. Before the chimneys were pointed she had acquired a bay mare for herself, with an elderly companion horse the kids could ride. Russ drove out on weekends, and while he complained a lot about the mosquitoes, which were fierce, his romance with horses burst into bloom.

He and Helen explored the countryside, mostly at a sedate trot, with a few uphill gallops thrown in. Russ was always a tactful rider and handler. He never tried to muscle a horse, and he turned out to have reservoirs of patience with them. He and Helen talked about starting over, maybe getting into breeding trotters for the nearby track.

About that time, he started losing his voice and then regaining it in little episodes of what he called bronchitis, although he rarely coughed. It was nothing, he assured Helen, his father at about this age had had the same thing. If it persisted, he said, sure, he'd see a doctor.

When Donnie graduated from high school (Nick waiting in the wings, just a year behind), Russ was so hoarse he could hardly congratulate his firstborn. They all made spirited jokes about Russ's speechlessness, but Helen, in a moment of blinding clarity, foresaw the truth. Six weeks later the surgeon removed his voice box and told them how lucky Russ was. The cancer had not yet spread. Months of chemo and radiation therapy ensued; months more while Russ learned to make approximate sounds without his larynx. He was clean. He had been a heavy smoker and a moderate drinker since his teens, but stopped smoking and went on the wagon without any histrionics. In three months' time, he and Helen had burned all their urban bridges behind them.

Jack came to them only a few years later by default; his owners could not keep him at home. Stabled in an indifferently fenced pasture, it was no trick at all for him to break out whenever wanderlust overtook him. One strand of electric wire? He rolled under it. Sliding post-and-rail? He inserted his draft-horse-size head between the middle and top sliders and used his shoulders to work the board loose. Thin boards he knocked down, turning around and taking careful aim. Thick ones he chewed to the desired thinness.

A careful fellow, once out his hoofprints attested that he always trudged along the shoulder of the busy country road. But his continual bustications said clearly that he could not live alone. Helen and Russ took him in because no one else wanted him. Homely and smart— particularly adept at lifting knitted caps off human heads—he served as surrogate uncle to the annual foals, sensible trail horse to accompany each flighty youngster as it arrived at driving age, and alpha horse for the herd.

Why, then, Helen asks herself as she crawls back between the covers, has he left his mares inside tonight?

After that, she sleeps fitfully and awakens to the flaming sky of a winter sunrise. Jack is no longer there. Possibly he was never there. The paddock and fields beyond are iced over with old snow crust, an empty landscape. Possibly, Helen thinks, I dreamed the whole episode.

She dresses and stamps out to the barn to feed. Jack stands dozing in his stall, its door hospitably open. No sign he had meandered by moonlight, except that the insulating cover of the watering trough in the alleyway has been nudged to one side. He had helped himself to a drink. By the rational light of morning he appears well-fed, tending toward hay belly. His expression is serene, even self-satisfied.

The impatient yearlings begin to set up a ruckus. The little bay mare bobs her head as she always does, awaiting her feed. The two big mares whicker rustily, as if unused to communicating. The barn cats appear purring, insinuating themselves under her feet. There is half a mouse corpse at the threshold to the grain room. It is a perfectly average beginning to the day.

Even so, a sense of things unanswered haunts her all morning. At noon the sun slips behind a cloud bank. The wind dies, the air grows heavy with moisture. A weather breeder, no mistake.

In waning daylight the first snow squalls blow in. By late afternoon the flakes have thickened, the wind slams doors in the treetops. Closing up for the night, Helen wedges a whittled peg into Jack's door latch to hold the bolt in place. Just in case.

Don't worry, she dreams he tells her that night, enunciating carefully in a perfect, accentless English. *We'll have 122 inches by morning.*

Inside the dream, she never wonders where he learned to talk. She thinks, on waking to light snowfall, how marvelous the illogic of dreams is. She is careful not to mention this episode to Donnie, who calls from the city for a little phone chat. He's heard she has a fresh foot of snow on the ground, right? A little less than a foot, she tells him, meanwhile thinking, *122 inches.* Grateful for his attention, Helen is wary, however. She doesn't want to hear again how she should give up this place, sell out, travel, find a nice apartment "closer in." She especially doesn't want a lecture on how arduous even the narrowest snow paths are for someone her age, the skinny trails she clears from house to barn, barn to manure pile. Her shoulders ache from the effort.

To Nick, who calls later that evening, she rhapsodizes about the fresh snow, about how snug the farmhouse feels, how well the young stock are doing, which one is going to the old trainer in March, and so on. Nick, at least, is a little bit horsey. And he is fond of Jack. Helen is careful to mention an old volleyball that turned up in the paddock while she was shovelling, and to omit the dream.

People who put words in the mouths of animals must be primitives, wild eccentrics, or going round the bend, right?

Helen and Jack expect to have several more years together. Jack is aging. Helen can see it in his gradually deepening swayback. He is having a little trouble now chomping down his hay pile, but his eye is bright, his sense of humor (today he is enjoying batting the caved-in volleyball round the paddock with two yearlings) intact. If he starts to lose teeth, there is always beet pulp, Helen tells him. You can last forever on beet pulp and hot bran mash. *Tea and toast for you,* he says. *And prunes.*

This is not a dream but rather the tone of voice two old friends take in conversation. And Russell is always with them, sharing the banter, the snow depth, the wind-chill factor, the flaming, stubborn determination to keep fast and remember.

Outside Peru

MICHAEL MARTONE

I was cutting the alfalfa with the
H when two A-10s skimmed over my
head low enough for me to feel the
heat from the exhaust.

The H is a tractor. It's red and the
first one McCormick streamlined so
that the radiator hood looks like a

melting ice cube, a charging locomotive, a bullet. The A-10 is an attack aircraft with stubby square wings, a forked tail, and two huge fan jets stuck on the rear of the fuselage. That day, they were painted five shades of green, a northern European camouflage of pine and lichens. Over the years I've watched the patterns and the colors on the planes mutate—the iridescent splashes of tropic jungles to Near Eastern sand studded with yellow rock to a white tundra splotched with brown. The designs advertise the way trouble grazes around the globe. My cows are always spooked by the fly-bys. I saw them scatter off the rise in the clover field next to the one I was cutting, angling for the electric fence it took me that morning to string.

The jets are pretty quiet to begin with and the Farmall chugs a bit when I use the power take off. The breeze I was heading into stripped the sound away. The jets cracked over my head at the same time the air they pushed in front of them slammed against my back. And then the fans whined overhead. The engines reared back like they were hawking spit. I had been a target. The planes are weapons platforms built to kill tanks. They are slow, haul a huge payload of ordnance, can hang over a battlefield like a kite. The pilots wobbled their wings. I could see the control surfaces, the rudders flex, the flaps and leading edges extended on the blunt wings. They were on the threshold of stalling. Then they broke apart from each other, one going left, the other right, and banked around the cornfield in front of me, meeting up again at the grove of trees near the section road. Without climbing, they tucked in together, the wing of one notched into the waist of the other, nosed over the horizon heading back to Grissom. I let the clutch out again on the tractor and the sickle mower, a long wing sweeping off to my right, bit into the alfalfa collapsing it into windrows. I nudged the throttle. The engine gulped and caught up with itself. The first cutting, rich, green and leafy. I settled back to work. Soon, I felt like I was flying myself, sailing at tree top level.

The first calf since I came back to the farm, I named Amelia. With another chance to farm, I was going to do everything right this time.

Mom dug out the herd book they kept when I was a boy, the records skidding to a stop around the time all of us kids were in high school. I remember some of those cows. They clouded the barn. Those winters in high school I came home late and stayed up for the milking in the steaming barn. I sat there in the dark, smoking, the radio tuned to WOWO. The cows, heaps in each stanchion, waited for my father to come into the milk house and turn on the vacuum. The herd book has silhouettes of cows, outlines of heads, all scored over with a grid to map the markings. We've always raised Holsteins. The black and white looks best on new grass. I looked at the sketches my mom had made back then. There was Amy with the blob on her shoulder. The crooked man spilling down Apple's flank. As I looked at the old book, I sat down next to the hutch I had just made for the new calves. I flipped through the spiral book to an unmarked silhouette. The new calf's tongue wrapped around the woven fence. She was mostly white except for a spray of black dime-sized spots along the ridge of her right hip and dwindling back down her thigh. Ringing her neck, another chain of black islands aimed toward her eye. There was this ocean of pure milk, white between the black markings. And I stared at her for a long time after charting those few patches. I thought Amelia would be a good name. An *A* since she was Apple's calf. And an *A* for Amelia Earhart, the flyer, lost between archipelagos, at sea.

We had just moved to this farm—I was eight—when the plane buried itself in the big field next to the road. The field was planted to corn that year, and the corn had just tasseled. A silver F-86 flamed out on take-off, the pilot ejected, and the plane arched over and swooped down onto our farm. It disintegrated as it plowed up the field scorching the ground, flattening the corn, and spraying fragments of the airframe along its path. It came to rest in the ditch looking like an exploded cigar, the engine ashy beneath the peeled aluminum skin. The swath it had cut through the corn was a precise vector pointing back to the base. Discing the field this spring I turned over more pieces from the crash, a bit of fused Plexiglas, part of a shock absorber, the casing of a running light. I threw them in the tool box of the 20-Harvester we use to plow and brought the finds back to the shed, to my dad who keeps all his scrap. The pile in the back corner looks like a reconstruction of a dinosaur—the whole imagined from a few bits. The wing tip, dented and discolored, resting on the floor far away from the main wreckage of bones, implies the missing wing. Dad has suspended a panel of the vertical stabilizer from the beam of the shed. It twists there, unconnected, could prove the rotation of the earth. The first time we went into Peru after the crash I found a plastic model of the jet at the hobby store. I put it together quickly and then with a soldering iron melted off the wings and canopy trying to sculpt the ruin in the field. For a long while the whole incident felt heroic. The pilot had chosen our farm to ditch into. I reasoned that from the air our dusty road must have looked like an emergency runway. Later I realized that the pilot hadn't thought twice about it. As he pulled the shield over his face triggering the ejection seat, he believed that no one was down there; his ship would fall into the green uninhabited place on his charts.

Early in the morning, waiting to milk, I've always looked up at the night sky. There are no city lights washing out the view. I watch the falling stars and the meteor showers. I can see a few satellites streak by and below them the puttering airliners. I think to myself, I'm a kind of homing beacon. Here I am, here I am, come and get me.

My father has offered money for a tractor tire someone was using for a sandbox. He scavenges. It's the only way we could farm these eighty acres. We are surrounded by corn this year. To the west and north, the land is owned by an Italian industrialist; to the east and south, by an insurance company—a thousand acres each. Beyond that, I'm not sure anymore, an incorporated family, rented parcels, more insurance companies. From the air our little grove of trees and the spread of buildings and the strips of grass and small grain stitched together with threads of muddy lanes must look like the center of a dart board encircled by the alternating eight row stripes of corn. The bull's eye would be Wilbur, our bull, lolling in the pen next to the red barn. We can keep this place because my dad never throws anything away and never buys anything new. "You never know," he says, "You never know." Under the old cottonwood trees he has parked the remains of 20s and *H*'s we've cannibalized and gathered there all the implements we'll ever need—the manure spreaders, the balers with crates of twine, the Deere two-row planters, and the corn picker that fits like fake glasses and a nose on the brow of the tractor. Wagons with bang boards, discs and harrows, a rusting mower conditioner, even a sulky plow though Dad says he never liked horses. People pay him to haul their stuff away. Now that I am home he has more time to scout around. I do both the milkings. His knees are shot. He walks like he's been dropped from altitude and his legs looked shoved up into his body. They fall straight from his shoulders.

We make do with this junk we've got. They can't touch us as long as we don't long for things we don't need. As long as we don't desire to live in the outside world.

I told my mother about the jets zeroing in on me because I knew it would remind her of the summer the red-winged blackbirds buzzed her as she mowed the alleys in her orchard. She wears a baseball hat now while tracing on the Toro compulsory figures around the apple trees. She hates to see my dad go into town because each way has its own junkyard or flea market. Once he came back in a new old pickup hauling a new trailer carrying the old Continental he was driving when he left.

I went to Purdue and majored in ice cream. The food labs I worked in were vast expanses of tooth-colored tile with eruptions of sparkling stainless and nickel chrome appliances spaced about the room. I wore white smocks and paper hats and wrote papers on stabilizing fruit ribbons and fudge swirls. In the gleaming kitchens, I was a long way from the wreckage of our farm. The milk too had been transformed into something else. I thought of ice cream as milk raised up to a pure art form. There was quarried butter fat to dabble on a palette of ingredients —exotic nuts and berries, fragrances shipped to us in plastic tubs, extracts of roots and seed pods, raisins soaked in rum so they wouldn't freeze. I worked also in the student union's snack bar waiting for pharmacy students to sample all the flavors. They stood there, deep in thought, licking the wooden spoons. I scooped up double scoops for couples who couldn't decide between two flavors and who crossed their cones like they were interviewing each other about the taste. Professors' kids ordered bubble gum flavor, embarrassing their parents who predicted the disasters just as the first dips cascaded to the floor.

Every spring, back on the farm, the barn swallows build their nests in the same places in the rafters. About the time we turned the cows out after a winter inside the barn, the swallows swooped through the top of the dutch door, jinking around the post and level out just under the mow floor stirring the cirrus clouds of cobwebs. Then they peel off, flapping their wings once, back out the door. I am scraping the shit into the gutters and plowing it toward the far door to shovel into the spreader. The yard is already mud; the cows mired, moo, their skins twitching and ears flapping. The swallows shoot in and out daubing the beams with mud and straw. There will be one nest right over Jean's stanchion; her black back weathers the summer of droppings from above as if her coat is wearing away.

My parents thought I'd never come home.

If you farm a dairy, you can never get away. That is, if you are milking cows, you have to be on the farm all the time. Milking is twice a day. When I first came back to the farm after quitting school, I tried milking three times a day to increase the yield. Slowly, I broke the herd's habits. The production fell way off. That's to be expected. There was nothing scientific in my methods. I weighed the cans before I poured the milk into the holding tank and marked a piece of scrap paper with the pounds of each. If I had the time between the milkings, I'd draw a line to connect the dots on my rude chart. It looked like a cardiograph. Molly came on in the afternoon when Clover was falling off. Amy made a sawtooth pattern, like she was singing scales. The vacuum pumps breathed all the time. I was inside the heartbeat of the barn. And I'd hear the cows' big heartbeats through their sides as I rested my head against them hooking up the claws. Over time, the weight came back up. I could feel it in the cans as I lugged them up the alley. The cows got used to the new routine, the extra scoop of sweet oats. But I gave it up. I was milking all the time. When I had a chance to sleep, I dreamed of the purple iodine dip I used to disinfect the teats. My whole body was stained. I fell asleep twitching, dreaming about the wet warm muck of the brown paper towels I used to massage the bags to get them to let down.

Now that I am back on the farm working, I don't like to ask my dad to do the chores. His knees are bad from the stooping he did all his life. But sometimes I have to get away. I like to take the Continental into Peru. It is the same blue black topless model that Kennedy was riding in when he was shot. It has the backward opening suicide doors. I nose into the line of hot rods cruising in downtown Peru and imagine those rear doors popped out, scooping up a bystander off the street into the back seat surprised but ready to go. Instead, the high school kids always say my car turns the loop into a funeral procession. Watching from the parking lot of the Come 'N Go, they see the Zapruder film. A creepy car. I am too old for this anyway. I end up buying some cigarettes for my dad and then point the endless hood of the car back to the farm and am home in time to muck out the stalls.

Those nights after I've come back home from those silly trips to town, I hear my parents worrying about me. Their whispers come up to my bedroom through a floor grate there to conduct the heat. I never heard words but sighs that have nothing to do with passion. My mother never changed my room when I went away to school. All the silver model airplanes are still tethered with yellow rotting string to the light fixture on the ceiling. I never had enough patience to paint them. The glue on my fingers had fogged the clear plastic canopies. The decals are dry and peeling. The planes twist above me, in that rising updraft of worry, like compass needles looking for a true north. On the walls are posters of prize-winning 4-H cows. Behind the planes, cows look like a backdrop of clouds, billowing thunderheads, dappled skies. In those pictures, the cows are posed with their front legs resting on little hills that are covered over with turf. The cows are supposed to look more beautiful—elevated slightly like that. But I always think the step-up hill takes away from the picture no matter how artfully it is hidden. I hung up my sketches of the new calves. I ripped them from the herd book. In the shadows, they could be mechanical drawings of camouflaged transport planes. My mother taped up the drawing Annie did when she visited the farm: the butt ends of the herd in a row of stalls at milking time, their pin bones forming a range of snow-capped mountains.

That night after the planes buzzed me in the alfalfa field, I asked my parents if I could go to Purdue. I called them from Peru, from the phone booth in the parking lot of the Come 'N Go. Pilots from the base still in their green nylon flight suits, perhaps the ones who flew over me that day, got into the midnight blue van. A national guard unit on maneuvers. The four of them had popsicles. I told my Mom I thought I'd head on down to Purdue, maybe stay a night.

"Whatever," she said. She wrote down the feeding instructions I gave her for Dad to use. I told her who the vet had treated for mastitis. The milk would go to the calves and cats.

I said, "I hope this isn't too much trouble." Moths were batting at the light in the booth so I opened the door to turn it off. I heard the sound of jets taking off over at the base, a sound like ripping cloth.

"You know your father likes to keep his hand in. I'll keep him company." I could see her that night. She would tune the radio to one of those magic stations where the songs have no words and then spread the lime thicker than I do in the alleyway. When I got back it would look like it had snowed inside the barn.

"Say hello to Annie for us," she said.

I brought Annie home to the farm once for a weekend when we were both in school. She was from the Region, in northern Indiana, and had never been on a farm. I went up to Hobart once with her, back then, and she took me to the dunes. We stared at Lake Michigan. I remember it looked like it could be farmed, flat and dusty. We huddled on some riprap and saw the lights of Chicago flare up where the sun set. It is the only body of water I've been to where I couldn't see the shore on the other side, and it scared me. Annie said she felt the same way walking the lanes around the farm. The land just seemed to go on forever.

"When I was a kid my mother told me to not go near the corn," I told her. In the late summer you can get lost in it and panic. It swallows you up.

The weekend she visited the farm, I helped Dad clear out some scrap wood piled next to the barn. We all stood around while he decided what to move where. My mother teased Annie about the rats that would be hiding underneath the lumber.

"Stick your pant legs inside your boots, Annie," she said. "They'll go right up your leg. It looks like a burrow to them."

Dad jiggled a two-by-four. I stood back a ways with a pitchfork. Annie curled over and stuffed her jeans inside her boots neatly. She did this straight-legged as if she was stretching before a morning jog, her hair falling over her head. The rat broke out from beneath some barn wood and window frames, parting the dried grass, faking first toward my father who tried to club it with a stick, then me, then my mother who was stomping, but then it angled straight toward Annie as if it had heard my mother's prediction. Annie stood perfectly still, her legs pressed together. I saw her shiver. The rat spun around toward me standing between it and the woodpile. I pulled the fork back above my shoulders aiming at it as it sliced through the grass. I hesitated because I didn't really want to kill it in front of Annie. The rat should be killed. His burrow was beneath the grain bin. I just couldn't be gleeful about it. My mother was squealing. I sensed Dad lumbering toward me, thrilled by the chase. Annie stood like a post, having rammed her boots into the ground after having taken care of her cuffs. Her face was pale and blank. At my feet, I could see how fat the rat was—how sleek and brown like a bubble of earth squeezing along under the dead grass. Then, surrounded, the rat stopped dead still. And then, it flew. It took off straight up, reaching the peak of its climb at my eye-level, where we looked at each other. It hung there it seemed for a long time. The rat's little legs were stretched out as if they were wings. It flashed its teeth then ducked its head and dove through my hands. I was twirling the pitchfork like a propeller, trying to find a way to bring the tines or the handle around to defend myself. I yelled. The rat disappeared again in the junk by the barn. We all stood there panting; clouds of dust wound round our faces. Our eyes were fixed on the spot in the air where the rat had hovered between us. I couldn't get Annie to come into focus again. She was a blur a few paces beyond the clear empty space.

That night, Annie and I sat on the couch pretending to watch television. I turned the sound down low so I could hear my dad snoring, the sound drifting through the registers from the room next door. The lights were off. Annie's white shirt turned blue in the flicker of the television. I tugged at her shirt, untucking it from her pants the way she pulled her pant legs from her boots after the rat had disappeared and we had all walked back to the house for dinner. As we kissed, I slid my hand up inside her shirt and covered her left breast. Then my hands weren't as hard as they were when I lived and worked at home. The only callus left was on my thumb, worn there by the trigger of the ice cream scoop. I rolled the nipple between my fingers and thumb. Even then I couldn't help but think what she was thinking. Just that day she had watched me strip the milk from the cow's tits. I'd wrapped my hand around her hands as she squeezed and pulled on the utters. Self-conscious, I traced a circle around her nipple a few times then ran my hand over her ribs and let it fall on the flair of her hip. She shivered and turned her head away.

"What?" I said.

"Your nails," she said, "that rat."

This all happened awhile ago. It has been two years now since I've seen her.

The road to Purdue follows the remains of the old Wabash Canal. In some places the ditch is dry and leafy. In other places, black water has pooled, steeping logs slick with green slime. The tow path bristles with saplings and a ground fog of wild berry canes. Through the sycamores, sometimes, you can see the river itself green from the tea of rotting leaves. Once, it had been important to hook the Great Lakes up with the Ohio and the Mississippi. The state went broke doing it. To the north is good farm land, a flat table leveled by the glaciers, but along the river the road rolls over the rubble of what the glaciers have left behind.

In the low slung Continental, I was flying. The car leapt off the crests of the rolling hills then settled again, the mushy shocks lunging with the revving engine. It was still early though most people were already in bed. The security lamps in the farmyards and small towns draped streaks of light along the long hood like straps of wet paper. In fields beside the road, I saw the hulks of lulling cattle, the debris of herds scattered around like boulders in the glacial till these pastures are built on. The car couldn't go fast enough to escape the gravity of the farm. I thought of my own herd drifting through the clover after Dad had turned them out. All their markings bleed together in the dark so that they become these lunky shadows, blotting out the stars rising behind them. I had raked the alfalfa in the neighboring field into wiggling windrows. The stink of the drying leaves hugs the ground and levels it again with a thick mist, the lightning bugs rising to its surface. For a second, my hands are on the yoke in the cockpit of the jet buzzing that field. The cows shimmer in the infrared goggles like hot coals in a pool of oil. The mown field pulses, smouldering with the heat of its own curing. The insects bubble through the haze to sparkle in the air. And I am looking down at myself sitting on the molten tractor, smoking, inhaling the fire of my finger tips, my sweat turning to light. I snapped out of the barrel roll, honked the horn twice, and coasted down the hill into Lafayette.

I got lost in the court of tin shacks where Annie lives, and turned around on the rutted, dusty roads in the dark. Somewhere, she rented a half of one of the Quonset huts the university put up during the war and never tore down. Any effort to remove them brings howls of protest from sentimental alumni who remember conceiving their first children in one barrack or the other; soon after the university administration loses interest in renovation. It is cheap housing, a place to store the international students who grow strange grains and vegetables in the empty plots that open up randomly in the court. The spaces mark where a shack has blown up, a yearly occurrence, torched by a malfunctioning gas heater, furnace, or range. The shacks all look alike though some are decorated with flower boxes rigged by this term's inmate. Bikes nose together in the long grass up against the corrugated siding of the houses. The galvanized metal of the buildings has oxidized over time, so now it has a finish akin to leather, grained and dull. I crept through the rows of shacks looking for the right number.

I had called her too. Her directions were highly detailed but useless to me since I didn't know this place intimately enough to see the details. They were camouflaged by the repetition of forms. I was lost in a neighborhood of Monopoly houses. I only found her because she was sitting on the stoop outside her house watching for the car. When she saw me skittering along the cross street she stood up and waved her arms over her head and whistled.

"The house is like an oven," she told me. "I was an idiot to cook." She had put on macaroni and cheese when she heard I was coming, and we ate sitting on the front stoop, our bowls balanced on our squeezed-together knees. I could feel the heat on my back as it poured out the screen door. There were clouds of bugs shading the street lights. Every once in a while another car, looking lost, would shuffle down the street dragging the dust behind it.

We talked. I said hello from my parents. Annie had been working this summer as an illustrator for the veterinary college, rendering organs, muscles, and bones of various domesticated animals. We set our bowls aside, and she brought out several drawings, turning on the porch light as she stepped through the door. She handed me a bone the size of a rolled-up Sunday newspaper.

"A cow's femur," she said. I was never much for the insides of things. I was raised on a farm and should be comfortable with the guts of animals. My father delights in eating the brains and hearts and tongues. I have watched my mother ring the water from kidneys and roll the shiny liver in her hands. I think to myself that I should love, to the point of consuming, the whole animals I tend. Still, something sticks in my throat. When I moved back to the farm, I castrated the first bull calf born. I wanted to raise a steer and slaughter it myself. I named him Orville. He was docile and fat. He dressed out nicely when the time came, but I let the locker do it. I can't get used to it. Sometimes during calving, a cow's uterus will prolapse. I'll find it spreading in the gutter behind her. I can tell myself I know what it is, I know what to do, but when I see guts it's as if my guts are doing the thinking. I stop seeing the animal as a kind of a machine to scrap or fix. Even dairymen need a distance. Maybe especially dairymen.

"Do they still have the cow at the vet school with the window in her side?" I asked her. I would go over there between classes and make myself watch the regurgitating stomachs squeeze and stretch. The cow was alive, chewing her cud. A flap had been cut in her side for studying. I always admired her patience, the way she stood in the special stall letting the technician dab antiseptic around the opening.

"I don't know if it is the same one you saw," Annie said, "but they still have one. The elementary school science classes still are herded in to take a look. They want to not look but can't help themselves."

I could feel my stomach working under my skin, wrapping itself around the stringy elbow noodles, plumbing within plumbing. The bone was in the grass at our feet, weighing down the newsprint sheet with the unfinished sketch. Annie used a kind of stippling style, all points of ink that clustered into shadow for depth, so that the bone on paper looked porous as bone, chipped like china bowls, worn as smooth as paper. The dots looked like a chain of volcanic islands on a map of a huge sea; they just traced the fault hidden under the water.

I told her about my own drawing, the sketches in the herd book. "I wish I had your eye," I told her. Even with the coordinate grid, it was still so awkward transferring the markings to paper. "It's just a mess. There are gray smears where I've erased. It looks like they have some kind of mange."

"You like cows a lot though, don't you?" she said then.

"Yeah, I guess I do. I guess I'd have to do what I am doing."

"But don't you miss," she said, "don't you miss the noise of other people? I remember the farm being so quiet and how you never talked. I never knew what you were thinking."

I sat there on the stoop in the yellow light of the bug bulb thinking about the farm and how, when I was here at school, I missed the cows, the green fields, and the piles of junk. I thought of the chatter of my own thoughts, how when I work I am always telling myself what I am doing. I am opening the gate now. I am walking into the barnyard. I am driving the cows into the lower field. My boots sinking into the kneaded mud of the yard.

"I love cows too," she said. "The big eyes. The way they just stand there. You look away and then look back and they look like they haven't moved but they have. The arrangement is all different."

"Yeah," I said. "That's true."

"It's like drawing waves in a lake. The calm motion." She shivered. "Spooky after a while."

That night I slept in the front room on a couch that came with the place. The apartment had aired out with the windows and the doors propped open. Annie had tucked in white sheets around the cushions. The vault of the Quonset hut created a kind of organic cavity, and the ribbed walls were papered with her washes of organs and glands. The sink on the dividing wall between the two apartments gurgled when the neighbors came home. I stayed awake, listening to the rattle of their language that seemed pitched just right to start the sheet metal of the building buzzing. They played strange music that ratcheted up and down the walls like a thumbnail on a washboard. Later still, when they had disappeared deeper into their side of the building, I tried to imagine them. I gave them a family life, a routine, classes to take, diplomas they would haul back to the other side of the world where they would wade in paddies, follow cattle along a packed earth road. And I thought of Annie too, on the other side of the inside wall. I hovered over her bed and watched her slowly rearrange herself, articulating arms, the white rollers breaking along the shore as she stretched a leg beneath the sheet, the tide of her breathing. How she used up every inch of space in her bed, asleep but constantly moving.

Before I left the next day, I wandered over to the student union and had some chocolate ice cream in a dish. Students were cutting through the building for a bit of air-conditioning before dashing on to the next classroom. Some would stop and buy a cone, stand and lick the ice cream smooth on all sides, manageable, before they rushed off. The union is camouflaged with Tudor beams of darkly stained wood and stuccoed walls. I hadn't remembered it being this much like a barn. Lumps of students sleeping in leather club chairs or single ones swaying in study carrels, reading, tucked in nooks behind squat square columns. I knew where the milk had come from to make the ice cream, but no longer remembered the origin of chocolate. South America? Perhaps Peru. Which was the more exotic ingredient, the stranger place?

I drifted over to the library across the street from the union. It was hot out, and I promised myself I would hang around the campus till the sun went down and then drive back home in the dark. When I was a student, I liked to look at the special collections the library had on flyers and airplanes. Neil Armstrong went to Purdue. A lot of astronauts did. I don't know why. And the plane Amelia Earhart disappeared in was owned partly by the school. At the time she was a professor of aviation or something. There are pictures of her in her flying jacket and slacks having tea with women students. They crowd around her. I love the pictures of her posed with the silver Electra, poring over maps of the world in this very room of the library. The room seemed even more crowded now with trophy cases, photos, charts, and models. There were navigation instruments and facsimiles of her notes and letters. I looked at a milky white scarf arranged as if casually flung along the black velvet shelf encased in glass.

A librarian was typing labels in an office off the main room. Behind her there was a picture of the librarian receiving the school flag from two astronauts. It looked like the ceremony was taking place during the half time of a basketball game.

"The flag had just come back from the moon," she told me. "I have it here someplace."

I told her I was interested in Amelia Earhart's time at Purdue. I like to think of her circling above the countryside, perhaps looking down on our farm. It isn't that far away. I sat down at a polished table where she brought me an album stuffed with local news clippings, brittle and yellowed, pasted to the black pages.

"They found her, you know," the librarian said. "They think they found her."

"What?" I said.

"Or what remains of her," she said, "on an island in the middle of nowhere. They found a navigator's aluminum case washed up on an atoll. They're going back this summer to find the plane and what's left of the bones. They came here to look at the photos, to see if they could see that same case in one of the pictures."

That night, I drove home with the top down on the Continental. I climbed and stalled and dove through the hills along the Wabash. The metal skin of the car was the color of the night and the road. I let myself lose track of what was what. All that was left was this little ellipse of upholstered light I sat in, gliding through space, adhering to the twisting white rails emitted by the low beams. Annie had sent her love to my parents, and I thought of it, her love, as a slick, gleaming, and, as yet, undocumented organ I was keeping right here in my silver navigator's case. It had been easy, the librarian had said, to find the little island in the middle of the Pacific once the searchers guessed the slight miscalculation that led Amelia Earhart off her course. They followed the string of physics into the sea. As I drove, my cows drifted from the light of the barn, sifting through the gates and alleys to the highest part of the farm, the rise in the clover field, there to catch the slight, stirring breeze. In their own way, they tell themselves what comes next. Wait, they say, and the next moment they say wait again. Me, I wanted right then to get lost on my way home in the middle of Indiana, but I knew, deep in my heart, that that was next to impossible.

Mister
Mister

DAVID HUDDLE

1.

I am not devoted to my plants.
I'm only mildly interested in them,

and they are only mildly healthy. The aloe grows so relentlessly that sometimes I have to remove gross sections of it to keep its pot from tipping over. But aloe is just that way. Some of my other plants, my little cactuses, for instance, are disgracefully feeble.

II.

Yesterday around dusk, I learned how to put the rabbit to sleep. He likes to have the front of his head scratched, between his eyes and up his forehead to the roots of his ears, then almost down to his nose. I was careful not to scratch too close to his nose because that disturbs him. So I sat very still, with him on the back porch window shelf right beside my shoulder, and I scratched him until I saw his eyes were staying closed and his body was relaxed. When I stopped and kept quiet, he remained in the trance for maybe a couple of minutes before his eyes opened up again. I'm hoping I'll again be able to hypnotize him like that with my wife or one of my daughters as a witness. Then I'll be the unrivaled Bunny Master of our household.

III.

Lately I've been feeling this desire to fall down. It comes to me in the presence of soft carpets and usually when I'm alone. But sometimes I'll be standing with my colleagues or some students on the grimy linoleum hallways at school, and I'll just want to collapse right there, not a hard crash or anything violent, just an easy folding down to the floor.

Beyond the fall, I don't have any definite ideas. I think I'll sort of curl up, but not into a tight fetal position. I'll probably be willing to talk, which of course will suggest that I ought to address the question of what I think I'm doing. "Oh, I just felt like falling down," I'll say, or something sociable and appropriate like that. I'll promise to get up in a minute or so.

IV.

Perhaps I am giving the wrong impression by referring to them as *my* plants. They're not really mine—in a formal sense most of them belong to my wife. But since I've looked after them for so many years, I suppose I've come to think of them as *my* plants—as opposed to *the* plants, or *my wife*'s plants.

The only reason I tend them is that I like to keep busy while the morning coffee drains through its filter. Since I make a lot of coffee, I have to find a fair number of chores to use up all that draining time.

So after I empty the dish-drainer and straighten up the kitchen counter, I walk through the downstairs rooms with the mister. I use this occasion to finger the soil of likely candidates for water to see if they really do need it. A more fastidious man than myself might be reluctant to insert his finger into the soil of a house plant. But I am all business and concerned, as I make my second round with the plastic watering can, with dispensing what is necessary for each plant's continuing survival.

V.

The rabbit wasn't my idea, of course. Every year at the bunny tent of the Champlain Valley Fair, Molly, my youngest daughter, has begged for one. Every year, just about the time Molly gives up on me, I've been on the verge of saying all right. This year, I didn't give her a chance to give up. We were at the fair on the last day, the bunny tent had only a few people in it, and the owners were packing up the stock they hadn't sold. Most of those rabbits were pretty inert, even if you tried to pick them up, but when the owner opened this fellow's cage, he stood right up and poked his nose out, clearly ready to go somewhere. We took him to mean that he wanted to go with us. When the lady murmured that she'd sell him for ten dollars, so quickly did I pluck the bills from my wallet that I startled us all.

He's a Dutch rabbit, with his body mostly black and his face, chest, and paws mostly white, about three-quarters as big as a standard white bunny. Though his fur has a slight barnyard smell, the black of his coat shines, and the white of it is immaculate all the way down to his paws. When he sits in the sunlight, you can see the veins through the skin of his ears.

VI.

Maybe nobody will mind if I stay down there on the floor. I can be everybody's metaphor. The environmentally concerned will see me as one statement, right-to-lifers another, and post-deconstructionist phenomenologists yet another. According to the needs and inclinations of my viewers, I'll be comic or tragic, minimalist, abstract, or overtly commercial.

VII.

Occasionally I wonder what someone outside would think of my performance. For a good part of the year, it's dark at that time of day—around five-thirty or quarter of six in the morning. So say for some crazy reason you're outdoors and walking by this house with its lights on, it's cold out, snow on the sidewalk, slippery enough to slow you down, and you glance up through a window and see this guy about the size of a Division II college tight end shooting at the window sill, pulling the trigger like mad even though his weapon makes no noise. Maybe you stand still long enough to discern that actually he's misting his azalea; more likely, you skedaddle so as to be able to worry about it when you can recollect the scene in tranquility.

VIII.

His official name is Ringo—by decree of Molly, his official owner—but he has picked up other tags from the rest of us: Matisse (my seventeen-year-old daughter's first choice), Pretty Boy (my wife's), Bonzo Bunny (mine), Buns, Bones, Dr. Bones, Rabeetz, Rabitzio, and Turdmacher. (This latter choice is usually exercised by someone cleaning up after him.)

Initially we kept Molly's rabbit in the box the lady gave us when she sold him. Then my wife bought a cage. Then we started letting him have the run of the back porch. That's his current circumstance, though he occasionally sneaks through the back door into the house, and we have to chase him down. For some reason, nowadays on his forays indoors, he heads upstairs for the guest room. We all like this choice better than his old one, back in behind the stereo rack where his inclination to chew wires recently resulted in a thirty-two-dollar repair bill for the tape deck.

IX.

Visiting the Metropolitan Museum of Art a few months ago, I found myself drawn to this life-sized black stone figure stretched out on the floor on its side. It rested among many other sculpted figures, every one of them sitting or standing. Some of this statue's power over me came from its place in the gallery's context, from its being a horizontal among the many vertical.

I recall that the lying-down figure provoked in me a mild anxiety because of its stiffness or immobility or statuesqueness or what have you. You really notice it when a supposedly resting person's muscles seem clenched. An upright figure can be frozen, but you can't help feeling that a prone one should soften into its pose, should yield to gravity.

X.

Over the course of months the paper boy must have had to interpret this image—of the big guy at the window silently triggering the pistol with a huge handle and a tiny barrel. Lots of mornings while I'm misting, I hear him stomping up the porch steps. He and I have never spoken.

XI.

Anger at a bunny has to be right up there with the most irrational of human emotions. I confess I've felt plenty of it. The chewed tape-deck cord caused a mere simmer compared to the rage he provoked with some rebellious toilet tactics one Saturday afternoon with company due in an hour and me trying to clean up the back porch. Standing over the third incorrectly placed pee-splash in ten minutes with your thumb and forefinger around a bad little bunny's neck, you tune into a surprisingly vivid memory of that Discovery Channel program where the hawk slashes down a rabbit and rips into its belly, then over a bloodied beak stares coldly at the camera.

XII.

When I fall down, I'm certain I'll relax. That will be the point, really— to stop pitching myself against time and gravity, to give over to the surface of the earth. Except that I prefer lying on a floor to lying on the actual earth, which even as a child I found inhospitable (which is to say damp, buggy, lumpy and itchy).

XIII.

I've never even read a house-plant book, and there are plenty of them around—a couple, even, here in the house that my wife bought back years ago, before we had kids and she used to take care of the plants.

I'm not saying I dislike these plants. I'm just explaining how their place in my life is one of small consequence.

XIV.

He makes spongy-sounding little grunts and squeaks when he eats or when his back or neck is being scratched. But because he is mostly mute, Dr. Bones's primary mode of communication, I have concluded, is body movement. When he's feeling friendly, he runs in circles around my feet. Playful, he dashes back and forth in front of me and thumps the floor with one of his hind paws to drum up my interest in him. Bored, he stays put, or else gets up slowly, stretches, and turns his back on me. Afraid, he scuttles under the porch furniture. Curious, he extends himself toward me or even stands up to get a closer view of something I might be carrying, something he might like to eat. His body movements fall into two separate modes; for most back-porch situations, he moves at standard speed—fast, but not too fast; however, when he's in the house and really doesn't want me to catch him, he goes into turbo.

The comedy of a two-hundred-pound man chasing a pound-and-a-half rabbit through a house is probably lost on the rabbit, whose one- or two-ounce brain can't have very many circuits available for appreciating Spontaneous Theater of the Absurd. Still, the night he got into Molly's room and required my wife and me to crawl around the floor, flailing under the beds to try to capture him without waking our sleeping daughter, I wondered about the content of Dr. Bones's brain waves.

XV.

I don't think this desire of mine represents significant personal change. It's a phase. When the weather improves, I'll get new urges; I'll want to sprint across the campus green or take off my shoes, roll up my pants, and go wading in the fountain. I'll want to sing my country-and-western songs outside the dean's office.

XVI.

I admit that it is true that I take it as an achievement whenever the hibiscus graces the house with a blossom. It is true that I take personal credit for having saved the life of Edna, the ailing ficus tree. When she was about half gone, shedding leaves like a third-rate stripper, I performed major surgery on Edna with my garden saw, then carried her up to my study where she could recuperate under my skylight.

Finally, it is true that I'm the only one in the family who truly understands the fern forest bowl. I'm the one who picked out a yellow-and-green-leaved replacement for the red coleus that couldn't live in it; I'm the one who can look at the forest and instantly know if a little monsoon action is appropriate.

XVII.

People who rattle on and on about their pets are not my favorite company, and so to non-family members I try to keep my observations about Dr. Bones to a minimum. If I like somebody, I'll take him or her out to the back porch to make an introduction. But even with my wife and daughters, I don't let on that I'm as interested in Bones as I am. In the privacy of my own brain, I entertain lots of fruitcake theories, a current favorite of which is that since it is clearly the case that we humans have failed to understand the planet and its creatures, then perhaps my relationship with Bones potentially holds the key to the survival of the human species.

The way I figure it, though, I'm not likely to discover the key, even if Bones goes into super-turbo communication mode and makes the incredible body movements that could reveal it to me. As a boy I was a serious student of Tarzan. My ultimate fantasy—cherished even more than the one where I mounted a silver-saddled palomino, waved good-bye to my parents, and began riding west—was to have a black panther for a companion. But the fancies of those days are invalidated by my adult life. I drive a Chevy station wagon, eat fast food, love appliances, can't be bothered to sort my trash for recycling, and waste a hell of a lot of water with my hygiene. A guy like me is not likely to be the recipient of the essential secret of the universe.

XVIII.

Besides, I am the publicly declared enemy of the lemon tree that my oldest daughter planted when she was in fourth grade. The only thing that has kept me from throwing that spindly thing into the trash has been my daughter's pitiful pleading. I am also the one who truly enjoys slicing off the leaves of the amaryllis in the fall before I haul it downstairs to the basement closet to make it sit in the dark for three months.

XIX.

But I can't help wondering—you know how silly ideas come to you—if in this slice of time I might be a kind of national symbol. Maybe my karma for the past month has been to be the quintessential American of the first quarter of fiscal 1991. Maybe the forces of history have randomly focused on me to induce this desire to fall down on the floor and lie there. Maybe I express what the nation wants right now—just to take a break.

In a day or two this symbolic duty will have to fall to somebody else. And this somebody will feel a desire of a different kind—to get up and do something that matters, to walk calmly into the darkness, to plunge boldly into the deep end, or to gaze up into the clouds and envision the beautiful city.

XX.

At dusk yesterday afternoon, I experienced this holy moment, scratching Dr. Bones's forehead and suddenly seeing him like it so much he was snoozing off right there at my shoulder. I guess it probably wasn't anything remarkable. Cats and dogs sleep in people's laps all the time. The fate of human civilization did not crucially rest on my little back-porch petting of my daughter's bunny. I know that perfectly well.

So I should keep this to myself, too, but since I've gone this far in revealing my crackpot secrets, I'll tell this last one. There was a fraction of a moment there, with Dr. Bones's minute eyelids drooping and my finger brushing along the frontal bridge of his skull, when the lower threshold of my identity just dropped out of me and I became something only one or two evolutionary stages up from protoplasm. In the half light of my back porch, I was something alive and in accord with something else alive.

XXI.

In conclusion, I want the record to show that I have never spoken so much as even one syllable to any plant in this house. Nor do I sing to them. There are those among them—the African violet tends to be especially vain—who might argue that my rendition of "Love Me Tender" has been performed for their benefit. This, however, is just the kind of egotistical misconception of which my plants are often guilty. The facts are that I am an Elvis fan from way back and that I enjoy singing to the empty house.

XXII.

I don't know what comes next. I see only as far as my little downward tumble and someone kneeling beside me to ask if I am all right. Then I hear my happy whisper: "I feel fine."

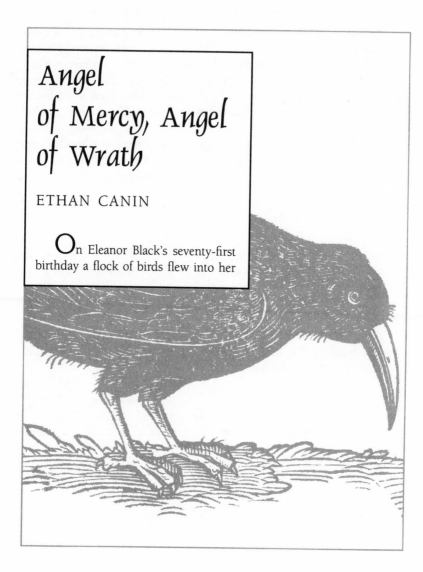

Angel of Mercy, Angel of Wrath

ETHAN CANIN

On Eleanor Black's seventy-first birthday a flock of birds flew into her kitchen through a window that she had opened every morning for forty years. They flew in all at once, without warning or reason, from the gingko tree at the corner of Velden Street, where they had sat every day since President Roosevelt's time. They were huge and dirty and black, the size of cats practically, much larger than she had ever imagined birds. Birds were so small in the sky. In the air, even in the clipped gingko ten yards from the window, they were nothing more than faint dots of color. Now they were in her kitchen, though, batting against the ceiling and the yellow walls she had just washed a couple of months ago, and their stink and their cries and their frantic knocking wings made it hard for her to breathe.

She sat down and took a water pill. They were screaming like wounded animals, flapping in tight circles around the light fixture, so that she got dizzy looking at them. She reached for the phone and pushed the button that automatically dialed her son, who was a doctor.

"Bernard," she said, "there's a flock of crows in the flat."

"It's five in the morning, Mom."

"It is? Excuse me, because it's seven out here. I forgot. But the crows are flying in my kitchen."

"Mother?"

"Yes?"

"Have you been taking all your medicines?"

"Yes, I have."

"Has Dr. Gluck put you on any new ones?"

"No."

"What did you say was the matter?"

"There's a whole flock of crows in the flat."

Bernard didn't say anything.

"I know what you're thinking," she said.

"I'm just making the point that sometimes new medicines can change people's perceptions."

"Do you want to hear them?"

"Yes," he said, "that would be fine. Let me hear them."

She held the receiver up toward the ceiling. The cries were so loud she knew he would pick them up, even long-distance.

"Okay?" she said.

"I'll be damned."

"What am I supposed to do?"

"How many are there?"

"I don't know."

"What do you mean, you don't know?"

"They're flying like crazy around the room. How can I count them?"

"Are they attacking you?"

"No, but I want them out anyway."

"How can I get them out from Denver?"

She thought for a second. "I'm not the one who went to Denver."

He breathed out on the phone, loud, like a child. He was chief of the department at Denver General. "I'm just making the point," he said, "that I can't grab a broom in Colorado and get the birds out of your place in New York."

"Whose fault is that?"

"Mom," he said.

"Yes?"

"Call the SPCA. Tell them what happened. They have a department that's for things like this. They'll come out and get rid of them."

"They're big."

"I know," he said. "Don't call 911. That's for emergencies. Call the regular SPCA. Okay?"

"Okay," she said.

He paused. "You can call back later to let us know what happened."

"Okay."

"Okay?"

"Okay." She waited a moment. "Do you want to say anything else?"

"No," he said.

.   .   .

She hung up, and a few seconds later all the birds flew back out the window except for two of them, which flew the other way, through the swinging door that she had left open and into the living room. She followed them in there. One of them was hopping on the bookshelf, but while Eleanor watched, the other one flew straight at the window from the center of the room and collided with the glass. The pane shook and the bird fell several feet before it righted itself and did the same thing again. For a few moments Eleanor stood watching, and then she went to the kitchen, took out the bottle of cream soda, and poured herself a glass. Yesterday it had been a hundred degrees out. When she finished she put the bottle back, sat down again, and dialed 911.

"Emergency," said a woman.

Eleanor didn't say anything.

"Nine-one-one Emergency."

"There's a flock of crows in my apartment."

"Birds?"

"Yes."

"You have to call the SPCA."

"They're going to break the window."

"Listen," she said, "we're not supposed to give this kind of advice, but all you have to do is move up quietly behind a bird and pick it up. They won't hurt you. I grew up on a farm."

"I grew up here."

"You can do that," she said, "or you can call the SPCA."

She hung up and went back to the living room. One still perched itself on the edge of her bookshelf and sat there, opening and closing its wings, while the other one, the berserk one, flew straight at the front window, smashed into it, fell to the sill, and then took to the air again. Again and again it flew straight at the window, hitting it with a sound like a walnut in a nutcracker, falling to the sill, then flapping crookedly back toward the center of the room to make another run. Already the window had small blotches of bluish feather oil on it. The bird hit it again, fell flapping to the sill, and this time stayed there, perched.

Through the window Eleanor noticed that the house across the street from her had been painted green.

"Stay there," she said. "I'm going to open the window."

She took two steps toward the bird, keeping the rest of her body as still as she could, like a hunting dog, moving one leg, pausing, then moving the other. Next to her on the bookshelf the calm bird cocked its head in little jerks—down, up, sideways, down. She advanced toward the window until the berserk one suddenly flew up, smashed against the glass, fell to the sill, flew up again, smashed, and perched once more. She stopped. It stood there. To her horror Eleanor could see its grotesque pulse through its skin, beating frantically along the wings and the torso as if the whole bird were nothing but a speeding heart. She stood perfectly still for several minutes, watching.

"Hello," she said.

It lifted its wings as though it were going to fly against the window again, but then lowered them.

"My husband was a friend of Franklin Roosevelt's," she said.

The bird didn't move.

"Why can't you be like your friend?" She pointed her chin at the one on the bookshelf, which opened its beak. Inside it the throat was black. She took another step toward the window. Now she was so close to the berserk one she could see the ruffled, purplish chest feathers and the yellow ring around its black irises. Its heart still pulsated but it didn't raise its wings, just cocked its head the way the other one had. She reached her two hands halfway toward it and stopped. "It's my birthday today," she whispered. She waited like that, her hands extended, until she had counted to forty. The bird cocked and retracted its head, then stood still. When it had been still for a while she reached the rest of the way and touched her hands to both sides of its quivering body.

For a moment, for an extended, odd moment in which the laws of nature didn't seem to hold, for a moment in which she herself felt just the least bit confused, the bird stood still. It was oily and cool, and its askew feathers poked her palms. What she thought about at that second, of all things, was the day her husband Charles had come into the living room to announce to her that President Kennedy was going to launch missiles against the Cubans. She had felt the same way when he told her that, as if something had gone slightly wrong with nature but that she couldn't quite comprehend it, the way right now she couldn't quite comprehend the bird's stillness until suddenly it shrieked and twisted in her hands and flew up into the air.

She stepped back. It circled through the room and smashed into the glass again, this time on the other window next to the bookshelf. The calm bird lighted from its perch, went straight down the hall, and flew into her bedroom. The berserk one righted itself and flew into the glass again, then flapped up and down against it, pocking the wide pane with its wings like a moth. Eleanor went to the front window, but she couldn't open it because the Mexican boy who had painted the apartments last year had broken the latch. She crossed into the kitchen and looked up the number of the SPCA.

A child answered the phone. Eleanor had to think for a second. "I'd like to report two crows in my house," she said.

The child put down the phone and a moment later a woman came on the line. "I'd like to report two crows in my house," said Eleanor. The woman hung up. Eleanor looked up the number again. This time a man answered. "Society," he said.

"There are two crows in my house," said Eleanor.

"Did they come in a window?"

"I always have that window opened," she answered. "I've had it opened for years with nothing happening."

"Then it's open now?"

"Yes."

"Have you tried getting them out?"

"Yes, I grabbed one the way the police said but it bit me."

"It bit you?"

"Yes. The police gave me that advice over the phone."

"Did it puncture the skin?"

"It's bleeding a little."

"Where are they now?"

"They're in the living room," she said. "One's in another room."

"All right," he said. "Tell me your address."

When they had finished Eleanor hung up and went into the living room. The berserk one was perched on the sill, looking into the street. She went into the bedroom and had to look around a while before she found the calm one sitting on top of her lamp.

She had lived a long enough life to know there was nothing to be lost from waiting out situations, so she turned out the light in the bedroom, went back into the living room, took the plastic seatcover off the chair President Roosevelt had sat on, and, crossing her arms, sat down on it herself. By now the berserk bird was calm. It stood on the windowsill, and every once in a while it strutted three or four jerky steps up the length of the wood, turned toward her, and bobbed its head. She nodded at it.

The last time the plastic had been off that chair was the day Richard Nixon resigned. Charles had said that Franklin Roosevelt would have liked it that way, so they took the plastic off and sat on it that day and for a few days after, until Charles let some peanuts fall between the cushion and the arm and she got worried and covered it again. After all those years the chair was still firm.

The bird eyed her. Its feet had four claws and were scaly, like the feet on a butcher's chicken. "Get out of here," she said. "Go! Go through the window you came from." She flung her hand out at it, flapped it in front of the chair, but the bird didn't move. She sat back.

When the doorbell rang she got up and answered on the building intercom. It was the SPCA, though when she opened the door to the apartment she found a young Negro woman standing there. She was fat, with short, braided hair. After the woman had introduced herself and stepped into the apartment Eleanor was surprised to see that the hair on the other side of her head was long. She wore overalls and a pink turtleneck.

"Now," she said, "where are those crows you indicated?"

"In the living room," said Eleanor. "He was going to break the glass soon if you didn't get here."

"I got here as soon as I received the call."

"I didn't mean *that.*"

The woman stepped into the living room, swaying slightly on her right leg, which looked partly crippled. The bird hopped from the sill to the sash, then back to the sill. The woman stood motionless with her hands together in front of her, watching it. "That's no crow," she said finally. "That's a grackle. That's a rare species here."

"I grew up in New York," said Eleanor.

"So did I." The woman stepped back, turned away from the bird, and began looking at Eleanor's living room. "A crow's a rare species here too, you know. Some of that particular species gets confused and comes in here from Long Island."

"Poor things."

"Say," said the woman. "Do you have a little soda or something? It's hot out."

"I'll look," said Eleanor. "I heard it was a hundred degrees out yesterday."

"I can believe it."

Eleanor went into the kitchen. She opened the refrigerator door, stood there, then closed it. "I'm out of everything," she called.

"That's all right."

She filled a glass with water and brought it out to the woman. "There you go," she said.

The woman drank it. "Well," she said then, "I think I'll make the capture now."

"It's my birthday today."

"Is that right?"

"Yes, it is."

"How old are you?"

"Eighty-one."

The woman reached behind her, picked up the water glass, and made the gesture of a toast. "Well, happy eighty-first," she said. She put down the glass and walked over and opened the front window, which still had smudges on it. Then she crouched and approached the bird on the other sill. She stepped slowly, her head tilted to the side and her large arms held in front of her, and when she was a few feet before the window she bent forward and took the bird into her hands. It flapped a couple of times and then sat still in her grasp while she turned and walked it to the open window, where she let it go and it flew away into the air.

When the woman had left Eleanor put the plastic back on the chair and called her son again. The hospital had to page him, and when he came on the phone he sounded annoyed.

"It was difficult," she said. "The fellow from SPCA had to come out."

"Did he do a decent job?"

"Yes."

"Good," he said. "I'm very pleased."

"It was a rare species. He had to use a metal-handled capturing device. It was a long set of tongs with hinges."

"Good. I'm very pleased."

"Are you at work?"

"Yes, I am."

"Okay, then."

"Okay."

"Is there anything else?"

"No," he said. "That's it."

A while after they hung up, the doorbell rang. It was the SPCA woman again, and when Eleanor let her upstairs she found her standing in the hall with a bunch of carnations wrapped in newspaper. "Here," she said. "Happy birthday from the SPCA."

"Oh my," said Eleanor. For a moment she thought she was going to cry. "They're very elegant."

The woman stepped into the apartment. "I just thought you were a nice lady."

"Why, thank you very much." She took them and laid them down on the hall vanity. "Would you like a cup of tea?"

"No, thanks. I just wanted to bring them up. I've got more calls to take care of."

"Would you like some more water?"

"That's all right," said the woman. She smiled and touched Eleanor on the shoulder, then turned and went back downstairs. Eleanor closed the door and unwrapped the flowers. She looked closely at their lengths for signs that they were a few days old, but could find none. The stalks were unswollen and cleanly clipped at an angle. She brought them into the kitchen, washed out the vase, and set them up in it. Then she poured herself a half glass of cream soda. When she was finished she went into the bedroom to the bedside table, where she took a sheet of paper from the drawer and began a letter.

Dear President Bush,
I am a friend of President Roosevelt's writing you on my eightieth birthday on the subject of a rare species that came into my life without warning today, and that needs help from a man such as yourself

She leaned up straight and examined the letter. The handwriting got smaller at the end of each line, so she put the paper aside and took out a new sheet. At that moment the calm bird flew down and perched on the end of the table. Eleanor jerked back and stood from the chair. "Oh," she said, and touched her heart. "Of course."

Then she patted her hair with both hands and sat down again. The bird tilted its head to look at her. Eleanor looked back. Its coat was black but she could see an iridescent rainbow in the chest feathers. It strutted a couple of steps toward her, flicking its head left, right, forward. Its eyes were dark. She put out her hand, leaned a little bit, and moving it steadily and slowly, touched the feathers once and withdrew. The bird hopped and opened its wings. She sat back and watched it. Sitting there, she knew that it probably didn't mean anything. She was just a woman in an apartment, and it was just a bird that had wandered in. It was too bad they couldn't talk to each other. She would have liked to know how old the bird was, and what it was like to have lived in the sky.

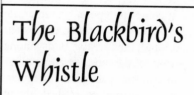

The Blackbird's Whistle

ITALO CALVINO

TRANSLATED BY
WILLIAM WEAVER

Mr. Palomar is lucky in one respect: he spends the summer in a

place where many birds sing. As he sits in a deck chair and "works" (in fact, he is lucky also in another respect: he can say he is working in places and attitudes that would suggest complete repose; or, rather, he suffers this handicap: he feels obliged never to stop working, even when lying under the trees on an August morning), the invisible birds among the boughs around him display a repertory of the most varied manifestations of sound; they enfold him in an acoustic space that is irregular, discontinuous, jagged; but thanks to an equilibrium established among the various sounds, none of which outdoes the others in intensity or frequency, all is woven into a homogeneous texture, held together not by harmony but by lightness and transparency. Until the hour of greatest heat, when the fierce horde of insects asserts its absolute dominion of the vibrations of the air, systematically filling the dimensions of time and space with the deafening and ceaseless hammering of the cicadas.

The birds' song occupies a variable part of Mr. Palomar's auditory attention. At times he ignores it as a component of the basic silence, at other times he concentrates on distinguishing, within it, one song from another, grouping them into categories of increasing complexity: punctiform chirps; two-note trills (one note long, one short); brief vibrato whistling; gurgles, little cascades of notes that pour down, spin out, then stop; overlapping twirls of modulation; and so on, to extended warbling.

Mr. Palomar does not arrive at a less generic classification: he is not one of those people who, on hearing a birdcall, can identify the bird it belongs to. This ignorance makes him feel guilty. The new knowledge the human race is acquiring does not compensate for the knowledge spread only by direct oral transmission, which, once lost, cannot be regained or retransmitted: no book can teach what can be learned only in childhood if you lend an alert ear and eye to the song and flight of birds and if you find someone who knows how to give them a specific name. Rather than the cultivation of precise nomenclature and classification, Palomar had preferred the constant pursuit of a precision in defining the modulating, the shifting, the composite. Today he would make the opposite choice, and, following the train of thoughts stirred by the birds' singing, he sees his life as a series of missed opportunities.

Among all the cries of the birds, the blackbird's whistle stands out, unmistakable for any other. The blackbirds arrive in the late afternoon; there are two of them, a couple certainly, perhaps the same couple as last year, as every year at this season. Each afternoon, hearing a whistled summons on two notes, like the signal of a person wishing to announce his arrival, Mr. Palomar raises his head to look around for whoever is calling him. Then he remembers that this is the blackbirds' hour. He soon glimpses them: they walk on the lawn as if their true vocation were to be earthbound bipeds, and as if they enjoyed establishing analogies with human beings.

The blackbirds' whistle has this special quality: it is identical to a human whistle, the effort of someone not terribly skilled at whistling but with a good reason for whistling, this once, only this once, not intending to continue, a person who does it in a determined but modest and affable tone, calculated to win the indulgence of anyone who hears him.

After a while the whistle is repeated—by the same blackbird or by its mate—but always as if this were the first time it had occurred to him to whistle; if this is a dialogue, each remark is uttered after long reflection. But is it a dialogue, or does each blackbird whistle for itself and not for the other? And, in whichever case, are these questions and answers (to the whistler or to the mate) or are they confirmations of something that is always the same thing (the bird's own presence, his belonging to this species, this sex, this territory)? Perhaps the value of this single word lies in its being repeated by another whistling beak, in its not being forgotten during the interval of silence.

Or else the whole dialogue consists of one saying to the other "I am here," and the length of the pauses adds to the phrase the sense of a "still," as if to say: "I am here still, it is still I." And what if it is in the pause and not in the whistle that the meaning of the message is contained? If it were in the silence that the blackbirds speak to each other?

(In this case the whistle would be a punctuation mark, a formula like "over and out.") A silence, apparently the same as another silence, could express a hundred different notions; a whistle could, too, for that matter. To speak to one another by remaining silent, or by whistling, is always possible; the problem is understanding one another. Or perhaps no one can understand anyone: each blackbird believes that he has put into his whistle a meaning fundamental for him, but only he understands it; the other gives him a reply that has no connection with what he said; it is a dialogue between the deaf, a conversation without head or tail.

But is human dialogue really any different? Mrs. Palomar is also in the garden, watering the veronicas. She says, "There they are," a pleonastic utterance (if it assumes that her husband is already looking at the blackbirds), or else (if he has not seen them) incomprehensible, but in any event intended to establish her own priority in the observation of the blackbirds (because, in fact, she was the first to discover them and to point out their habits to her husband) and to underline their unfailing appearance, which she has already reported many times.

"Sssh," Mr. Palomar says, apparently to prevent his wife from frightening them by speaking in a loud voice (useless injunction, because the blackbirds, husband and wife, are by now accustomed to the presence and voices of the Palomars, husband and wife) but actually to contest the wife's precedence, displaying a consideration for the blackbirds far greater than hers.

Then Mrs. Palomar says, "It's dry again, just since yesterday," referring to the earth in the flower bed she is watering, a communication in itself superfluous but meant to show, as she continues speaking and changes the subject, a far greater familiarity and nonchalance with the blackbirds than her husband has. In any case, from these remarks Mr. Palomar derives a general picture of tranquillity, and he is grateful to his wife for it, because if she confirms the fact that for the moment there is nothing more serious for him to bother about, then he can remain absorbed in his work (or pseudowork or hyperwork). He allows a minute to pass; then he also tries to send a reassuring message, to inform his wife that his work (or infrawork or ultrawork) is proceeding as usual: to this end he emits a series of sighs and grumbles—". . . crooked . . . for all that . . . repeat . . . yes, my foot . . ."—utterances that, taken all together, transmit also the message "I am very busy," in the event that his wife's last remark contained a veiled reproach on the order of "You could also assume some responsibility for watering the garden."

The premise of these verbal exchanges is the idea that a perfect accord between a married pair allows them to understand each other without having to make everything specific and detailed; but this principle is put into practice in very different ways by the two of them: Mrs. Palomar expresses herself with complete sentences, though often allusive or sibylline, to test the promptness of her husband's mental associations and the syntony of his thoughts with hers (a thing that does not always work); Mr. Palomar, on the other hand, from the mists of his inner monologue allows scattered articulate sounds to emerge, confident that, if a complete meaning does not result, at least the chiaroscuro of a mood will.

Mrs. Palomar, instead, refuses to receive these grumbles as talk, and to underline her nonparticipation she says in a low voice, "Sssh! . . . You'll frighten them," applying to her husband the same shushing that he had believed himself entitled to impose on her, and confirming once more her own primacy as far as consideration for the blackbirds goes.

Having scored this point to her advantage, Mrs. Palomar goes off. The blackbirds peck on the lawn and no doubt consider the dialogue of the Palomars the equivalent of their own whistles. We might just as well confine ourselves to whistling, he thinks. Here a prospect that is very promising for Mr. Palomar's thinking opens out; for him the discrepancy between human behavior and the rest of the universe has always been a source of anguish. The equal whistle of man and blackbird now seems to him a bridge thrown over the abyss.

If man were to invest in whistling everything he normally entrusts to words, and if the blackbird were to modulate into his whistling all the unspoken truth of his natural condition, then the first step would be taken toward bridging the gap between . . . between what and what? Nature and culture? Silence and speech? Mr. Palomar always hopes that silence contains something more than language can say. But what if language were really the goal toward which everything in existence tends? Or what if everything that exists were language, and has been since the beginning of time? Here Mr. Palomar is again gripped by anguish.

After having listened carefully to the whistle of the blackbird, he tries to repeat it, as faithfully as he can. A puzzled silence follows, as if his message required careful examination; then an identical whistle re-echoes. Mr. Palomar does not know if this is a reply to his or the proof that his whistle is so different that the blackbirds are not the least disturbed by it and resume their dialogue as if nothing had happened.

They go on whistling, questioning in their puzzlement, he and the blackbirds.

Contributors

James Balog's award-winning photographs are included in major public and private art collections, and collected in his book, *Survivors: A New Vision of Endangered Wildlife* (Harry N. Abrams). Along with photographs from that monograph, included here are images from a new work-in-progress—a close examination of primate facial expressions.

Rick Bass is the author of *The Ninemile Wolves,* published by Clark City Press, and other books on natural history. He lives in Montana, where he is working on a new novel, *Where the Sea Used to Be.*

Sara Burnaby lives in the eastern Sierra Nevada. "Bears" is her first published fiction, a chapter from the novel she is writing. She is also the author of *A Practice of Mountains,* published by Seaview Press in 1981.

Italo Calvino, one of the world's most beloved storytellers, died in 1985, having created such enduring works as *Invisible Cities, Cosmicomics, The Baron in the Trees, If on a winter's night a traveler,* and *Italian Folktales.*

Ethan Canin has written a story collection *Emperor of the Air,* and a novel, *Blue River.* A physician as well as an author, he currently resides in California.

David Huddle's most recent books are *The Nature of Yearning,* poetry; *The Writing Habit,* a collection of essays; and *Intimates,* new stories.

Maxine Kumin's tenth collection of poetry, *Looking for Luck,* was published by W. W. Norton in 1992. She and her husband live on a farm in New Hampshire where they raise horses.

Michael Martone has written three collections of short stories, the most recent being *Fort Wayne is Seventh on Hitler's List,* and edited two collections of essays, *Townships* and *A Place of Sense.*

Michael Maslin's collections of cartoons include *The More The Merrier, The Crowd Goes Wild, Mixed Company,* and *The Gang's All Here!* He has been a regular contributor to *The New Yorker* since 1977.

Haruki Murakami's first collection of short stories in English *The Elephant Vanishes* was published this spring by Alfred A. Knopf. Translator **Jay Rubin** is professor of Japanese literature at the University of Washington.

Jill Peacock has published stories in *Alaska Quarterly Review, Santa Monica Review,* and *Story.* She lives outside Los Angeles in the Santa Monica Mountains.

Brenda Peterson is the author of three novels and two collections of essays, the most recent being *Duck and Cover* and *Nature and Other Mothers: Reflections on the Feminine in Everyday Life,* both published by HarperCollins. She lives on Puget Sound in Seattle, Washington; every chance she gets she visits her human and animal family in the Florida Keys.

Constance Pierce's stories have been collected in her book, *When Things Get Back to Normal.* She teaches in the creative writing program at Miami University in Oxford, Ohio, and lives in rural Indiana.

J. F. Powers's books include the story collections *The Presence of Grace, Prince of Darkness and Other Stories,* and *Look How the Fish Live,* and the novels *Morte D'Urban* and *Wheat That Springeth Green.* He has taught at several American universities.

Lynne Sharon Schwartz has written four novels and two collections of stories. Her most recent book is *A Lynne Sharon Schwartz Reader,* including essays, stories, and poems, published by the University Press of New England.

Leslie Marmon Silko's novel, *Almanac of the Dead,* was published by Simon & Schuster in 1991. She lives in Tucson with five macaws, four cats, five dogs, two horses, three lizards, two snakes, two cockatoos, two Bantam chickens and one turkey.

Gregory Blake Smith is the author of two novels, *The Devil in the Dooryard* and *The Divine Comedy of John Venner.* He teaches American literature and creative writing at Carleton College.

Graham Swift is the author of five novels, *The Sweet-Shop Owner, Shuttlecock, Waterland, Out of This World,* and *Ever After,* and a collection of short stories, *Learning to Swim and Other Stories.*

Yuko Tsushima has written a dozen collections of stories, seven novels, and literary criticism. The daughter of Japanese novelist Osamu Dazai, she lives in Tokyo. Translator **Martin Holman,** professor of Japanese at Vanderbilt University, has also translated the work of Nobel Prize-winner Yasunari Kawabata.

David Wagoner is the author of fourteen books of poems, most recently *Through the Forest,* published by Atlantic Monthly Press, and ten novels. He is professor of English at the University of Washington and editor of *Poetry Northwest.*

Robley Wilson, Jr., is the author of several volumes of short stories, most recently *Terrible Kisses,* and a novel, *The Victim's Daughter.* He lives in Iowa, where he is editor of *The North American Review.*

Jeanette Winterson was born in 1954. She is the author of *Oranges Are Not the Only Fruit, The Passion, Sexing the Cherry,* and, most recently, *Written on the Body,* all published by Vintage Books.

Permissions

Sources, Resources, and Further Reading

The following books have either been quoted in the Introduction or have provided significant background information and perspective for my particular undertaking in this volume. I can, as well, recommend the majority of them for the general reader's continued interest.

ACKERMAN, DIANE. *A Natural History of the Senses.* New York: Random House, 1990.

———. *The Whale By Moonlight.* New York: Random House, 1991.

AISENBERG, NADYA, ed. *We Animals.* San Francisco: Sierra Club Books, 1989.

Anthrozoös: A Multidisciplinary Journal on the Interactions of People, Animals, and Nature. Publication of the Delta Society. P.O. Box 1080, Renton WA 98057-1080.

ARLEN, MICHAEL J. "The Lame Deer." In *The Camera Age.* New York: Farrar Straus Giroux, 1979.

BALOG, JAMES. *Survivors: A New Vision of Endangered Wildlife.* New York: Harry N. Abrams, 1990.

BERGER, JOHN. *About Looking.* New York: Pantheon Books, 1980.

CAMPBELL, JOSEPH. *The Power of Myth.* New York: Doubleday, 1988.

COLETTE. *Creatures Great and Small.* Translated by Enid McLeod. London: Martin Secker & Warburg, Ltd., 1951.

DAY, CLARENCE. *This Simian World.* New York: Alfred A. Knopf, 1920.

Fox, Michael W. *Inhumane Society: The American Way of Exploiting Animals.* New York: St. Martin's Press, 1990.

Garnett, David. *A Man in the Zoo.* Great Britain: Chatto and Windus, 1924.

Grumbach, Doris. *Coming Into the End Zone.* New York: W. W. Norton, 1991.

Hearne, Vicki. *Adam's Task: Calling Animals By Name.* New York: Alfred A. Knopf, 1986.

Katcher, Aaron H., and Alan M. Beck, eds. *New Perspectives on our Lives with Animals.* Philadelphia: University of Pennsylvania Press, 1983.

Kundera, Milan. *The Unbearable Lightness of Being.* Translated by Michael Henry Heim. New York: Harper & Row, 1984.

Lopez, Barry. *Crossing Open Ground.* New York: Scribner's Sons, 1988.

Lorenz, Konrad. *Here Am I—Where Are You?* Translated by Robert D. Martin. New York: Harcourt Brace Jovanovich, 1991.

Maeterlinck, Maurice. *The Life of the Bee.* Translated by Alfred Sutro. New York: Dodd, Mead & Co., 1921.

McKibben, Bill. *The Age of Missing Information.* New York: Random House, 1992.

Morris, Desmond. *The Animal Contract.* New York: Warner Books, 1990.

Peterson, Brenda. *Nature and Other Mothers: Reflections on the Feminine in Everyday Life.* New York: HarperCollins, 1992.

Sagan, Carl. *Cosmos.* New York: Random House, 1980.

Serpell, James. *In the Company of Animals.* Oxford: Basil Blackwell, Inc., 1986.

SINGER, PETER. *Animal Liberation*. Revised Edition. New York: Random House, 1990.

————, ed. *In Defense of Animals*. New York: Basil Blackwell, Inc., 1985.

THOMPSON, WILLIAM IRWIN. *Passages About Earth*. New York: Harper & Row, 1973.

ZIEGLER, MEL, et alia. *The Republic of Tea*. New York: Currency Books, Doubleday, 1992.

The following organizations generate a considerable amount of printed material dealing with various aspects of animal welfare and issues pertaining to human/animal relations. This is a starting point for more information. Readers should not overlook the availability of local resources. Animal shelters, local chapters of many national agencies, and hundreds of smaller, region-specific service, lobbying, and rescue organizations are located throughout the country.

ASPCA
(The American Society for the Prevention of Cruelty to Animals)
441 East Ninety-second Street
New York NY 10128

The Delta Society
321 Burnett Avenue South, Third Floor
Renton WA 98055-2569

Culture and Animals Foundation
3509 Eden Croft Drive
Raleigh NC 27612

Friends of Animals, Inc.
P.O. Box 1244
Norwalk CT 06856

HSUS
(The Humane Society of the United States)
2100 L Street NW
Washington DC 20037

IFAW
(International Fund for Animal Welfare)
411 Main Street
P.O. Box 193
Yarmouth Port MA 02675

The National Association for the Advancement of Humane Education
P.O. Box 362
East Haddam CT 06423

National Audubon Society
950 Third Avenue
New York NY 10022

National Humane Education Society
15-B Catactin Circle #207
P.O. Box 837
Leesburg VA 22075

PETA
(People for the Ethical Treatment of Animals)
P.O. Box 42516
Washington DC 20015

About the Editor

Michael J. Rosen's philanthropic efforts for The Company of Animals Fund include three "companion volumes"—this one, as well as *The Company of Dogs* and *The Company of Cats,* and a children's picture book, *SPEAK! Children's Book Illustrators Brag About Their Dogs.* He also conceived and edited *Home: A Collaboration of 30 Distinguished Authors of Children's Books to Aid the Homeless* on behalf of the organization Share Our Strength. His other books include a volume of Thurber's uncollected work, *Collecting Himself: James Thurber on Writing and Writers, Humor and Himself;* poetry, *A Drink at the Mirage;* and children's books, *Every Kid's Best Dog Book, Elijah's Angel, The Kids' Book of Fishing,* and *50 Odd Jobs.* His fiction, articles, reviews, poetry, and illustrations appear in magazines and newspapers around the country. He lives in his hometown, Columbus, Ohio, where he serves as literary director of The Thurber House, the writers' center in the restored boyhood home of James Thurber.